A DARK PATH

"I don't understand it, Max," said Ukiah. "Alicia has veered and gone down a trail through the creek's undergrowth. She has to hunch down to run, but she scurries like a rabbit, sometimes on hands and knees. She must be afraid. She stands and starts to run. Here's the man again, and she turns.

"Alicia runs. Again the man turns, doesn't follow. He's going to cut her off again—Max, he's herding her."

"Herding?"

"He's getting in front of her, and forcing her to go the way he wants."

"Oh damn, Ukiah, the main road is in that direction. She was heading away from it, but now she's pointed right at it."

"No. No." Ukiah groaned at what he could read in the torn earth. "They jumped her. She fought. They bloodied her. They lifted her up, and th‌ ‌ ‌ ‌ ‌he car, and they drove away. . . "

TAINTED TRAIL

Wen Spencer

A ROC BOOK

ROC
Published by New American Library, a division of
Penguin Putnam Inc., 375 Hudson Street,
New York, New York 10014, U.S.A.
Penguin Books Ltd, 80 Strand,
London WC2R 0RL, England
Penguin Books Australia Ltd, Ringwood,
Victoria, Australia
Penguin Books Canada Ltd, 10 Alcorn Avenue,
Toronto, Ontario, Canada M4V 3B2
Penguin Books (N.Z.) Ltd, 182–190 Wairau Road,
Auckland 10, New Zealand

Penguin Books Ltd, Registered Offices:
Harmondsworth, Middlesex, England

First published by Roc, an imprint of New American Library,
a division of Penguin Putnam Inc.

First Printing, June 2002
10   9   8   7   6   5   4   3   2   1

Copyright © Wendy Kosak, 2002
All rights reserved

Cover design by Ray Lundgren
Cover art by Steve Stone

 REGISTERED TRADEMARK—MARCA REGISTRADA

Printed in the United States of America

To Carol Larkin,
who always believed in me.

Many thanks to the people who helped me with this novel, from answering technical questions to helping me work out plot problems: D. Eric Anderson, Ann Cecil, Jeff Colburn, Amy L. Finkbeiner, Kevin Geiselman, Nancy L. Janda, Dr. Hope Erica Ring, June Drexler Robertson, Thomas Rohosky, Diane Turnshek, Larisa Van Winkle, and Aaron Wollerton.

CHAPTER ONE

**Continental Flight 5373: Pittsburgh to Portland, Oregon
Tuesday, August 24, 2004**

He was cold because he was starving. The early winter had brought deep snow, and hunting had been scarce. The wolves of his pack eyed him often, as if judging his weakness. Perhaps his years of running among them would have kept him safe from being pulled down and eaten as the gray ones grew thin. Still, he stopped sleeping among them, climbing pine trees to sleep above the ground, far from their reach. Finally, the Wolf Boy trusted them no longer, and he ran by himself.

He knew the metal box was a trap. He had seen others like it, sprung, holding wolves fast. There was, however, the dead rabbit inside, just beyond his reach. The sharp stick he stuck between the box's bars moved the rabbit's head about, but the body seemed stuck. If he wanted to eat, he would have to enter the box.

He had never been so hungry and cold, not in all his long vivid memories of countless seasons. A wolf howled far off, and then again, closer. If he stayed outside the box, the wolves would find him and perhaps kill him. If he left, one of them would get the rabbit.

Did he want to stay cold and hungry? Could he stand being trapped by those that walked on two legs like he did? The Wolf Boy had a deep, nameless, formless fear of them. What would they do to him? They put the wolves in their large, smelly vehicles and carried them away.

The wolf howled again, a minute's quick run away. He had to choose quickly. Food and entrapment, or starving freedom? It was a decision that could mean life or death. Which one was death, though, and which one was life?

For the first time in his life, the Wolf Boy chose the unknown. He would let himself be caught. He would eat and then, maybe, escape . . .

"Ukiah?"

Ukiah Oregon woke, shivering, face pressed against an oval Plexiglas window. The endless muted roar of the jet engines vibrated against his senses.

"You okay, kid?" Max Bennett, Ukiah's partner, had been making notes on his PDA in the aisle seat. He now eyed Ukiah worriedly, something he did more often since they stumbled into the secret war between the alien invaders known as the Ontongard and the rebel alien forces who called themselves the Pack. "It sounded like you were having a bad dream."

"More like a recall, back when Mom Jo caught me in the humane trap." Combing his long, dark hair out of his dark eyes with his fingers, Ukiah realized he was still shivering. Locating the source of the chill, he reached up to close the overhead air conditioning vent. The plane bucked and he missed the first grab for the vent. He got it on his second try. He closed his, and then the one above the empty seat between them, where Homicide Detective Raymond Kraynak should have been sitting. "Where's Kraynak?"

"He felt like throwing up again, so he went off to do it in private. He's going to be in sad shape when we hit Pendleton. Depending where Alicia got lost, we might be doing this case on horseback." Max made a note on his PDA, and then turned a gray-eyed query at him. "Can you ride?"

"I don't know. That's something I might have learned during the missing part of my life, before running with the wolves. Native Americans in the movies can always ride like the wind."

Max grunted and made a note on his PDA. "A resounding maybe. Hopefully, Alicia didn't choose one of the wilderness areas of Umatilla National Park to vanish into. They're the only part of the park without access roads."

"Why is Alicia in *Oregon*?" Ukiah had missed most of the explanations in the mad scramble to catch the flight. When he started tracking for Max, years before they became full partners, Kraynak's niece Alicia worked part-time at the office. She quit last fall when she entered grad school. While Alicia usually stayed in close touch, he hadn't seen her since Max's annual Fourth of July picnic. She hadn't mentioned going to Oregon, but then Alicia had acted weird—even for her—the entire picnic. "Did she drop out of Pitt?"

Max gave him a startled look, which changed to one of understanding. "Oh, yeah, you hung up before Kraynak got into that and drove back to your mom's to pack." Max waved one hand to indicate he only vaguely understood Alicia's situation. "Alicia went out to Oregon on a geology field trip. Two friends of hers had plans to go out and collect data on their graduate thesis; the one with the reliable car canceled, putting the remaining woman in a bind. Alicia swung some deal with Pitt—Kraynak didn't know all the details—and went."

"In her Metro?" Ukiah was surprised that the ancient compact car had been deemed reliable enough to make the trip.

Max shook his head. "Alicia swapped cars with Kraynak and took his van. They've been out there almost the whole month, roughing it during the week and then spending the weekends at Pendleton. Last night the other girl called Kraynak and said that Alicia disappeared while hiking."

And Kraynak called them. The late-night phone call gave them less than nine hours to drop everything personal and professional, pack, and catch a flight across the country. With his moms and sister on vacation, Ukiah had been enjoying a rare opportunity to be sole parent to his infant son, Kittanning. True, he hadn't gotten much work done while he juggled his schedule around Kitt's feeding and sleeping periods, but for the first time, Ukiah felt more like a father to his son than a big brother.

Luckily, his fiancée, FBI Special Agent Indigo Zheng,

agreed to take hasty delivery of Kittanning. Ukiah had driven the hour north to his moms for the oddest packing experience he had ever gone through. One Berretta 9mm pistol with three clips, one case of formula, and three baby bottles. Bulletproof Kevlar vest. Two dozen medium-sized diapers, diaper wipes, and diaper-rash cream. Two-way voice-activated radio headset. One baby monitor. Five black T-shirts with PRIVATE INVESTIGATOR, BENNETT DETECTIVE AGENCY stenciled across the back in large white letters, size medium. Five pairs Barney onesies pajamas, size three months.

He barely got Kittanning settled in at Indigo's, and himself back to the office, before they needed to leave for the airport. In the confusion, Ukiah didn't get a chance to eat, and Kraynak forgot to pick up Dramamine.

"I'm starving. Are they going to serve a meal?"

Max looked up the aisle. "The flight attendants have the cart out, and they're serving something. It won't be very much, kid. A sandwich, a cookie or two, and a soda."

The flight attendants seemed not to notice that the plane jerked and bucked on invisible airwaves. They served the food with practiced smiles.

Ukiah glanced at the empty center seat. "You think Kraynak will eat his?"

"Probably not. He'll be lucky to get out of the restroom this flight. He'd hoped to grab something for motion sickness in Houston, thinking we'd have time in the layover."

For some reason unfathomable to Ukiah, one couldn't fly directly from Pittsburgh to Portland. Stranger yet, they had flown south to go north. A storm front over Houston delayed their landing and their layover consisted of a dash through the sprawling, crowded airport.

Max looked at him warily now. "How do you feel?"

"I'm cold and hungry," Ukiah admitted, then realized Max was asking if he was going to be airsick. "I think after the first handful of jiggles, my body decided to ignore my inner ear as an alarmist. Remember that time on Lake Erie when Kraynak took us fishing with his brother-in-law?"

"God, don't say anything else, or I'll start puking." Max undid his seat belt, stood cautiously, opened the overhead compartment, and tossed a folded blanket to Ukiah. He pulled out his briefcase, closed the overhead, and sat back down. "I've got a Snickers bar or two in here." He thumbed open the locks. He fished out the candy and handed it to Ukiah. "Remind me to stock up at the Portland airport."

"Thanks." Ukiah glanced into the briefcase. Taking up the most space in the briefcase was a fat folder marked ORE-GON, UKIAH—BENNETT DETECTIVE AGENCY FILE #117. "Is that my case file?"

They had first met when Ukiah's adopted mothers hired Max to find out Ukiah's real identity. Max had failed. In hindsight, there was no way Max could have succeeded. Ukiah's background had been too strange for anyone to guess, and sometimes, even believe. The case had, however, introduced Max to Ukiah's tracking abilities and inspired a partnership that specialized in finding missing persons.

Max nodded, flipping open the file. "I grabbed it as we were running out the door. I kept all the geographic maps of the Umatilla National Park, road maps, campground guides, and so forth. I figured that it would prove to be useful."

"Can I see?" Ukiah took out one of the maps and opened it. It showed the mountains of the national park in a series of squiggly lines. Spreading it out on his lap, he studied it for several minutes as he ate the candy, shaking his head.

Max noticed the motion. "What's wrong?"

"I lived here for so long, Max. Maybe over two hundred years. I knew every inch of it. This map, though, is so abstract, I can't relate to a single feature. I wonder how much it's changed in the last eight years. Am I going to be able to find my way around?"

"All you need to worry about, kid, is Alicia's trail. Wherever she went, you follow. I'll handle the maps."

Ukiah glanced to the back of the plane. The right restroom door stayed firmly shut as a short line rotated through the left. "You think Kraynak is right, and she's in serious trouble?"

Max shrugged. "He thinks so, he's footing the bill, and we owe him a favor. I'm hoping we'll get out there and find out that she just let the batteries of her phone die or some such nonsense."

"What are we charging him?" Their normal tracking fee was a thousand dollars a day, a bit steep for a police detective to pay.

Max looked sheepish. "Hell, I didn't talk to him about it. It's Alicia! If need be, we'll do a this as a freebie."

Ukiah nodded without a quibble. Technically, he was a full partner of their detective agency, but only because Max had given him half the company after Ukiah saved his life. Outwardly, seventeen years Ukiah's senior, Max still made most of the business decisions, especially the financial ones. Ukiah supposed it was just as well—being raised by wolves gave him a very loose grasp on the concept of money.

Kraynak came back from the restroom, seeming even larger than normal in the close quarters of the jet. He reeked faintly of vomit and old cigarette smoke resurrected by water. "Can I sit on the end?"

Max handed Ukiah his briefcase with a "Hold this" and started to shift over his other belongings to the middle seat. Ukiah thumbed through the folder. Max kept meticulous records and the folder was no exception. A photo of Ukiah at thirteen was clipped to the inside cover. Maps in the front. Area info next. There was a copy of a newspaper article tucked in before a bundle of receipts. Ukiah pulled it out as Max sat beside him and Kraynak carefully settled his tall, solid body into the end seat.

INFORMATION SOUGHT ON WOLF BOY was the headline of the small article circled in red.

Anyone with information on the feral child sighted recently at the Umatilla National Park, please contact Jesse Kicking Deer. Kicking Deer believes the mysterious boy reportedly "running naked with the wolves" to be a distant family member. Kicking Deer describes the supposed feral child as a handsome boy from the Cayuse tribe. Anyone sighting the Umatilla Wolf Boy can reach Jesse Kicking Deer at Rt. 1 Box 534, Pendleton, Oregon 97801.

"Max? What's this? This sounds like me."

Max looked over and frowned for a moment in recall. "That sounded real close, but I had to discount it."

"Why?"

Max tapped the "1933" written in red ink at the top, next to the *East Oregonian* legend. "Because the kid disappeared in 1933 and that would make him over eighty."

"Or over two hundred," Ukiah whispered.

Max glanced at him puzzled. Understanding came with a slight widening of his eyes. "Oh, shit." He looked down at the paper again. "Ukiah, this could have been you. I thought you were a normal kid at the time."

When his Mom Jo found him running with the wolves, there had been no way of knowing his birth date or exact age. He showed signs that he had started into puberty, so his Mom Jo had assigned him the age of thirteen. In actuality, they learned later, he was several hundred years old; after growing to maturity, he aged only when he was wounded. The rough-and-tumble life of a private investigator was the only reason he couldn't still pass as a thirteen-year-old. A series of almost fatal accidents and shootings made him look almost eighteen, but certainly not the twenty-one stated on his driver's license.

Ukiah flipped through the case report looking for an indication that Max had followed up on the newspaper clipping. "You talked to this man?"

Max considered the overhead compartments as he thought. "This was five years ago, Ukiah, and I don't have your memory. I talked to him, but not face to face. It was over the phone. I remember it was a short conversation. I told him I found the article in the library's archive and that I was trying to establish someone's true identity, but I know I didn't go into details with him. I think one of my first questions was "When did the boy disappear?" After he said 1933 I thanked him for his time and cut the conversation short."

Ukiah found the name, address, and phone number of Jesse Kicking Deer in the case report. Max had noted, *Description and location match, but age is completely wrong.* "I would love to go see this guy. I wonder if he's still at this address."

Max picked up the phone built into the seat in front of them. "Let's see."

The phone number listed in the file was no longer in service. Undaunted, Max called information and gave the name and address.

"I'm showing a Claire Kicking Deer at that address," the operator said over the drone of the engines, "but that number is unlisted."

Max thanked the operator and hung up. "With a name like that, it's a fair bet they're related." Max consulted his PDA. "We're landing in Pendleton at five-thirty, if we don't miss the commuter in Portland. We'll need to rent the cars, load them, and then it's an hour drive down to the campground." He tapped through a series of pages. "We're not going to be able to do any actual tracking tonight; I don't want to be stumbling around in the dark."

"I can track at night," Ukiah said.

Max gave him a cold look. "I know, kid, but I can't see in the dark. I'm not letting you track without backup." Max considered the rest of the day. "Three is overkill for what we're doing tonight. Let's split up. We'll rent a second car. Kraynak and I will load the gear, find out what we can on the search-and-rescue efforts, and then check into the hotel. You can see if you can find Jesse Kicking Deer."

Ukiah slipped both the photograph and the news clipping into his wallet for his meeting with Jesse Kicking Deer. "Is that okay with you, Kraynak?"

Kraynak didn't answer.

Glancing past Max, Ukiah discovered that the homicide detective was gone again. "We've got to make sure he takes something before we get on that commuter plane to Pendleton."

Portland International Airport, Portland, Oregon
Tuesday, August 24, 2004

Ukiah hated strange airports.

Any crowded place was an assault on his senses. Here, every person breathed out a cloud of information that trailed behind them as they rushed to their destinations, every surface was layered thick with the histories of those who had handled it, and the very air vibrated with countless conversations. Over the years, he had learned to cope with crowds, keeping his hands in his pockets, filtering the effusion of air data to the point where he could ignore it. It only worked, though, in places where he had been before, and among people common to that area. He could only keep out what was familiar, as if there was something deep-coded inside of him, cautiously checking everything new for danger.

In a place such as this, where his surroundings competed with the crowds for attention, he was lost in the flood. Everything was new, even the faintly salt-tainted air, pressing in to be noticed, overwhelming him until he lost track of himself. Max kept a hand on his elbow, guiding him through the jostling confusion.

Once past the gates and into the public concourse, Max veered into a sitting area across from a Hudson News stand. Fifty or sixty seats made a pocket of quiet beside a children's play area in the shape of a jumbo jet. Max moored Ukiah in the far back corner, away from the foot traffic. There, Max put his hands to Ukiah's face and made him focus his gaze on his own.

"Kraynak and I are going to grab our luggage, guns, and equipment and check them with the commuter airline." Max took out both their phones and turned them on. "Baggage claim is downstairs, and it's going to be a madhouse. I'm leaving you here. Stay put. I'll be back." He paused, waiting for the phones to indicate they had a signal. "If you need me, call instead of trying to find me." Max pocketed his own phone and tucked Ukiah's into his partner's shirt pocket. "Okay?"

Max waited until Ukiah nodded, then left. The flood rushed in again. Ukiah floundered, sorting through the stimuli. Slowly, enough became known qualities he could then ignore that he felt solid and grounded. As if welcoming him back to himself, his phone chirped. He dug it out of his pocket. A female security officer at Pittsburgh's airport had handled his phone when he passed through the metal detec-

tors, leaving behind a ghost presence of White Linen perfume, Coast soap, and her own unique genetic profile.

"Oregon."

"It's me, love." Indigo's voice competed with a gate-
change announcement booming over the airport's speakers.
Ukiah plugged the other ear with his finger, but still felt the
words ripple across his skin. "How was the flight?"

"It was a bit rough," Ukiah answered after the announcement ended. "We kept hitting storms. How's Kitt?"

Max had vetoed Ukiah's first choice of babysitters: the
Dog Warriors. The twenty Pack members would have de-
voted themselves to Kittanning and guarded him armed to
the teeth. Max, however, had never forgiven the Dog Warriors for kidnapping Ukiah at gunpoint and wasn't about to
trust the alien outlaws with his godson. While Indigo cheerfully took Kittanning, she would still need to find daylight
babysitters among her family or take vacation time from her
work.

"He's being an angel so far," Indigo told him. "We've
had dinner and he went right to sleep. I'm reviewing foren-
sic evidence files." A quiet rustle over the phone indicated
she had gotten up and moved across the room. "Rennie
Shaw and Bear Shadow have this watch."

He heard the slight tension in her voice. "I'm sorry."

He had contacted the Dog Warriors to feed Mom Jo's
half-breed wolves while he was in Oregon. He should have
realized that Dog Warriors would track down Kittanning to
watch over, regardless of Max's wishes.

"It's not like I haven't been through this before," Indigo
said. The Dog Warriors had guarded Indigo while Ukiah had
been dead. "They're being very discreet. I needed my night
scope to spot them. I suppose I better get used to it if we're
getting married. It's kind of a package deal—marry the
Pack's child, get the Pack keeping watch."

Ukiah winced at the "if." Usually she said "when." He
hoped it was a merely a slip of tongue. If he could hear the
tension in her voice, then her legendary calm must be taking
a beating. "Is something wrong?"

"Other than lack of sleep and being stalked by your extended family? No." She took a deep breath, released it slowly, and when she spoke again, the tension was gone. "Everything is fine. I called to ask you, though: Didn't Mom Lara say something about Kittanning having a doctor's appointment on Wednesday?"

Ukiah closed his eyes to summon up his moms' kitchen calendar. Printed in tomorrow's allotted square was Mom Lara's hieroglyphics of *K. Dr. 8:00 AM 2 m. check & shots.* He told Indigo the time. "I'm not sure why he has to go. I don't think he *can* get sick."

"You think your immune system can handle anything, Wolf Boy?"

Kittanning was Ukiah's clone, created out of his blood. They were identical except for their age. Despite being born to a human woman, Ukiah's cells were vastly more complex, able to function both jointly and independently, to the point they were able to transform into small animals if separated from Ukiah. Earth viruses had no hope of breaching his alien-born defenses. Ukiah could remember being sick only once; when Pack leader, Rennie Shaw, gave Ukiah his memories in the form of a mouse. The ensuing cellular war—lasting until the Pack memories were added to Ukiah's own genetic memory—made Ukiah thankful that he didn't get sick.

"Aye, our immune system kicks butt." He slipped into Rennie's slight brogue. "It spits on all puny earth viruses. Pooey. Pooey."

"It may, but he still needs to go."

"Why?" It defied logic.

"Ukiah, no preschool, kindergarten, first grade, or even college would let him in without proof of immunization."

"Oh." It amazed him sometimes what he didn't know about the world.

"Is he still going to the same place?" she asked. "Or did your moms move him to a place closer to them?"

He, his moms, Max, Indigo, and at times their lawyer, Leo Stepanian, held several war sessions trying to deal with Kittanning's sudden appearance. They walked a legal tightrope to get Kittanning a birth certificate, hampered by the fact that he hadn't been born so much as made. The system required certain information such as mother's name and time of birth.

They set time of birth to be when Hex shot Ukiah. Shortly after that moment, the blood flowing from Ukiah's wounds formed into the mouse that would eventually be infant Kittanning. His moms refused to be named Kittanning's mother, pointing out that it would appear dangerously close to incest with their adopted son. Leo reminded them that if Ukiah wasn't listed as Kittanning's father, Ukiah would have no legal right to his son. In the end, Indigo volunteered to stand as Kittanning's mother.

Of course there was the slight problem that Indigo had never been pregnant. One reason they chose a busy multi-doctor medical association in the North Hills was the anonymity it gave them. While much of the information on Kittanning's birth certificate was accurate, they couldn't *prove* any of it.

"No, it's the same doctors. If it would be easier, you can just call and reschedule. You don't have to take him."

"Yes, I do. He's my son, Ukiah. He was born because you came to rescue me. I made a commitment to him when we put my name down as mother on his birth certificate. I have responsibilities for him, even if we're not married."

There was that word again. If.

It seemed they had fallen off an edge the day Kittanning was created. Ukiah had been killed protecting Indigo, and Indigo went on to rain cold vengeance down on those who killed him. Wedding vows seemed trivial after *I will die for you* and *I will make sure your sacrifice was not in vain* were made deed. Yet without those spoken wedding vows, how could *I love you now* become *I will love you forever*?

Max touched his shoulder, making Ukiah aware of him. Kraynak stood beside Max, fumbling with a bottle of Dramamine. Max tapped his watch.

"I need to go," Ukiah told Indigo. "Do you want me to call you later?"

She mulled the question over with a long, drawn-out

"um." "No. I don't relish trying to get Kitt back asleep if the phone wakes him. Call me tomorrow morning."

"Okay." He mouthed "Indigo" to Max, who had queried him with one raised eyebrow and a glance at the phone. "We're three hours behind you, so I'll call before I start to track, see how the appointment went."

"Be careful," Indigo warned, and then added, as if in consideration of the dangers he might be soon facing, an earnest "I love you."

"What appointment?" Max asked after Ukiah hung up.

Ukiah recounted the conversation as they threaded through the crowds. Max guided him to a distant wing of the airport catering to Horizon Airlines. Four abbreviated gates shared one large sitting area.

"You've got to marry that girl." Max showed their boarding passes.

The woman at the counter said, "Gate eleven" and waved them through.

"We talk about getting married all the time." Ukiah followed Max out to an open walkway. Every ten feet, the walkway had a large doorless exit to the tarmac. A turboprop airplane sat at each such "gate." Behind Ukiah, Kraynak groaned at the sight of the small airplanes. Gate eleven was the last opening before the walkway ended. The door of the plane had been folded down to make a five-step ramp up into the aircraft.

"We're eight A, B, and C," Max said. "We're the next to last row, two right, one left. And?"

Max prompted Ukiah back to the conversation. It was interesting, Ukiah thought, that Max felt so comfortable discussing other people's lives. If this were a discussion on Max's love life, it would already be over. Usually Max had to be drunk before he was willing to talk about his dead wife or the idea of dating again.

"Well," Ukiah reluctantly admitted, "we actually kind of dance around the idea of marriage. I think we're both still scared about the idea."

"What's to be scared of?" Max stowed his briefcase and took the left aisle seat.

Kraynak ducked through the door and paused in the front of the plane to talk earnestly with the flight attendant, dwarfing her with his bulk. Ukiah glanced back at Kraynak, and then whispered to Max. "Start with I'm not human and work your way down."

Max gave him a hard, disapproving stare. "You *are* human," he said in a quiet, uncompromising tone. "Go on."

Ukiah sighed, stowing his carry-on. "My moms hate the idea of me marrying Indigo. They don't want us to rush into anything. They've never been really happy that Indigo and I had sex before we even had a first date."

"Well, it was kind of sudden." Max allowed.

"Mom Lara has this cascade theory, that Indigo seduced me because she overreacted to me saving her life and the Pack kidnapping me, and then she dated me because she felt guilty about seducing someone so young, and now she's pushing for marriage because I ended up with Kittanning by trying to rescue her."

"It's so like a woman to overanalyze things."

Ukiah dropped into the window seat. "And that's just my family."

"I meant to ask you how the picnic went on Sunday."

"Well, her brothers and sisters seemed to like me. Her older brother Zane said that if Indigo could run around shooting people, she certainly could date anyone that she pleased."

Max laughed at this.

"Her parents, though . . . to them I'm a long-haired, teenage, Native American, Unitarian, Wolf Boy raised by lesbians, with an infant son obviously from a previous failed relationship."

"Are you quoting?"

"Indigo's mother doesn't realize how well I hear."

"Ouch." Max winced for him. "Don't worry, kid, they'll come around."

Ukiah nodded, but heard again Indigo's quiet "if." "Mom Jo is worried that we haven't given enough thought of 'how' we could stay married. I don't know the first thing about living on my own, and Mom Jo says that would throw Indigo into the role of caretaker. She says it could put a lot of stress on Indigo that she's not expecting."

"Your Mom Jo is a good woman," Max said. "But she's always underrated your ability to learn. If you want to make this marriage work, you can."

Again—*if*. Some part of him certainly craved being married to Indigo, despite it being a vast unknown. Unsuspected, he had a deep want for *his* wife and *his* son living in *his* house—all the fine trappings of being an adult.

The realization bothered him. Could wanting to be married have nothing to do with loving Indigo?

Pendleton Municipal Airport, Pendleton, Oregon
Tuesday, August 24, 2004

When Ukiah remembered Oregon, he recalled only steep mountains and towering pines. He was startled when the turboprop airplane dropped down through the clouds to reveal a land nearly flat and utterly treeless. More startling, the land was marked with a multitude of huge circles.

"What are those?" he asked Kraynak.

Kraynak leaned over to peer out the window. "Those are from the long, rolling irrigation . . . thingies. They anchor one end and it rolls in a circle about the endpoint."

They landed without Pendleton coming into view. The airport was laughably small after the Houston airport: four modest-sized public rooms linked together. Over the sole door leading to a single X-ray device was a sign proclaiming ALL GATES. It was the first airport of the day in which Ukiah wasn't immediately overwhelmed.

Four children with black hair, dark eyes, and dusky skin played in the largest room. Ukiah watched the children while Max rented two Chevy Blazers from a Hertz kiosk-styled office, doing the typical corporate paperwork dance to allow Ukiah to drive under the age of twenty-five. Were the kids Native Americans, Chinese, or Mexican? None of them came close enough for him to tell.

Max threw him the keys to the first Chevy. "You sure you're okay to drive?"

"If I take a few minutes to get settled in, yeah. There's no crowd to deal with."

The Hertz agent laughed. "Wait two weeks, and there will be. The annual roundup starts then. It's a rodeo with an Indian powwow. Pendleton goes from a population of twenty thousand to sixty thousand."

"Ouch," Max said. "Well, hopefully we'll be gone by Thursday."

"People will be drifting in starting this weekend," the Hertz agent said.

"Explains why getting hotel rooms was so fun," Max muttered, resetting his watch to local time. "It's five-thirty now. See you at the hotel in two hours or so? We'll probably both be out of regular cell-phone range, so take one of the satellite phones with you. Call me if you run into trouble."

Ukiah snagged one of the equipment bags with a phone and GPS system in it and went out to the parking lot. The Blazer was unlocked and stifling hot. He started up the SUV and let the air conditioning run while he stood outside, acclimatizing to the world around him.

The airport sat on the edge of a river valley. The flat land broke suddenly to drop down in ragged hills. The stubble of wheat on the nearby fields shined gold, and heat wavered liquid in the late-afternoon sun. He could pick out the constant hum of distant highway traffic and the faint gurgle of river water. Once the interior of the Blazer was bearable, he slid in, closed the door, and started out to find Jesse Kicking Deer.

Pendleton was at once familiar and strange, like a house that been remodeled. The streets lay in a straight grid, as much as the river valley allowed. None of the street names seemed right, and only a handful of buildings struck a resonance in him. He drove up out of the river bottom, and pulled off just short of the I-84 on ramp. Getting out of the Blazer, he looked back at the island of civilization, surrounded by vast, empty prairie.

Mom Jo had slipped him out of Oregon without visiting

Pendleton, so he wasn't recalling a recent memory. Was he finally remembering something from his childhood?

He focused on the memory, and found it wasn't his. It belonged to Rennie Shaw.

When Ukiah had realized that he, the Pack, and the Ontongard weren't human, he had gone to Rennie Shaw and begged for answers. What was he? How was he related to the Pack? Who were the Ontongard? Where had they all come from? Why did the Ontongard want to kill him? Instead of answers, Rennie bled into a coffee can and gave it to Ukiah, telling him to use it. The blood transformed into a mouse—as Pack blood was wont to do once separated from the main body—and contained Rennie's genetically coded memory. After much bafflement as to how he was supposed to use the mouse, Ukiah absorbed it, and Rennie's memories had been added to his own.

Oddly, while the memories were sharp and clear as his own, they were harder to access. A stray thought or image would trigger Ukiah's memories to the surface. Rennie's memories lurked like silvery minnows under the shimmer of his own thoughts and memories, there to catch and examine, but never really offering themselves up freely.

Ukiah fished out Rennie's memory and examined it. Rennie had been in eastern Oregon twice. The first time had come a decade after Rennie's last day of being human: May 5, 1864.

The Ontongard reproduced by invading a host, much the same as a virus would, using the host's own biology to reproduce and then replace all the cells in their body. The hosts became identical to those that begot them on a cellular level—with an important difference. These "Gets," as the Ontongard called the hosts once they had been wholly taken over, retained all innate abilities and skills needed to not only survive but excel in the host's native ecology. Thus, as the Ontongard spread across the galaxy, not only did they receive bodies adapted to the new worlds, but they also gained intelligence, education, and memories, all wrapped in a camouflage shell of a being known to the uninfected natives.

Once little more than lowly pond scum, the race had stolen all they needed to leap across the stars.

To fight the Ontongard, Prime had no choice but to make Gets of his own.

A West Point trained Union officer, Rennie had been wounded, trapped under his dead horse in the tangled undergrowth west of Wilderness Church. Prime's first Get, Coyote, came to Rennie in moonlight, a wolf changed into a man by alien blood, named for a native god, offering the cursed gift of life as a Get. Only twenty-three, with a wife and child to live for, Rennie accepted, thoughtless of the cost. Coyote's blood burned its way through his body, the viral genetics changing him cell by cell into a copy of Coyote that wore Rennie's face.

He was Coyote's first Get. By that time, however, Hex— the sole Ontongard to reach Earth after Prime crashed the mother ship on Mars and sabotaged the scout ship—had made a small army of Gets.

Rennie never returned to his family. He dedicated himself to the war against the Ontongard, protecting his wife, son, and the rest of humanity from the alien invaders. He and Coyote's other Gets forced Hex into hiding by 1874. Leaving Hex to the others, Rennie formed the Dog Warriors and backtracked to Oregon, hunting Hex's scattered Gets. The country had been raw frontier, and the Dog Warriors killed Ontongard with open, reckless abandon.

Rennie returned to Oregon during the early part of the last century, called back by Degas, the leader of a pack clan named the Demon Curs. By then, the killing between Pack and Ontongard had become a secret war; it behooved neither side for the humans to know that aliens lived among them.

Rennie had stood on this same ridge overlooking Pendleton, amused by his own surprise. *It's been fifty years, you old dog. Of course it's going to change. Hell, they've even changed the name from Goodwin Station.*

The gold boomtown of the Old West had been a good place for hunting Ontongard, Rennie thought. *It's going to be harder to put the Ontongard down and burn them to ashes in this* Pendleton *than in Goodwin Station.*

"They even have a sheriff now," a voice said behind Rennie, surprising him. "Although the first one got himself killed in a jail break. One would think he was a martyred saint or something, the way they carry on."

Rennie jerked around, pulling out his hidden pistol before the wind shifted, bringing him the stocky man's scent, deeply drenched in woodsmoke. Rennie recognized him then. "Degas." Last time they had hunted together, Degas had been newly made. His curly hair had been a bright carrot red with muttonchops down to his sharply pointed chin. That had been—what?—twenty years. Their alien gene drift toward black hair had muted the red to auburn. Combined with a clean shave, Rennie hadn't recognized the solid-built leader of the Demon Curs.

"You took your time," Rennie growled, unsettled that he hadn't caught the other man's approach. It had been a long time since someone took him unaware.

Degas came down the hill, wiping his hands with a white handkerchief, staining it with blood. "You can't hide your thoughts from me, Shaw. You're angry that I surprised you."

"You know I am," Rennie snarled, annoyed afresh.

Degas gave a soft smug laugh. "Oh, stop snarling and growling, and be the man you were born, not the wolf that you've become, or next we will be sniffing asses."

"You asked me here just to make me wait and then insult me to my face?"

"You're the one that's late." Degas lifted the bloodstained handkerchief. "The killing's started—on both sides. We caught one of Hex's Gets nearly drenched in Pack blood."

"Who did it kill? Was it permanent?"

"Don't know." Degas let the wind take the handkerchief. It flew out over the prairie like a wounded dove. "None of the Curs are missing. Most likely it had been a new Pack Get, turned out to grow back into itself. If it wasn't a permanent death, it'll be back on its feet soon enough."

In those words hid an ugly truth: The Curs were casually making Gets wholesale.

Rennie growled softly. "That's not our way."

"It should be! Hex infects humans daily. We should match him, Get for Get."

"So if he takes over half the world, we take the other half?"

"How can a hundred fight a thousand?"

"By using the intelligence we were *born* with. Hex keeps his Gets too close, refusing to let them think. They're like infants without his thoughts guiding them."

"Infants with tommy guns."

"All the more need to be clever, then." Rennie watched the distant tumble of bloodstained white. A thought started to form, and then, with a realization that Degas would read his mind, Rennie veered away from that line of thinking.

Degas glanced hard at him, suspicious of the guarded feelings. "What?"

"We're wasting time here."

"That's not what you were thinking."

"What I was thinking isn't up for discussion." Rennie turned and stalked away, keeping his mind carefully void.

Outside the memory, Ukiah wondered at the timing. Had the war between the Pack and the Ontongard had anything to do with him? Rennie had no memories of Ukiah in Oregon. The Pack had no knowledge of Ukiah prior to this June. Still, Ukiah couldn't ignore the odd coincidence of the date; Rennie arrived in Pendleton on September 23, 1933—the same year that the Kicking Deers lost a child they believed had become the Umatilla Wolf Boy.

CHAPTER TWO

Kicking Deer Farm, Umatilla Indian Reservation, Oregon
Tuesday, August 24, 2004

Straight east on I-84, and Ukiah found his missing mountains. They rose like a wall running north to south before him. But where were the trees? The mountains in front of him looked as bare as the vast fields around him. He passed a sign reading ENTERING UMATILLA INDIAN RESERVATION alongside the highway, but there was no other indication he crossed a boundary. The fencing and fields on either side of the road continued unchanged.

With the GPS system, the ranch was simple to find. All the local ranches seemed linked to the main roads via long, winding driveways. Sometimes the houses were tucked unseen behind a gentle swell, up to a half mile away, but black gravel made the driveways obvious.

He followed the Kicking Deer driveway back to a sprawling ranch house with several well-kept outbuildings. He parked in plain view of the front door, and sat, listening to the engine ticking, suddenly nervous.

If this was his family—then what?

He'd given no thought to how he'd feel and what their reactions might be. Would they recognize him? 1933 was at once unimaginably long ago, and yet, via Rennie's memories, as clear as an hour ago. He struggled to see the passage of time in normal human terms. It was difficult. His only points of reference were Rennie's memories of his childhood, drifting banks of tattered clouds compared to the

Pack's razor-sharp, sequential, and easily searchable memory. Ukiah suspected that even Rennie's memory wasn't a true representation of how humans thought, since Rennie had been made a Get young, and Ukiah viewed his childhood memories after they had been recalled and stored to alien sharpness.

Ukiah couldn't judge what his family might remember. He wished he'd been able to talk to Max freely about what to expect, but Kraynak's presence had made that impossible.

Nor was he sure what this family were hoping to find. The newspaper clipping spoke only of "boy" and "child." How old was that? Five? Eight? Twelve? Eighteen? Were they expecting a child to return, or an old man?

And now that he started to wonder, he wasn't sure why they would want to find him. Mom Jo said once that if she lost Cally, she would look for her daughter until she died. Believing Ukiah's parents would feel the same about their lost son, she hired Max in attempt to reunite Ukiah with them. He knew now that Hex killed his father, and his mother was surely dead.

So who was this Jesse Kicking Deer? Why did he want Ukiah back? How much? Enough to demand that Ukiah move back to Oregon? Even as unlikely as that might be, Ukiah was glad that he was legally an adult and able to choose for himself.

But if these people were his real family—would *he* desperately want to be with them?

A woman's face appeared in one of the windows. He had been noticed.

Suddenly the house seemed like the humane cage that Mom Jo had caught him in; his life was about to totally change. He hadn't expected this. He wasn't sure if he truly wanted whatever the future held anymore.

Still, he couldn't just sit out here. He'd invaded these people's privacy. He should at least explain his presence. Reluctantly, he got out and walked up to the front door.

The door opened even as he raised a hand to knock: The rich smell of fried bacon and potatoes flooded out into the summer dusk. The woman from the window stood in the doorway, without welcome in her stance. She was in her late fifties, long graying hair drawn back into a ponytail. Her dark eyes regarded him with hostility. "Yes?"

"Claire Kicking Deer?" Ukiah got a slight nod. "I'm sorry to bother you. I would have called, but your number is unlisted. I'm looking for Jesse Kicking Deer."

Her eyes narrowed. "Why don't you people just leave him alone?"

Ukiah blinked with surprise. "Pardon?"

"Go away." She started to shut the door.

"Wait!" He stiff-armed the door to keep it from closing in his face. "There's some kind of confusion here. I'm not who you think I am." *Whoever that was.*

"Let go of the door." She tried pressing it shut.

Ukiah resisted, talking quickly. "Please, I just want to talk to Jesse Kicking Deer about an article in the *East Oregonian*. He was asking for information on a feral child."

Claire Kicking Deer tried to yank open the door in a way that suggested she would slam it shut in his face, arm or no arm. He caught hold of the door, reacting without thinking. "Let go of the door, or I'll call my son to the door, and you don't want me to do that."

He kept hold of the door, sure if he let her close it, she wouldn't listen to him, and he'd lose this chance to reconnect with his lost family. "I don't understand why you're so angry with me. I just want to talk to Mr. Kicking Deer. I'll ask him a few questions and go away. Please, you have no idea how much this would mean to me."

"Jared!" She called over her shoulder.

Oh, shit! Heavy footsteps heralded the arrival of the son. Instincts told Ukiah that violence was becoming a distinct possibility. He released the door and backed up. The door jerked completely open, and Jared Kicking Deer stepped out onto the porch, looking fully capable of said violence. He was a tall man, in his late twenties, broad in a way that suggested weightlifting sometime in his past, and had a bearing that spoke of being unafraid of a fight.

"My mother said to leave my grandfather alone."

Ukiah held out a hand to ward off any blows. "Look, I'm

a private investigator from Pittsburgh, Pennsylvania. I'm out here on business with my partner." Once sure that Jared Kicking Deer wasn't going to swing at him, Ukiah took a business card out of his wallet, and handed it to Jared.

Jared didn't bother to glance at the card. "PI from Pittsburgh. You here to find Alicia Kraynak?"

One surprise after another. "Yes. I'm an expert tracker; we specialize in missing persons. The thing is, when I was thirteen, I was found running feral in Umatilla National Park by my adoptive mother. She took me home to Pittsburgh. I thought, since I was in the area, I'll try to find out who I really am."

"Well, you're younger than most of them, but I've heard this song before."

Song? Ukiah tilted his head in puzzlement. "What do you mean? You've had a glut of amnesiac wolf boys coming here?"

The man gave a dry snort of laughter. "More or less."

Ukiah considered him for a moment, finding it difficult to judge this stranger. "You're not kidding." A horrifying possibility suggested itself to Ukiah; Kittanning might not be the only clone made out of his blood. "Oh, please don't tell me that they all look like me! Do they?"

Another laugh. "No. If anything, you're the only one so far that looks like a Cayuse."

So there wasn't a flood of his violence-born copies like Kittanning. He relaxed slightly. "I don't know what's made you so hostile, but I promise you that I mean no harm. I'm only looking for my own identity."

There was bored disbelief in the man's eyes. "We're sick of you people. You should be ashamed of yourself, preying on the hopes of an old man. Now, I suggest you leave before you find yourself in jail for trespassing and fraud."

"What harm could it be just to let me talk—"

"I said go!"

Ukiah backed down. "Okay. I'll go. If you change your mind, just call me at any of those numbers."

Red Lion Hotel, Pendleton, Oregon
Tuesday, August 24, 2004

Their hotel, the Red Lion on South Nye Avenue, sat on the ridge above Pendleton. Ukiah checked the front desk for their room numbers, dropped his bag in the empty rooms, and went in search for Max and Kraynak at the restaurant.

He found them taking up the corner booth. Maps fought dinner dishes for table space. A tall, lanky woman in her late twenties sat with Max and Kraynak. She wore black-leather hiking boots, tight blue jeans, a black-leather bomber jacket, and her blond hair cropped short. She glanced up at Ukiah in surprise with pale green eyes as he pulled up a chair to sit down.

Kraynak wearily nodded his welcome, eyes bloodshot and bruised from the vomiting. He carefully ate a bowl of chicken rice soup, several slices of white toast, and a side of rice.

Max's dinner of steak and steak fries sat cooling, barely touched.

"How did it go?" Max asked.

Ukiah pantomimed an airplane dive-bombing the ground and exploding.

"That bad?" Max winced. He caught the woman's look of curiosity. "This is my partner." Max let Ukiah introduce himself. Establishing a strong presence, Max called it, and they practiced it until it was smooth.

"Ukiah Oregon." He offered his hand.

The woman startled slightly. "Ukiah? Like the town?" It was weird to get the reaction. In Pittsburgh, no one realized he was named after an actual place. Pennsylvanians thought it was an odd family name, often confused with Uriah, Uriel, and once, by an old Jewish man, Uzziah. (The man went on to *tsk* over his supposed Jewish parent for marrying outside the religion.)

Max coughed instead of laughing and said, "His mom named him after the town."

She accepted this explanation and Ukiah's hand.

Ukiah shook her hand just as he was taught—meet the

eyes, give a serious half smile, firm grip but not too hard, and finish with, "Glad to meet you."

"Sam Killington." Her grip was strong, her skin warm and dry, the touch telling Ukiah a host of disturbing information. Gunpowder from a handgun cuffed the back of her hand under his thumb. Ash from burnt carpet, mattresses, and painted wood was lodged in various creases of her palmprint. With the motion of shaking hands, the cuff of her jacket brushed him, reporting the presence of charred human flesh.

Ukiah jerked his hand back, and wiped it clean on his pants.

Max caught the exchange, flared an eyebrow at him, but leaned back slightly, away from Sam. "She's a reporter. She's offered to help however she can."

"Not really a reporter. I write occasional fluff pieces. I thought I could pick up food and supplies, that kind of thing," Sam elaborated calmly, though obviously noticing Max cooling toward her. "If you're here to find Alicia Kraynak, you don't have time to waste trying to find the grocery store."

Ukiah gazed at her. *Who was she? What did she want?* Under Obsession perfume, female sweat, leather jacket, woodsmoke, and gun oil, he caught the engine smell from a motorcycle. There had been a Harley-Davidson in the hotel's parking lot. Stepping back through the day, he found it again at the parking lot of the airport. He flipped through memories of the airport and found her, hidden behind a newspaper and the loudly playing children.

She met his eyes levelly for several minutes and then looked away. "So, Max tells me you're a tracker. It seems slightly stereotypical that the Indian is the tracker."

"Ukiah is the best tracker in the country," Kraynak stated, waving a piece of toast.

She dragged her gaze back to Ukiah. "You're real good at that evil eye."

"You were waiting for us at the airport," Ukiah stated.

She shrugged. "I heard the rumor that you were coming and was curious. It's not a crime."

"You're currently carrying a pistol, either on a shoulder holster or kidney holster. You fired that weapon this morning. You've been in a burned building, a house I think, and you've been exposed to human ash."

There was silence at the table, and then Kraynak stated, "I said he was the best."

"I'm impressed." Sam pulled a business card from her jacket pocket and slipped it gracefully onto the table. "I'm a private detective. I'm investigating the death of a local family. They were killed in a house fire last Thursday. I was at the site this morning, after some target shooting."

Kraynak claimed the card first, glanced at it, and handed it to Max. "What does that have to do with Alicia?"

"I'm playing a hunch," Sam admitted, spreading her hands. "A family of six dies in a house fire on Thursday. Four days later, a hiker from Pennsylvania disappears. I thought there might be a connection."

Max took the card, showed it to Ukiah long enough for Ukiah to memorize it, and then studied it himself. SAMUEL ANNE KILLINGTON, PRIVATE INVESTIGATOR, it read, followed by a Pendleton address and telephone number. "Samuel Anne?"

"My parents were twisted," Sam said. "My sister is Kendall Jane."

"So what's the connection?" Kraynak asked.

Sam gave a weak laugh. "Well, it struck me as odd that the hiker's uncle was flying in two private detectives. Professional pride aside, a local investigator would know the area better and be a hell of lot cheaper. And two men instead of just one seemed like overkill, so maybe they were hired muscle. The father of the family worked at the casino. Dead casino worker. Two hired goons." She rolled her wrist as she listed the last two points and ended with her hand cocked upward in speculation. "Organized crime?"

"You've got to keep that rampant paranoia in check," Max said, and grinned. "Ukiah and I specialize in lost and found. We're damn good at it."

"So, the kid's a tracking wonder," she conceded, then

looked questioningly at Max. "What do you bring to the partnership?"

"A mature, level head"—Max took out his cigar case, flicked it open, and selected a cigar—"worldly knowledge, and a big gun I'm not afraid to use."

She laughed, showing sound, clean teeth. "How big is that gun of yours?"

Max's eyebrows shot up in surprise, and then he grinned. "Wouldn't you like to know?"

Sam's smile widened. "If you show me yours, I'll show you mine."

Max idly flipped the cigar through his fingers as he narrowed his light gray eyes at Sam. Reaching some decision, he leaned back, unholstered his pistol, and carefully placed it on the table so it pointed at no one. "SIG Sauer Model P210, nine-round magazine in nine millimeter." He kept his hand on it so even with a quick grab, Sam couldn't pick it up.

Sam reached behind her and pulled her pistol. Her gun had sleek lines and a molded grip. "Heckler and Koch P9S. Also nine in nine."

"Nice piece," Max said around his unlit cigar.

"You've got a nice rod there yourself."

"Some of us are still eating," Kraynak grumbled, then muttered softly, shaking his head, "Gun-bunny foreplay."

Max and Sam blushed, and the guns vanished from the table.

Ukiah frowned, feeling like he just missed something huge that everyone else could see, like he had suddenly gone blind to elephants wandering through the lounge.

"I'm serious about the help," Sam said. "I've been in Pendleton for four years. I know the locals and the area. If you need any help, give me a call. I'll gladly trade information for local color."

She stole one of Max's fries, popped it into her mouth with a grin, and strolled away.

"Woof," Kraynak said after the lounge door closed behind her.

"Woof, woof," Max said, picking up the business card and stowing it away.

"You think we can trust her?" Ukiah asked.

"I would like to trust her," Max admitted with a grin, and then sobered. "You didn't find Kicking Deer?"

"He's got a big, angry grandson that didn't like me on sight. Apparently they've gotten a string of people showing up and claiming to be the Umatilla Wolf Boy." Max's eyebrows went up in alarm but relaxed as Ukiah continued with, "But they didn't look like me."

"That's weird," Kraynak said.

Ukiah agreed with a twinge of guilt. While Kraynak was one of his and Max's best friends, they'd never revealed Ukiah's alien origins to the homicide detective. Max and Indigo both stressed that the fewer people who knew the truth, the better. Luckily, being raised by wolves seemed to excuse most of his oddities.

Speaking of oddities. "Another weird thing, Jared Kicking Deer guessed I was here to find Alicia—although from what Sam said, it's common knowledge that two private investigators from Pittsburgh are flying in to look for her."

"There is that," Max said, although his tone suggested that he didn't believe it.

Kraynak pushed abruptly away from the table. "We'll check his priors tomorrow with the police, if Alicia doesn't turn up."

"What did you two find out?" Ukiah asked.

"We talked to the incident commander, Tim Winholtz," Max said. "He seems to know what he's doing. They had thirty people out looking today, but they didn't turn anything up."

In rugged country, a broken or twisted ankle could strand a hiker on or near a trail. Searchers without tracking abilities could find such a hiker "lost" this way. Experienced hikers left markers when they ventured away from the trail. Alicia was experienced and intelligent. It boded ill that so many searchers hadn't found her.

"Any helicopter support?" Ukiah asked.

Max shook his head. "They weren't able to bring in the helicopter until late. That front that we flew through this afternoon kept them buttoned down all morning."

"It rained?" Ukiah asked. Rain would make tracking harder.

"It just blew over," Max said. "Strong gusts and overcast. Not flying weather. Not in the mountains."

"What's the weather for tomorrow?" Ukiah asked.

"It's a fifty-fifty chance that it will clear up enough." Kraynak said. "We'll know tomorrow."

Max sighed, fidgeting with his unlit cigar. "Oh, hell, Kraynak, I hope we find Alicia tomorrow—open and shut."

"You getting a bad feeling about this?" Kraynak asked.

Max nodded. "Real bad."

Ukiah winced. The last time Max had a bad feeling about a case, Ukiah got killed.

CHAPTER THREE

Bear Wallow Creek Campground, Ukiah, Oregon
Wednesday, August 25, 2004

They took I-395 out of Pendleton an hour before dawn, running nearly straight south by the GPS. After passing through a small town called Pilot Rock, the road began to climb through bare, rolling hills. All signs of civilization fell behind, except for the unbroken fence that paralleled the highway on either side. From road edge to horizon, the vegetation stayed at a constant four-inch height. After years in Pennsylvania, where chest-high weeds and scrub trees would spring up if not constantly cut back, the landscape seemed otherworldly and almost lifeless.

They had traveled nearly thirty miles before pine trees appeared. The trees started deep in the steep valleys, scattered and few. Slowly, as they drove farther south, the pines increased and crept up the sides of the hills until they blanketed everything.

During the next thirty miles, they passed only one or two houses and a handful of dirt turnoffs. The first true intersection was the lonely road back to the town of Ukiah. Only two signposts marked the crossroad. The first signpost merely labeled I-395 as it continued and the crossing road as State Route 244. The second sign read UKIAH and pointed eastward, down 244, though nothing seemed to lay in that direction.

"They left out signs for you, kid," Max said to Ukiah, but

his eyes were on Kraynak, who had grown silent and tense during the trip.

Kraynak's eyes narrowed at the desolate crossroads and the road that had been empty of all other traffic. "Damn it! Alicia couldn't have found a place more fucking isolated."

"We'll find her," Max said quietly.

It was odd that Ukiah could remember the town he was named after perfectly, and yet completely wrong. The city of his memories was large, imposing, loud, and frightening. Three streetlights shined on the same exact buildings, only now the structures appeared few, small, and rustic.

The tin man made out of welded parts, marking the only gas station, had terrified him as a child. Why? Even with his perfect memory of his terror, he couldn't recall the mindset that viewed the metal scarecrow with horror. It looked quaintly harmless to him now.

The lone bar, decorated with a hundred pair of antlers tacked to its wood siding, made him laugh. Even the junk-yard seemed pitifully tiny. And then the town was passed. At forty miles per hour, it had taken less than a minute to drive through it and back into wilderness.

"I thought it was bigger." Ukiah turned to watch the town vanish behind them. "It seemed bigger."

"You had nothing to compare it with," Max said. "You're used to Pittsburgh. Of course it seems smaller now."

Bear Wallow Creek Campground was fifteen miles out of Ukiah. The only building they passed, once clearing the out-skirts of the town, was abandoned and collapsing. They ar-rived as the gray of predawn set in. A narrow dirt road crept through a series of primitive campsites, showing no water or electric hookups. The bus that served as base camp for the Umatilla County search-and-rescue team sat wedged into one of the campgrounds. Kraynak's tan Volkswagen van with Pennsylvania plates sat parked across the narrow lane from the bus, seeming horribly out of place.

They climbed out of the rental car, yawning and stretch-ing in the chilled morning. Ukiah breathed deep the moun-

tain air, filling his lungs with the sense of home. This was
what he remembered. This was *all* he remembered before
his Mom Jo caught him: the steep hills and mountains; the
clear, cold air; and the firs, towering so straight and high that
one looked and looked and looked to see their tops.

If he was the Kicking Deer boy, he had lost every memory of the flat, treeless farm on the reservation.

"Let's check in and then gear up." Max headed across the
loose gravel parking lot, his footsteps loud in the silence.

Tim Winholtz was a lean thirty-year-old who barely
looked up from his maps when they entered. He held a bulky
satellite phone to his ear, shaking his head as he listened.

"Bad news?" Max asked.

"Oh, the forecasts are changing, but just for the bad. No
helicopter support for the day."

"This is my partner," Max said.

Ukiah took the cue and held out his hand. "Ukiah Oregon."

"You're kidding. Like the town?"

"Yeah. My adopted parents named me after the town."

"So you grew up around here?"

"I guess."

"What tribe are you from?"

"I don't know." In June, he discovered that he understood
the language of the Nez Percé tribe, which he had in common with the Pack. It was the first human language Coyote
learned, and thus all his Gets knew it. It was unlikely, however, that Ukiah could have remained hidden from the Pack
all this time if he had lived with the Nez Percé. The Kicking
Deers were Cayuse, a tribe he and the Pack knew little
about.

Max rescued Ukiah from the conversation. "Daylight's
burning! We'll keep in touch with you, Winholtz. Come on,
kid."

"Good luck," Winholtz called as Max hustled them back
out of the mobile command bus.

The volunteer search-and-rescue team members started
to arrive in their personal cars as he and Max did their tra-

ditional wrangling. The small GPS tracer went on without
question; it was vital in keeping them together during the
tracking. Max insisted on the bulletproof vest and the voice-
activated two-way radio. Ukiah managed to talk Max out of
the headset-mounted camera and his pistol. Max backed
down on the gun only because by the strict letter of the law,
their Pennsylvania concealed-weapon permits weren't valid
in Oregon; chances were good that they would encounter at
least one police officer helping out on the rescue mission.
Ukiah covered up his body armor with a black T-shirt labeled across the back with PRIVATE INVESTIGATOR, BENNETT
DETECTIVE AGENCY in large white letters. He added a matching windbreaker to keep out the morning chill.

Max tested the volume levels on the radio, then checked
to make sure that Ukiah's tracer showed up on the GPS system. "Okay. We're ready to go."

Alicia's campsite was just beyond the Volkswagen. Just a
campfire, picnic table, and the Kraynaks' four-person tent, it
still had a homey, lived-in feel. Bear Wallow Creek bordered
the small patch of land; it was so narrow he could have leapt
across the stream, so clear he could see fish darting in the
shadows. Across the stream, the hills climbed steeply upward, heavily wooded with tall firs. The Oregon wilderness
seemed almost parklike, clear where in Pennsylvania there
would have been tangled undergrowth.

The other grad student, Rose, was slightly older than Alicia and much smaller. She sat at the picnic table, her hands
hugged around a mug of steaming coffee, dark circles bruis-
ing her eyes from lack of sleep and worry.

"It was so cold out last night," Rose whispered into her
coffee. "I hope Alicia kept warm."

Kraynak looked away. "Can you—can you tell Max and
Ukiah what you told me on the phone?"

"We normally only go out together," Rose started quietly.
"We've been doing a field map of this quadrangle as part of
my master thesis. It's the whole reason Alicia was here—Pitt
doesn't allow solo field trips because of safety."

Rose shifted forward her right foot and pulled up her pant

leg to show off a bandage wrapped tightly around her ankle. "I twisted my ankle on Sunday, not badly, but it still hurts to walk. Alicia didn't want me to put weight on it. She said I might hurt my ankle worse when a day or two of rest would completely heal it. We were planning to leave on Friday, and it's a three-day drive home without cruise control. If my ankle doesn't heal, I won't be able to help drive home. All we had left was to double-check some of our findings—we could have even left early. Monday morning Alicia went out, alone, and didn't come back. I feel so guilty."

Ukiah wondered if it was sexist of him to assume that Rose had nothing to do with Alicia's disappearance just because she was a woman. Certainly if she had been a man, he would have examined her for blood traces first.

He glanced guiltily at the woman. She was tiny, lucky to be five foot and break the hundred-pound threshold. Freckles bridged her nose. Laugh lines surrounded her dark eyes that were now filled only with concern and growing dread. It seemed unlikely, almost impossible, that she could have killed five-foot-eleven Alicia and hidden her body.

Ukiah listened to Max and Kraynak question Rose as he ducked into the tent. Alicia's ghost presence hovered inside. her scent, her DNA, and his memories of her attached to nearly everything in sight. Her sleeping bag lay smoothed flat on a surplus army cot, pillow on one end. Ukiah lifted her pillow, and found one of his T-shirts. At one time, the T-shirt had been identical to the one Ukiah was currently wearing. Alicia had torn the collar and sleeves off the shirt, and apparently was using it as a sleeping shirt.

When did I give this to her? he wondered, and then remembered.

The rain started suddenly and hard, a typical early-June Pittsburgh downpour. Mist rose from the hot asphalt as the rain sheeted down. The foyer door to Max's Shadyside mansion—which doubled as the company's offices—opened and then slammed shut.

"Hello?" Ukiah called from the kitchen, putting his lunch dishes down on the granite countertop.

"It's me!" Alicia came laughing down the front hall into the kitchen, dripping wet.

"You're soaked!" Ukiah laughed with her.

"It's glorious! Come on!" She caught his hand, skin warm and wet, and tugged him out the back door and into the warm rain.

It was wonderful; there was something intimately maternal about the wet warmth, as if the whole world embraced them. They stayed outside until he was thoroughly soaked, laughing, stomping in puddles, and dancing. Alicia hugged him, raindrops glistening in her eyelashes like diamonds.

Oh, yes, she needed something dry afterward, so he loaned her the T-shirt, a pair of clean boxers, and the use of the second-floor laundry room. She must have kept the shirt.

Ukiah laid his cheek against it. The T-shirt held Alicia's scent, healthy and clean, no hint of violence, no drugs, nothing that would bring on a collapse on the trail—just Alicia.

"You got any idea which direction she headed?" Max asked Rose outside the tent.

"No, none. She got up early. She told me to sleep in, that she'd be back before dinner, and walked out of the tent. I heard her walk off, but I was already going back to sleep."

Under the bed was a collection of shoes: a colorful plaid pair of tennis shoes, low-heeled sandals, a worn pair of moccasins. He examined them for size and wear. Alicia was a woman's size nine with a walk that wore down the outside heel of her shoes first.

"The search-and-rescue people kept asking yesterday, as if I knew and just forgot I knew. I don't know. I didn't think to ask. I should have asked." Exasperation mixed with guilt in Rose's voice.

Plastic milk crates made makeshift bookcases. The diverse selection of notebooks, magazines, and paperbacks were all tucked into Ziploc freezer bags of various sizes. The two Hillerman mystery novels were Alicia's, as was a fat, tapestry-covered daily planner. He took the planner out, unsnapping the leather band that kept it closed. The book all but exploded, stuffed to overflowing with inserts and paper.

He flipped through the planner. There was a notepad in the back, a plastic pouch containing small fossils, a business card holder, an address book—yes, he was listed under the "O's" with smiley faces around his listing—a paper pouch for receipts, and a photo album. The photographs included several school photos of Kraynak's daughter, Sasha, a family portrait of the Kraynaks—Alicia included, one each of her dead parents, a trimmed Polaroid of Max prior to the graying at his temples, and three pictures of Ukiah himself—ages thirteen, seventeen, and twenty according to his driver's license and the date they were taken.

In his last two pictures, he hadn't aged more than a couple days. In comparison, Sasha's school photos showed the change that a year made in a child. Why had no one ever noticed how alien he was? Or had they, and just never commented to him?

Most of the planner's bulk, however, was made up of a fat day-per-page calendar covered heavily with yellow notes and one red flag marking last Sunday. Ukiah checked Monday, found it blank. He flipped through Tuesday and Wednesday and found them blank too. He flipped backward for a few days. Alicia filled the pages with her life; nothing sinister seemed to lurk under the surface, waiting to snatch her away the moment she was alone. He put his thumb to the edge of the pages and ruffled them by so each page registered in his sight only a second, and he counted back the days by odd numbers. No pages were missing.

"She had a phone with her," Rose was saying. "I thought if she got into trouble, she'd call for help."

Ukiah closed the planner, struggled a moment to get it snapped tight, and replaced it into the plastic bag. On top of the crates, he was only mildly surprised to find her jewelry case. Alicia never wore makeup; she flattered her vanity with earrings. Gems, semi-precious stones, and minerals dominated the collection. Many he recognized as ones he had seen her wear. There was a new influx of stone animal fetishes, dreamcatchers, and other Native American–influenced earrings. He closed the lid. Her jewelry-making tools sat in the box under the jewelry case, along with bags of various beads and wires.

"Are you sure she has the phone with her?" Kraynak was asking. When Rose answered that she was positive, Kraynak asked why.

"Well, we both have satellite phones; they're a must for a geologist," Rose explained. "We recharge them when we drive to Pendleton. I charged mine going to town on Saturday, and she charged hers coming back. When we were out on Sunday, she forgot to get her phone out of the van, but it's not there now."

"You sure she didn't take it out and still forget it in camp?" Max asked. Alicia's memory was almost as bad as Ukiah's was perfect.

"When she didn't turn up at lunchtime, I tried calling her. When I called, I didn't hear her phone ringing here in camp. It rang a couple of times and then dropped me into her voice mail. I thought it was weird, she should have been able to hear it and answer if she was carrying it. So I started to look for it here in the camp, some place I couldn't hear it ring."

"And you didn't find it?" Kraynak asked.

"No."

Ukiah gazed about the tent. It was filled with little homey touches that reflected Alicia's hand. A dreamcatcher hung from the center post, to catch her common nightmares. He shook his head and ducked out of the tent.

Rose continued with her account of the day. "I tried calling Alicia every half hour. When she didn't come back by evening, I called the park rangers and then you. I should have called while it was still daylight."

"That's okay. You did fine," Kraynak soothed. "Do you remember what she was wearing?"

Rose said that she didn't remember, but in the last day she had pieced together which of Alicia's clothes were missing. Hiking boots. Blue jeans with a Celtic-knot design painted down the outside seam. A mottled mauve T-shirt. An oversized flannel button-down shirt, mostly in red. Backpack. Phone. Field journal and compass.

The conversation turned to the search that had started at dawn yesterday.

"They asked the same questions that you're asking," Rose said. "They seemed pretty organized."

All thirty searchers seemed to have moved through the campground, trampling out Alicia's presence. Ukiah pressed fingers into the various tracks, picking up the dirt and sifting it though his fingertips, sniffing it, and then tasting it, trying to determine when the prints were made and by whom.

"It's so weird having you here," Rose said. "She talked about you guys all the—what's he doing?"

"He's tracking," Max answered without pause.

"It looks like he's eating dirt."

"It only looks that way," Max assured her.

Ukiah started a spiral search from the heart of the camp. The women had been in Oregon almost three weeks before Alicia had vanished; she had walked around the camp in every pair of her shoes. Ukiah found hundreds of her footprints. It was going to be difficult to tell which was the last set of tracks she had set down. He ranged out to the fringe, to find departing tracks, which were fewer in number.

Nose almost to the ground, he examined Alicia's various trails. The sun was rising as he leaned back, stretching.

Max caught the motion. "How's it going, Ukiah?"

"She left the camp the day before yesterday with this trail here," Ukiah answered, standing. "I'm going to be switching into high gear. You ready?"

Max consulted his map and compass. "Hmmm, that trail runs kind of parallel to one of the forest roads, keeping about two to five miles from it. You going fast?"

Ukiah nodded. "It's a clear trail."

"Okay, go ahead, we'll follow in the four-by-four."

He turned to go, then remembered that he unthinkingly promised Indigo a phone call. "Oh, Max, can you call Indigo for me and see how Kittanning's appointment went?"

"Sure thing."

So he went, at an easy lope he learned from the wolves.

*　　*　　*

Over the voice-activated radio, Ukiah caught Max's side of the phone call to Indigo as he headed out of the campground into the park proper. She kept the conversation short, limiting it to a report that everything went smoothly with Kittanning's checkup, hopes that they find Alicia quickly, and then a pledge of love to be passed along.

After that was silence as he tracked Alicia over steep hills, through rugged valleys, and across dirt forest roads. Occasionally he caught the sound of the Blazer as Max drove the forest roads, trying to keep them close together via Ukiah's GPS tracer.

Max broke the radio silence after a half an hour with a muttered, "What the hell does he want?"

"What is it, Max?" Ukiah paused on a rocky spar at the top of a ridge. Trees screened the Blazer from sight. A red light flickered oddly through the green, too bright and quick for brake lights.

"There's a police car that just came up behind us and it's flashing its lights at us," Max explained.

"Oh, joy," Ukiah muttered, and plunged down the next hillside.

"How are you doing?" Max asked now that the silence was broken.

"That last part was fairly steep, you nearly had to rock climb, and I found red-flannel fiber on some of the stones. They have her sweat on them."

"Good. Can I help you?"

Ukiah paused on the edge of the stream meandering through the valley, wondering at Max's last sentence. A third, deep male voice came over the radio, and he realized that the police officer must be standing at Max's window, speaking into the vehicle so the voice-activated radio could pick it up. Max had spoken to the police officer.

"Which one of you is Alicia Kraynak's uncle?" the police officer asked.

"I am." Kraynak's answer sounded slightly distant, as Max's mike was on his left. "Homicide Detective Raymond Kraynak, City of Pittsburgh Police Department. You found her?"

"Sorry, no," the stranger's voice rumbled, and yet seemed familiar. Over the radio, it was difficult to tell.

Ukiah jumped over the creek and started up the next hillside. It was even steeper than the last.

The remote conversation continued, with the policeman asking, "Then you're the private investigator from Pittsburgh?"

"I'm Max Bennett, Bennett Detective Agency." Max's introduction seemed loud after Kraynak's. "My partner is tracking Alicia in the next valley over. We're using a global-positioning tracking device with a geological software interface."

There was a grunt from the policeman. "Fancy setup. What's your range?"

"About fifty miles, here in the mountains," Max said.

"He's on foot?" the policeman asked.

Max confirmed this and added, "And moving fast."

Another grunt. "Tracking done right is slow work."

Ukiah shook his head and scrambled up the last few feet of the steep hillside. A whiff of plastic caught his attention. He sniffed, trying to locate the source. It seemed to come from a deep crack in the stone. He reached down into the rough-edged darkness. His fingertips brushed plastic tainted with Alicia's presence. The shape and the material suggested a wireless phone. Try as he may, he couldn't get a grip on the object to pick the item up. "Max?"

"Yeah, kid?"

"Have Kraynak ring Alicia's phone."

"Ukiah wants you to ring Alicia's phone," Max relayed to Kraynak. "What's up, kid?"

"I think I found her phone. It's down in a crack where I can't reach it."

The overture from *William Tell* chirped out from down between the boulders.

"That's it. It's her phone." He considered the stone surrounding the crevasse. There was no indication that Alicia ever searched for the dropped phone. "I think she never noticed that she lost it."

Max relayed the information to Kraynak.

"Is she hurt?" Kraynak asked.

"Did you hear that?" Max asked, meaning Kraynak's question.

"There's no blood sign here." He continued his climb up the rocks. "And she seemed to make the summit without any problem. In fact, she just scrambled up onto another higher set of rocks, maybe to take a look around."

"Ukiah says no," Max told Kraynak.

"She's crossing over the ridge into this next valley. Are you going to be able to follow?"

There was the rustling of paper. "Yeah, this road swings in that direction. We have to keep on moving to keep in radio range with my partner. Is there a number we can reach you with updates?"

Ukiah winced at the skewed conversation, needing to think a moment before realizing Max started off talking to him but had switched over to the police officer.

"I'll follow along behind," the policeman stated.

This time it was Max that muttered, "Oh, joy," but hopefully after the officer returned to his own car.

Ukiah ran for another hour, the track still clear. Max and Kraynak talked, but trying to maintain a three-way discussion was maddening, so Ukiah refrained from making comments. Something about the case had triggered the men's nostalgia, and the conversation covered the hardships of their fifteen-year friendship: the Gulf War, Kraynak's struggle to quit smoking after his father died of lung cancer, Max's ordeal to make his Internet startup company a success only to have wealth become meaningless to him, and the harrowing accident that killed Kraynak's brother. Hinted to, but never spoken about directly, were the death of Max's wife and his years of near-suicidal depression.

Ukiah had just gained another ridge, when Max whistled to catch his attention.

"The road nips in to almost a mile of you, to the west. You want to swing over and pick up food and water?" Max asked.

"Yes!" Ukiah replied. He had drained his water bottle a

long time ago and he was on the verge of starving. "I'm coming in."

He swung over to the west edge of the ridge. The rocky hill dropped sharply, nearly a cliff, and then the land leveled out into a small meadow. The Blazer sat pulled off the dirt road. The squad car parked behind Max was marked with UMATILLA COUNTY SHERIFF'S DEPARTMENT.

Max spotted him on the skyline and whistled. Ukiah waved and came down the hillside in a series of leaps and bounds down the rocks.

"Shit!" Kraynak's curse came over the headset. "He's going to kill himself."

Max's laugh echoed from in front of Ukiah and the radio. "If it makes you nervous, don't watch him. He's half mountain goat. I've never seen him fall. What do you want, kid, tuna fish or smoked turkey?"

"Tuna," Ukiah answered into his microphone, running through the last sparse stand of trees, "but lots of Gatorade first."

Max was dropping the tailgate as Ukiah cleared the last trees. The police officer was beside Kraynak and they were watching Ukiah come at the easy wolf lope. Ukiah could smell the tuna sandwich, though, unwrapped on the truck's roof. It sucked in his attention.

"I knew you were good, kid," Kraynak called as Ukiah scrambled down the road's bank. "But I didn't know this good. You've been running at that speed for the last three hours. How long can you keep it up?"

Ukiah caught an ice-cold bottle of Gatorade from Max. "I don't know."

"It usually gets dark before he tires out," Max said, pulling out a second bottle of cold Gatorade while Ukiah drank the first one. "That's as long as you keep him in liquid and food."

Ukiah snatched up the sandwich and tore into it. "This was too long, Max. Get me some food to carry when I pull out, okay?"

"You want a second sandwich now?"

Ukiah started to nod his head, and noticed for the first

time exactly who stood beside Kraynak. It was Jared Kicking Deer. *Sheriff* Jared Kicking Deer, according to the nametag on his neatly pressed gray uniform, complete with handcuffs and service revolver. What a wonderful person to have pissed off with you. Ukiah gave a wary nod to his possible relative.

Sheriff Kicking Deer nodded back, seemingly just as wary.

Max noticed the exchange and his body stiffened. "Did I miss something?" Max murmured to Ukiah as he handed the second bottle of Gatorade to him.

"He's Jesse Kicking Deer's grandson," Ukiah quietly explained. "He threw me out of his mother's house last night."

Max glanced at Jared, and turned back to Ukiah, swearing softly. "Sorry, kid, he didn't give a name, and I didn't think to read the nametag. What do you think he wants?"

"The mind boggles." Ukiah shrugged, unclipped his water bottle, and handed it to Max. "Could be he's just worried about the missing college student."

"Well, it's a chance to win him over with your charm and beauty."

Ukiah laughed and finished the rest of the sandwich. Max handed him back the refilled water bottle and a fanny pack of candy bars, beef jerky, and trail mix.

"I can't imagine her having gone much farther on Monday than this," he announced to them. "She wasn't moving very quickly in the last valley and actually stopped quite a few times to bang chips off rocks and such like. She ate lunch already, so we're into travel she did during midday. If she planned to go back to camp, she has to change course soon."

"So, she hasn't started to backtrack?" Kraynak asked.

Ukiah shook his head. "No. We've been swinging east and south for the last hour, so I think she planned to circle back around instead of backtracking."

Max pulled the map from the Blazer, and unfolded it onto the tailgate. "Well, if she didn't come down that ridge this way, she could have taken this spur, which would have landed her near this road here." He tapped where the darker squiggle of the road nearly touched a stacked series of light squiggles that indicated a very steep hill. "It's a fairly level hike back to the campground then, at least according to the map."

"We've had some bad falls from that hill," Sheriff Kicking Deer stated. "It's taller, so it's a vantage point. On the maps, that point looks no steeper than the rest, but it's actually a cliff. People not familiar with the area often park and try to find their way up and down it."

Kraynak studied the map. "Why don't we drive over while Ukiah takes the high country? We'll meet at the bottom, here."

Max nodded. "Okay. Sounds like a plan. You set, kid?"

"Set." Ukiah gave them all a wave. "See you later."

As Ukiah started to run, Sheriff Kicking Deer returned to his car and radioed in their plans.

Ukiah backtracked the mile, scrambling easily back up to the ridge and starting along it. His mind, though, kept returning to Sheriff Kicking Deer. Win him over with charm and beauty? He laughed to himself. How do you convince a person that you're his ninety-plus great-uncle when you look eighteen? Maybe in the future he could use cryogenic sleep as an excuse, but he disappeared in 1933.

Reports of alien abductions flourished after the chaos he and the Ontongard caused with the Mars Rover. The NASA Channel faithfully caught and CNN endlessly replayed every moment of the mother ship—from when the cloaking shields dropped to its blinding self-destruction. Later, a hacker group claimed responsibility for the video feed, saying that they swapped the live coverage with doctored footage. Later still, a small group of experts, willing to undergo world ridicule, pointed out evidence why the ship couldn't have been computer-generated graphics. Despite everything, few people believed in aliens, except those who also believed in government conspiracies.

No, he couldn't say aliens had abducted him. He hated the idea of lying.

Besides, the *East Oregonian* newspaper article specifically named him the Umatilla Wolf *Boy.* Maybe the Kicking Deers were expecting an unaging child. Perhaps the true problem was that he looked too old.

"This isn't good." Ukiah squatted at the cliff edge, scanning for the track.

"What is it?"

"Can you see me?"

"No."

Ukiah worked his way out onto a narrow outcrop and waved down at the three men. "How about now?"

"Okay. We see you. What's up?"

"The track stops here. I think she fell."

"Oh, shit."

Ukiah leaned carefully out, over the ledge, to look down at the jumble of rocks. "Can you work over until you're under me and see if she's—"

Something hit him on the right side of the chest, just over his heart. As it slammed him around in a half spin, he heard a loud crack echoing across the valley. Even as he realized that he had been hit by a bullet, and that he was falling over the outcrop's edge, another struck him hard.

CHAPTER FOUR

Umatilla National Park, Umatilla County, Oregon
Wednesday, August 25, 2004

"Ukiah! Ukiah!" Max scrambled over the rocks to him.

So he *was* on the ground. Ukiah had hit an outcrop of rock coming down, his arm taking the brunt of the fall in an explosion of pain. He fell again, a second hard hit, this time in the stomach, and then tumbled a few more feet. He expected a third drop through free fall, but apparently he had run out of cliff. Ukiah slowly rolled over, moaning in pain as he did. "Somebody shot me, Max."

"I know." Max unzipped Ukiah's windbreaker.

"Don't let him shoot you!" Ukiah pushed at Max, trying to get him to take cover.

"We're fairly well-screened by rocks here," Max said. "I've got my vest on too. Now, lie still."

"Oh, I'm not going anywhere." Ukiah quit struggling and let Max undo his body armor.

Sheriff Kicking Deer joined them, ducking down behind the rocks, talking fast and low on his radio. "Officer needs backup, shots fired. I've got a shooter with a high-powered rifle that just shot the damn tracker. I'm going to need an EMS crew at the foot of Slide Hill. I need backup. Get hold of the state police and tell them we have a sniper."

Kraynak crouched beside Max. "How bad is he?"

"The vest took the bullets," Max muttered, eyeing Ukiah's bared chest. "I think the fall damage is going to be the worse." He leaned up to brush blood-soaked hair back from Ukiah's forehead and scowled at the wound he located. "There's where the blood is coming from."

"I think I broke my right arm." Ukiah considered the rest of his body. "I wrenched my left leg somehow—maybe the hip is broken or maybe it's the knee. The whole damn thing hurts. And my stomach is killing me."

Max pressed a linen handkerchief to Ukiah's head and placed Ukiah's left hand on it to keep up the pressure. "Damn it, when you waved at us, you made a perfect target."

Kraynak fingered the dents punched into Ukiah's armor. "It had to have been a semi-automatic supersonic rifle. They couldn't have hit him twice otherwise."

Sheriff Kicking Deer frowned at Ukiah between squawks of his radio, as if the sniper was all Ukiah's doing. "How is he?"

"Don't know." Max took out his pocketknife, sliced open Ukiah's right shirtsleeve, and winced at what he found. "Yeah, you broke it, Ukiah. Your radius, it looks like, has punctured through your skin. The tibia's probably broken too."

Ukiah closed his eyes to avoid seeing the wound. An odd mental glitch made it easier to endure the pain if he didn't look at the injury causing it. Knowing exactly how bad he was hurt only made it worse.

Kicking Deer's radio crackled and reported that an ambulance had been dispatched. He added that it would take the EMS crew an hour to arrive.

Max and Ukiah looked at the Sheriff in surprise and dismay. Since Hex, the leader of the Ontongard, shot Ukiah dead, and he came back to life, they had avoided hospitals. Unvoiced was the worry that, like so many science-fiction movies predicted, Ukiah would fall under government control if too many people saw his oddities. Besides, they had discovered, he almost never needed medical intervention.

While Kicking Deer checked on his backup, Max whispered, "If you can walk, we can talk our way out of an ambulance ride."

Ukiah sat up only to have his consciousness slide sideways toward darkness.

Max caught him and eased back. "Okay, that's not going to work."

Through a screen of pine, Ukiah gazed up at the cliff face. The white tips of broken branches stood out in sharp relief against the green needles and dark wood. He stared for several minutes until he realized Alicia must have tumbled down through the tree, the branches snapping as they broke her fall.

"What are you doing?" Max kept Ukiah from sitting up again. "Just lie still, son."

"Alicia. This is where she would have landed . . ."

His moms had been reluctant to let Ukiah off the farm without them. With his newborn sister taking up all his Mom Lara's time, life would be simpler, however, if they allowed fifteen-year-old Ukiah to work part-time with Max. In what would become the pattern for years ahead, Ukiah rode with Mom Jo to her workplace at the Pittsburgh Zoo. While they waited for Max in the zoo's parking lot, Mom Jo taught Ukiah how to call her on a public payphone and filled his pockets with quarters. The Max that picked him up that day had been a man fighting grief and depression, so the ride to the office was filled with edgy silence.

Later, Ukiah would have a scale of luxury to measure the Shadyside mansion against. At the time, the office was merely a very big house, nearly void of furniture. Max led Ukiah through the empty rooms to a keeping room off the kitchen. Besides the grandfather clock presiding over the foyer, the desks and file cabinets occupying it represented the only furniture on the first floor.

What surprised Ukiah was that there was someone already in the room. A teenage girl sat at the nearest desk, studying a computer screen intently. She shook the last bit of a candy bar at Max in greeting, not looking up.

Max checked Ukiah with a hand on his shoulder. "Alicia, there's someone here I want you to meet."

Alicia glanced up, startled at Ukiah's presence and

scrambled to her feet, popping the last of the candy bar into her mouth. "I was working on those background searches."

"Good." *Max indicated Ukiah with a pat on his shoulder.* "This is Ukiah Oregon. He's the John Doe case I went to Oregon to trace."

Ukiah and Alicia stared at each other. Her hair fascinated him, a rich shade of purple he had never seen outside of certain flowers. He didn't realize people came with such hair color. Certain cartoon characters suddenly seemed more feasible.

In addition to her hair, Alicia had an abnormal number of tiny holes in her ears, from which dangled elaborate pieces of silver-and-amethyst jewelry. Was there some correlation to the color of her hair and the jewelry?

"Oh, wow! He looks like a Wolf Boy." *Alicia breathed out a chocolate-flavored sigh. She held out her hand to him.* "Hi! I'm Alicia Kraynak."

He leaned over to examine her outstretched chocolate-coated fingers. Deciding she was sharing with him the last remains of her candy bar, he licked her fingers clean. Her hair, according to her life pattern, should have been brown, like her eyebrows. So how did it get purple?

"Ukiah!" *Max choked on something that sounded like a laugh.*

Alicia's eyes had gone wide. "Um, it's okay, Uncle Max."

"You're supposed to shake her hand, Ukiah, not lick it." *Max picked up Ukiah's hand, molded it around her salvia-damp palm, and made him shake it up and down.* "Look her in the eye. No, not like that—like you're pleased to see her. Um, we'll work on the smile. Now say: 'Ukiah Oregon, pleased to meet you.'"

Ukiah did as directed and Alicia's eyes crinkled into a huge smile.

"That's great!" *Alicia claimed back her hand.* "Let's try it again."

So they practiced shaking hands with Max interrupting to make small improvements. Later Ukiah would realize Max's patience stemmed from Ukiah's ability to learn; nothing had to be repeated, only refined. Alicia's patience ran deeper, willing to practice what she already had pat for the simple joy of helping him.

"Ukiah?"

Ukiah blinked away the dream recall and looked up at Max in surprise. Max had that harassed look he got when things went bad. "Max? What's wrong?"

"The EMS crew is almost here."

"The EMS?" Ukiah started to sit up and stopped as pain shot through his body. "Max? What happened?"

Max looked at him, eyes widening. "Oh, damn. What's the last thing you remember?"

"We were at the office with Kittanning, trying to figure out if we could do a stakeout with him along. I was hurt, wasn't I? What happened? Is Kittanning all right?"

"Kittanning is fine. You fell off a cliff and you're bleeding someplace." Max slipped a hand under his back, running it from shoulder to hip. "You're bleeding and losing your recent memories. I thought I checked you thoroughly."

Ukiah grunted in pain, trying to distance himself from the hurt by looking around. The place looked hauntingly familiar and it smelled of home. "Max, what are we doing in Oregon?"

"We're on a case." Max rocked back on his heels. "Ukiah, you're bleeding inside. It's the only place possible. You said earlier that your stomach hurt."

"Yeah, it hurts."

"How does this work, with you being Pack?"

Ukiah searched Pack memory. "Um, there are three ways this could go. If I'm not hurt too bad, my body heals up the damaged area and then reabsorbs the blood trapped inside."

Max looked down at him and shook his head. "I don't think so."

"Secondly, I'm hurt so bad that I die. That stops the blood from being pumped into the body cavity. My body reabsorbs the blood and then focuses on healing the leak. It's a matter of energy. Once wounded, my body can only do one or the other."

"Then what's the third thing?"

"I'm screwed."

"Huh?"

"There's this magic halfway point that's really hard to hit, but when you do, you're screwed. You're hurt too bad to heal, but the blood keeps pumping into the body cavity, so while you reabsorb some, the rest becomes mice. They have no way out. They die trapped inside. Their bodies rot. Blood circulation would spread that toxin through my system, and I'm too hurt for my cells to adapt to the poison, so my body shuts down. When I come back alive, the problem is still there, and I'm only weaker than I was before. I'll die, and come back, then die, again and again, until I simply don't come back."

Max looked at him bleakly. "Isn't there a way out of it?"

"The Pack usually just kills the person cleanly, usually by snapping their neck: that's fairly easy to heal afterward. The blood stops pumping, and what's trapped inside reabsorbs before the mice form. You're only screwed if the mice form."

Max looked at him, too stunned to speak. Finally he asked in a weak voice, "How soon does that start?"

"About a half hour after I started to bleed."

Max glanced at his watch, then covered his face. "Shit. Shit. Shit."

"How much time?"

"It's been nearly an hour." Max's hands slid up until his palms were pressed against his eyes. "I'm sorry, Ukiah. I thought you'd be okay, so I've been looking for Alicia."

"Alicia?"

"You were tracking her when—never mind. It's not important." Max sat rocking, hands pressed to his face. Finally he took away his hands to look down at Ukiah. "Have you stopped bleeding?"

Ukiah considered the question. "I think so."

"So if we get whatever mice are in you now, out, there won't be more?"

"Maybe. I don't think so. This rarely happens, and I told you how the Pack handles it."

"I am not killing you!" Max growled, undoing his cuffs

and rolling up his sleeves. "It took me weeks to get over the nightmares from killing Hex's Gets disguised as you! I can't do it! Don't even ask!"

Ukiah managed a smile. "I wasn't going to. I don't like being dead."

"Good." Max looked up to scan the surrounding woods. "Kraynak! Kraynak!"

"He's here too?"

The big policeman came scrambling out of the under-brush. He had his service pistol in hand. "What is it?"

"One of Ukiah's weirdnesses just turned deadly. We've got to cut him open, now."

"You're kidding." Kraynak went pale.

"No. I need your help. You've brought Bonnie along?"

"Of course." Kraynak slid up the leg of his jeans and undid a knife sheath. He handed knife and sheath to Max. "I sharpened her before we left Pittsburgh."

"Good." Max considered Ukiah and shook his head. "Oh, kid, I don't know if I can do this."

"I can't do it myself," Ukiah said.

"I'm not doing it," Kraynak added. "Deal with hacked-apart dead bodies? No problem! Observe autopsies? No problem! Cut open a *living* person? No way! I faint at the sight of live blood. I pass out every time they run us through drug testing."

"For a homicide detective," Ukiah observed, "you're a wimp."

Kraynak gave him a craggy smile. "I'm just too sensitive of a guy."

"Okay." Max took a deep breath. "I'll do it. Do you have any idea where I should cut?"

Ukiah closed his eyes and focused tight on his body. "Here."

"Kraynak, hold him still and don't faint."

"I just won't look." Kraynak stated, becoming sober. He put his weight on Ukiah's shoulders and, true to word, looked away.

Ukiah couldn't look either. He watched clouds race

across the sky. There was a sharp, thin pain across his stomach. He bit his lip against the pain.

Max suddenly jerked backward and started to curse. Tiny warm wet feet raced up Ukiah's bare chest. "Shit, that scared me! Kraynak, don't you dare look and faint! That's one."

Ukiah risked a glance at his chest. One bloody mouse sat on his sternum, trying to clean itself. "My life is so weird."

"You can say that again," Max muttered. "How many do you think are in you?"

Ukiah watched the clouds again. "Five in all, I think."

Max slipped fingers into the cut and there was deep hard pain as he tugged free a squirming ball of matted fur. "I didn't think I'd have so much trouble catching the suckers."

"And they like you."

"What the hell are you talking about?" Kraynak asked. "They who?"

"Don't look!" Max snapped. "I'll explain later."

So much for Kraynak not knowing that he wasn't human.

Another deep pain and Ukiah couldn't keep the scream in. It pressed against his lips until it forced its way out. He managed to keep it a low, guttural howl. His body fought to escape and Kraynak shifted to trap his whole upper body to the rocky ground. Another wrench of pain and a third soggy mouse joined the first two. Ukiah went limp and panting with the momentary relief.

"Hang in there," Max murmured. "Just two more."

As if letting the first scream out opened a channel, he couldn't resist the next one at all. The agony started and immediately he started to whimper. The whimper built to a long howl of pain. Finally the pain stopped and Max deposited the bloody mouse onto his chest.

"I can't find the last one. Ukiah? Ukiah?"

"It's, um," he closed his eyes, fighting to ignore the pain to focus on his body. He could sense the mice on his chest, but where was the one in his stomach? "Low, to my right, deep."

Max probed the side gently. "Tell me if I'm getting close."

"Lower. Lower. To the right a little. There. Deep in."

Max held a finger on the point. "Ukiah, I'm going to have to make another cut."

"Oh, please, just do it quick."

"Hold still, son."

He managed not to scream, but then Max was mercifully quick. The sharp thin cut was followed immediately with fingers slipping into the new opening. A decisive thrust in to catch hold of the struggling mouse. A quick jerk to get the mouse out before it could slip away. It joined the others on his chest.

Someone crashed through the woods to stand nearly over Ukiah. "What the hell are you doing to him?"

"Emergency surgery," Max answered.

The man was a tall, solidly built policeman. His dusky skin, short, dark hair, broad face, high cheeks, and sharp nose marked him as a Native American. He held a service pistol in hand, pointed skyward. Eyes as dark and rich brown as chocolate gazed down at Ukiah in concerned confusion.

"Max?" Ukiah winced as he discovered his right arm was broken. He motioned to the newcomer with his left instead. "Who's this?"

The man's black eyebrows leaped upward as the officer noted the collection of bloody mice. "What the hell?"

"This is Sheriff Jared Kicking Deer." Max snatched up the mice, stuffing them into vest pockets. He produced bandages out of his other vest pockets. "We're done, Kraynak."

Kraynak released Ukiah and fled the fresh blood, gagging. Max applied pressure to the two incisions. Ukiah lay with eyes closed as Max bandaged him, but opened them again as Max pressed fingertips to his pulse point. Concern and doubt showed clear on Max's face.

"How do you feel?" his partner asked.

"That was not fun."

"Do you think you're going to be okay?"

"Hunky-dory," he murmured and discovered that over Max's shoulder loomed a cliff. "I fell off that?"

"Actually someone shot you and then you fell," Max stated.

"I hate when that happens." A noise made him glance over and rediscover the sheriff. At some point the policeman had put away the pistol and watched Max and him with dark, unreadable eyes. Ukiah returned the gaze, wondering why a stranger would seem so familiar.

"Do you think I'm going to buy this act?" the sheriff asked, breaking the silence.

"What?" Max asked.

"This pulling-mice-out-of-the-stomach routine." The sheriff shook his head. "I've arrested faith healers for performing similar slight-of-hand surgery, pulling tumors out of people, only it's calves liver that they have palmed. All you've done is make shallow cuts and rolled the mice in the blood. If you think I'm going to fall for this, you're mistaken."

Max looked startled, torn between relief that the sheriff wasn't jumping to the "he's an alien" conclusion and annoyance that the lawman thought him a fraud. "Whatever."

"Please save me a lot of grief and tell me this whole shooting was scripted."

Max snarled a curse. "I don't know what you're using as brains, but this wasn't staged for you. Some lunatic is out there with a high-powered rifle. He shot my partner! That body armor is the only reason Ukiah is still alive. In Pittsburgh we call that attempted murder, and we don't go hassling the victim when they haven't even been seen by the EMS."

"I've got a girl that may or may not be missing. A shooting that could have been staged. And some weirdness out of *The Outer Limits*. Normally, I'd believe it all was above board, except act one was staged at my house last night."

"Act one?" Ukiah glanced to Max. "What happened last night?"

Max put a hand on his shoulder to quiet him. "I don't know what your problem is with my partner, but don't you dare mix Alicia Kraynak's safety into it."

There was a shout from the trees behind Sheriff Kicking

Deer. He half-turned as if reluctant to turn his back on Max and Ukiah, his eyes angry. "Over here!" he shouted, and moments later a foursome of men carrying a stretcher between them scrambled up the slope to Ukiah.

St. Anthony's Hospital, Pendleton, Oregon
Wednesday, August 25, 2004

Even with six men carrying the stretcher, it was a difficult scramble back to the ambulance parked a mile from the cliff. They drove him to St. Anthony's Hospital in Pendleton. There they set the bone, x-rayed various parts of his body, bandaged, braced, stitched, and poked him from head to toe. At one point Sheriff Kicking Deer appeared, standing over Ukiah as the doctors filled him in with medical mumbo jumbo. The report ended with "and thirty-eight stitches for the deep abdominal incisions," which only served to harden the Sheriff's gaze.

The doctor, looking only a few years older than Ukiah, added cheerfully at the end, "But considering that he'd been shot twice and fell off a cliff, he's in remarkably good condition."

Kicking Deer grunted and walked away. "I want to know," he called without looking back, "when you release him."

His grand exit was defused by a candy striper pulling him aside at the end of the hall. Their whispered conversation involved lots of head shaking on the part of the sheriff, and curious looks in Ukiah's direction on part of the candy striper.

A gray-haired phlebotomist came to take his blood. So far, his blood had been gathered into cotton swabs and had either died or swarmed back as barely noticed gnats.

He eyed the test tubes with a sense of helplessness.

"Please don't take my blood."

"Honey, I have to take your blood." She swabbed his arm clean with alcohol. "Have your folks signed something saying your blood shouldn't be taken?"

He puzzled over the question. Folks? His moms were

here? He realized that this was one of those legal-age issues. "I'm not a minor."

"You aren't?" She applied a tourniquet to his arm. "How old are you, honey? Sixteen? Seventeen?"

"Twenty-one."

She laughed. "You're going to be carded until you're forty. Now, it will just pinch a little. If it really bothers you, look away."

"Can I sign something that says that my blood shouldn't be taken?"

She *tsk*'ed at him. "We just take a little to make sure you're all right."

So he had to watch unhappily as she filled two vials with his blood and pressed stickers to them. What was the lab going to think of the creature-filled vials? He was still wondering what the blood would turn into when the candy striper suddenly darted into his area. She was only fourteen or fifteen, a Native American with black hair in braids, and huge dark eyes. Her nametag labeled her as ZOEY.

"Here!" she gasped, pressing the still-warm vials into his hand. "Jared's taking me home in a minute and if he catches me with these, he'll *kill* me!"

He sensed his blood inside the vials, changing already to something that could exist outside of his body. He tucked them quickly out of sight, under the sheets. "Jared?"

"He's my brother, but he acts like he's my dad!" She rolled her eyes, and then looked at him with such curiosity that it fairly shimmered out of her. "You're him, aren't you? The Umatilla Wolf Boy! Jared doesn't want to believe you, but he never has believed in anything. Grandpa says that all of you is alive, so I figured that they shouldn't test your blood. I stole some of your stickers from the nurse's station and stuck them on Billy Cosgrove's blood. I'm not sure what he's in here for, but I don't think it's too serious. When they can't find his blood, they'll just draw more."

"Thank you," he said.

She grinned impishly. "Don't mention it! That's what family is for!" She suddenly hopped up to lean over the rail and kissed his cheek. "See ya!"

And she was gone, dashing away.

Cautiously, Ukiah checked the vials. The purple-topped vial held a small salamander, twisting in the tight confines. The tiger-striped-topped vial had a praying mantis. He freed both of his blood creatures and held them loosely in either hand. He felt their tiny pricks of anxiety at being separated from him. With a sense of relief, they reverted back to blood and seeped into his skin. For a few minutes, his hands felt slightly bloated and hot, and then the extra mass redistributed itself, surging through his bloodstream to where it could be put to best use. Ukiah tucked the vials away before the next round of poking and prodding by the hospital staff could start.

Ukiah asked for something to eat but was refused on the ground of possible internal injuries. Finally they let Max in to see him.

"Please," Ukiah begged, "tell me you've brought me something to eat."

"Would I let you down?" Max produced lukewarm French fries from his jacket pocket.

"Oh, bless you." Ukiah winced in pain as he levered himself upright. As Ukiah wolfed down the fries, Max pulled two double bacon cheeseburgers, a handful of candy bars, and a bag of trail mix from his various pockets. "Thank you. Thank you."

"You're welcome." Max, in a flourish, added a bottle of root beer to the stock of food.

"Here." Ukiah pressed the empty blood vials on him. "Get rid of these someplace safe."

Max frowned at the labels. "You let them take blood? How did you get it back?"

"I couldn't stop them. Jared's little sister stole them for me. She's a candy striper. She believes I'm family."

Max laughed and tucked away the vials. "I'll take care of them."

"Where's Kraynak?" Ukiah asked.

"He went back to the campsite to pack up Alicia's belongings. He's driving her straight home—when—we find her."

As an unspoken rule between them, it was always "when" and never "if," even in the bleakest cases. Ukiah took a deep breath as he realized that his shooting changed Alicia's disappearance into something more insidious than simply being lost and possibly hurt. Max's hesitation indicated that Max knew that Alicia's rescue had crossed the line from likely to doubtful.

Max looked away, refusing to put the change into words. "The doctors want you to spend a night for observation."

"I'm fine," Ukiah said quickly, and got a scowl from Max. "Well, I'm getting there."

"Yeah, I know. After you eat this, though, you're going to fall asleep until tomorrow. I rather you'd stay here than try to get you moved back to the motel before you zonk out."

Ukiah admitted that he had a point.

"It's weird," Max said, "but it's a hell of lot easier seeing you in here, knowing now that you're virtually indestructible. It used to be that every time you got hurt, I'd go through this massive guilt session and think about calling it quits."

"Quits? Dump me as a partner?"

"Don't give me those puppy-dog eyes. The worst part was having to call your moms and tell them what happened," Max said, and shuddered.

Ukiah discovered how much it hurt to laugh. "You're going to call them now?"

Max considered. "I don't think so. You're not their little boy anymore. Besides, we know you're going to be all right—don't we?"

Ukiah nodded. "I'm fine. I'll be back on my feet tomorrow and back to normal in a day or two. My moms are having their first vacation in six years. Might as well not alarm them."

"On the other hand, I have already called Indigo."

Ukiah burst out laughing, rolling into a ball against the pain. "Oh, please, don't, that hurts!"

"She was not happy. If this was anyplace on the East Coast, she'd be on her way."

"I wish she was here." Ukiah polished off the second double bacon cheeseburger.

"So she can watch you eat and sleep?"

"I'd feel safer," Ukiah admitted, yawning. "Do you think there's a chance that the shooter will come after me here?"

Worry flashed across Max's face and was controlled. "I don't think so. You can't ID him. Even in a town this small, it will take him a few hours to learn you don't have bullet holes in you, but still most people wouldn't be fit to walk for another week or so. I think you were shot just to keep you from tracking Alicia. Flat on your back in a hospital, you're no threat."

"We go out tomorrow?"

Max winced. "Ukiah, I know that you're almost indestructible, but I hate the thought of putting you in deliberate danger. I don't like seeing you in pain, and I really, really don't want to find out the limits of your abilities."

"We can't leave her out there." Ukiah clung to the hope that they would find her alive, against growing odds.

Max studied the ceiling for a few minutes. "We'll see how you are tomorrow. I'm not taking you out if you're not at a hundred percent. If for no other reason than it took six men to carry you out this time. It would have been a night mare if the shooter decided to pick us all off. If there's a next time, he might."

"Jeez, Max, you know how to scare me into doing what you want."

One corner of Max's mouth curled up in a wry smile. "Good. As for being safe here, I heard Kicking Deer has arranged for one of the security guards to hang out outside your door. It's not much, but—at least you're nearly indestructible."

"Why do you keep saying that?"

"Because it's the only reason I'm as calm as I am right now. If I didn't know how hard it is to kill you for good, you'd be heading home right now."

CHAPTER FIVE

As a testament of how badly he had been hurt, Ukiah spent a deep and dreamless night at St. Anthony's Hospital. He woke at his normal East Coast time, which meant it was still three hours before dawn. Rubbing sleep out of his eyes, he peered around the hospital room, confused.

He was in Oregon, he had to remind himself, for the memory of arriving on the West Coast had skittered away on little mouse feet. Alicia was missing, someone had shot him, he had fallen off a cliff, Max had performed surgery, and he was in the hospital. At least for the last two events, he had his normal total recall. The first three were just words, like a story read from a book. "Once upon a time, a girl named Alicia disappeared, and her good friend looking for her was shot. Bang. He fell down."

His stomach grumbled, reminding him of the normal result of being shot and falling down. The night nurse answered his summons and complaint of hunger with crackers and ginger ale. The crackers made one mouthful. The ginger ale went down in one long swallow.

He was considering buzzing her again, when Max slipped into the door, wreathed with the perfume of breakfast.

With a deep inhale, Ukiah drank in the smell. "Denny's!"

"Basic comfort food," Max said, cleaning up the debris of Ukiah's snack. "Looks like I timed it perfect it too."

"I'm sorry you had to get up early to come feed me."
Ukiah opened the box to find maple-syrup-soaked pancakes,
a western omelet, and a dozen sausage links. "This is wonderful!"

"I'm still operating on East Coast time." Max stole one of
the sausage links, and settled into the visitor's chair. "I'm
fine. So, how do you feel?"

Ukiah raised up his plaster-encased arm. "I wish they
hadn't done this. It's going to be a bear to get off."

"We'll pick up a hacksaw at a hardware store. How does
the arm feel? Truthfully."

Ukiah considered it. "Fragile. The breaks are all knitted,
but not strong, like they're balsa wood."

Max grunted at the discouraging news. "And the leg?"

"Not much better than the arm," Ukiah admitted. "I probably should use a crutch today." He sighed. "If we were in
Pittsburgh, I could push myself, pay for it later. I've had
time to think about what you said. I'm not up to tracking
today, not here. If I collapse, it's not going to be in someone's backyard where you only need to carry me twenty feet
to get me into a car."

"Amen to that." Max leaned forward to steal another
sausage link. "Just as well. It will be hours before anyone
will be able to check you out. You know how it is—doctors
will want to poke at you, maybe run tests and such before
they'll okay your release. If you don't let them, then our insurance might back out of paying for the bill."

They had learned the hard way that insurance companies
didn't like patients walking out in the middle of the night.
Unless medical costs in Pendleton were much lower than
Pittsburgh's, they had racked up a serious bill yesterday.

"I'll stay put."

"Thanks." Max stole a third sausage link, and they ate in
silence for several minutes.

"How's Kraynak taking this?" Ukiah asked.

"A bear looking for something to maul."

"I'll be up and running tomorrow—but I can't help thinking that tomorrow will be too late."

"You're doing the best you can, kid—which is a hell of a

lot more than most people could—but everyone has limits and you just hit yours."

Ukiah looked out at the predawn lightening the sky. "You and Kraynak are going out?"

Max nodded. "We're meeting with the search-and-rescue team in an hour. They've agreed to change the focus of the search over to the bottom of the cliff. It will trample the trail for you tomorrow, but if we find her today it will be worth it."

In the meanwhile, he would need to sit around and wait to hear. The day stretched out long before him.

"Oh, before I forget." From various pockets, Max produced five plump black mice. "Take these back. They make me nervous. Much as I love my godson, I don't want another Kittanning on our hands."

Kittanning had been the least dangerous of Ukiah's stolen mice; Hex injected one into Max in an effort to turn him into Ukiah's Get. Max had a right to be nervous about free-roaming blood mice.

Ukiah picked up the first mouse, smiling at the shimmer of joy racing through the little creature. The mice didn't like being away from him—it was a big, scary world. Ukiah held it cupped in his hands, letting it revert to blood, then seep into his skin.

Memories seeped blood warm through his mind. *Jared Kicking Deer standing on his back porch, the smell of fried bacon coming from the open door.*

"Maybe I'll give seeing Jesse Kicking Deer another try."

"I did a quick Internet search for you last night," Max said. "The only hits on Kicking Deer were on our friend, the sheriff. I couldn't find anything on his mother, Claire, or Jesse or even your little candy striper. If there are more Kicking Deers in the area, they all have unlisted phone numbers and live uninteresting lives. I didn't have time, though, to dig deeper than general public records."

"So Jesse does live at the farm."

"Well, he might be in a nursing home without a private phone. Looks like you're going to have fun today sharpening your private investigator skills."

Sam Killington standing up from the table, long, thin legs ending in a shapely bottom, Obsession perfume warmed by her body, laying a business card on the table that read SAMUEL ANNE KILLINGTON, 451 MAIN STREET, SUITE 2B, 541-555-7895.

"Maybe I'll get help."

"Indigo? You know how she is about using official FBI databases for private use."

"I think I'll talk to Sam Killington. Trade local color for inside information."

"Sam?" Some emotion Ukiah had never seen on Max's face before flashed by and was gone. "That might be a good idea. Be careful, though. Someone took those shots at you. It's a small town, but we only talked to the search-and-rescue team, and Sam last night."

"And Jared Kicking Deer."

"But he was beside me when the shots were fired." Max waved a finger at the remaining mice. "Keep going, you'll see."

Yes, Kicking Deer had been down beside Max as the shots were fired. He stood with eyes shaded by his hand to look up at Ukiah. There was even one quickly spinning image of the sheriff—the man seemed horrified by what he was witnessing. No. Jared Kicking Deer hadn't shot him.

But who had?

Surprisingly, he managed to talk his way out of the hospital a few hours after dawn. The young-faced doctor of the previous day turned out to be more than willing to sign release forms, saying that anyone that could shrug off impromptu amateur abdominal surgery probably shouldn't be holding down a hospital bed. While Ukiah wanted to be released, he felt the need to argue against such a cavalier attitude. If he was human, he should have stayed in the hospital. But he wasn't—so why was he upset?

Mysteriously, the hospital also asked if he wanted help "with his problem" and gave him several pamphlets on drug abuse. It wasn't until he remembered that the candy striper had swapped his blood that he realized they thought he was a drug addict. Perhaps it was why they were so eager to see him go—leaving a drug addict in a hospital might be akin to leaving a child in a candy shop. Hopefully, the information wouldn't get onto his permanent insurance record!

He had only gotten as far as the front sidewalk before wondering if he had made a huge mistake. The short walk had his knee screaming in pain, and not using his right hand proved nearly impossible. Every ounce of pressure he put on it tested the strength of the fragile knits. He kept expecting the bones to splinter back apart. The energy provided by the a.m. breakfast was depleted, leaving him hollow, hungry, and shaking.

"You look like shit." A familiar voice made him look up. Sam Killington was standing a few feet away, hands on her hips. "Are you supposed to be out here, or is this some lame excuse of a breakout?"

"They signed me out."

"I'd get a second opinion on that." Sam closed the distance between them. "I didn't expect you to be out of bed this week."

Was that because she had put him into the bed in the first place? He stifled a flare of fear. He was nearly indestructible, he was nearly indestructible—he chanted it like a mantra. Pain started to thrum in his wrist in time with his pulse rate, a dull beating agony. Sure, all he had to fear was pain, lots and lots of pain.

"I heal quickly." Ukiah gazed out over the parking lot, suddenly aware that he had no clue which direction the hotel lay.

"Where's your partner?" She joined him at scanning the parking lot.

"Looking for Alicia Kraynak."

"Down in Umatilla National?"

"Yes."

She sighed. "Let me get my Jeep, and I'll give you a lift."

It was a deep green Jeep Wrangler, probably ten years old, and burning oil. The front was clean of litter. The backseat, while orderly, obviously served as a general closet.

"Hotel?" she asked as he carefully climbed into the passenger seat, hoping he wasn't making a second, larger mistake by getting into her car.

"Actually, if it wouldn't be too much trouble, could we go through a drive-through? I really need something to eat."

"McDonald's?" she asked. When he nodded, she shifted into first and pulled out. "It's a bit out of the way, but I know they're open this early."

"I was coming to see you, actually." Ukiah told her. "You said that you'd trade information for local color."

"Ah, local color becomes more interesting when it's shooting at you."

"Something like that."

"Great! I'm dying to know—why were you wearing body armor while looking for a lost hiker?"

"How do you know about the vest? For that matter, what do you know about the shooting?"

"Just what I heard over the police scanner in my office. I caught Kicking Deer's first call about you being down." She glanced over at him, green eyes sincere. "I'm glad you're okay."

"Thanks."

"So, why were you wearing the vest?"

"Max and I were nearly killed by a man that kidnapped a hiker who had been reported as just lost." Actually Crazy Joe Gary had killed Ukiah—the first of several deaths; luckily, none of them permanent. "Max doesn't let me track now without a vest."

"Isn't that expensive?"

"Not unless someone shoots at me."

"Does your insurance cover the replacement?"

"I don't know," Ukiah admitted. "Max handles the business end of things. He's really good at it."

They stopped at a red light, and she gave him a long study. "How old are you, anyhow?"

How old indeed? "Twenty-one."

"And how long have you two been partners?"

"Three years. I worked with Max before then, part-time, just on tracking jobs."

"So, he took on an eighteen-year-old as a full partner?"

The light changed. She checked the traffic and started up, shaking her head. "And he seemed like such a sane man."

"Out of the way" meant that the McDonald's was clear on the other side of town, under the interstate's overpass, and up the hill beyond.

"Because of the sniper," Sam said, "most of the search-and-rescue volunteers have been called off the search. The sheriff's department, your partner and Kraynak, and a handful of weapon-trained volunteers are the only ones still looking. They do have three helicopters up today."

"Three?"

"The army assists search-and-rescue efforts like this by sending helicopters over—that is when flying weather is clear, which it hasn't been." Sam pulled into the drive-through and up to the speaker. "So, what do you want?"

He ordered three of their biggest breakfast meals of pancakes, scrambled eggs, and hash browns. He fumbled out his wallet, paid with a twenty-dollar bill. Sam pulled into a parking spot to let him put away the change and organize his food.

"Your shooting," she said, "seems to indicate that there is a connection between the fire victims and Alicia Kraynak."

It took him a moment to realize she meant the six family members that died in a house fire four days before Alicia disappeared. "It does?"

"Statistically speaking, yes. There's no evidence of arson in the Burke fire, but it's the third fire in two months that killed the entire family. Statistically, the chance of a house going up and killing everyone is slim. It's less than a fifty-percent chance that everyone is home. Cut it down drastically that not one of six people gets out alive. Then whittle it to nothing that it happens three times in two months."

A chill went down Ukiah's back. "So, what's the connection to Alicia?"

"Three hundred and fifty people died in Umatilla County last year. Three hundred and thirty-five were natural causes. Only ten were killed by accident during the whole year. That's an average year. In the last two months, twenty people have died in fires, four people have drowned, six people have died in nonwitnessed, single-car accidents, and five hikers have vanished without a trace. Alicia is just the most recent one. If the hikers are all dead, then that's thirty-five people in an eight-week span."

The numbers stunned him. He could see why the deaths were alarming, but not why they pointed to a connection between all of them. "Why do you say that the shooting links it?"

"Do you know how many homicides we have a year?"

"I wouldn't think many."

"In a good year, none. In a bad year, one. So, statistically, there's a connection."

He looked at her.

"Listen to the details," she urged him. "The Coles' house burned down on July third—eight dead. A fire in a trash can, seemingly started by a cigarette butt, spread to some fireworks, and the whole house went up. July nineteenth—the propane grill sitting on a wooden front porch takes out the Watsons' house. Six dead and the family dog. August nineteenth—the Burkes' house. Six dead. Cause this time: an apparent toaster meltdown. Nothing's the same, right?"

He nodded, not sure where she was leading.

"All fires started after midnight." She ticked the points off with her fingers. "All family members were found dead in their beds or bedrooms. And the kicker, all family members had missed work, school, doctor appointments, et cetera, the day of the fire. No one had seen or talked to them the day they died."

"All twenty?"

"All thirty-five people, actually, with maybe the exception of Alicia, who had been seen the morning she disappeared. And a large number of them hadn't been seen for two or three days prior to the fire: Kids were off school for summer, some of the homemaker mothers didn't have appointments to miss, or one of the adults wasn't employed."

"Why 'maybe' for Alicia?"

"If she was killed Monday, then she was seen the morning she died. If she died Tuesday or Wednesday, then no one saw her the day of her death."

"We have to assume she's still alive."

Sam glanced at him in surprise. "Despite the shooting?"

"There are reasons why my shooting might not be related to Alicia's disappearance," Ukiah stalled, and then changed the subject. "Do you think these people are killed and put into their beds and the house burned down to cover the murders?"

Sam shrugged, sighing. "So far the autopsies don't show any cause of death beyond smoke inhalation and massive burns. The firefighters say that some of the victims obviously woke up enough to try to escape but never made it to safety."

She saw that he was finishing the third meal and indicated a nearby trash bin. "Want me to toss the papers?"

"Sure, thanks."

She strolled over to the trash bin, stuffed the bag in, and turned. She looked past the car, swore, and started for Ukiah at a trot. Even forewarned, Ukiah was still startled by the man that suddenly leaned in the Jeep's window.

"Hello! Who are you?" the stranger asked. He had an infectiously cheerful smile and ice-cold blue eyes that swept down over Ukiah, inspecting his wounds.

"None of your business, Peter." Sam jumped into the driver's seat.

"Peter Talbot." The stranger put out his hand to be shaken. "I'm Sam's husband."

"Ukiah Oregon." Ukiah extended his right hand out of habit, and checked the motion as his bulky white cast reminded him that his right arm had been recently broken. *Sam is married?* Peter Talbot reached out and caught Ukiah's hand before he could retract it.

Just looking at him, Ukiah couldn't imagine Sam married to this man. Ukiah recognized that Peter Talbot was good-looking in a scruffy sort of way. Tall, lean, chisel-featured, he could have graced a magazine ad. From wispy blond hair that fell into his eyes, shirt unbuttoned to show lean chest muscle to battered shoes, though, he seemed completely mismatched to Sam's orderly neatness.

In the driver's seat, Sam nearly bristled with anger. "Let go of him and get away from the car."

"I'm just shaking his hand." Peter kept hold of Ukiah's hand, giving it a painful shake.

Sam started the Jeep. "You know you're not supposed to be within a hundred feet of me."

"That's cute, Sammie Anne. You come to my place of work and tell me to stay away from you."

"Since when are you working at McDonald's?"

"Sammie Anne, private eye, you're supposed to know all this! I started last week. I'm the morning manager."

Sam glared, revving the Jeep's engine. "Let go of him."

"So, who the hell are you, Ukiah Oregon?" Peter flashed him a smile that might have been charming if not for the coldness in his eyes.

"I'm a private investigator from Pittsburgh," Ukiah said, trying to extract his hand.

"The uncle of the lost hiker flew him in." Sam gunned the engine again.

"Couldn't cut it, Sammie Anne?" Peter grinned.

"He's a tracker. It's not my area of expertise," Sam stated.

"So, what happened to you, Ukiah?" Peter asked, ignoring Sam's anger. "Did someone else catch you messing with their wife?"

"I'm not your wife anymore," Sam said. "Now, let go of him."

"Now, honey, give the man a chance to answer." Peter tightened his hold.

"I had a rough day." Ukiah stopped trying to free his hand, instead squeezed back. Recently he'd discovered he was considerably stronger than the average man.

Peter winced slightly. "Well, you better not even think about touching my wife."

Sam reached into the backseat of the Jeep and fished out a cattle prod. She snapped it on and jabbed it out within an inch of Peter Talbot's nose. "Let him go!"

"Easy, Sammie, I was just doing just that." Peter released his grip.

Sam must have shifted into reverse earlier while Ukiah was grappling with Peter. She let out the clutch and the Jeep leaped backward. She snapped off the cattle prod, dropped it into Ukiah's lap, and wrenched the Jeep around. Shifting into first, she roared out of the parking lot.

They drove in silence until Sam suddenly pulled into a small shaded park.

"I'm really sorry about that," she said. "People do silly things when they're young. Start to smoke. Get tattoos. Get married to complete jerks." Sam parked the Jeep and killed the engine. "Of course later you grow up enough to realize how stupid you've been, but getting rid of your mistake requires lots of pain and messy procedures."

"You're divorced."

"Coming up on two years. Not that Peter has acknowledged it. He thinks since I haven't shacked up with anyone else, I'll be crawling back to him any day now. He's even taken steps to speed up the process, so I needed to get a restraining order on him. I try to keep track of where he's working so I can avoid him; but he's never happy at anything very long, so he quits most jobs after a few months. He just started working at the post office a few weeks ago. I guess that got tedious fast."

"He must find work easily."

"He's a charming, irresponsible bastard. People love him. Most people forgive him for all the shitty things he does, mostly because when he's truly cruel, he makes sure he isn't caught. I caught him at it one too many times, and just ran out of forgiveness. Screwing with your broken arm is so like him. I didn't want to pull away while he had hold of your arm. Are you okay?"

"Yeah."

"Do you have a girlfriend, kid?"

"Girlfriend isn't the right word." It wasn't a strong enough word. Fiancée also seemed weak.

"Oh! Okay. Well, this might be useless advice then, but don't rush into anything permanent. Love isn't enough to base a life together on."

"Max thinks it is. He says when you find someone, you grab hold and you don't let go."

"Oh." She said and started the car. "Sooooo, Max is married?"

"He was. His wife was killed in a car wreck. He thinks you should make the most of life because you don't know when it's going to end."

Sam made a sound of enlightenment and pulled out of the parking space. "Well, love is a good start, but love can blind you to the monster inside. People are rarely what you think they are on first sight."

What if you're the one with the monster inside? He wondered about Indigo's comment of "If we get married." Was she beginning to see what life with him would be like and having second thoughts? Could he blame her?

"I should have asked earlier," Sam went on, unaware of Ukiah's turmoil. "Should you really have eaten so soon after abdominal surgery?"

"You heard about that?"

"It's a small town and I like to nose into other people's business. What the hell was that all about, anyhow? And why did it piss off Kicking Deer so much?"

"Ahhhhhh." Ukiah drew a blank on how to explain. "That one is hard to explain. Can we get back to it?"

Sam threw back her head and laughed loudly. "Oh, come on, that's the interesting one, especially since it's put a bug up Kicking Deer's back end something awful."

"Kicking Deer is annoyed because I'm trying to find his grandfather."

She stopped laughing. "Jesse Kicking Deer?"

"Yes. I would like to talk to him. Do you have any clue how I could do that?"

"Ah!"

"Ah?"

"The Tuesday-night disaster. You drove out to see Jesse Kicking Deer and got jumped all over by one big, mean county sheriff."

"Yeah. So Jesse still lives at the ranch?"

"Is this part of the Kraynak case?"

"No," Ukiah admitted. He shifted uneasily in his seat. Boy Scouts, with all the emphasis on truthfulness, hadn't been the best training for a private investigator. "A couple years ago, Max was hired by a client in Pittsburgh to find the identity of a John Doe. The case brought him out to Pendleton and dead-ended. Some new information has turned up, and we think the John Doe and the Kicking Deer boy are one and the same. Sheriff Kicking Deer, however, won't let us talk to his grandfather."

"The Umatilla Wolf Boy ended up in Pittsburgh? That's a new one. Is this John Doe still alive, or are we talking heirs of the estate—so to speak?"

"He's still alive."

"What the hell is he doing in Pittsburgh?"

"He was adopted after found running feral. His parents tried to establish his identity when they found him, and when they couldn't, they decided to keep him instead of informing the authorities. They believed a feral child in a state institution would receive minimal loving attention."

There, the Boy Scouts would be proud of him. Each and every word the truth!

"And?"

"And what?"

"Well, that happened back in the 1930s. What's the Wolf Boy doing now? Can he talk? Is he in a nursing home? Is he running naked in the back woods of Pennsylvania? Is he a millionaire?"

Ukiah hunted frantically for a safe answer. "What he is doing really doesn't matter if I can't get to talk to Jesse Kicking Deer."

Sam clicked her tongue several times, thinking. "Jared's sister, Cassidy, just bought Zimmerman's, the Pendleton hardware store. She might not talk to you, but she'd be stranded behind the store counter, having to listen to you."

"Hopefully, she won't take a swing at a wounded man."

Sam smiled. "Or shoot him again."

Ukiah frowned. "What do you mean?"

"I'm just saying that Jared Kicking Deer might have a good alibi, but there are over a dozen Kicking Deer families in the area. It's common knowledge that the Kicking Deers are quite annoyed by all the claims to the Wolf Boy legacy. Jared seems to have his nose particularly out of joint—perhaps he said something to a sister or uncle or cousin and now suspects they did something rash."

"A dozen? Jared is the only Kicking Deer in the phone book."

She laughed. "They all have unlisted numbers. Now tell me, why did your partner feel the need to do surgery on you?"

"Let me think on that one."

She frowned in annoyance. As she pulled onto Main Street, though, she shrugged. "You owe me, Oregon. Just remember that. You owe me."

CHAPTER SIX

Zimmerman Hardware, Pendleton, Oregon
Thursday, August 26, 2004

Zimmerman's sat midblock on Main Street, hemmed in tight on either side. There were no parking spots available, so Sam stopped near the door.

"There's parking in back, but it's really uneven. This will be easier on you. Go ahead in, I'll catch up with you."

Ukiah climbed carefully out and she pulled away. Tools and signs crowded the window front, an overload of information complete with a historical plaque. A cowbell over the door clanged as Ukiah came through the door, but it was doubtful anyone heard it over a loud banging coming from the back of the store. Like the window front, the store was a tight pack of everything imaginable. What caught the eye was a moose head, stuffed and hung on a support column, looking dolefully down at Ukiah.

The banging continued in the back. No one was at the front counter, so he limped to the back of the store. A second checkout counter formed a small conversation niche in the back. Four men gathered there, Native Americans, in blue jeans, T-shirts, and baseball hats. The oldest seemed in his seventies, the youngest only nineteen or twenty. They nodded in greeting, eyes curious.

The noise came from an old Coke machine, which rattled and banged as if it was about to fling machine parts across the room. The hot grease smell coming from the soda machine's compressor competed, strangely enough, with the heavy scent of fresh-cut cedar.

"Turn it off! Turn it off!" the man leaning against the counter was saying. "Just give it up, it's dead!"

"It's still running, Lou!" A woman wedged in behind the Coke machine called.

"It's time to get a new one, Cassidy," Lou said.

"Oh, no, it isn't," Cassidy shouted over the noise.

The eldest man shook his head. "She's not going to throw it away because that's the way the white man thinks. Throw it away instead of fixing it."

"What did I tell you about that, Uncle Daniel?" Cassidy said. "White man this and white man that. Bleah on the 'white man.' You give him power by assigning everything to him. Think of it instead as human nature. We see something better and grab hold of it, even if what we've got is perfectly good."

"Getting a new one is the only practical answer," Lou said. "What you'll save in electricity costs will pay for getting a new one. Hell, you probably could sell this one to an antique dealer."

"Heretic!" Cassidy hunted through a battered red metal toolbox. "You're missing the whole point!"

"Cassidy," the youngest said. "You just said getting a new one is human nature."

"What's the point?" asked the eldest man.

"It's a landmark. A tradition." Cassidy stood, her back to Ukiah. "We've got here the old hardware store. The old pickle barrel." She gave said pickle barrel a kick. "The old Indians sitting around talking life to death." She waved a crescent wrench toward the men. "And the Coke machine. If I replaced it, then it would be: Oh, it's a shame about the hardware store. Cassidy got hold of it and just gutted it down to the bones!"

"Gutted" was emphasized with a wild swing of the hand holding the crescent wrench; it would have caught Ukiah in the temple with the backhand if he hadn't ducked. The local men all flinched for his sake.

"Don't give me that look," Cassidy growled at the local

men and crawled behind the Coke machine again. "Don't
think I don't hear it. 'What does that insane red woman
think she's doing, buying a hardware store? What does she
know about hardware?' Well, hellooooooooo! I have an industrial engineering degree, people. I know a crescent
wrench"—she stuck the crescent wrench out and waved it—
"from a screwdriver! Really, if a white *man* can run this
place, then I should be able to do it in my sleep!"

"If you have an industrial engineering degree, why did
you buy this place?" Ukiah asked. "Why not do—industrial
engineering?"

"Bwah!" she shouted into the guts of the Coke machine.
He wasn't sure if this was a laugh or not. "I did the token
red-woman bit, and no thank you. Here, if people act like
your friend, you know they mean it because otherwise they
don't bother, I don't have to spend a fortune in clothes, and
all I have to do is show that I know how to repair things."
The Coke machine purred to life. "There! And that's why I
can't throw this old baby away."

She came up grinning, grease smudging her face. She
was an older version of Zoey, from wry mouth and dark
laughing eyes, down to a face that was more strong than
pretty. She wore her thick sienna hair pulled into one ponytail instead of dual braids like Zoey. Despite the grease on
her hands and face, she managed to get none on her crisp
blue oxford. Nearly hidden by her collar, she wore a leather-
and-bone choker, beaded with chunks of tumbled turquoise
and a center silver medallion. She smelled of bruised pine
needles, cut cedar, and machine grease.

She looked at Ukiah in surprise. "Oh, you're the one asking dumb questions."

"Sorry," Ukiah said.

She waved away the apology. "It's just these guys heard
the rant so often, I was surprised anyone asked. What happened to you, good-looking?"

"The crutch?" Ukiah risked standing on both legs to
swing his crutch about. Breakfast was kicking in and his
body was speedily mending itself.

She laughed. "Yes, the crutch and the cast."

"Oh, I fell. Actually, I was shot and then I fell."

She looked at him for a minute, blinking in surprise, and then giggled, covering her mouth with a greasy hand, smudging black fingerprints across her face. "You're the new Umatilla Wolf Boy?" She went into gales of laughter when he nodded. "Oh, Jared told me about you, but he didn't say how cute you were."

There was an interesting mix of reactions among the men. Two were laughing. The eldest one looked at him thoughtfully. The youngest glared jealously at him.

"So, what's your name?" Cassidy asked.

"The woman that adopted me called me Ukiah Oregon."

"Like the town?"

"Yes." He balanced on his crutches to take out his wallet and dug awkwardly into it to pull out his business card. "She found me in Umatilla Park just out of Ukiah and took me to Pittsburgh, eight years ago." Then, because he had tucked the picture into his wallet, he pulled out the photo of him at thirteen. "This was what I looked like back then."

She ignored the card, taking the photo instead, carefully as not to smudge it with grease. Some of the laughter went out of her eyes. She looked up at him again, studying him.

"Actually, you haven't changed much." She went off into a side room. There was the slight hum of a machine. "I'm surprised to see you up and around. Jared gave the family a full report on your injuries, including the hocus-pocus stuff."

"I heal quickly." Ukiah cringed at the thought that *all* the Kicking Deers knew about the mice.

"You've got Zoey convinced, but she always believed." She came to the door of the small office, using a paper towel to wipe cleanser off her hands along with the black grease. She considered him silently, her face skeptical. "Jared says you're a fake, but Jared has never believed any of the family stories about Uncle."

"I haven't asked anyone to believe anything," Ukiah protested. "I just wanted to ask a few questions. Who was my mother? What was she like? How did I get lost? What age was I when I was lost? Why did you call me uncle? Are we related? Did my mother have other children?"

"But you *have* asked us to believe you," Cassidy said. "Don't we have to first judge your right to an answer before we give it?"

Ukiah met her dark eyes much like his own. "Can you fairly judge someone you've refused to talk to?"

Cassidy gazed at him in silence that went on for several minutes. Ukiah waited, sensing that she was trying to be fair. His patience in listening, Max said once, was one of his greatest strengths.

Cassidy spoke to the youngest man without looking away from Ukiah. "Simon, can you do me a favor?"

"Anything," Simon answered, leaping to his feet.

"I didn't bother to refill the machine until I was sure I could repair it." Cassidy went back into the office and returned with a printout and the photo. She handed the printout to Simon. "Could you go to Swire's and pick up a case of each in bottles?"

"I'll do it in a little bit." Simon looked pointedly at Ukiah.

"Oh, don't be jealous." She handed Ukiah his photo. "Didn't you hear? He's my long lost great-great-uncle."

Grudgingly, Simon went and Cassidy considered Ukiah, arms folded over her chest. "The boy we lost was grandfather's uncle, so that's what we call him," she admitted grudgingly. "Jared told me about the mouse thing. He's positive you faked it. I've been dying to know. How *did* you do it?"

Ukiah was startled at her directness. "What?"

"The trick with the mice. How did you do it?"

He glanced at the listening men.

"Oh, don't worry. Its just family now." She indicated the men in turn, starting with the oldest. "This is Uncle Daniel, and Uncle Quince, and Cousin Lou. That's why I sent Simon out for soda. He's not family."

"I don't want to talk about it," Ukiah said.

"If you want us to tell you about our missing Uncle,"

Cassidy said, jerking up her chin, "you have to tell us about the mice."

Ukiah considered the four Kicking Deers. An exchange of trust. It felt like he was getting the short end of the bargain, but perhaps they felt the same way too. He tried for a vague explanation. "The mice are just something that happens when I'm hurt." Oh, that sounded stupid. He winced, and decided to keep his mouth shut.

She laughed at the look on his face. "So, it's been seventy years! What have you been doing with yourself, Wolf Boy?"

He shrugged. "I don't know. Running with the wolves is all I remember. Season after season."

She walked around him, scratching her chin. "Well, you look damn good for being eighty!"

"I'm not eighty," Ukiah said quietly. "My father's people told me how old I was."

That startled them.

"Your father's people?" Cassidy echoed.

"Who are your father's people?" Uncle Daniel asked.

How did one describe the Pack without using the word "alien"? "They are dangerous, brutal people. Killers. They told me how my mother was taken. How I came to be." Hex had stunned his mother and taken her to the ship. Prime used the ovipositor to splice his alien genetics into her human DNA and impregnated her. It was sterile rape. "My father planned to kill my mother before I was born." Prime thought a breeder was too dangerous to let him live. "My father's people thought he had succeeded, so they didn't know I existed until recently."

Puzzlement took over Cassidy's face. "If you don't remember anything, and they didn't know you were born, how did you find your father's people?"

"Well, actually, they found me."

"I reiterate."

Ukiah cocked his head. "You what?"

"Oh, I forgot." She clapped her hands together. "Wolf boys don't have a strong grasp of English!"

"I do well enough," he said. "We think it's because I lived long enough among humans"—that sounded bad—

"before I lived with the wolves, that I picked up English quickly once I was found. I didn't know it when Mom Jo found me."

"Reiterate is to repeat," Cassidy told him. "How did your father's people find you?"

"There is a knowing, without touching, without speaking."

She looked angry for a moment, and then a grin took over her mouth. "You do the mystic bullshit pretty good."

"I was hired to find a missing girl that they were looking for too. Our paths crossed."

"Oh, the first story was so much better." She shook her head. "Do you really expect us to believe that you're an eighty-year-old man?"

"No. I'm older than that," Ukiah said.

"Ninety?" Cassidy asked.

Ukiah hesitated, wondering how much to tell them. If they were his family, wouldn't they know this already? "My father's people say that I was born several hundred years ago."

"He's good," Uncle Quince mumbled. "I nearly believe him."

"Someone talked again," Lou said.

"What do you mean?" Ukiah asked.

"Whenever someone comes along with a good story," Cassidy said, "it always turns out that someone in the family told the wrong person the whole story. You've got interesting takes on the story that no one else has tried. And you've got that wolfie kind of feel."

"Look, all I want is to talk to people about my mother, and about myself," Ukiah said. "My father's people thought she had been killed before I was born, so they were surprised to find me. They couldn't tell me how I ended up with the wolves, or how long I had been with the wolves, or what I had done before then."

"Couldn't the wolves tell you?" Cassidy asked blandly, getting a laugh from the men.

"They didn't talk," Ukiah said. "They knew me well enough to share their kill with me, that was all."

"Uncle died in 1933," Uncle Daniel said quietly. "My father never accepted it, but that's the truth. He thinks he saw Uncle, running with the wolves, even when it was impossible."

Uncle Quince added, "If all the family legends are true, and Uncle did return to us, you could not be him. If the legends are not true, again, you could not be him."

Ukiah tried to puzzle this out, but there were too many mysteries fighting for his attention. "He died? How did he die?"

"He was killed," Lou said.

"Killed!" Cassidy gave a breathless half laugh. "That doesn't do it justice. Do you know why my brother is a cop? When we were little, Grandpa used to talk about how much Jared was like Uncle. Then one day, we were digging in Grandpa's things, messing with stuff we shouldn't have been into, and we found a book with photos of what happened to Uncle." Judging by the men's reactions, everyone in the family had seen the book at one point or another. "Jared woke up screaming for a month. It *really* bothered him that Uncle's murderer was never found."

Photos? Police photos of his murder? Ukiah wondered how many times, during his life, the police were going to make a record of his death. This was the second time that he knew of; luckily, his other deaths had gone unnoticed by the police. Both recorded deaths, it seemed, were incredibly violent—then again, anything short of that didn't put him down long enough for the police to get involved. "What happened? Who killed him? And why does your grandfather think he's still alive?"

The Kicking Deers—his family—looked at one another, and the eldest among them shook his head.

"We don't talk about it," Uncle Daniel said.

"It's the only defense we have against fakes," Cassidy said.

"You said yourself that you don't remember," Lou said. "So how can *you* be sure you are our Uncle?"

"I'm not," Ukiah said. "It just seems that if you're missing a feral Indian boy, and I was found running with the wolves—well—it just seems likely I'm your Uncle."

The cowbell clanged as the door opened and Sam came in. She nodded around to the Kicking Deers. "Lou, Dan, Quince. Good to see you. *Cassidy. What's that monstrosity you've got blocking up the back?*"

"The wood chipper? Shoot I forgot." Cassidy made a face and pulled keys out of her pocket. "Uncle Quince, can you move that for me?" He nodded, standing, and caught the keys she tossed to him. She went on to explain the wood chipper's presence as Uncle Quince ambled out the back door. "I got it off the Highway Division. I'm not sure what I'm going to do with it. It was cheap. I'm making mulch from cedar for the time being."

"Ah!" Sam said, enlightened. "I had to come back around again and find parking in the front."

"Sorry. What can I do for you?"

Sam glanced meaningfully at Ukiah.

"We're through with our business." Cassidy said, crossing her arms.

"Ah! So, how's that deputy of your brother's?"

"Which one? Tommy? What, you sweet on him, Killington?"

"Hell, no!" Sam picked two of the midget-sized peppermint patties out of a box beside the cash register. She fished a fist of change out of her pocket, jiggled it around until she found two quarters, and paid for the candy. "I meant Brody. He any better?"

Cassidy sighed. "No. He's still shuffling around like a zombie. You whites are too reserved at grieving. You keep all that pain in, swallow it down to poison you. It's better to wail than to suffer in silence."

Sam sighed at the news, and tossed one of the candies to Ukiah. "One of the deputies, Matt Brody, lost his kid in June. He's one of my drowning victims."

"Oh."

"He and his wife took it hard. They're both like stick puppets."

"A lot of grief in this town lately," Lou said. "Lots of people walking around shell-shocked."

"Yeah, it seems like Harry's death just sucked the life out of Matt." Cassidy rang up the sale and then indicated Ukiah with a thrust of her jaw. "I wondered how he figured out where to find us."

"A woman's got to do business." Sam leaned against the counter. "I'm just dealing in information. It's not like I held out for a cut of the reward."

"Reward?" Ukiah said. And then things clicked. The glut of people wanting to see Jesse Kicking Deer. The unlisted phone numbers. The hostility. "There's a reward for producing the Umatilla Wolf Boy?"

"You didn't know?" Sam asked.

"The newspaper clipping we were working from didn't mention it."

"Yeah, right," Cassidy said.

"Look, if it's the money that's the problem, I can sign a paper, waiving the reward."

"Don't you even want to know how much it is?" Sam asked.

"No. Money isn't important to me."

"It's a hundred thousand dollars," Sam said. "The Kicking Deers have been holding a nest egg for the boy for over seventy years. Jesse Kicking Deer decided to blow it all just to get the boy back."

"The money isn't important," Ukiah repeated.

"Sure it isn't," Cassidy said.

Ukiah looked at them, saw the hostility in their eyes, and another connection was made. "Is that why one of you shot me? To keep me from claiming the money?"

He was watching Cassidy, who had been the easiest to read. Confusion came first. Then a look of anger, which gave way to sudden horror.

"No!" Cassidy cried. "That couldn't have been one of us!"

"You're not sure, though, are you?" Ukiah said.

The moment of doubt, though, was gone. "If we shot everyone that claimed to be the Umatilla Wolf Boy, Pendleton would be littered with bodies!" Cassidy snapped. "Every idiot in Oregon, California, Washington, and Idaho has besieged us with claims. We've had people show up with a child's skeleton—made in Korea, thank God—a forged John Doe death certificate from Baker County, a little old wrinkled man who turned out to be Navaho, and one bastard that actually dug up a Kicking Deer grave for an authentic dead boy's body. Him, we would have shot, *if* we were going to shoot anyone."

"And can you prove that you were here yesterday," Ukiah asked, "at the time of the shooting?"

"Yes I can," Cassidy snapped angrily, then looking at Ukiah's shattered arm, pulled back some of that anger. "Look, Jared called me the night before last to say another 'Wolf Boy' had shown up. He wanted to know how you found Mom's place. He said that you had the weakest claim yet. You're the wrong age. You have no physical proof. You didn't even have a reasonable story. I'm sorry someone hurt you, but it wasn't one of us."

"Wait, wait, wait!" Sam said. "You mean *you're* the Umatilla Wolf Boy?"

"Yes" Ukiah said.

"What's this 'John Doe client' bullshit?" Sam asked.

"It's not something I like talking about," Ukiah said. "It's embarrassing to tell someone that the only childhood memories you have is running naked in the woods. My mothers hired Max to find out who I was. That's how Max and I first met. He came to Pendleton looking for the identity of a John Doe child between the ages of thirteen and sixteen in 1999."

Sam frowned and looked to Cassidy, "I thought the Wolf Boy was supposed to be old, like in his eighties or something."

"Uncle died in 1933," Cassidy stated. "Grandpa never got over it. When people started to sight the Wolf Boy back in the nineties, he set up the reward, but it's not the same person."

Was he the same person? He could be, but only if the boy had been him. He could have survived a murder and being lost in the woods for decades. A normal Native American child, though, would have stayed dead. How could he know without talking to someone that knew the boy?

Sam put a hand on his shoulder. "You can't win them all, Wolf Boy. Come on, I'll give you a lift back to your hotel."

Behind Ukiah, the door opened and the cowbell clanged in warning of another customer.

Cassidy glanced over Ukiah's shoulder and then sighed. "If you have nothing you want to buy, it would be best if you go."

He started to turn away, and then remembered Max's comment at the hospital. "Actually, I need a hacksaw."

Sam announced that she'd be out in the car.

Cassidy Kicking Deer rang up the purchase and slipped the hacksaw into a plastic bag to make it easier for Ukiah to carry. "What do you want this for?"

Ukiah lifted up the cast. "To cut this off."

Anger, disbelief, and glimmers of belief warred on Cassidy's face. Apparently she could not decide if he was truly a family legend returning home or a clever con artist scheming to trick her family out of a lot of money. In the end, disbelief won out. "Have a nice day," she said coldly, meaning it as a dismissal.

Ukiah used his card key to get into his room, wishing Max had been there to greet him. He stretched out on the bed, heartsick from the day. Alicia was still missing, someone had tried to kill him, and the Kicking Deers thought he was a con artist. Sleep would be a welcome distraction. Luckily his body was battered enough, and his breakfast large enough, that he dropped off almost immediately.

He woke to his phone chirping on the nightstand. Indigo's phone number showed in the display. He hit the talk button. "Hi. I miss you."

As if the words opened a wound, he suddenly missed her horribly. It was the first time that they had been separated.

"I miss you," Indigo murmured. "How do you feel?"

He considered his body. "A little sore. I'll be able to track tomorrow, after a big dinner tonight and a good night's sleep."

And truthfully, he realized, it wasn't the first time they had been apart. Indigo's FBI work had taken her a field several times in the last two months. It was the first time he was away, with no friends or family except Max and Kraynak to disguise their separation.

"Good. Any news on Alicia?"

"Um, I've been asleep. I haven't heard anything all day." Suddenly a flash of fear went through him. What if Max and Kraynak both had been shot? Who would call him? "Can I call you back? I just had a panic attack over Max—I'm going to stay worried until I talk to him."

"I understand. I'll be here for the rest of the evening."

"Thanks."

"I know you'd do the same for me."

They said quick good-byes and he hit the speed dial for Max.

"Bennett." Max answered on the first ring.

"It's me. I was just getting worried that I hadn't heard from you."

Max laughed. "Actually, same here. I've got a gun, Kraynak, and half the Umatilla county police force with me. You've got a busted-up arm, walking on a crutch, no gun, and are completely alone in a strange city."

"I'm amazed you left me alone."

"I don't know what I was thinking about."

"Alicia."

"Yeah, I guess so. Are you okay?"

"I'm fine. I'm holed up in the hotel room right now. I had an interesting talk with Sam Killington about statistical deviations from the norm. There's a weird pattern of elevated death rates in the area. House fire fatalities is one."

"Sounds like she's doing insurance-fraud investigation."

"Well, missing hikers is another elevated rate."

"Oh, damn. One of Kicking Deer's deputies—he's one of those big, dumb-blond ox types—has a theory that a hunter shot you, despite the fact it's out of season for just about everything."

"With that high-power of a rifle?"

"Yeah, I know. Stupid as it is, we've been hoping it might be true."

"Sam has no proof that the fires and hikers are connected, just statistics."

"Something is juggling the numbers, kid. I've told you that sometimes the only way you can see the passing elephant herd is to look at the numbers on the seismograph."

Ukiah consulted his nearly perfect memory. "No you haven't."

"Well, I should have. Look, we're calling it a night here. It's getting dark. Kraynak and I will be back in Pendleton in an hour or so. The three of us can compare notes over diner. See you then."

Ukiah hung up and dialed Indigo again.

"Special Agent Zheng," she answered.

"Max is fine, but they haven't found anything. They're on the way back."

"You'll be out first thing tomorrow," she reminded him. "You'll find her."

He found himself smiling under her calm assurance. Indigo was the most centered person he knew, unruffled in the face of death and destruction, with a stillness that was a peaceful refuge for him. In the face of confusion and chaos of the everyday world, he found her tranquility a joy and blessing.

"How's Kittanning?"

"A little fussy. I think he misses you. Hellena showed up on the pretense of discussing Mom Jo's dogs and got him settled." Hellena was the alpha female of the Dog Warriors. "I hope you don't mind, but I told her about the shooting."

"I don't mind." The Dog Warriors were his family by genetics; they probably should know he had been hurt. It steered his mind, however, to the Kicking Deers. "Did Max tell you? We think we've found my mother's family."

"He told me that your contacts with Sheriff Kicking Deer haven't gone well."

"It's worse." He sighed, wishing she was there, with him. He told her about his meeting with Cassidy Kicking Deer. "Maybe they're right, Indigo. I mean, I'm kind of jumping to conclusions here. There is a boy missing, believed to be running with the wolves. I'm a boy that ran with wolves. But what if Cassidy is right? Her great-great-uncle is dead, and has nothing to do with me. Maybe because I was out there, being strangely famous for running with the wolves, Jesse Kicking Deer clung to the hope that his uncle wasn't dead, when he really was."

There was a minute of silence and he listened to her beautiful breathing.

"There's holes to it," Indigo stated. "First is the sheriff's reaction to the mice. Why would anyone fake pulling mice out of incisions? Normal Native American children do not have mice in their abdominal cavities."

He followed her logic. "If the Kicking Deer boy was Pack blood, though, he would."

"Exactly. Secondly, there is the Kicking Deers' reply to your claiming of possibly being several hundred years old." Indigo repeated the response. *"He's good. I nearly believe him. Somebody talked."*

"As if someone told me something I shouldn't know."

"Which is the Wolf Boy could be considered two or three hundred years old," Indigo continued. "Then there is the fact that the grandfather believes that the boy is still alive even though there are photographs of his death. Cassidy indicates a gruesome death. If the body was disfigured, then the question of true identity comes into play. Or did the body disappear?"

"Which would have happened if the boy came back to life."

"Lastly, the grandfather believes that the child is still alive, even at age eighty-four, which isn't a totally unreasonable life span for a normal person. Remember, though, they're looking for the Umatilla Wolf Boy. Who would believe a person could spend seventy-two years running feral in the Oregon wilderness?"

"Cassidy Kicking Deer doesn't."

"But Jesse Kicking Deer, who knew the boy personally, does."

You're virtually indestructible, Max's voice repeated in

his head. Max would still believe in him after seventy-two years.

"I don't think you're jumping to a wrong conclusion, Ukiah, but I also think you may never get these people to admit you're their relative. I know that this isn't the same, but your moms and Max love you. They're your parents now. You've got them, Cally, Kittanning, and me."

"I know. It's not like I was planning to move back to Oregon with them. I just wanted to know what my childhood was like."

"Ukiah, the Kicking Deers loved you enough that seventy years after you vanished, they're still looking for you. Perhaps the old man could give you more details, but it's going to work down to this—they loved you. Knowing how you thrive on being loved, how could you've been anything but happy as a child?"

With the three-hour time difference, Indigo needed to say goodnight shortly afterward. Rather than torturing himself about what he hadn't discussed with Indigo, Ukiah thought about what Sam Killington had told him, and wondered what she hadn't.

He wasn't sure if three fires in two months was a huge number. It felt like it, though. If the fires started after midnight, most people *would* be in bed. In a deep sleep, most people *would* die of smoke inhalation before waking. But all of them? Only the large numbers of deaths indicated something wasn't right. It was a deviation of statistics, and that was all.

Yet, that was what seemed to be driving Sam's investigation. The only link between the house fires, the hikers, and drownings—if Sam was telling him the truth, and if she hadn't missed some other connection—was that the numbers were all statistically deviant from the norm. Max would be aquiver now, sure that someone was plotting something. Ukiah, however, was at a loss. He worked with the concrete. A footprint. A blood sample. A stray hair. These were things he could grasp.

When Max, Kraynak, Chino, Leo, and himself played

poker on Fridays, they never let him shuffle the deck or deal. Each and every card felt slightly different to him. As he slid the card facedown across the table, he knew what it was as clearly as if it was faceup.

Max stated that there were ways to predict, based on your own cards, what other people were holding and if your hand beat theirs. Ukiah found the theory impossible to use. He judged his hand against the others' reactions, weighing their nervousness or lack of. Against their regular players of two private detectives, a police detective, and a lawyer, he did poorly. He only did well when outsiders sat in—people more open with their expressions than they knew, and less knowledgeable about Ukiah's skills.

He tried to find angles to Sam's case he could grasp easily.

There was the fact that the families of the house fires had missed appointments, work, and school. Something kept all these people home to die. It kept them in bed as the house filled with smoke. Perhaps it was a killer, holding these families hostage. But fires weren't as destructive as people supposed; even on badly burned bodies, coroners could find evidence of stabbing, gunshots, poison, drugs, and strangulation. Even if the victims had been smothered—which was also death by asphyxiation—prior to the fire, there would be the lack of smoke in the lungs.

The thought of someone stalking through a dark house, snuffing out one life after another, sent another shiver down his back.

He thought instead of Alicia. He wanted desperately to believe she was just lost. He didn't want to think about someone killing her.

Alicia and Rose had set up camp at an isolated point, yet with full access to the road. Anyone could have driven up to the camp, killed both girls, and rode away without fear of detection. If they had wanted to eliminate evidence, they could have carried off the bodies to be dumped elsewhere; in this land of four-wheeled pickup trucks and great tracts of rarely traveled forest roads, there were no logistic problems. Surely there was comfort in that Rose was still at the camp, and saw Alicia walk away. Surely in a place as small and remote as the primitive campground, no killer would feel the need to so carefully hide his presence.

But who shot him, and why?

"We looked." Max blew the dust out of the cut in Ukiah's cast, eyed the depth, and placed the hacksaw blade back into the groove. "We didn't find any sign of Alicia. We also tried to find where the sniper would have been when he shot you. Unfortunately we're talking too large of an area—a hundred and eighty degree arc up to a half mile in range."

Kraynak watched the proceedings from the narrow balcony, doubt clear on his face as he chain-smoked through two cigarettes. "You sure we should be taking that off?"

Max glanced up at Ukiah without lifting his head, a steely command to be silent. Kraynak, like many of their Pittsburgh friends, knew that Ukiah was different. After the shooting in June, it was a fact impossible to hide. Max and Ukiah, however, told almost no one the whole truth. Indigo knew—she had been swept up in the events—as did Ukiah's mothers. Everyone else, Kraynak included, they left to make their own best guesses. A guess, Max insisted, could not be as dangerous as the confirmed truth.

"I'll be fine as long as I don't put stress on the knit," Ukiah said truthfully.

Max sawed slowly and carefully. "He's good with his left hand, but he's been taught to use his right. The cast is in the way. He can't shoot accurately or move easily with it on."

"If he shoots with that hand, he'll break the arm again," Kraynak said.

"Do I have to really carry?" Ukiah asked.

Max looked up Ukiah again. "Yes. If I could have left you a gun at the hospital, I would have."

Ukiah sighed. It didn't seem right to shoot at someone to defend himself when he was nearly indestructible. He supposed there was a chance he would have to defend Max or Kraynak, who weren't. It might have been the luck of the draw that he was shot and not one of the others. Unless, of course, the Kicking Deers had something to do with the shooting.

Which reminded him. "I found out something interesting today. Apparently Jesse Kicking Deer has a large reward for the information leading to the return of the Umatilla Wolf Boy to him, and the family isn't happy. It's possible we tripped a trigger there. One of them might have shot me."

"That's slim," Max said. "About as slim as the hunter theory."

"Why don't we just say it?" Kraynak ground out his butt. "The only reason anyone in Pendleton would be shooting at Ukiah would be to stop him from finding Alicia."

"They had thirty experienced people out the day before," Max said. "Why not shoot at them?"

"They weren't on the right trail," Kraynak said.

"How did anyone know what trail I was on?" Ukiah asked.

"Scanner," Max said. "Sam told you that she heard Kicking Deer report the shooting."

Ukiah scanned his memory. "I wasn't reporting where I was, and you can't tap the GPS signal."

They considered the problem in silence.

"Jared Kicking Deer knew we were heading for that hill," Max said. "We stood there and discussed meeting Ukiah at the foot of the cliff."

"We said that was slim," Kraynak said.

Ukiah threw his mind back. "He reported to the dispatcher where he was going. It went out on the police channels."

"And anyone with a scanner would have heard it," Kraynak said.

"Ukiah will be up to tracking tomorrow," Max said, pausing for a confirming nod from Ukiah. "We'll find her then."

CHAPTER SEVEN

Umatilla National Park, Umatilla County, Oregon
Friday, August 27, 2004

It was the type of morning where the sky turned solid, the very air thickening to a gray blanket. Riffs of fog drifted off the treetops, the forest breathing out into the chilled air like a slumbering beast.

Kraynak and Max were tense to the point of vibrating and trying not to show it. Healed and sound, Ukiah nevertheless still felt battered and bone-bruised. He limped through a grid search, hoping he'd find Alicia before he collapsed again.

He crossed over the point where he lay wounded the day before yesterday and came to where Alicia landed. He crouched close to the earth, trying to glean every detail from the loose crumble of cliff face and weeds.

Alicia had come down through a series of pine branches, resulting in a far easier landing than he experienced. Somehow the search-and-rescue team hadn't trampled this point and he found Alicia's handprints where she pushed herself up to a sitting position.

"She's bleeding, but not too much. I don't think she was knocked unconscious; there's no blood pool. She's moving on two feet with a steady stride. If she had hurt a leg, or couldn't swing an arm, it would show."

"Incoming," Kraynak said calmly, but was moving quickly sideways to take cover behind a boulder, pulling his pistol.

Max dropped down, bringing up his pistol.

Ukiah took a deep breath, focusing on the crash of a body moving through the woods. "It's Kicking Deer."

Max and Kraynak pointed their pistols skyward instead of at the oncoming sheriff.

The county policeman came out of the woods like a storm front. "Why are you out here?"

"My niece is still missing, we're still looking," Kraynak snapped, holstering his pistol.

Kicking Deer crossed to Ukiah. "You fit to track?"

"I'm fine," Ukiah lied, feeling anything but fine.

Kicking Deer caught Ukiah's right wrist. Lifting Ukiah's arm up, Jared ran a thumb over unblemished skin, pressing carefully against the healed but still aching radius bone.

The slight pain triggered a deep growl of warning.

Max added his own style of growl. "That's enough, Kicking Deer."

Jared released Ukiah's arm. Whatever the sheriff thought of Ukiah's condition, though, was carefully hidden away behind a policeman's neutral facade.

"We've lost a day." Kraynak broke the silence. "We've got a lot to make up."

Kicking Deer backed up to give Ukiah room. "Lead the way, magic boy."

Ukiah knelt, ignoring the twinge of pain the action put through his knee and hip. He sorted through the confusion of footprints left by the search-and-rescue team to find Alicia's trail. Luckily, the SAR team had fanned out, leaving her tracks fairly unmarred after the first twenty feet. While the narrow forest road had been somewhat visible from the cliff above, it was totally invisible now. Apparently disoriented by the fall, Alicia headed away from road.

Several hundred feet from the cliff, he stopped, frowning at what her tracks told him.

"What is it?" Max asked as the others caught up.

"She stopped here for several minutes, moved forward a few feet, and then started off at another angle, faster, like she's running from something."

"An animal?"

He shrugged, unsure, and continued along her trail.

Within minutes the truth was obvious. He hand signaled to Max to wait. "There's a second set of footprints right over Alicia's. A man was following her." Ukiah backtracked the man's trail, acting on a hunch. Disappointingly, yet as he expected, the track lead back to a slight trail coming down off the ridge. Ukiah returned to the others. "I don't know how I missed him, but I think he was up on the ridge with Alicia. She might have been running from him when she fell."

Kraynak ground his teeth as he took out a cigarette and lit it.

Max hissed out a curse. "Is she still heading away from the road?"

Ukiah nodded.

"I think we'll just slow you down. Why don't you take off, and we'll follow in the Blazer."

Jared insisted on being able to tune into their radio link. Ukiah did a top-down check, making sure his body armor was fastened tight, that he had food, water, and his pistol.

"I'm ready," Ukiah said.

"Be careful," Max told him. "Don't get too focused that you don't see the danger."

Ukiah called the trail over his radio headset as he ran. "Alicia isn't running, but her stride is long. She walks quickly. I don't think she was hurt badly by the fall. There's no more blood from her. She doesn't pause long. She moves in a straight enough line. The man comes behind her, matching her stride. He wears boots, Timberlands, size ten. He is wearing blue jeans and a flannel shirt, mostly in blues. He walks easily, no brushing into trees or bushes; he is not in a hurry."

A few minutes later, he spoke again, slowing his run slightly so he had breath to talk. "I think she gave him the slip, though I don't know how. She's leaving a fairly obvious trail."

"For you." Max spoke over the radio for the first time in a while.

"Perhaps." Ukiah returned to the point of separation, eyeing the man's trail as it broke off. "The man starts to run.

He's tall, his legs are long, and his footprints are far apart. He seems fairly solid too, judging by the depth of his print. He's a big man."

Over Max's headset came the distant, explosive curse from Kraynak. This new information of a stalker could not come easy to Alicia's uncle. Ukiah winced for Kraynak.

A shimmering line of sun caught Ukiah's eye. A hair dangled on a branch, so thin it was amazing that he could even perceive it, would not have except for the gleam of light on it. He plucked it free. A human hair. The dead cells gave up a vast store of information. Blond. Male. Blue-eyed. O-positive blood. Early thirties.

Ukiah pocketed the hair and started again after Alicia.

"She seems to know she has lost him. She pauses, turning, turning, I think she's trying to get her orientation, figure out where she is. She starts forward again—still in the same direction. Perhaps she's decided that just getting away from the man is the best course."

He ran, eyes on the ground, hurrying forward, ignoring his battered body, afraid of what he was going to find at the end. "She walks quickly, still not tired. She is in good condition."

"But she's moving deeper into the park."

"She stops. She backs up. Something is in front of her." Ukiah scouted forward and cursed. "He's here. He got ahead of her and has been waiting. He stands with feet braced, so still, like a statue, sinking into the ground. He's very, very patient to stand so long without moving—but when he does, he does not follow her. He turns and goes back."

"He just turns and goes?"

"I don't understand it, Max. Alicia has veered and gone down a trail through the creek's undergrowth, she has to hunch down to run, but she scurries like a rabbit, sometimes on hands and knees. She must be afraid. Here's a deer trail. She stands and starts to run. Here's the man again, and she turns.

"Alicia runs. Again the man turns, doesn't follow. He's going to cut her off again—Max, he's herding her."

"Herding?"

Ukiah needed to stop and pant out his explanation. "He's getting in front of her, and forcing her to go the way he wants."

There was the rustle of paper. "Ukiah, I've got you on the monitor. Head after Alicia so I can see what direction she took."

Ukiah started down the deer trail after the running Alicia.

"Oh, damn, Ukiah, the main road is in that direction. She was heading away from it, but now she's pointed right at it."

Ukiah ran, despite the fact he was reaching the end of his strength, sickened by the realization that this drama took place five days earlier. No matter how fast he ran, he would not get to Alicia before she reached the road.

And yet he couldn't stop running.

Minutes later, he hit the graded berm.

"Oh, damn." He stumbled to a halt, panting. "She's at the road. There was a car pulled over, waiting. There were people here, standing still for a long time, waiting. Damn it, Max, she hit the road, saw the car, and probably thought she was saved."

"Maybe she was." Max held out for hope.

"No. No." Ukiah groaned at what he could read in the torn earth. "They jumped her. She fought. They took her down to her knees, to her hands, to her face. They bloodied her. They lifted her up, and they put her in the car, and they drove away."

He followed as far as he could, limping now, but the dirt of the berm pounded out of the tires and the car moved on, unremarkable from the countless other cars that had traveled the highway since Monday. He finally gave up and sprawled out onto the hot asphalt, letting the heat bake through his worn body.

Max's Blazer came down the road, slowed and stopped a few feet shy of where he lay, protecting him from any oncoming traffic. He heard the county police car pull over to the berm, its tires crunching on the loose girt.

Max and Kraynak got out of the Blazer, looked down the

ribbon of empty road, and shook their heads. Kraynak sulked off, trailing the smoke of his Marlboros.

"Come on." Max tugged Ukiah up into a stand and helped him to the back of the Blazer. There, Max gave him a candy bar and made room for him in the cargo area. Rather than chewing, Ukiah simply let the chocolate melt in his mouth.

"There." Max shifted the climbing equipment into the backseat. "Lie down."

"I feel horrible that I've lost the trail," Ukiah whispered, collapsing into the Blazer.

"You did your best." Max took out his map, unfolding it to study the whole, instead of the small area they occupied.

Sheriff Kicking Deer got out of his car and came to stand beside Max, talking on his shoulder-mounted radio. "We're out on 244, heading west back into Ukiah. The tracker says that she was forced into a car. Let Tim Winholtz know."

Max looked up from his map to gaze down the desolate stretch of road. "They could have taken her anywhere. Pilot Rock. Pendleton. They could be all the way to Portland by now."

"We're only going to find her," Kicking Deer said, "if we can figure out who took her."

The Pittburghers stayed out from under foot while plaster prints of the tire tracks were made, photographs taken, and the whole area combed for evidence. Ukiah thought there would be none, for the people had waited with extraordinary patience. They had not paced, meandered about, smoked cigarettes, chewed gum, spat, or even rocked from foot to foot. They had stood at inhuman attention, sinking into the soft earth of the berm.

"How did he do it?" Ukiah asked. "A million acres of forest, hundreds of miles of road, and yet he herded Alicia up onto the road right where a car was waiting. How did he do that?"

"Radio and GPS," Kraynak snapped from his far sulking point. "Like you and Max. The car could have coordinated with the field scout and been here, waiting."

"They would have needed practice to pull it off this flaw-lessly," Max said.

"Ex-military," Kraynak guessed.

"It would explain their orderliness," Ukiah said. As an ex-Marine, Max lived at a level of military clean that amazed Ukiah's mothers.

"Maybe," Max said. "Maybe there's a lot more missing hikers than anyone knows."

Alicia had managed to leave one sign of her kidnapping. Somehow, while her assailants wrestled her to the ground, she had slipped her college ring off, pressed it into the dirt until it was almost invisible. It had been a chance in a million that anyone would ever find it, for the search for her had centered around the campground, now ten miles away.

Jared Kicking Deer had found it, shifting gloved-covered fingers through the dirt in hopes of any evidence beyond impressions in the ground. He dropped the ring into a small plastic evidence bag and brought it to Kraynak to identify. "It's hers. Those are her initials engraved there. Alicia Caroline Kraynak. ACK."

"I'm sorry," Jared said quietly. "Were you in contact with Alicia prior to her disappearance?"

Kraynak knew where the question was leading, and talked about his last conversation with Alicia. She had been happy and excited, and gave no indication that someone was stalking her, waiting for a moment to get her alone, to make her vanish.

"She had a daily planner," Kraynak told Jared. "It's back at my hotel room. I looked through it briefly last night. It might have something in it."

Jared noted the diary into his case tablet. "I'll get it later." He tucked away the small pad and glanced over at Ukiah, who was limp with exhaustion. True worry got past the cop facade. "Will he be okay?"

"He needs some more food," Max said. "And lots of sleep, but he'll be fine."

Jared accepted it as truth with a slight nod and a lessening of the worry. "He does good work." He started for his car. "I'm going to drive back to the campground and question the other camper."

"She shouldn't be left alone," Kraynak stated.

Jared frowned, then nodded. "People around here leave their keys in the car and their houses unlocked. I hate the thought that a girl can't be safe alone in my county, but you're right."

"If you don't mind, we'll tag along and see what Rose says." Max looked around at the desolate stretch of road. "There's nothing here for us."

CHAPTER EIGHT

Bear Wallow Creek Campground, Ukiah, Oregon
Friday, August 27, 2004

Rose shook her head, a hand covering her mouth as if to keep a sob or scream trapped within her, her eyes huge black buttons of fear. Her terror wreathed her like perfume. Ukiah put space between him and her fright as the others questioned the geology student; he was too tired to shield himself from its effects.

He glanced into the tent and experienced a bolt of surprise that the tent was half empty, stripped of Alicia's items. Then he remembered that Kraynak had packed her stuff the night before, intending to take Alicia straight home after this experience.

"No, no, there was no one," Rose murmured from behind the imprisoning hand, "We talked to people, but no one seemed dangerous. No one was scary."

"We'll need a list of everyone Alicia might have spoken with prior to her disappearance."

Rose's eyes went a little wider. "I have no idea who she talked to. When we went into town, we would split up. She would go to the library, the bead shop—I don't know where. I went to the post office, the ice-cream shop, and the bookstore. We took turns doing the laundry. The only place we went together was the grocery store."

Ukiah looked away from her alarm, wearily studying the ground. Time, wind, and dew had eroded Wednesday's massive number of footprints down to a rumpled mass, and only

Rose's and one other person's now crisply marked the campsite. Judging by her footprints, Rose had spent most of the day sitting at the picnic table, doing the same paperwork she had been working on when they arrived. The other person, in comparison, had walked from the parking lot to the tent, entered the tent, and then returned to their car.

He frowned as he realized that all of Rose's tracks to the tent were from the morning, and the stranger had been in camp within the last hour. If the person came to see Rose, why no tracks to the picnic table? If Rose hadn't been at the picnic table when they arrived, why not look around for her? He crossed the campsite to crouch wearily beside the tracks and examined them closer.

What he found pulled a growl out of him.

"What did you find, kid?" Max asked.

"She was here. The woman driver of the kidnapper's car. She was here within the last hour."

"Here?" Rose squeaked. "One of them was here while I was gone?"

"Where did you go?" Jared asked.

"The rangers came up and asked me to come to the office with them. There were some forms that they needed filled out. I just got back only about five minutes ago."

"Miss, I don't think you should stay here today," Jared said quietly. "Could you pack your things and we'll take you into town."

She nodded. "I want to go home."

They waited until she was out of earshot.

"Why did they come back for her now?" Kraynak wondered quietly. "She's been out here alone since Monday morning."

"Which was stupid of us!" Max snapped. "We should have moved her to the hotel the first day!"

"With Rose here safe," Jared guessed, "it seemed more likely that Alicia was merely lost."

"Why not take them both?" Kraynak whispered.

"There were other campers here Monday and Tuesday," Max reminded Kraynak.

"And herding two people through the woods would have

been nearly impossible," Ukiah said. "Wolf packs usually only pick one animal out of a herd."

"They came for Rose as soon as we had proof Alicia had been kidnapped," Max said. "They're tying up loose ends."

"Damn it!" Kraynak swore. "The police scanner!"

Jared looked puzzled, so they explained their theory on how the sniper knew where to find Ukiah. "And I reported in that Ukiah found the kidnapping site. Everyone in the county with a scanner knows."

"We should have thought of it beforehand," Kraynak said. "Thank God Rose wasn't here when the kidnappers came for her!"

They packed all the camping equipment into Kraynak's Volkswagen van, which Alicia had used instead of her own small car. They made a small convoy pulling of out the campground, Jared leading in his cruiser, then Kraynak and Rose in the van, and finally Ukiah and Max in the Blazer.

Max was silent for the ride back to Pendleton. Ukiah slumped in the passenger side, exhausted but too unnerved to sleep.

As they pulled into the hotel's parking lot, Max gave a deep sigh. "Kid, could Sam Killington have been one of the kidnappers?"

Ukiah recalled the long-legged blond woman. "No, wrong shoe size. I think she's about an eight, and the tracks were fives. The kidnapper wore tennis shoes, high end, probably considered walking shoes or cross-trainers. Sam had on hiking boots both times I saw her."

"And the others?"

"I think the rest were men."

"Good," Max murmured, then, as a grin spread across his face. "Well, speak of the devil."

Max toggled down his window, and the wind spilled into the cabin, bringing Sam's scent of leather, gunmetal, female sweat, and Obsession perfume. She swaggered across the parking lots flipping a keyring around her right index finger in a jangle of metal. "Hi, guys! Can I interest you two in a proposition?"

"Proposition away," Max grinned, half-leaning out his window.

"Thought you might be interested," she said with a wink. "Let's do dinner and swap information. That is"—she glanced past Max to Ukiah—"if you're up to it."

Max looked to Ukiah. Ukiah would have preferred to order room service, followed quickly by sleep, but there was no denying that Sam could be the key to finding Alicia. She knew the area. With snipers and multiple kidnappers roaming the area, they were safer traveling as a team. So Ukiah nodded.

"We're up to it." Max told her.

They followed Sam on her Harley across town. On the way, Ukiah called and let Kraynak know where they were heading. Kraynak had volunteered to drive Rose to the airport for the evening flight. He told them to eat without him.

A neon sign in the window marked the restaurant, a cowboy hat with the word STETSONS. Of the four parking spaces beside Stetsons, two and a half were taken up by a pickup truck and a badly parked station wagon. Sam tucked her Harley into the short third space behind the station wagon, and Max pulled into last space. She was pulling off her helmet when Ukiah opened his door and stepped out onto the sidewalk.

Sam paused, helmet cocked over her shoulder, frowning at him. "Where's the crutches?"

"I told you that I heal quickly," Ukiah said, though he felt far from well. His entire body ached as if someone had beaten him with a baseball bat. He had pushed himself too hard, ignoring his body completely during the day's tracking.

"Ah, I forgot." Sam snapped her fingers. "You're a Kicking Deer."

"What does that mean?" Ukiah asked.

"The Kicking Deers are local legends," Sam said. "Stronger. Faster. Healthier. They say that the Cayuse horses are so sturdy because the Kicking Deers bred with them."

"What?" Max said.

"Oh, it's an old Indian tale." Sam said. "A Kicking Deer

woman ran off with one of the stallions and turned into a horse, and had colts with him. You listen to enough of these stories and you start to wonder if they didn't spend much of their time on peyote."

Max gave Ukiah a worried glance, and then did a frowning double take. "You sure you're up to this? You look wiped."

"I'll be better once I eat."

Max headed them toward the front door, keeping a light hand on Ukiah's arm, as if to catch him if he fell. "Ukiah tells me that you're doing insurance work."

Sam fell into step with them, helmet tucked under her arm. "Oregon Life and Home handled all three houses that burned. Not surprisingly. This is a small town. They cover most of the homes. Three home policies. A dozen life-insurance policies. They're suddenly paying out a large chunk of money, and they don't want the trend to continue."

Max opened the door, and held it wide for Sam and Ukiah to go through. A flood of information spilled out of the restaurant. People. Alcoholic drinks. Cooked food. Twanging country music. Max caught Ukiah's arm, actually supporting him now, without comment. "What are we talking about, moneywise?"

"A few hundred thousand." Sam didn't say it the same way Max would have. A hundred thousand was petty cash to Max. She said it as if it was quite a bit of money. "Maybe as much as a half-million dollars. The houses weren't mansions, but they're insured at replacement cost."

"So a fifty-thousand house, built new today, is actually a hundred-thousand-plus home."

"More or less, plus all the appliances were at replacement, not depreciated costs. So you're talking three refrigerators, three stoves, three dishwashers, so on and so forth. What was there might have been twenty years old and the shit busted out of it, but the people paid for it to be replaced with new if the houses were burned."

"Televisions, carpets, beds, clothes," Max added to the list.

"The whole works. Each family had thirty thousand dollars' replacement allowance. Then you get into the life insurance. One family was insurance-happy, and even the kids had policies."

A hostess showed them a corner booth. Ukiah leaned against the wall, eyes closed, trying to shut out the flood. The waiter came up, wearing too much Polo aftershave.

"They've got a good beer selection," Sam said, a familiar voice out of the dark rumble.

Max ordered Sierra Nevada Pale Ale and then asked if they had milkshakes.

"We have soda, unsweetened tea, hot tea, milk, and coffee." The waiter's unfamiliar voice and breath tore through Ukiah's awareness like barbed wire, snaring and snarling all his thoughts.

"The kid will have a milk, and a bowl of whatever soup you have." Max paused, apparently consulting the menu. "A plate of calamari rings, a shrimp cocktail, the langostino, and the breaded, smoked salmon, whatever that is."

A song Ukiah had heard the day before came on the sound system, mourning a lost love, the words and tune now familiar. With the waiter gone, the tide of the information receded enough for Ukiah to open his eyes.

"I've heard that your client was definitely kidnapped," Sam was saying.

Max's eyes narrowed, and his smile faded slightly. "How did you hear?"

"Police scanner." Sam held up her hands to hold off Max's wrath. "Like I said, it's a small town. I figure if you three are staying in town for a while, we can join forces. I've got the contacts. The kid's a tracking wonder, and yes, it would be nice to have armed backup with kidnappers running loose."

The waiter returned, forcing silence on the table as he thunked down glasses, beer bottles, and a steaming bowl of vegetable beef soup. Ukiah curled himself around his soup.

Max relaxed back into his seat, giving a slightly smug grin. "You're just wanting another peek at my piece, eh?"

Sam snickered, pouring out her beer. "Of course. So, we work together?"

"I'm not saying we wouldn't welcome the help." Max poured his own beer. "But are you sure you're not haring off on a wild-goose chase? Alicia's disappearance might not have anything to do with your case. It would make it tough getting paid."

"I've had a hunch about this since I heard the first all-points. Frankly, it looks more and more like I'm right."

The waiter returned, doing a balancing act with plates of appetizers, bread, napkins, and silverware. He carefully set the food in the center of the table. Max snagged a piece of the fried fish and moved the plate directly in front of Ukiah.

"Are you ready to order dinner?" the waiter asked, his presence still grating. He'd had a cigarette since serving them—Marlboro 100s—and the traces of smoke leaked out with his breath. "Or should I come back?"

Max frowned at the menu and ordered the baked lemon-herb salmon, a salad, and decided to try the mashed baby reds. "They have twenty-ounce porterhouse, kid. Want it?"

Ukiah nodded, mouth stuffed with smoked salmon. Max ordered it rare, and picked out a baked potato as the side. He checked the menu, and added sautéed mushrooms and shrimp to Ukiah's dinner.

Sam ordered sautéed langostino without glancing at the menu. She watched Max edge the other appetizers in Ukiah's direction. "For one crazy minute, I thought we were going to share all that food."

"If you want some, grab it now." Max demonstrated with a calamari ring. "Much as I love it, I can't take this level of fat anymore. Goes right to the midsection."

"Your midsection looks fine to me."

Max covered another smug grin by sipping at his beer.

"So, do you have a photo of your client?" Sam helped herself to one of each appetizer.

Max reached into his pocket and pulled out his PDA. "I downloaded a few photos before we left." As a hobby, Max took professional-level photographs. Despite of, or perhaps because of, his rampant paranoia, he could see and capture the inner beauty of people. It was as if he peered past all illusions.

He tapped through menus and Alicia gazed out of the small screen. Despite her glad clothes and the spread of glitter on her cheeks, she seemed the portrait of bitter sorrow. "This is her at the Fourth of July. She's twenty-three. Kraynak was her legal guardian until her birthday two years ago, but she still lives with him and his family. She's his older brother's only child. Her folks were killed in a 737 crash just outside of Pittsburgh in . . . when was that, Ukiah?"

"September ninth, 1994," Ukiah said.

"She survived the crash?" Sam asked.

Max shook his head, selecting another sad photo of Alicia from the Fourth. "She wasn't on the plane. Everyone was killed. The plane exploded on impact. They had to piece everyone back together in order to identify the bodies. Alicia's parents had gone to Chicago for the wedding of a distant relative on her mother's side and left her with Kraynak. The airplane crashed on their way home."

Ukiah felt bad that he never found out why Alicia had been so sad at Max's picnic on the Fourth. In the picture, she looked ready to cry.

"That's rough," Sam said of the Kraynaks' deaths.

"Speaking of insurance, Alicia was attending graduate school on the money from her parents' policy." Max tapped his PDA and the photo changed to one of Ukiah and Alicia at Kraynak's Christmas party. In this photo, Alicia was her normal exuberant self. She leaned against Ukiah, arms looped around his shoulders, just noticeably taller than him, pale face pressed close to his dark cheek, smiling brightly to his quiet retreat in the face of the party confusion.

All traces of Sam's smile vanished from her face. "Oh," she breathed, taking the PDA and gazing at it closely. "I didn't realize you two were friends of the family."

"Kraynak and I served together in the Gulf. Military police. We were the only ones in our unit from Pittsburgh. We stayed friends after discharge. We've been through some rough times together."

"When Alicia turned sixteen, she wanted a job other than flipping burgers. I hired her to do work at the agency. She did gofer work, library searches, and such like that. She quit when she started grad school last year."

"I'm sorry." Sam handed back the PDA. "What was—is she like?"

Max sipped his beer before answering. "She's the kind of person they invented the phrase 'full of life' for. I think her parents' death made her obsessed with being impulsive. Seize the moment. Party hardy. Dance naked in the streets."

Sam made a sound like "gak."

Max flashed a smile and then shrugged. "She's really a sweet, intelligent kid with lots of common sense—which she works hard to ignore. She gets herself into one mess after another, but she usually gets herself back out of trouble, and you only hear about it later. She only mildly drove me nuts when she worked for us."

"Only mildly?" Sam made a face. "You've got more patience than I do, then."

Max poured the rest of the beer from the bottle into his glass. "It was hard to listen to her complain about her newest mess when you knew she flung herself into it with her normal reckless abandon. There's always this part of you afraid that one day it might land her in a body bag."

It was odd hearing Max's impression of Alicia. Max often dissected clients, laying bare to Ukiah what truly motivated them, patiently explaining human behavior to him, but he rarely turned his abilities on friends and family, letting Ukiah make up his own mind about them.

"Alicia liked people," Ukiah said. The deep aches in his bones were vanishing as the food worked through his system. "I'm not sure if it was because she was fearless, or she just expected the best from people, but she'd talk to anyone. She was very patient and kind."

"So she could have gotten herself hooked up with the wrong people?" Sam asked.

"To Alicia, being wild and crazy is like surfing—it's a game you play when you've got the time," Max admitted. "Judging by Alicia's ex-boyfriends, she wants a guy to ride the waves with her. What she keeps finding are guys who make waves just to upset the world around them."

Sam made another rude noise. "Those aren't hard to find."

"When you're in the water, it's hard to tell the difference." Max forgave Alicia. "She dumps the losers once her common sense kicks in, but she's made more than one phone call for help while locked in a strange bathroom."

"Pendleton isn't Portland. She'll have limited access to a party crowd," Sam said, and then cocked her head, frowning. "What was a girl like her doing as a geology grad student?"

"Process of elimination, I think," Max said. "As an undergrad, she changed her major at least six times. Even taking summer classes, she graduated three months late, and that doesn't reflect the classes that she attended for a week and then dropped, switching to something else before the term got too far along for her to play catch-up."

"She said she liked the permanence," Ukiah told them. "A rock stays a rock despite almost anything you do to it."

Sam shook her head as if it still didn't make sense to her. "I would have thought with her uncle a cop, and working with you two, she'd end up in law enforcement. It's exciting work."

"At first, her major was criminology." Max stalled by sipping his beer, then reluctantly explained. "Alicia's junior year in college, we ran into a serial killer by the name of Joseph Gary. He was kidnapping people, killing them, and eating them—a real wacko. He had grabbed the hiker we were tracking, and we ended up in a shootout with him. Alicia didn't like that."

"I didn't like it," Ukiah muttered around a mouthful of shrimp.

"Up to that point," Max finished. "I think she glamorized the work. The shootout brought the danger too close to home. Afterwards, she started switching majors until she settled into geology."

"This is the case that started the bulletproof-vest habit?" Sam asked.

The waiter appeared with a tray of dinners. He cleared off empty glasses and appetizer plates to make room. Ukiah's dinner came on multiple plates, the twenty-ounce steak covering one entire plate. After the protein-loaded appetizers, Ukiah had the patience to attack it with knife and fork instead of picking it up and biting off large mouthfuls. As a sure sign of how badly hurt he had been, even after all the earlier food, the meat tasted sublime, a creation of heaven. He chewed with his eyes half-lidded with pleasure.

Max uttered affirmation to Sam's earlier question, and clarified with, "Joe Gary nearly killed Ukiah. He shot him in the chest with a rifle—luckily it just grazed him. I think that's what bothered Alicia the most; Ukiah was just eighteen."

Actually, they knew now that Gary *had* killed Ukiah, only not permanently. Fired at extreme close range, Gary's bullet had not scratched Ukiah, but instead punched a hole through Ukiah's chest. His cells, recognizing that continuing to pump blood would merely geyser it out of his body, shut all heart functions down while they shuffled about to patch the wound. A relatively small wound with only soft flesh damage, it had taken only a short time before his collective self restarted.

Half unconscious from a blow to the head, Max had felt for Ukiah's pulse a few moments prior to this. For a few anguished filled minutes, Max thought he had gotten Ukiah killed. Then Ukiah woke up.

For three years, they thought they had gotten lucky that day, and Max merely failed to find Ukiah's heartbeat. In June, after all the insanity that came with Ukiah learning the truth about himself, they realized that there had been no pulse to feel. Early in July, they went back to the cabin to collect the blood mice accidentally left behind. The colony had merged together into a solitary rattlesnake. After years of not remembering the fight, Ukiah now had fuzzy, scattered recollections. Between the change to mice, then rattlesnake, and the years of surviving alone, however, parts of his genetic memories had been lost.

"So," Sam said. "Tell me what you know about our kidnappers."

"There were four kidnappers, as far as I can tell. Three

men. One woman. The first is a blond, male, slightly taller than Max, heavier than Max by forty or fifty pounds. He wore size ten Timberlands, blue jeans, and a blue flannel shirt. Early thirties. O-positive blood."

Max had taken out his PDA and jotted notes as Ukiah talked. He winced slightly, reminding Ukiah too late that blood type wasn't something most trackers could determine.

Sam was also taking notes, in a small paper notebook of the type reporters used when they hadn't switched over to PDAs. "Kraynak's right. You're damn good."

"The second was a female," Ukiah continued between bites. "She drove the car. Size five shoes, cross-trainers or walking shoes. She's small, around five foot, maybe shorter, and around a hundred pounds. She kept back, away from the violence." He chewed for a few minutes, searching his memory to see if there were any other clues he had picked up without realizing it. No. "The third seems to be a man, five ten or eleven, around two hundred pounds, size nine cowboy boots, blue jeans. The fourth also seemed male, tall, maybe about six-two, but skinny, around a hundred and seventy. He wore size twelve tennis shoes."

"How are you determining sex?"

"Size and weight, style of the shoe. They could be very tall women wearing men's shoes."

Sam nodded, making notes.

Max explained about the ring, and then asked Ukiah about the car the kidnappers used.

"Four-door, front-wheel drive, all-weather treads, probably with a trunk instead of a hatchback. They put Alicia into the back and drove toward town during the daylight, so I'm guessing that it's not a station wagon either. Whatever it is, midsized. "

Max made a noise at the vagueness of the description.

Sam, however, seemed happy. "This is great!" When they looked at her in surprise, she added, "You found evidence that someone acted against Alicia. There are over thirty people dead in the last three months without a shred of evidence that someone killed them. Hell, there might be people missing that we're not aware of. Hitchhikers. Seasonal workers. Drifters."

Ukiah and Max traded glances, and Max told Sam how the kidnappers seemed well-practiced at herding a person to a waiting car.

"The bodies are probably well-hidden to keep the death count down," Sam theorized.

"Why do you think Alicia's kidnapping has anything to do with your house fires?"

"Sheer gut instinct," Sam admitted. "There's nothing that links all of this together except the skewed numbers."

"Nothing at all?" Max asked.

"Nothing that I can see," Sam amended. "I've been on this case for a month. I've listed out everything about the victims. Where they worked. Where they lived. Where the kids went to school, including teachers, classmates, and kids outside of their class that they played with at recess. Church. Relatives. Neighbors. God, the number of possible suspects could drive you nuts. If you draw it out, it looks like a massive spiderweb—everything's connected—and yet, when you look closely, there's nothing obvious linking all three families."

Max gave her a sympathetic smile. "Sometimes doing all the legwork, you get too close and you can't see the obvious."

"Actually, I'd love for you to go over my notes with me," Sam said. "See if you can spot something I've missed. I haven't talked to anyone in town about it, because anyone might be involved."

Max grinned at the mildly paranoid comment, which was very similar to what he'd say. "Good thinking."

Sam flashed a look at him and then returned her attention to her meal. "It might be a glut of information is masking the true connection. That's why I think Alicia's going to be the key to the case. Everyone else has a billion connections above and beyond the ones I've recorded. Maybe their link with the killers happened ten years ago, or is somehow related to what their parents did together as children, or maybe it was their grandparents. Who can tell?"

"Alicia had only been in the state for a month," Max said. "There's going to be a finite number of people she met."

"Bingo," Sam said. "We can take the thirty or forty people she's talked to and see if they connect back to the arson victims."

"If her kidnapping is related."

Sam conceded with a shrug that Alicia's kidnapping might be unrelated. "I'm willing to run the risk. Can I have a copy of that first picture?"

Ukiah stifled a yawn as he shoved the gnawed bone of his steak aside and upended his baked potato into the bloody juices on his plate. "Kraynak has Alicia's daily planner. You know what a compulsive note maker she is. We can probably chart out who she talked to in town from it."

Max flagged the waiter and pulled out his wallet. "I need to get Ukiah back to the hotel. He'll be dead asleep in a few minutes."

"The night's still young," Sam said. "We can drop him at your room and do some legwork."

Max sighed, almost wistfully. "Let me check with Kraynak." He accepted the check from the waiter, glanced at the total, and handed it back with his American Express card. "I don't want to leave Ukiah alone. Someone's taken a crack at him once already, and the stakes went up today."

"Do you always take good care of your partners?"

"I've only got the one." Max laughed as Ukiah tried to smother a huge yawn. "And he's about to go facedown in the dirty dishes. Come on, kid."

They went out into the night. Max dialed Kraynak as Ukiah gave up on stifling the yawns.

"Oh, stop that." Sam covered her mouth. "I'm not even tired and you got me going too."

"It's me—Bennett." Max said into his phone. "Where are you? What are you doing there?" He listened for a minute, shaking his head. "Okay. We'll meet you back at the rooms. The kid is crashing, but Sam and I plan to do some more legwork tonight." He listened to Kraynak for a moment, and then laughed. "Get your mind out of the gutter, Kraynak. See you in ten minutes."

"It's a go?" Sam asked, swinging one of her long legs over the Harley's seat.

"He's at the hotel now." Max said. "The van broke down at the airport and he had it towed. He hoofed it from the auto shop to the hotel. As if he hadn't done enough walking today, he was taking the stairs up to the room—apparently he came in a side door where it's easier to walk up than go down to the elevators. And, yes, it's a go."

"Meet you there." Sam started the Harley, the engine pulsing noise against Ukiah's skin. She gave the men a grin and sped away.

"What did Kraynak say about a gutter?" Ukiah asked as Max pocketed his phone.

"Nothing that bears repeating." Max pulled out his keys and unlocked the Blazer.

"You like Sam, don't you?"

"Yup!" Max cuffed Ukiah lightly, grinning widely. "Come on! Get in the car! Let's get you to bed!"

From across town, faint gunshots rang out.

"It's a .357." Ukiah cocked his head. "Kraynak is carrying his .357."

"Shit!" Max swore. "Get in the car!"

They scrambled into the Blazer. Max narrowly missed the back of the badly parked station wagon as he roared out of their parking space. They slid around the turn onto Main Street.

"Sam won't be able to hear the shots over her bike." Max growled. "Is she carrying?"

Ukiah recalled Sam's scent. "Yes." He pointed at the single red light far in front of them, already cresting the hill to South Nye Avenue. "There she is."

Max threw him a glance. "Are you still carrying?"

"Yes."

"Good boy."

The hotel was barely a quarter mile, but they had to turn again and again, climbing the river bluff, before reaching the hotel's driveway. As they came down South Nye, Ukiah made out that their room lights were on and the glass window shattered. Sam had stopped at the far end of the parking lot, a lone figure in an empty row. She leaned forward, trying to free a white plastic bag that had blown against her bike, unaware of the gunshots. Dark figures ran out into the lower parking lot, Kraynak's tall, unmistakable figure in pursuit. Kraynak carried his .357. One of the runners turned and lifted his hand. There was a muzzle flash, but no noise.

"There they are!" Ukiah pointed. "Two shooters with silencers, and Kraynak."

"Damn it, Kraynak, this isn't the OK corral!" Max cried.

A truck suddenly moved out the shadows. The runners scrambled into the truck as it passed.

"The truck!" Ukiah shouted as truck gathered speed, racing toward Sam on her motorcycle. "It's going for Sam!"

"The hell it is!" Max growled and jerked the wheel hard. They went over the curb and across the grass, rushing to intersect the truck. "Hang on!"

Sam looked up as the truck's headlights spotlighted her. The truck swerved slightly, aiming now to take her dead center. Max laid on the horn so it screamed his outrage. Sam scrambled sideways, abandoning her bike.

The Blazer met the truck mere feet from Sam, catching it in the front quarter panel. The truck's driver turned as they collided, and the vehicles veered off at an angle, front ends grinding metal into shreds as they fought. Shoved sideways by the truck's momentum, the Blazer broadsided Sam's bike with its backend, smashing the motorcycle over. Sam herself was tumbled across the pavement and came up with her pistol in hand.

"How is she?" Max cried as the Blazer bucked and shuddered.

"She's up!" Ukiah said. "And she looks pissed."

"Ha! That's my girl!" Max shouted.

The truck tore free, wheeling tightly to the left, plowing over small shrubs in its way. It gained the asphalt again, and raced toward the loop at the end of the parking lot, which would bring it back past Kraynak as its only way out. Ukiah scanned for Kraynak and saw the big policeman staggering in the middle of the lane. His white shirt was stained red.

"Kraynak!" Ukiah flung open his door and sprang out, unheeding of Max's startled call. "Kraynak, move!"

Kraynak wavered in place, pressing his left hand to his bleeding side wound.

Ukiah ran. Out the corner of his eye, he saw the truck loop around, heading toward Kraynak. He wasn't going to make it. Sam's nine millimeter thundered behind him, punching stars through the truck's windshield. The night was filled with sirens, but everyone was going to be too late.

The truck roared toward them. He reached out for Kraynak, caught him, spun, flinging himself shoulder-first for the truck's hood.

The truck hit them with a force that made the fall from the cliff seem gentle. The top of the grille clipped him first, sending him rolling across the hood with Kraynak in his arms. He smashed against the windshield and then rebounded, sliding off to the driver's side. The driver's mirror caught him as he fell groundward, knocking him finally unconscious.

CHAPTER NINE

Red Lion Hotel's Parking Lot, Pendleton Oregon
Friday, August 27, 2004

He came to still trying to escape.

Max had him pinned against a wall, hands framing his face, looking into his eyes. "Come on, son. Come back to me. I need you awake."

Ukiah blinked, surprised to find his eyes already open when a moment before he had been unconscious. "Max?"

Max grinned. "Ah, there you are! Good boy."

Trapped by Max's hands, Ukiah flicked his eyes about to orient himself. He was pressed against the wall surrounding the outdoor pool, downhill of the parking lot where a frantic knot of paramedics worked on Kraynak. "Kraynak? Sam?"

"Sam's fine. I don't know about Kraynak yet. You kept running, so I figured I better nail you down first."

"Yeah." That did seem like a good idea.

"How are you?"

"I'm fine. Thanks. How are you?"

"Ukiah," Max said sternly, leaning closer to take up Ukiah's entire range of vision. "How. Are. You?"

"Oh. How am I?" Ukiah considered. "I hurt real bad. I should lie down before I fall down."

"Are you going to live?"

"Yeah." He said. "I think. Yeah, probably."

Max kept a light hold of his arm and guided him to their second rental car. "If you think you're going to drop for whatever reason, you tell me. Okay?"

"Okay, Max."

"Do you trust her?" Max unlocked the car and opened the backseat, motioning Ukiah inside.

"Who?" It was a relief to lie down in the dark interior.

"Killington. Sam." Max opened the back, found a blanket and tossed it forward so it landed on Ukiah.

"I don't know. Do you?"

Max sorted through their gear in the back. "Oh, kid, I've crossed the line with her. I can't see her clearly. I'm seeing what I want to see, and I can't trust that, not with your life."

Ukiah tried for a shrug and winced when the motion lanced pain through him. "She hasn't lied to us since that first one, about being a reporter."

"I should go with Kraynak. There's no telling how hurt he is. People have died while the hospital tried to find next of kin to okay surgery. I'm the only one in this town who knows shit about him."

"I can come with you."

"No, no, no." Max closed the back and came around to the open back door. He had a sixty-four-ounce bottle of Gatorade, still warm from being in the hot car all day. "We can't risk anyone who knows exactly how hurt you were the first time getting a second look at you. Right now the hospital thinks you're recuperating, and everyone else figures you weren't as hurt as you seemed."

While someone had concealed the truth about the Ontongard mother ship with the story about hackers downloading graphics to the Mars Rover, one only had to turn on the television to see that the initial news clip had etched itself into the human psyche. From commercials to the revival of old shows based on UFO investigations and alien invasions, extraterrestrials still saturated the media.

So far, few people believed that the ship on Mars had been real—and they were hampered by the lack of proof. Max and Ukiah's family lived in fear that the *fact* that humans weren't alone on Earth might leak out. Unfortunately, Ukiah's body contained enough evidence for anyone with a suspicious mind and an understanding of basic biology.

"I'll go with Sam." Ukiah saw the concern on Max's face, and forced himself to say, "I'll be safe with her."

"I hope so." Max watched Ukiah take a long swallow of the warm Gatorade. "How is it?"

They had developed a rate system based on warm Gatorade. The better it tasted, the worse Ukiah's state. Completely healthy, he couldn't stand the stuff.

"You don't want to know," Ukiah gasped, and guzzled the rest of the stuff down, savoring the taste.

The timer on the interior lights decided that they were going to leave the back door open all night and clicked the lights off. In the darkness, Ukiah was losing the battle to stay awake.

"You sure you're going to be all right?" Max took the empty bottle from Ukiah's limp hands, recapped it, and tossed it in the back.

"Nothing's broken. I'm not bleeding—just bruised all over."

"Hey!" Sam's voice floated out of the night. "There you are! Thanks for the save."

"Not a problem," Max said.

Sam's footsteps approached the Blazer. "The hotel manager was down here a minute ago. The door to your room is busted open and the place has been trashed. The FBI doesn't want anything moved. They're coming to dust for prints."

"Shit!" Max swore. "That's why they went back to the campground. Not to grab Rose, but to get Alicia's things."

"Apparently." Sam stopped beside Max.

"Can you do me a favor?" Max asked.

"Anything."

With a soft jangle, Max held out the keys to the rental car. "Take my partner someplace safe—someplace these assholes aren't going to find him—and stay with him tonight?"

Sam glanced at Ukiah through the open door. "You're shitting me. He's been hit by a car. He needs to go to the hospital."

"He's okay, just a little bruised."

She gave a disbelieving laugh. "Bruised? I saw him take that hit! If he dies, it's manslaughter through negligence."

"Trust me as much as I'm trusting you. The only danger he's in is from these bastards that shot him two days ago and just tried to kill you and Kraynak. He'll be okay."

Sam stared at Max with laser intensity, her eyes flicking over the set of his mouth, the sweat on his brow, and the open pleading in his eyes. She looked then to Ukiah, curled in the rental car's backseat. "How do you feel?"

"I'm fine, Sam. I just want to go to sleep."

Sam let out her breath in a long sigh. "When am I going to stop trusting men? Okay. Fine. I'll do it." She took the keys. "How do I get hold of you?"

"Ukiah has my phone number on his speed dial." Max leaned into the car, pulled out Ukiah's phone, and made sure it worked. He slipped the phone back into Ukiah's pocket, rumpled Ukiah's hair, and closed the door. "Go on, before the police start looking for him."

Sam swung into the driver's seat. "This makes us even."

"As long as you keep him safe."

Sam took him to a small A-frame cabin, tucked someplace in the mountains. Night pressed in close as she helped him out of the car. Pines veiled the sky. No lights shone inside the cabin. He followed her to the door and waited while she unlocked it.

The door opened into a large room that smelled of old fires, trout dinners, and Sam herself. Sam paused beyond the door, seeking with a blind hand to orient herself. Ukiah's eyes had already adjusted to the dark and he made his way to a kitchen chair. He felt hollow, the pain dull and banging in time with his heart, filling up the emptiness. He sat carefully, trying not to jar himself.

"I'm renting this place from an old client." Sam walked through the darkness, hand gliding along the butcher block countertop of the L-shaped kitchen. "After I broke up with my ex, I had a place in town, but it was too easy to find. All my mail goes to my office. The taxes and utilities are in my client's name. I check to make sure I'm not followed every time I drive out, and you can't see the car in the driveway from the main road."

She flipped on a recessed light over the sink. Dishes from her last meal sat clean in the drying rack. A bowl. A spoon. A cup. "The only people that know where I live are in Portland."

"None of your friends know?" Sitting up, he felt his blood pressure dropping. Cold seeped in.

"All my friends live in Portland. Everyone I know here were his friends first and last."

He wondered why she didn't return to Portland. Money, probably. It seemed to control most people's lives. "How long have you been here?"

"Too long." She considered Ukiah. "How long, total, have you worked with Max?"

"Five years. Two years doing tracking part-time before going full time three years ago."

"And you trust him?" She repeated Max's question, only the pronoun changed, with the same tone of voice. Like they trusted one another, but not themselves for doing so.

"There's no one I trust more." He started to shiver.

She came to press a hot hand to his forehead. "Damn, I told him you should be in a hospital. You're going into shock."

"It's just because I'm sitting up."

"It's just because you were hit by a car."

"I just need to lie down. Cover up. Stay warm."

She swore softly, just like Max would. "The bed's upstairs. You don't need to pee first, do you?"

"It probably would be best if I did." At the thought of flushing his system, his body made sudden demands for him to urinate. "Definitely."

"Hold on." She went to switch on lamps, lighting the way.

The downstairs was sectioned off into a large kitchen/living area and a full bathroom. Opposite the kitchen, four wing chairs stood guard about an oriental rug. Each chair was slightly different in height, width, and style of feet, but they'd been reupholstered in deep green damask in an attempt to make them match. A beveled-glass tabletop resting on four large river rocks made a coffee table island in the center of the rug. The lamps sat on mismatched but stylish side tables.

The bathroom was tiled up to the ceiling in large squares of smoky pink, with smaller accents of deep green and silvery gray. Sam apologized for the color scheme, saying that the original owner ran a flooring business and had used overstock to do that bathroom.

"Come up to the loft when you're done."

Ukiah used the toilet and then drank deeply from the faucet.

The steps up to the loft, he noticed, were done in hardwood, but they didn't match the floors downstairs. Upstairs, no attempt had been made to disguise a jumbled selection of wood flooring.

"Overstock?" He pointed out abutting cherry and white oak boards.

"Overstock." She held out a blue-flannel shirt. "I got this for my ex, but we broke up before I gave it to him." When he only blinked at her in confusion, she draped it over the bed's footboard. "Put it on. You're not wearing that dirty thing into my bed."

The ceiling slanted up to a peak. Low, mirrorless dressers and cedar chests lined the short walls. While Ukiah gingerly pulled off his torn, bloody T-shirt, Sam stripped the king-sized bed, took clean sheets from one of the cedar chests, and remade the bed. She seemed to make it a point not to look at him while he changed. He fumbled with the buttons, shivering too hard to do them up. She came and pushed away his hands, frowning as she did the buttons.

"Do you need help with your boots?"

He eyed his feet, suddenly so far away. "Probably." She caught him before he could sit on the bed with his dirty pants, undid his pants and stripped them down to his knees, and sat him on the bed. She frowned at him as she crouched at his feet, undoing his laces and pulling off his boots, as if she expected him to do something she didn't like. "Not a word . . ."

Word about what? Perhaps something sexual in nature,

but he couldn't guess what. After she pulled his pants the rest of the way off, the frown eased to a more worried look.

"You're not going to die in my bed, are you?"

"No." At least, he didn't think so.

"Well, get in."

He crawled wearily into the bed as she collected her pajamas, turned off the light and went downstairs. The place was too new, too unfamiliar for him to fall asleep. He heard her use the toilet, wash her face, and brush her teeth. She turned off the lights downstairs, returning the house to full darkness. She padded barefoot up the stairs, went to the far side of the bed, and slipped in beside him. She smelled of damp soap, mint toothpaste, leather, cold steel, and gun oil.

"Just so you know," she whispered in the dark, "I sleep with my gun."

Good. They'd be safe if someone had followed them.

After several minutes of silence and stillness, she reached over to lay a warm hand on his cheek. Finding him shivering, she slid across the bed and carefully curled around him. Her warmth muted the thudding pain.

CHAPTER TEN

Blue Mountains, Eastern Oregon
Saturday, August 28, 2004

Ukiah woke when Sam slipped out of the bed, disturbing his background filter. He leaned over the edge of the bed, found his clothes, pulled out his phone, and called Max.

Max answered on the third ring. "Hey, kid, how are you?"

Ukiah considered himself as the shower turned on downstairs. "After the last few days, I kind of feel like a kite: thin sticks and paper held together with string."

Max laughed, sounding tired.

"How's Kraynak?" Ukiah asked.

"They don't want him roaming the countryside, looking for Alicia." Max said. "But they're making noises that all he needs is time to heal."

"You still at the hospital?"

"No. They kicked me out around two. It took me a while, but I managed to find a motel with a room available. I signed in under my cover name." Which meant Max was running in full paranoia mode. "Where are you?"

"Sam's house. It's about half an hour out of town, up in the mountains. She says she's taken a lot of effort to keep people from knowing where she lives."

"Ah, *she says.* Finally, you're learning paranoia."

"I have a good teacher."

"You up to a full day's work?"

"Probably."

"You dressed?"

"No. Sam just got out of the bed and it woke me. She's in the shower now."

"So you'll need at least an hour to get into town. *The* bed? As in same bed as you?"

"It's a little house. I think your bedroom is bigger than this whole cabin."

"No couch? No recliner?"

"No."

"Big bed?"

"King-sized."

"Good." Max changed the subject. "Did you have a chance to look at Alicia's daily planner?"

"I flipped through it."

"Great! I'm going to see if we can get rooms at the Red Lion again, or another real hotel. This motel is too open. I also need to deal with the rental-car people. They're not going to be happy with us, but shit happens. Hopefully they'll have a replacement car this morning."

"Do you want to go with just one rental car? Sam has a Jeep, as well as the Harley."

"Nah. I like having a car for each of us. We would have been sunk last night without the second car."

Ukiah had to agree with that. "So, what's the plan?"

"Take your time getting back to Pendleton. I'll pick up a new rental car and check in on Kraynak. If you saw Alicia's daily planner, we can take a stab at recreating it. Maybe there was something in the planner that the kidnappers knew would lead us to them, which is why they took it."

"It's worth a try." Certainly his photographic memory would make it an easy task. He described Alicia's planner in detail. "I'm going to call Indigo, let her know what's going on."

"That's a good idea. She might be able to give us a heads-up if the local office starts digging into our background."

Ukiah winced at the idea.

Once Indigo learned of Ukiah's alien parentage, she had risked her career to protect him. She destroyed her copy of the tracking contract Max had drawn up for the FBI, and

erased all mentions of hiring Ukiah to find the missing FBI
agent, Wil Trace, which ended with Ukiah's kidnapping by
the Pack. She never documented the connection between the
Pack and the Ontongard. She treated Dr. Janet Haze's fall
into insanity, the coroner's murder, the burning of Haze's
body, and the kidnapping of all the various FBI agents, herself included, as separate, unrelated, and mostly unsolved
cases.

Ukiah was not sure how she explained her raids on the
Ontongard dens and the eventual shoot-out at the airport. He
knew, though, that she made no mention of the Mars Rover
hijacking equipment, and the Pack reduced it to burnt rubble
by the end of the same week

Indigo justified her actions by saying she couldn't blindly
hand anyone the means to destroy Ukiah and his family's
life. Still, it made Ukiah nervous. He didn't want to get her
involved now unless they had to. "Why would the local FBI
offices check into our background? We're the victims here."

"Alicia's ring, a set of tire tracks, a few footprints, and
your testimony is all they have on her kidnapping," Max
said. "If it had stayed at that, they might have dug into your
background just out of lack of anything else to do. The only
good thing about last night's fun and games is that the FBI
now has well-described bad guys to find, and you've once
again demonstrated that you're an innocent bystander with a
hero streak. I want to keep moving, see if we can find anything else to preoccupy them."

"Okay. I'll let Indigo know that they might be looking
into us."

"Call me back when you hit town and we'll go from
there. Oh, and Ukiah, when you call Indigo, don't mention
anything about *the* bed."

"Why?"

"Trust me. Just don't."

Indigo was at her family's restaurant, judging by the
background chatter of Chinese and the whisper of Hawaiian
music. He felt a moment of disorientation—he expected to

catch Indigo at work—then realized that it was Saturday, and she was doing her normal family breakfast.

"What happened yesterday?" Indigo asked. "You didn't call."

"Alicia was definitely kidnapped," Ukiah said. "Our rooms were ransacked, Kraynak was shot, and I was hit by a car."

"I suppose this isn't such terrible news, then," she said after a moment of stunned silence. "I just found out that Rennie flew out of Pittsburgh yesterday. He might be in town already."

Ukiah sat up. "In town? You mean Pendleton?"

"He landed in Portland three PM yesterday." She explained that Rennie had gotten as far as Portland before tripping airport security alarms. "Portland security lost him in the parking lot around four. It's two hundred miles between Portland and Pendleton. He could have gotten there last night."

"I've been in hiding all night, healing up." As Ukiah filled her in, he tried to feel the prickly Pack sense that would mean a Pack member was close. No Pack sense. What he did feel was uneasy.

Usually the Pack didn't travel alone, even in emergencies.

The nearest clan was the Demon Curs, controlled by Germain Degas. While complete strangers to Ukiah, they brought dark apprehensions rising in Rennie's memories. It would be surprising if Rennie wanted Degas and the Curs in Pendleton any more than Ukiah did.

But Ukiah couldn't imagine Rennie arriving unaccompanied. "Have you talked to Bear or Hellena?"

"No."

"So you don't know what Rennie's plans are."

Indigo's Chinese grandfather distracted her with a flow of English so heavily accented it sounded like Mandarin. "No, Gong Gong, they haven't found the girl yet," Indigo answered her grandfather, and then guessed at Rennie's plans. "I'm assuming it's to provide you backup. It sounds like you need it, especially with Kraynak in the hospital."

Indigo promised to keep them appraised of any new information, whether it be from the FBI or the Pack. They said their good-byes and hung up.

The question remained, though: Would Rennie be alone, or would he have Degas and the Demon Curs with him?

The mirror in the bathroom showed an older him.

It amazed him sometimes how long it took him to realize he wasn't human. Everyone around him grew older daily, constantly undergoing minuscule changes to their faces, their bodies, and their genetic code. He didn't. From age thirteen to eighteen, he probably aged only a handful of days in bumps and bruises and occasional dog bites from Mom Jo's half-breed wolves. His face had been seemingly unchanging as a photograph.

Then, the day after Crazy Joe Gary shot him through the chest, he startled himself in the bathroom mirror. No one else seemed to notice, but he barely recognized his own face. It frightened him then, not knowing why the sudden change. He knew now that he had aged months in a single day. In the scramble to heal his body, his cells made slight errors copying themselves. Mistakes that mirrored the human aging process. Mistakes that became part of his cellular genetic pattern. In June, even his moms noticed the sudden leap ahead, a year or more worth of damage dealt out in the course of a painful week.

Sam's mirror showed that he had aged again. Not much. Maybe no one else would notice. Very slowly, but just as surely as any human, he was growing older. He stood staring at his reflection, getting to know himself again.

Sam tapped on the door. "You decent?" She leaned in when he opened the door, and picked up her deodorant. "Forgot to put some of this on."

As she reached the deodorant under her shirt to apply it to her underarms, she studied his bare shoulders and chest.

"So there's some truth to those Kicking Deer legends. Last night I was sure you were going to drop dead on me. Now, I'm not sure why I was so worried. Hell, you look like you could do a Chippendale number without flashing so much as a bruise." Ukiah shrugged, not sure how to respond.

She set the deodorant back onto the edge of the sink. "You're gay, right?"

He gave a bewildered shake of his head. "No."

Several emotions flashed across her face before it settled on annoyance. "Ah, hell, just when you think you've got life all figured out, it hits you up the back of the head with a two by four."

"Huh?"

"Well, do me a favor. Don't tell your partner that we slept in the same bed."

"I already did."

"Shit." She turned and walked away, muttering. "Oh, well! He was from Pittsburgh anyhow."

Ukiah drove them down out of the Blue Mountains and back to Pendleton. They planned to stop at the Red Lion so Sam could check on her Harley. If the motorcycle was drivable, they would drive separately to the Wildhorse Casino. Saturdays and Sundays, Sam explained, the casino's restaurant featured an all-you-can-eat breakfast brunch.

Ukiah scanned the oncoming traffic as he drove, trying to sense Rennie or any other Pack members.

"Jumpy?" Sam asked when she noticed.

"There's someone Max and I know coming out to act as backup. We're not sure when he's showing."

"You're calling in another private investigator?"

"He's not a PI. H-h-he's sort of my father."

Technically, all of the Pack could be considered his father. His true father was the alien Prime, a mutant of the Ontongard race. Wounded and desperate to check the Ontongard invasion of earth, Prime had injected his viral genetic material into a wolf pack. One wolf survived to become the Get known as Coyote. Driven by Prime's memories and desires, the wolf transformed into a man, living at first among the Native Americans. Later Coyote followed Hex toward the East Coast, creating the Pack to war with Hex's Gets.

At their base, the Pack duplicated Prime's mutated alien genetics. Through Coyote, though, they had a wolf taint— instincts to protect and nurture their only son. From their human shells, each held their own hopes and desires for children. Rennic had abandoned his newborn son to carry on Prime's fight; among the Pack, Ukiah counted him as his stronger protector.

"Sort of your father?" Sam echoed. "How does one have a sort of father?"

Ukiah wished he were better at lying. "He didn't know I existed until June—and things started out rocky between us."

"He knocked up your mom and left her before she knew?"

Ukiah shook his head. If only it were so simple. His conception had been a delay tactic on Prime's part, to distract Hex while Prime programmed a self-destruct code into the already crashed mother ship. Prime knew that Hex would have to find and capture members of a suitable host race, create a half-breed child through complex gene manipulation, prepare a fertilized egg, and do the implantation. Not one to leave things to chance, Prime replaced Hex's stored genetic sample with his own mutated rebel material, and planted explosives in the room where Ukiah would have been born.

The Pack had memories of Ukiah being placed in his mother's womb. They assumed that the explosives had killed his mother long before he was born—effectively destroying him.

But something had gone wrong with Prime's plan.

"Ooookay." Sam broke the silence. "He didn't knock her up. She got his sperm sample off a sperm bank and was artificially inseminated."

He glanced sharply at Sam, who beamed in response of his look.

"That's it," she said, "isn't it?"

"Something like that," he temporized. He supposed it was the closest analogy available. Like any child naturally conceived, he was genetic mix of his mother and father. The ovipositor that handled his creation, however, had made him—as close as alien technology could—perfect.

To forestall more questions about his relationship with Rennie—which were all too hard to explain—Ukiah said, "The past isn't important. What's important is that he heard that I was shot, and took a plane out of Pittsburgh yesterday. He might be in Pendleton when we get there."

"He's got a name besides 'Dad'?"

"I don't call him Dad. He's Rennie. Rennie Shaw."

"Well, we should check at the hotel before going out to the casino, then; see if he left a message."

Ukiah doubted Rennie would be that direct. The Pack rarely used normal means of communicating. Hotel employees can be bribed. Phones can be tapped. Then again, Rennie had already put himself on the radar screens by flying out to Portland. He might be waiting at the hotel, having no leads where to find Ukiah otherwise.

Just the thought of an irate Rennie and an unsuspecting Pendleton made Ukiah shudder.

"Sam, Rennie is a dangerous man. We're not calling him in on this; he's just showing up. He's my father, but it doesn't mean we trust him. It doesn't even mean any of us are entirely safe from him. If he thought he had an important enough reason, he'd kill even me."

"He'd fly out here to see if you're okay, and then kill you?"

He pulled into the Red Lion's parking lot beside Sam's battered motorcycle. "He doesn't think like a regular person would."

"So you're saying he's insane?"

Ukiah considered it as he killed the engine. Without knowing about the Ontongard trying to take over the world, the alien/wolf mix of Rennie's genetic makeup, or the fact that the Pack leader was born in 1842, Rennie's thinking would appear insane. "Yeah, that would work."

They went up to his hotel room together. Since they were already stopping, Ukiah wanted to change out of his gritty clothes. Sam wanted to hear more about Rennie, specifi-

cally, "What does your homicidal, lunatic father look like?"
Ukiah called Max and told him to meet them at the casino.
On the way out, they stopped at the desk and asked for messages. As Ukiah expected, there were none.

Sam checked over her motorcycle with a thoroughness
that would have pleased Max. "It seems like it's all cosmetic
damage. You can follow me out to the casino, just in case it
decides to die after a mile or two."

"Okay," Ukiah said, gazing across the parking lot where
Kraynak had been shot. The damaged vehicles were gone,
along with the dark, painful confusion. The parking lot was
just an empty slab of asphalt again. "Thanks for taking care
of me last night, Sam."

She laughed, straightening. "I didn't do much."

"You were there when I needed you." Ukiah folded her
into a hug. "It means a lot to me."

She stood stiff in his arms a moment, and then hugged
him back. "Sure, whatever, you can crash in my bed anytime." She buried fingers into his long black hair and tugged
it gently. "You're a sweet kid—but I wish it had been your
partner!"

The casino sat out on a lonely expanse of prairie, isolated
except for a hotel attached at one side. It was done in what
had to be a Native American design, with bright colors and
poles sticking out at odd angles, but looked vaguely Scandinavian to Ukiah. It bothered him that he couldn't recognize
it as something belonging to his people.

Max waited beside a blue Ford Taurus, chewing on the
end of a lit cheroot. Sam tucked into the space between the
Taurus and the Blazer. Tension went out of Max's face, replaced by a lazy, pleased smile.

"Hey," he greeted Sam. "You look great."

Ukiah had to admit that she did. She wore skintight riding leather pants, and under her leather jacket, a snug, white
tank top.

"Hanging with you guys is a little too rough for anything
but leather," Sam said.

"You didn't get too banged up last night?"

"My jeans are shot, but no, I'm fine. How's Kraynak?"

"Bitching about being stuck in bed," Max said, and patted Ukiah on the shoulder. "I got the planner." He held up a daily planner identical to Alicia's. "And the inserts. Put them in order once we get to the restaurant, and I'll put them into the planner."

"I can put them in," Ukiah offered as they walked up to the casino's doors.

Max ground the cheroot out in a large sand ashtray by the door. "I want to get some food into you first."

Max took hold of Ukiah's arm, and when they opened the doors, Ukiah realized why. The casino was dark, crowded, smoky, and loud. Rows of video slot machinea blinked bright, complex screens. After the clean emptiness of the parking lot, the confusion hit Ukiah's senses like a fist.

Max caught his elbow as he checked, and murmured, "It's okay. Just follow me."

They pushed through the crowds to the restaurant beyond the slot machines. Luckily the eating area was nearly empty and quiet. A hostess greeted them at the door and seated them at a table with four place settings.

Max handed Ukiah the packs of inserts. "Here, put them in order, then get some food."

Ukiah shuffled the inserts into order, starting with the "To Be Done Sheets" and working to "Address/Phone Pages with Alpha Tabs." Handing the sorted packs to Max, he went up to the buffet.

When he returned, Max was using a fork to start a tear in the shrink-wrap of the last insert. Once open, Max discarded wrap, cardboard stiffener, and title sheet off to one side.

"I don't see the point," Sam said, as Max threaded the pages onto the six metal rings. "It's a lot of money for blank pages."

"Ukiah has a photographic memory," Max said. "He saw Alicia's planner. He can recreate any page he looked at."

"The Kodak kid."

Max pulled out a box of yellow pencils, and a small, blue, barrel-shaped pencil sharper. He handed them over to Sam to make herself useful. "Alicia used number-two pencils. Apparently geologists expect everything to get wet, and ink smears."

Sam opened the box so it could be reclosed, spilled out the pencils in a neat pile, and began sharpening them. "And it matters if we use the same type of writing implement or not?"

"Who knows?" Max turned the calendar section and leafed through until he hit the first week of August. "Let's start with her leaving Pittsburgh." He tapped the day. "Then work on through to after she disappeared. Here."

Max gave Ukiah a small yellow pad of Post-it notes. Sam held out the first sharpened pencil, looking doubtful about the whole experiment. Ukiah shifted his plate over to eat with his left hand, so he could write with his right.

"There didn't seem to be anything of interest during these days." Ukiah started filling in the day labeled AUGUST 1, SUNDAY, with the normal work hours of a day ticking down the side. Alicia had mostly ignored the hours, the day flowing unscheduled down the page, falling wherever it would fit.

Check tent for leaks. Field notebooks—Pitt bookstore? Laundry soap. Dryer sheets. Imodium. Tums. Neosporin. Check supply of bandages in first-aid kit. (A check mark beside this.) *Sun block. Bug repellent.* (A doodle of what might have been a dead bug on its back, little x's for eyes, legs curled.) *Ziploc bags—all sizes. See if Rose can drive stick!!!* (This was underlined many times.) *Get duffel bag from Uncle Ray. Check Ukiah weather.*

The last was a weird jolt, his name leaping out at him. Ukiah, the town.

Bookstore, coin laundry, supermarket. Nothing of menace. On the otherwise blank opposite page was a Post-it note, stating, *Erotic Laundry. Handsome man's dryer, in hot ghost embrace tumbles, my silk lace panties.* Ukiah flipped to the next day. The page was split in half with a drawn line. Next to the hours, she had written, *Wake up, pack, swap cars, get gas, pick up Rose.* On the other side of the line, was *Tent, duffel bag, shoe bag, books, MAPS, MONEY!!!, phone, CAR RECHARGER—don't forget to transfer to van!!* Alicia's memory had been a joke with her family. Eventually she hoped to be a college professor, which would make her the stereotypical absentminded professor.

"I know it's a long shot, kid." Max said. "There is a chance that her kidnappers picked her by random. But they did take the planner, so there might be something in it."

"She had it so stuffed with paper, I could barely get it snapped shut again." Ukiah flipped to the next page, his fingers moving on automatic. "I tried to glance at every page, figuring that I might want to review it in my head. Still there were lots of things I know I won't be able to recreate."

"Do the best you can." Max went to fill his plate from the buffet. Sam finished sharpening the last pencil, and slid it into the box with the others. She followed Max to the buffet. They stood, plates in hand, heads together, talking quietly.

"The hash is good." Sam scooped some onto her plate. "You know, nothing happened."

"When?" Max leaned close to get some too, their shoulders brushing.

"Last night. Just because we were in the same bed, doesn't mean anything happened. I don't go for his type."

Max paused behind her to rub a large pleased smile from his face. "His type? What type is that?"

Sam half-turned to shoot a narrowed look at him, and then intently prodded some helpless scrambled eggs. "Please! He's drop-dead gorgeous. Complete eye candy."

"So you only like ugly, old guys?"

"Brat," she muttered. "I like the *GQ* look as much as the next hot-blooded woman. So maybe I drooled a little when he got off the plane. And straight out the shower, he smells good enough to—"

"He's all but engaged to an FBI special agent," Max said, cutting off her monologue.

"You're kidding!"

"A little pistol on wheels stationed in Pittsburgh. She nailed him two days out of the gate."

"Cradle robber."

Max shrugged. "She's one of those focused people. She figures out what she wants and goes after it."

"You think that's the best way? Want it. Get it."

"I like to be sure I know what I'm getting. No surprises. But, yes."

"And what if the thing doesn't want to be gotten?"

Max slanted a look at her beside him, and then focused on the wedges of cantaloupe. "People aren't things. You don't buy them. They never belong to you."

"Even your partner?"

"What's that supposed to mean?"

"He's carrying a pistol, so that means he's at least twenty-one, even though he looks like a college freshman. Yet you order his food. You take care of him like he's a puppy. Being on the outside, looking in, I can't tell who's to blame. Sometimes people are dependent because they can't take care of themselves, and sometimes it's because they're not allowed to take control of their life."

Max took his turn torturing the eggs, the muscles of his jaws working as he considered and discarded things to say. Finally he tapped a small spoonful of the eggs onto his plate. "Look, what's between Ukiah and me isn't up for discussion. What we were talking about was what happened last night—which was nothing. Nothing happened between you and Ukiah, even though you were in the same bed together."

"You actually believe that? Or is that sarcasm?"

Max turned to face her, a hint of anger in his eyes. "First off, I don't feel the need to mark my territory and growl like a dog protecting a bitch in heat. If you're interested in me, great. If you want my partner, well, you'll have to work that out with Special Agent Zheng, but that's none of my business. Secondly, I know my partner. I can't explain to you in simple, short sentences, but I know nothing happened last night."

"What's that supposed to mean?" she asked in a carefully neutral voice. "Simple short sentences? Are you saying I'm stupid?"

"Have you never trusted someone so much that it couldn't be put into words?"

She gazed at Max a minute, and then turned away, looking troubled. They drifted apart, making pretended studies of the containers of food. Separately they returned to the table, and ate without speaking.

"How are you doing?" Max asked Ukiah, breaking the silence.

"Last day," Ukiah said, writing out Sunday. *Geologist: I am like an ant, crawling over mother earth, biting at her bones. ???:Does earth feel pain, as I <break, chip, pry> off my rocks, ???*

"There was a red flag marking this day, but I think it was just to make the current day easy to find. She kept it closed up and in a Ziploc bag. The days after this were blank. I've put in the Post-it notes. On some pages, they were blocking out text. Mostly it seemed like shopping lists, things to do, really odd things that I think are poems, stuff like that."

Max commandeered the planner and covertly finger signed "Go, food" to Ukiah, indicating that he should hit the buffet again. When Ukiah returned, Max had made a list on a Post-it note and passed the planner to Sam. She flipped the pages, looking stunned.

"Oh, this is so weird." She lifted a Post-it note with the cryptic number *OR 364.1523 B26*. Ukiah had faithfully copied what he had seen as he flipped through the pages. On this page it had been *Call Uncle Ra . . . un block, D batteries, CHOCOLATE, newspaper. Check Ukiah weather. Ukiah history: obits.* There had also been a doodle, the bulk of it hidden by the Post-it note. By lifting the square of yellow, Sam revealed the perfectly square blank spot. "It looks like one of those model homes, all decorated as if someone lives there, until you noticed the books are blocks of painted wood."

"OR 364.1523 B26," Max read off the Post-it note. "What do you suppose that is? A telephone number?"

"That's not a local exchange."

Ukiah consulted his memory. "It's not a phone number in her address book."

"OR could be Oregon or the word 'or.' B26 sounds like a

vitamin." Max shook his head. "Maybe it's a map reference number."

"Or something that has to do with geology," Ukiah said.

"Is the other geologist in town?" Sam asked.

Max shook his head. "Kraynak put her on a plane last night." He winced. "I have no idea how we're getting Kraynak's van home. Kraynak wants to fly Alicia back when he finds her, and now he's in no shape to drive it back to Pittsburgh."

"I occasionally work as a driver," Sam grinned. "Money up front for expenses, fifty dollars an hour that I spend driving, and return airfare."

"Drive stick?"

"Yup."

Max studied Sam, a minute of stillness. "We might take you up on that. Otherwise, it's up to Ukiah and me, and I'd rather avoid that if I can. We're stretched painfully thin now; we really need to take on another investigator."

Max usually avoided leaving town; financially it didn't make sense to drop all their cases to pursue just one. Their part-time investigators, Chino and Janey, were currently covering the ongoing cases, but neither of the two had the experience, skill, or temperament to cope with a long absence. Ukiah wondered why Sam had no qualms accepting out-of-town work; was it because she had little work to neglect?

"How many miles is it to Pittsburgh?" Sam wondered aloud, somewhat gleefully.

"Two thousand three hundred and fifty-five." Ukiah pulled the number out of his memory.

Sam looked surprised, then even more pleased. "Twenty-four hundred? That's over thirty hours of driving. Three or four days to do it."

Max gave him a questioning glance, picking up a glass of water.

"Mom Jo and I drove it after she—" Ukiah started, then stopped as Max frowned him into silence over the rim of his glass.

"That's a good ventriloquist trick you've got there," Sam

said dryly to Max. "But you better practice the drinking water routine. He stopped talking."

Max slapped a napkin over his face and snorted water. "Brat!" he said after he finished laughing.

"So what did your mother do that I'm not supposed to know about?" Sam asked.

"Embarrassing family vacations aren't the agenda of the day." Max said. "Finding Alicia is. She came to town four times, and these are the places we know she would have visited."

Ukiah glanced over the list Max had made. "She had some color brochures stuck in the pages too. I think they were tourist sites in the area."

"Okay. We can hit those too."

Ukiah described them, and Sam guessed from the description which site they represented. Max added them to the list. For being in the area for such a short time, Alicia had managed to visit an impressive number of places.

"Do we split up, or work together?" Sam asked.

"Well, we'll cover more ground split up," Max said, obviously unhappy with the thought.

"I'm fine," Ukiah said. "I've got my pistol, it's daylight, and I've got my phone."

Max frowned at Sam. "And you probably think I'd be domineering if I don't let him solo."

Sam held out her hands, palms up. "Hey. You decide without trying to please me. I might talk big, but the fact remains someone plowed over your big cop friend. I'm not going to open my yap and be responsible for something ugly on down the line."

"Three is overkill." Ukiah said. There was slim hope for Alicia, if kidnappers took her and demanded no ransom. Every hour could be critical. They had wasted so much time since last night, yet they couldn't have done more, not with Kraynak in the hospital and himself hurt so bad. "You don't have to worry about me."

"Fine. We'll split up."

Sam picked up her coffee. "What I would love is a picture of Ukiah's father, so I know all the players."

Max looked at Ukiah, puzzled.

"Rennie," Ukiah said. "Indigo says he flew into Portland yesterday."

"Oh, shit! That's the last thing we needed!" Max pulled out his PDA and played with it a few moments. "Here. This is him."

Sam viewed the picture a moment, sipping her coffee, and then suddenly spit it all back out. "This is the FBI Most Wanted list!"

"Yes, it is." Max reached for his PDA. "I don't have any other picture of Shaw."

Sam leaned out of reach, scrolling down through the entry. "Wanted for arson, assault, assault with a deadly weapon, auto theft, burglary . . . *kidnapping . . . manslaughter . . . murder*—oh my god, you weren't kidding! He is a homicidal lunatic! And he's coming here?"

"See, I'm not the only one he has that effect on," Max said to Ukiah.

"He's not that bad," Ukiah said meekly. "Once you get to know him."

CHAPTER ELEVEN

Pendleton, Oregon
Saturday, August 28, 2004

Sam had guessed that *OT Trading—Main* in Alicia's diary meant the Oregon Trail Trading Post. Peering into the windows, the place looked a likely site to interest Alicia. Just from the window Ukiah could see baskets, buckskin dresses, moccasins, seashells, and furs cluttering the front of the store. Ukiah nearly itched with curiosity, wishing he could go inside. It looked like no store he had ever been in.

But the doors were locked. A red-and-white CLOSED sign hung in the window, listing hours. Saturday, it turned out, was the only day it wasn't open. Closed Saturday, but open Sundays? In Pittsburgh, stores tend to only close on Sundays. Often they even had extended hours on Saturday. Closed Saturday? Was it a culture thing? Did Native Americans celebrate their holy day on Saturdays? Or was he making a huge assumption, and Jewish people actually owned the store? He knew the Jews celebrated Sabbath on Saturday. The office of the Bennett Detective Agency in Pittsburgh was located next to the neighborhood of Squirrel Hill, which had a heavily orthodox Jewish population.

Ukiah leaned his forehead against the glass, frowning as he thought about those Jewish families walking to temple. Somber black clothes, side locks, and skull caps. His family attended church each week, but there never seemed to be that solidarity, that belonging those Jewish families must feel. To be surrounded not only by those that believe, but were the same, down to genetic similarities. To be able to see it stamped on the face, the color of the eyes and hair.

He thought of Jared and Cassidy Kicking Deer. His family. His people. What church did they belong to? What did they believe? Were they in church today? Did they sing the same hymns? Did they even believe in the same God? He peered into the darkened store, at the beaded shirts and headdresses, and felt bewildered and lost.

The second store was open. Alicia's planner had labeled it as *Beads—22 SW Dorion.* BLUE HAWK BEADS proclaimed the sign over the door, and once again, Alicia's attraction to it was obvious. Loud rock music played on the sound system. Incense perfumed the air. On the right there were tiny square bins of beads upon beads, and on the left a display case full of stone-and-silver bracelets, stone pendants, beaded barrettes, and buckles. A treasure trove to the eye.

The saleswoman was checking out a customer, so he crouched down to study the beautiful exotic knives in the nearest display case. The handles were of antlers, banded with a strip of bright woven seed beads. The blades themselves were stone, chipped away to sharp edges. One was displayed with an elaborate sheath beaded and fringed with leather. He gazed at them, wondering if they were traditional. Were they on sale here because all Native Americans wore one? Or simply because they were beautiful?

"Can I help you?" The saleswoman could have been a soul mate for Alicia: a halo of red hair instead of brown, but the same tall, sturdy build, bright smile, and clothes completely unique. The woman wore a tight tie-dye dress that flared out midthigh to a full skirt, a jasper necklace, and a beaded chain that tied into her hair and hung down her back.

"What are the blades made of?"

"They're obsidian. Aren't they beautiful?" She came to lean on the display above him. "The artist creates the edge by flaking the stone by hand."

"What are they for?" he asked.

"I suppose you could use them as knives, but they're mostly for display." She seemed confused by the question. "They're traditional artwork. These were the blades that the natives used before the white man came. They're somewhat fragile, the blade will chip if you knock it against something hard. They're too expensive to actually use, I would think."

"How much are they?"

She gave him their prices. They ranged close to a hundred dollars each. He suspected they would go for much more at the fashionable stores of Shadyside.

He introduced himself then with a firm handshake, as he was taught. "Ukiah Oregon, yes, like the town. I'm a private investigator."

"Really? That is so awesome!"

"And you are?"

"Cecilia. Like the song." She broke into song. "Cecilia, I'm down on my knees, I'm begging you please, to come home." She smiled. "My mother was a huge Simon and Garfunkel fan."

"Actually, I wanted to ask a few questions." He pulled out the photograph of Alicia. "This is a friend of mine. Her name is Alicia Kraynak. She's disappeared; we're afraid she might be in danger."

Cecilia frowned in puzzlement at the picture. "I had heard she was lost hiking." She dug through a stack of papers behind the counter and produced an *East Oregonian,* dated Wednesday, featuring Alicia's photograph. "She was camping in the national park."

Max had taught Ukiah to "ease" people into being witnesses. Weaned on too many movies where murderers betrayed themselves by revealing facts about the case, Americans often went silent if approached too directly. Max used what he called the "crayon" approach, where you gave the person as blank an outline as possible, and let them color in the details. It went against Ukiah's natural directness, so it was weird trying to phrase questions, like thinking sideways.

"We think she might have been kidnapped. There's evidence that she might have been forced into a car." There, a vague sketch of the details. "We're trying to re-create everything she did in Pendleton. Perhaps someone saw something without realizing what it meant."

"Kidnapped? Oh, God, the poor woman."

"Alicia had plans of visiting your store. She would have visited here sometime between August first and last Sunday. Do remember if she came in to your store?"

"She came in. It was a Saturday. Not the last one, but the one before it." Cecilia said it slowly, as if she wasn't sure. A leather-bound guest book sat open on one of the counters. She pulled it over to her and started to flip through it. "Yeah, here. Alicia Kraynak, University of Pittsburgh, Pennsylvania, August fourteenth, 2004."

So it was. It was Alicia's handwriting, down to the circles over the I's which, in her teenage years, used to contain smiley faces. There were two other names after hers. One claiming to live in Portland, and the other said they were from Boise, Idaho.

"Was there anyone with her?"

"No." Cecilia squinted as she thought, as if peering back through time to see Alicia walk through the store. "She came in alone. She was my only customer for like an hour, so we talked a lot. She liked the CD I was playing, so I wrote down the name, but I forget which one it was now."

"What else did you talk about?"

"Beading. She bought mostly loose beads, wire, and some earring backs." Her eyes traveled about the room, watching that past Alicia. "She bought a strand of turquoise nuggets and all the wolf fetishes I had. She was going to make presents during the trip home. She liked the knives, everyone loves the knives, but she couldn't afford them."

"Did she mention anything about someone following her, watching her?"

"Nothing like that." Cecilia was startled out of her time seeing. "She asked about places to eat. She wanted information on the local tribes. I gave her one of the newspapers"— she pointed out a stack of papers beside Ukiah—"and I told her about Tamástslikt."

The newspaper was the *Confederated Umatilla Journal,* which was subtitled "The monthly newspaper of the Confederated Tribes of the Umatilla Indian Reservation— Pendleton, Oregon."

"What's Tamástslikt?"

"It's the cultural institute for the tribes in the area. They're the Cayuse, Umatilla, and Walla Walla tribes. The reservation is just east of town."

He recalled now seeing signs for it while driving out to the casino. "Did she say why she wanted the information?"

"I took a phone call, so I was half-listening to her. She said something about Ukiah. The newspaper said she disappeared from a campground near there, so I guess that she was researching the town she was in."

"At the reservation?"

She shrugged. "The Indians have been here the longest. Hey, wait; didn't you say your name was Ukiah? That is so wild! Well, now I don't know. She might have been talking about the town, or maybe she was talking about you. Hell, she might have been talking about getting you a present. I really wasn't paying attention."

Ukiah found it disquieting. Since the insanity of June, he had barely thought of Alicia until her disappearance. It was disturbing to imagine her thinking of him right before she vanished. "Her uncle is my partner's best friend." Spoken aloud, the link seemed so tenuous. "I guess we're fairly good friends. We're thrown together a lot."

Cecilia grinned at him. "I wouldn't mind being thrown together with you."

"You say she was your only customer?" He angled for a second witness.

"I don't remember anyone else coming in while she was here. Mostly we just talked about beads. Food and beads. She did ask what were good places to eat, other than the fast-food places."

"What places did you recommend to her?"

"Shari's is good and inexpensive. I told her that if she was out at the reservation to check out the Wildhorse Casino. The restaurant has a good buffet."

"Did she mention needing to meet someone? Or someone she would like to see?"

Cecilia shook her head, eyes looking back again, but seeing nothing. "I don't remember anything else."

He gave her a brief description of the kidnapper, tall and blond, remembering to hold back the blood type. She couldn't match it to anyone specific, certainly not anyone that would kidnap someone. He wrote down the mysterious number in Alicia's planner. She shook her head, bewildered as they were. The bell hung over the door twinkled as several, women entered. Ukiah took out his business card.

"Thank you. If you think of anything, you can reach me at the first number listed."

"Sure. No problem. I hope you find her. She was really nice."

Underground? was all Alicia wrote. Sam had expanded it to *Pendleton Underground, corner First and Emigrant.* It was nearly impossible to miss with a huge wall painting of a hand pointing down Emigrant Street at the corner of Main Street. The door read TOURS AND GIFT SHOP and swung open on a room with two banklike teller windows. A mannequin of an Abraham Lincoln look-alike sat at one of the windows.

On the wall was a map of the world with thousands of bright colored pushpins. Visitors were invited to stick a pin at the place they were from. Alicia had stuck a yellow one into the mass surrounding Pittsburgh.

A woman came out of a side room, investigating the bell that jingled as he had entered. "Oh, I thought I heard that bell. I'm sorry, all the tours are sold out today and tomorrow. I can make you a reservation for Monday afternoon."

"I'm a private investigator looking into a kidnapping. Can I ask you a few questions?"

"A kidnapping?"

He produced Alicia's photo. "This is Alicia Kraynak. She was kidnapped earlier this week. I've been hired by her uncle to look for her."

She looked dutifully at the photo. "I don't recognize her, but we have lots of people in every day. They mill around, maybe buy something in the gift shop, and then they leave. The tour guide spends ninety minutes with them. If she was on one of our tours, he'll probably remember her."

"Can I talk to him?"

"Them. There are several. It depends on which day she was in."

"It probably was a Saturday, sometime between August first and this Sunday."

"We have a guest book. Most people sign it. We can check that to see if she signed it." She led him into a small gift shop with an unusual range of gifts. Some were clearly Old West Cowboy. Others were Native American crafts. There were also a puzzling number of Chinese items.

At the center of it all was a stuffed grizzly bear inside a glass case. It stood on its back legs, mouth open in an unending roar. Like most things of his childhood, the grizzly seemed smaller than he remembered grizzly bears being, even while standing on a rock pedestal. The fur on its belly was sparse, the crudely stitched seam from its skinning zigzagging haphazardly through a rough tic-tac-toe pattern.

Its claws, the length of his fingers, however, remained impressive.

The ticket woman was beyond the bear, flipping through a book much like the one at the bead shop, chanting, "Alicia. Alicia. Alicia." She paused. "K-ray-nak. Was that the name? University of Pittsburgh?"

"That's her."

"She was here on August seventh." The woman handed him the book. "I'll see who was on duty."

That Saturday had been busy. Signatures representing nearly a hundred people had dates of August seventh. Rose had gone on the tour with Alicia, signing immediately below her. Most of the people, like the pins outside, came from the West Coast, but there was a married couple from Australia, and another from Boston. None of the people, however, were locals. That was, of course, if everyone signed the book.

"You're in luck." The ticket woman returned. "Frank was on duty and he's here today. He's downstairs, replacing some lightbulbs for the next tour."

"Can I talk to him?"

She gave him directions, starting with going back outside and around the corner. Outside he noticed the words WEBB and GRANT marked into the corner cement. *Those were the street names as Rennie remembered them!*

There had been a card room at the foot of the steps, and the second floor of the building had been a brothel. He went down the steps to the old card room, wondering why the street names had been changed. He opened the door and found that the card room remained—sort of. Mannequins dressed in blue jeans and cowboy hats sat around battered tables. The room was as cold and dark as he remembered, but everything was off.

He heard a distant curse, and he wandered through a doorway into the next room. "Frank?"

"Who's there?"

He followed the voice through a maze of rooms, revealing a vast underground space with stone walls and rough-timbered ceilings. "Hello?"

"Next room," came the call.

This was a large cellar, completely bare. A man stood on a ladder beneath a bare lightbulb in a ceramic base, lightbulb and flashlight in hand. On the floor were two four-packs of light bulbs.

"Are you Frank?"

"In the flesh!" Frank leaned down, offering out a gray lightbulb. "Can you hold this for me? I don't have enough hands."

Ukiah took the lightbulb and the flashlight, freeing Frank to climb down the ladder unhindered. He was under six feet tall, compact, and dark-haired.

"I'm a private investigator," Ukiah said. "My name is Ukiah Oregon."

"Howdy!" Frank grinned as Ukiah tucked the flashlight under his arm in order to shake hands. "I can take those now. Thanks. This is really a two-person job, but no one was free to help. Ukiah? Like the town?"

"I was named after the town." Ukiah tried to keep the conversation from veering off into that trap. He never had this problem in Pittsburgh. "I'm looking into the disappearance of Alicia Kraynak."

"Who?" Frank slipped the burned-out lightbulb into an empty slot in one of the four packs.

Ukiah gave a few brief details, ending with, "It appears now that she was kidnapped. We're checking into places we know that she visited in Pendleton."

"To see who she met who might have followed her back and kidnapped her."

"Yes." Ukiah shifted uneasily. "We don't have any leads at this time."

"And in about three days, this town explodes. Anyone tell you about the roundup?"

Ukiah checked his memory. "The population triples."

"Yup. We're already feeling the squeeze. Got a picture of the girl?"

Ukiah pulled Alicia's photograph out and showed it to him.

"I remember her. Don't think I have anything useful to tell you, but I remember her."

"Tell me anyhow."

"Mind if I finish doing lightbulbs as we talk? We had a whole series of them flash out on the morning tour, and the afternoon tour is due in about twenty minutes."

"Okay." Ukiah tucked away Alicia's photograph.

Frank folded the ladder, swung it into a carry position, then quirked an eyebrow as he looked at the four packs. "Can you grab those?"

"Sure." Ukiah picked up the lightbulbs and followed Frank through a series of interlinked underground rooms. Without outside windows, he found it difficult to keep his bearings. He never realized before that usually he knew without thinking which ways were east and west, and how the rest of the world, inside and out, lay around him. If there was a place he could get fully lost, this was it. They cut through a mock-up of a Chinese laundry and an ice-cream shop. After the fourth oversized room, Ukiah realized that the area was huge; they seemed to be moving through the cellars of an entire city block.

"What is this place?" Ukiah asked.

"Pendleton Underground." Frank opened a door into

cave blackness. He set down the ladder, took out his flash-light, and turned it on. Picking up the ladder, he continued forward, his light playing through another store mock-up. It seemed to be a butcher shop, complete with fake animal car-casses hanging from hooks. "When they built up the town, all the buildings were going up just about the same time, and they had cheap labor: the Chinese who worked on the inter-continental railroad. So they decided to build the cellars uni-form and interconnected. They went a little mad with it, though. All told, there's like seventy miles of corridors."

"All connected?"

"At one time. It's fairly chopped up now."

The room dog-legged to the right after the door, so the light from the previous room barely leaked in. Ukiah waited for his eyes to adjust, then followed Frank.

The tour guide swept his light over the ceiling and picked out three burned-out lights. "These three always go at the same time. I'm going to come down and replace one of them in a week or two, so next time they're staggered." Frank no-ticed then that Ukiah was in the room with him. "Careful, the floor isn't even over there."

Frank indicated the area with a quick sketch of light on the far side of the room.

Ukiah had a sense of the room now, pieced together by the shifting column of light from Frank's flashlight. The un-even section was a large square on the floor, which at one time might have been a pit, but was now filled in with loose earth. Hooks hung on a ceiling track dangled over the square. "What was that?"

"It used to be a ten-foot pit, lined with cork and filled with salt water." Frank lined up underneath one of the burned-out lights and set up his ladder. "They had coils run-ning from a newfangled pneumatic compressor, through the salt water, which freezes at a lower temperature than plain water."

"Why?" Ukiah steadied the ladder as Frank climbed it.

"It was the only way to make ice." Frank flashed his light over a tall, narrow tin. "They filled those tins with spring-water, and lowered them into the salt water. The spring-water freezes overnight, and makes a hundred-pound block of ice, which sold at a dollar per pound. New bulb?"

Ukiah handed the lightbulb up and took the dead bulb in its place. He studied the dirt while Frank screwed the new bulb in, wanting to spare his currently light-sensitive eyes.

The half-glimpsed pieces of the room connected with one of Rennie's buried memories. Curious, Ukiah summoned it to the surface, and discovered what a Pack member could do with a pit of freezing water and a half-dead Ontongard. The individual cells of the alien could choose to generate heat to keep from freezing, or heal. Without great quantities of food, they couldn't do both. Starving, they could do neither.

He recoiled from the memory, and found himself disoriented by the changes in the room. "There used to be windows with moonlight coming in."

Frank came down the ladder, looking at him oddly. "Moonlight? Well, yeah. We had to change some things around." He went and shut the steel door into the butcher shop. "Because of fire codes, we had to put in this door and keep it closed at all times."

Frank crossed the dim room to where the window used to be and a door now stood. "We knocked out this window and put in this door. We don't have access to that area." He waved at the wall to the right. "So we put this in to connect to the speakeasy."

He opened the door into a small, triangular room. Sunlight spilled down through a grid-work skylight. "Basically they built the basements under the buildings, and out here were service tunnels or light wells, under the sidewalks." He pointed to the skylight. "That's a ship's prism light. Normally it sets into the deck of a ship to let light into the hold. Here, the prism light is set into the sidewalk."

"That's the sidewalk? Out on the street level?" Ukiah tried to reconstruct the turns he had taken in order to place which street was above them.

"Yeah. See, the ceiling is reinforced to take the poured concrete." Frank turned to point out a second window beside the door. It looked like a normal window frame, plywood replacing the glass. "We boarded this one up to meet fire code. In the old days, the sidewalks were wood, so the windows had glass to let in the light but keep out the cold."

Across the light well was another door, apparently the way to the speakeasy.

Ukiah gazed at the far door. He *almost* remembered it, which was very strange for him. He usually either recalled something perfectly, or not at all. Perhaps it was one of Rennie's memories, refusing to surface because things had been too altered to recognize. "That was a window too?"

"Perhaps at one time. Things have changed a lot since the 1870s. When we started working on the tour, it was just a hole in the wall into the speakeasy. They used it as a secret passage during police raids."

Frank opened the far door.

The smell of mothballs washed into the room. Ukiah glimpsed a tin ceiling in the room beyond. Utter terror hit him—then was gone. He stumbled backward, fighting the urge to bolt. *What was that? What happened to Rennie here?*

No. Rennie never had been in this odd-shaped area beyond the butcher shop's windows.

I remember this. I was terrified here. Ukiah walked forward, trembling with the recalled terror and the excitement of finally having discovered one of his own memories.

The room beyond was set up like the card room. The smell of mothballs came from cloth bags dangling from the tin ceiling. He gazed around, but nothing else came. He stepped back into the light well.

A sliver of memory. One brilliant, hard moment.

. . . the ground of the room had been up to the level of the window sill. He lay in the dirt, frightened beyond rational thoughts. He stared at the speakeasy's door, which then had been a much smaller hole in the wall, cut into the back of a cupboard . . .

And then the memory stopped.

"You okay?" Frank asked. "Some people get hit with claustrophobia. They don't expect it. It's just a basement, but after all the twists and turns, sometimes . . ."

"I was here, once, as a child," Ukiah said. "Something bad happened. It frightened me."

"What happened?"

"I don't remember. I don't have any memories of my childhood. It's a complete blank. I was a John Doe who my adoptive parents renamed."

"So, Ukiah Oregon isn't your original name?"

"No." The Kicking Deers, he realized, had only called him Uncle. What had been his name?

Frank looked like he was about to launch into more questions.

"Tell me about Alicia," Ukiah detoured him.

Frank indicated Ukiah to follow him. He juggled the ladder through to the speakeasy, pausing to close doors behind him.

"She was one of twenty people that I took through, hmm, almost a month ago." Frank continued. "She seemed to be with this little woman, Italian-looking. I don't think she said anything to me. She laughed at my jokes. She seemed to be a feminist. Now, the Chinese and the Indians really got a raw deal out of this town. All this land once belonged to the plateau Indians. When the white men came over the mountains, more times than not, they were starving. The Indians would greet them in peace and sell them food so they wouldn't die."

"What does this have to do with Alicia?"

Frank stopped under another gray, burned-out lightbulb. On the wall was a map, showing the city street, bearing the names that Rennie remembered.

"Well, the first part of the tour I talk about how badly the Chinese and Indians were treated." Frank set up the ladder. "The Chinese were indentured servants, which meant they were one step removed from slaves, and treated as such. The Indians were rounded up and confined to the reservation. All through this, Alicia is fine.

"Second part of the tour, though, we go up to the Cozy Rooms, a brothel, and suddenly you can see the hurt feelings all over her face. These were *white women* that suffered."

Frank held out his hand for a new bulb.

Ukiah glared at him, angry that this stranger passed judgment on Alicia. "You're saying she's a bigot."

"That's simplifying something that's a whole lot more complicated than that," Frank said, folding his arms across the top of the ladder. "What's a Chinese man that lived a hundred years ago to an American woman of 2004? She feels sorry for him, but, hell, he's dead. This is America! We've pissed on everyone, at one point or another, but we're over all that, right? She hasn't seen the Chinese mistreated lately, so she assumes that all that badness is over. On the other hand, we've still got whores."

"I suppose." Ukiah's anger retreated into confusion. Indigo's family never spoke about discrimination, but did that mean that they faced none?

Frank reached out again for the new bulb, and Ukiah handed it to him. "She's a friend of yours?" Frank asked, his attention on the socket.

"Yes."

"I'm sorry. I hope you find her." He handed down the old bulb. "Folks come to this area. They gamble at the casino and tour the Tamástslikt. They see the miles of rolling farmland, and that the reservation is marked with only a sign and not a tall fence with barbed wire on top, and they go away with the wrong idea."

"What's that?"

"They think that the past is dead. They don't see that the past is just the beginning of the future."

After the cold, damp bleakness of Pendleton's Underground, Ukiah welcomed the heat shimmering off the wood-plank-patterned cement sidewalk. He stood on the corner, looking at the old street names stamped into the curb. He had forgotten to ask why all the street names had been changed.

He smelled Cassidy first. A stiff breeze brought him the scent of cut cedar, which brought her to mind moments before her pickup turned the corner. She saw him standing on the sidewalk, lifted her hand to him in recognition, and started past. As if she suddenly changed her mind, though, she stopped her truck half a block down, and honked at him.

"Hey! Ukiah!" Cassidy leaned out the truck window to wave him over.

Ukiah checked for traffic and went out to talk to her.

Her little sister, the blood-swapping candy striper named Zoey, sat in the passenger seat, grinning in welcome. A dog sat between the girls, tense and alert to a stranger's presence. He nodded to all three. "Hi!"

"Howdy, Wolf Boy," Cassidy said. "Jared told me about your friend. I'm sorry. Any luck yet?"

He shrugged. "Hard to tell. Finding a missing person is like assembling a jigsaw puzzle. Everyone holds fragments of the puzzle, but not everyone realizes it. Oh, the person with part of the picture that shows the gun or someone tied up knows, but what everyone else holds is too abstract for them to know what they have. To them, it's a blob of brown, or a flash of red, or just a big chunk of sky-blue."

"Do you look for missing people because you were lost once?" Cassidy asked.

"No. I didn't feel lost. I just *was,* as if there was no other way to be."

"So, why do you do it?"

"Because I'm good at it."

"Have you found any important pieces of this jigsaw puzzle?" Cassidy asked.

"Am I supposed to trust you if I have?"

"Perhaps." Her smile slipped into something sly-looking. "We are family."

"Are we?"

The smile faded, as if she realized that she had gone too far. "Perhaps. Jared is drumming a different dance, so it's possible. Come on, trust me. Jared will tell me anyhow. Besides, maybe I can help."

"Well, you can tell me now to get to the Tamástslikt. The woman at the bead shop said Alicia asked about information on the tribes. Something to do with my past."

Cassidy worked her jaw, thinking. "So, this Alicia, she knew you?"

"Yes. We're friends."

Cassidy hitched her chin. "Get in. I'll take you out to the institute. I want to show you something there."

Ukiah peered into the truck's crowded cabin. "There's no room for me."

Cassidy slid back the window behind her, opening it up to the back. "In the back, Elvis. Back." The dog scrambled into the back. "Zoey, move over." The girl slid over, making room on the passenger side for Ukiah. "Come on."

Ukiah went around to the other side of the truck and got in. The cabin was thick with the smell of cut cedar and white flakes of sawdust whirled about the floor like snow.

"This is my little sister, Zoey." Cassidy concentrated on merging with the oncoming traffic. "She's the baby of the family."

Zoey used Cassidy's distraction to turn to him, press a finger to her lips and plead for his silence with her eyes.

Don't say what? he tried to communicate silently back, unsure what he wasn't supposed to say. Surely she didn't think he would say anything about the stolen vials of blood.

Her dark eyes went round, growing bigger, and she repeatedly stabbed the finger to her mouth, so he took it to mean *Anything!* But she was looking ahead, innocently, when Cassidy glanced over at him, apparently suspicious of the silence.

"Hi!" he tried.

Zoey rewarded him with a bright smile. "Howdy! I've counted. I'm your great-great-great-great-great . . ." Zoey paused, squinting and checking on her fingers. ". . . great-great-great-grand-niece."

My brother or sister's grandchild. The thought stunned him for a moment. "I-I'm pleased to meet you, Zoey. You can call me Ukiah. It's what my adopted mothers named me."

What had his real mother named him?

Zoey pressed fingers to his arm. "You feel just like a real person."

"He is a real person," Cassidy murmured.

"Grandpa said that all of him was alive, and that if you

took any one piece away, it'd be alive too. Every drop of his blood, Grandpa says, can be something else."

Cassidy clearly wasn't as startled as he was by this statement. She looked at him with mild curiosity, and then said, "Well?"

"Well, yes," Ukiah reluctantly admitted. "That's basically right. That's where the mice come in."

Zoey dug into her pocket and produced a small box. She opened it up and took out a rectangle of glass. "Here. Show me."

"What is that?" Cassidy asked.

"A glass slide. It came with my microscope." Seeing Ukiah's confusion, Zoey explained. "I'm going to be doctor some day, so I asked for a high-quality microscope for my birthday. I told Grandpa about blood typing and he said that you couldn't type Uncle's blood because all of him was alive. That as soon as he bled, it became something else." She pleaded with her eyes. "Can I see?"

Cassidy threw him a curious look too but said nothing.

"You can't tell other people about it," Ukiah said cautiously.

"Of course not. It's a family secret," Zoey said. "Look, I even got a lancet from a diabetes kit, and gloves." They were the pale latex gloves they used in the hospital. "One should always take precautions when handling blood. Please? It would only pinch for a minute."

"Do you practice that line?" Cassidy asked.

"Of course," Zoey said. "Cough. Breath deeply. Say 'ah.'" Zoey caught his hand and squeezed it. "Please?"

"Okay."

"Hold on a minute." Cassidy guided the car to the berm. They were out of town, on the interstate. Shorn wheat fields extended off on either side to the horizon. "I want to see too."

Zoey donned the gloves and lanced his finger with a thin sharp pain. She milked the blood out of his finger onto the glass slide. The flow stopped, the wound healing shut despite the pressure, before Zoey could fumble open a bandage while wearing the gloves. Cassidy had held the slide, and once it was covered with blood, leaned back, as if she wanted it out of his sphere of power.

The blood gave an unnatural tremble, gathered into a ball, segmented, and hardened. Within a few minutes, a ladybug sat in the blood's place. The ladybug unshuttered its wings, and with a minute thrum, it rose from the slide, winged over, and settled on his hand.

"That is creepy," Cassidy whispered.

"No, it isn't," Zoey said. "It is sooooo cool."

The blood reverted back to its original form and seeped into his hand.

"Oh, wow." Zoey breathed happiness. "I've told Grandpa all about you. You've got to come see him."

Cassidy gazed at him over the top of her sister's head. "Yeah. I think you probably should."

Tamástslikt was just out of sight of the casino, over a slight rise in the hill. It was a long, low building, like a piece of modern art in and of itself, faced in river stone. Zoey and Cassidy had membership cards. Ukiah paid admission and turned to the sisters, who were conferring quietly.

Zoey frowned at whatever Cassidy had to say, but then shrugged in compliance.

"I know you're really busy," Cassidy said. "But you say that you don't remember anything about living with our family. I thought it might be good for you to see all of the museum."

"All of it?" He balked at wasting the time.

"Well, you can skip the videos. It won't take long. Family legend says that you've got a magic memory; you can remember anything you've seen. Just run through and think about it later?"

That seemed reasonable.

Zoey announced that she had seen it all dozens of time and by now it was "boooooring!" She said she would be in the gift shop. Cassidy guided Ukiah out the cavernous teak entry hall. Beyond, a huge rock formation guarded the entrance proper to the museum. Pictographs decorated the natural stone face. Plaques described the importance of the crude drawings.

"The museum is set up in three areas," Cassidy said. "The way we were before the white man, the way we became what we are today, and where we hope to go in the future."

Beyond was a collection of artifacts made of stone, wood, leather, and reed. Judging by the amount of fishing equipment—nets, weights, spears—life had revolved around the salmon. A teepee of reeds woven into mats stood beyond it, and from inside it, recorded voices told stories of his people.

"This was our culture before the white man came," Cassidy explained. "Our people have lived on this plateau for ten thousand years."

"Look at what they were defending themselves with." Hex held out short wooden shafts with tips of stone.

The arrows were amazing objects of craft, but they would have been no true weapon against the aliens, had the Ontongard landed in force. Even if the arrows killed an Ontongard, it only rendered the alien dead for a short period of time.

"Long before the white man arrived in Oregon, their horses changed our lives." Cassidy pointed out the next exhibit, centered around two riders on life-sized horses. A plaque described a Cayuse chief leading out a war party, and encountering another tribe with horses. Grasping immediately what the horse could mean to their people, the party had stripped off everything they carried and offered it as trade for a mare and a stallion.

Ukiah gazed at the mounted pair, wondering if he had known the wise Cayuse chief. Was he related to him?

"Then the white man himself came."

The museum chronicled the beginnings of trade, and then, a purchase between the European French and the East Coast Americans led the United States government to see all of the land to the West Coast as theirs. After exploring the extent of the purchase, the government threw it open to settlement. Any married *white* couple that traveled to Oregon received a square mile of land. Half a million white people made the journey to claim the land.

Ukiah stared at the map after reading about the Louisiana Purchase. "But how did the French own it?"

"Because they were the first white people to arrive."

"But what about the natives who already lived here?"

"They were forced to live on a section of land that the government chose for them." Cassidy showed him maps depicting a shrinking mass of land. "We used to call all this ours, then the government told us we had to live here. Then they reduced it to this. This is how much we own today."

Ukiah traced out the rivers on the map. Few fell within the reservation boundaries. "But we lived on fish."

"And we starved."

This was nearly as bad as what the Ontongard would have done to the natives. He felt somehow betrayed. He read on, and the history grew even bleaker. The white man brought smallpox and measles to the area. Entire villages died. A white doctor tried to save the natives, but all his patients died. Believing the doctor was poisoning his patients, the Cayuse killed him, and triggered a war they couldn't hope to win.

Finally, Ukiah couldn't stand any more. He walked quickly through the next section, staring at the floor, trying to avoid the wall displays. Fleeing the truth, he only stopped when they reached the teak entry hall again. As Cassidy said, though, all of it was now etched it into his memory.

"Why did you think I should see any of this?" he forced out in a hurt whisper. "It's like drinking poison."

"You lived through all this." Cassidy rubbed his shoulder, trying to comfort him. "The white man stole, and lied, and killed our people. The Cayuse don't even speak their own language anymore—the white man took it from us in the early 1800s."

"I don't remember," he hissed. "I don't remember any of it!"

If I found a mouse with my old memories, would I even want to reclaim it, knowing what the past held?

"But if you ever do get back your memory," Cassidy

whispered, "this is what you're going to remember. You witnessed the white man do these unspeakable things—and now you live with them."

Why hadn't Mom Jo and Mom Lara told him about this? Why keep him ignorant of his true heritage? Why hadn't Max, in the last few days, warned him what he might discover here? It shook his faith in his moms and Max.

Ukiah realized he had been right, that first night outside the Kicking Deer home, when he saw the house like a humane cage. His life was irrevocably changed. He could only escape what he just saw by bleeding out the memory and never taking it back.

Cassidy brushed his hair out of his eyes. "Maybe being forewarned will make it all less of a blow."

He ducked his head, and his bangs fell back into his eyes. "Is there something really here relating to Alicia?"

"Yes. It's a photograph she might have seen." Cassidy pointed down a narrow hallway off the grand entrance.

The hallway had a door into the gift shop to the right, bathrooms on the left, and continued on down to staff offices. A temporary exhibit hung on the wall, past the point of normal public areas. Looking for Alicia on his own, he would have ignored the exhibit. A plaque explained that these were family photographs taken during the annual rodeo.

"I'm not sure if this is important," Cassidy said as he looked at the pictures. "Call it my chunk of blue sky, or flash of red." She referenced their earlier conversation on jigsaw puzzle pieces. The photographs were mostly in color, showing people in brilliant costumes. Some photos were much older, carefully posed, black-and-white. In one, a familiar face looked out. "That's me."

"Yeah." Cassidy produced a copy of the photo he had shown her at her hardware store. He realized that the machine hum he had heard while she was in her office had been a scanner—she had scanned the photo without him knowing it. She held it up beside the black-and-white photo. Even down to the length of hair, the faces were identical. "I came out yesterday and compared these two. If Alicia saw this, she might have recognized you. You haven't changed much over the years."

As in all the other places Ukiah had visited so far, the museum had a guest book on the front desk. He wondered what weird Oregon tradition led to the prevailing habit as he flipped back through the pages. They were marvelous tools for a private investigator; too bad most of the places in Pittsburgh didn't have them.

Alicia signed in August 21, a week after being at the bead shop, and a little over a week before she disappeared. Either Rose hadn't signed, or Alicia had come alone.

Armed with the date, Ukiah began questioning the staff. He held out little hope, however, of them remembering her. After buying the tickets, he and Cassidy had not seen one identifiable museum worker.

Luckily, he found a gift shop employee that thought she might remember Alicia.

The young Native American woman, however, shook her head even as she admitted recalling Alicia. "I see a lot of people this time of year. She looks vaguely familiar."

Ukiah pulled out a copy of the Christmas photo, the one of Alicia standing beside him. It gave a size reference. People of extremes got noticed, and Alicia was a tall woman.

"Yes. I did see her. She was asking about one of the rodeo photos. I'm not sure which one. Apparently it didn't have a name identifying the person in the photo. I told her that she would have to talk to a curator, who would be in on Monday."

"Did she talk to you about anything else?"

"She bought one of the books. She said it was going to be a gift for a friend who was from one of the local tribes."

Alicia bought a book for me? "Did she say anything about him being related to the photograph?"

The woman considered and nodded slowly. "Yes, she said something about that. She said she wanted to know the name of the family so she could contact them and see if they had lost a child several years ago. She asked me if I knew anyone in the area that lost a little boy."

"What did you tell her?"

"I didn't grow up around here." She pressed a hand to her breast. "I'm Cree! I met my husband at a powwow and moved here only three years ago."

"We didn't put a name on it because we didn't want reward seekers to know what Magic Boy looked like," Cassidy explained the lack of a name on the photo. Zoey had rejoined them, explaining that the rodeo photos were new, and thus interesting.

"They could take a photo of it," Cassidy said. "Play with it digitally and come up with proof of some sort that my grandfather would believe. He's nearly a hundred years old. He was born before television was invented. He doesn't realize what people can do with pictures now."

Ukiah murmured his agreement while staring at his photo. What could Alicia have learned from it? They had kept Kraynak in the dark about his true nature, so Alicia couldn't have known that this was him. She could have guessed, though, that this was a near relative. Certainly it seemed to confirm in her mind that he was from one of the three tribes on the reservation.

Had she handled the photo? He touched the frame edge lightly. Alicia's ghost presence indicated she had most likely taken it off the wall. He lifted it up.

"What are you doing?" Cassidy hissed.

"Alicia took it down," he said and flipped it over. "She undid the catches." He undid them and lifted off the back. Written on the back, in ancient, faded script, was MAGIC BOY KICKING DEER, DIED SEPTEMBER 23, 1933.

Jared caught Ukiah's right wrist, lifting his arm up to run a thumb over the unblemished line of his radius bone . . . "Lead the way, Magic Boy."

Jared called Ukiah by his true name, but Ukiah hadn't recognized it. Even now, it triggered no emotion in him.

"My name was Magic Boy?"

"What else would you call a two-hundred-year-old child?" Cassidy asked.

September 23. The day Rennie arrived at Pendleton.

Unsettled by the apparent coincidence, Ukiah replaced the back and rehung the picture. "So Alicia has a name."

"We had nothing to do with her disappearing," Cassidy said.

"I didn't say you did." Ukiah stared back at himself. "She wouldn't realize this was me. She thinks I'm only twenty-one. She would look for relatives of Magic Boy, though, thinking I was a descendent."

"She didn't talk to anyone in the family that I heard," Zoey said. "That's who I would ask."

"We're not all on speaking terms, though," Cassidy said. "Magic Boy's death triggered a big family feud."

"The family isn't listed in the phone book," Ukiah murmured. "She wouldn't know how to contact them. She probably would have checked with county records."

"Let's go, then!" Zoey cried.

"It's closed today," Cassidy said. "I'm not sure she could have found anything. Magic Boy disappeared during the 1933 roundup, within hours of that picture being taken. My family has always believed that he was killed, but the police wouldn't start an investigation. They said he just ran off. Alicia wouldn't have found any birth or death certificates on file."

"Census records," Zoey stated. "In 2000, we had to fill out the names of everyone that lived in the house. She could have found who he was living with and then looked up their descendants. Boy, this is like a puzzle."

"Obituaries list next of kin and how they are related," Ukiah said. "If the library has microfilm of the local newspaper, and your family placed an obituary for Magic Boy, that's one place she could have looked."

Cassidy glanced at her watch. "I think the library might still be open. We can see what she found out."

The library closed twenty minutes before they arrived. It was one wing of a large imposing red-brick building. Zoey rattled the doors and then proclaimed, "Major stinker."

"No Sunday hours," Ukiah observed.

"You can visit on Monday," Cassidy said. "If you're still here. Surely, this has nothing to do with her disappearance."

"It's a place she visited and maybe met someone," Ukiah said. "She was only in town three times. Unless the kidnappers saw her at the campgrounds themselves, Pendleton is where they noticed her."

Sam had picked out their rendezvous site, a park at the end of town next to the courthouse. A statue of a man on a horse presided over the park. A plaque explained that he was Til Taylor, first sheriff of Pendleton, killed during a jailbreak. Ukiah glanced at the bronze statue and heard Degas's slight mocking voice, saying, *"One would think he was a martyred saint or something, the way they carry on."*

Max and Sam sat opposite the statue, heads together in deep discussion. Ukiah caught the scent of their mutual attraction. Sam laughed at something Max said and turned to press her face against Max's shoulder. There was softness to Max's face that Ukiah had never seen before, as if some inner tension had released. The two looked up as Ukiah approached, a mix of guilt and mild annoyance.

Ukiah felt a twinge of jealousy and tried to soothe it away. The last few days had bruised him heart and soul as well as body, he told himself, and he was being oversensitive. "The gang's all here and none the worse for wear."

"Good," Max said. "Dinner?"

"Definitely," Ukiah agreed. Food, sleep, and a phone call to Indigo would return him to balance. Sex with Indigo, though, would have been an even better tonic.

True to form, Max had found the best place to eat while doing his legwork. "I've heard Raphael's is excellent."

Sam cringed slightly. "Excellent but expensive."

"Our treat," Max said, "for putting Ukiah up for the night."

"Oh!" Sam stood and bent her arm up behind her back. "Okay, okay, you twisted my arm enough. Raphael's it is."

Raphael's turned out to be around the corner in a large Queen Anne–style house. Three tall gables looked out over a covered porch. The interior was rich with stained wood, leaded glass, and modern art from native artists. Just inside the door was the ever-present guest book.

"I love these things" Max murmured, signing in a flourish. "Alicia was a good little trooper and signed all the ones she came across."

"So I noticed," Ukiah said.

"Did you check to see if any of the names around hers repeated?"

"Same people visiting the same time as her?"

"Yeah."

Ukiah called up the guest books. "No. No one had."

Max made a slight noise of disappointment.

The hostess sat them at a window, gave them menus, and fetched them hot, fresh bread with a spicy herb crust.

Sam leaned across the table to murmur to Max, "Is that your foot?"

Max looked slightly surprised over the top of his menu. "Yes."

She smiled. "Oh, good."

Max looked smugly embarrassed and laughed.

Max ordered the smoked quail with browned huckleberry sauce. Sam had venison marsala. Ukiah ordered the salmon topped with huckleberry puree, the soup along with the salad, and asked for a second round of the bread.

The waitress clucked, "Growing boys," and went off for the bread.

Sam took out her notebook. "If I ever disappear, I hope I'd leave more of a trace. Today almost inspires me to dye my hair purple or green."

"At one time, Alicia dyed her hair purple," Ukiah said.

"Too bad she stopped," Sam murmured. "At most of the places I checked, no one remembered Alicia or Rose."

Max considered Sam. "Green would be fetching on you."

"Brat." The corners of her mouth turned up into a Mona Lisa smile. "Kentucky Fried Chicken is a few blocks down from the coin laundry. As I hoped, Alicia stopped there while doing laundry. Andy Henry on the counter remembers her, but they talked about nothing more than chicken and the weather."

"What's this Henry like?" Max asked.

"He's extremely short with huge feet. Looks like Mickey Mouse," Sam said. "So desperate for a woman to notice him that he'll remember any one that does."

"Well, that doesn't match up with any of our kidnappers," Ukiah said.

"I solved our mystery location." Sam tapped her list. Alicia had written *Big Sink* for the total of Wednesday, August 18. "I called Eastern Oregon University at La Grande and questioned one of their geology professors. The 'big sink' turns out to be a weird local geological thing that I hadn't heard of before. The 'sink' is an area south of Jubilee Lake, which looks like a large piece of earth *sank* into the ground. The girls got directions at the Chevron service station last week on how to get to Jubilee Lake. The attendant was fairly sure it was Wednesday morning, and that they were going to drive out immediately. But it's just a big hole in the ground, with a weird magnetic thing so compasses don't always work correctly."

"They don't?" Max asked.

Sam shrugged. "Harold Grantz, that's the professor, thinks there might be a large iron deposit, like a meteorite hit there at some point. He gave me directions: Forest Road 63, three miles south of the lake. Park and hike."

"That last bit gets somewhat vague," Max said. "So they spent that day out in the middle of nowhere."

"Well, Jubilee Lake is a popular spot," Sam said. "It's well-stocked with rainbow trout, has a boat ramp, campground, picnic tables, and a footpath. They could have spent part of the day there and met up with someone."

Max winced. "But the population isn't constant, so we probably won't find witnesses to any meeting."

"At least it was only last week," Ukiah said. "There might be someone still at the campground that saw them."

"We better hit it tomorrow, then," Max said.

"What about where Alicia was camped?" Sam asked.

"I talked to the FBI about that." Max earned a surprised

look from Ukiah. "Since this is now a kidnapping, and we might not be here for the full course of the investigation, I thought that we should work with them as much as possible."

Max gave Ukiah an "I'm handling it" look in return as he spoke. Better Max than him. Ukiah supposed it was for the best—if they walked too meekly, the FBI might think they were up to something. As his Mom Lara often said of his baby sister, those who are quiet are often into the worst trouble.

"So, did they say *anything*?" Sam clearly thought this was a waste of time.

Max leaned back from his quail. "Not much, just that the search efforts, and especially the shooting, spooked away everyone at the girls' campground. The FBI has a list of who was there, and is trying to find them for questioning now." He glanced to Ukiah. "How did you do, kid?"

"The Underground Tour seems to be a bust," Ukiah said. "The tour guide remembers her, but only vaguely. The Trading Shop is closed."

"Oh, yes; it's Saturday," Sam said. "They're at flea markets on Saturdays."

That mystery solved. "But the woman at the bead shop remembered her, and that took me out to the cultural institute with Cassidy Kicking Deer." Ukiah was unsure how much he should say in front of Sam. It was going to be tricky to dance all around the truth. "They have a photograph of the lost Kicking Deer boy. Alicia apparently saw how much it looked like me. She took it down and found the name in the back."

"Which is?" Max asked.

"Magic Boy. It also listed date of death, but Cassidy says that there isn't a death record on file."

"Obits. Wasn't there a comment on Ukiah obits?" Max took out the daily planner and flipped through. "Here. *Ukiah history: obits.*"

"This is the kid that disappeared in 1933, right?" Sam got nods from both Max and Ukiah. "You look that much like him?"

"Not now." Ukiah tried not to squirm in his seat. "The photograph taken when I was found does. Cassidy was the one that figured out that Alicia could have seen the picture and made the connection."

"So, your family has this weird genetic weakness for disappearing into the wilderness and running with a pack of wolves?" Sam asked.

"Well, yes," Ukiah said unhappily.

Sam shook her head. "It's amazing you keep finding girls to overlook that little oddity and produce the next generation to get lost all over again."

Max coughed. "Alicia asked the post office clerk if they knew anyone by the name of Kicking Deer." He consulted his PDA. "He told her that Elaine Kicking Deer works at the Watering Hole on Fridays and Saturdays."

"She's a waitress," Sam said. "The Watering Hole is across town."

"Being tonight is Saturday," Max said, "it would be best if we work the crowd, see if anyone saw or talked to Alicia."

"The crowd there tends to be a little rough around the edge," Sam said. "They drink to get drunk."

"Then we definitely all should hit this one," Max said. "In case one of us needs backup."

CHAPTER TWELVE

The Watering Hole, Pendleton, Oregon
Saturday, August 28, 2004

The Watering Hole was a sprawling set of buildings down by the shallow Umatilla River. The ceilings were low, smoke from a dozen different brands of cigarettes hazed the air, the rooms were dark, and the darkness was cut mostly by the neon lights of beer logos. The jukebox played at deafening levels. Max and Ukiah had trawled through bars like this in Pittsburgh, usually smaller in size, looking for skips. Most of the crowd was just the poorer ranks of good average people. Mixed in was a rougher crowd. Unfortunately, it was difficult to tell the good from bad. It amazed Ukiah sometimes that the rougher-looking of two men might be the hardworking father of four just looking for a drink or two before heading home. What gathered them together in a room so dark that it was hard to see who you were with, with noise so loud that you had to shout to be heard?

They found Elaine Kicking Deer weaving through a crowd of mostly men, doing an amazing balancing act with glasses filled with alcohol. She was remarkably blond and blue-eyed, although dusky-skinned, and had a look around her eyes that said that she had some ethnic blood. She nodded to Sam, and eyed Ukiah with interest.

"So this is him? The incredible stud muffin, Wolf Boy?"

"Me?" Ukiah pressed a startled hand to his chest.

"Stud muffin?" Sam echoed uneasily.

Elaine laughed, deftly avoiding an already staggering patron to keep her drinks intact. "I would think by now, Sammie, you would know how small a town this is."

Sam threw a glance at Ukiah that almost seemed angry, then grew puzzled at whatever she saw on his face. "So?"

Elaine only laughed more, delivering the drinks around a crowded booth, nodding as the customers asked for nachos, wings, and a drink for a late arrival. The private investigators hung back, letting her work.

"What have you heard about my partner?" Max asked.

"A hell of lot more than about you," Elaine said to Max, heading for the bar. "Between my family and the men in town, you'd think only one man flew in from Pittsburgh, not three."

"What men?" Sam asked.

"Ricky Barkley, for one," Elaine said.

This was a new name for Ukiah, and apparently an unexpected one for Sam. She looked even more puzzled.

"What is this Barkley saying?" Mix asked.

Elaine held up a finger, leaned across the bar, and repeated the drink order from the table. "He's here somewhere. Ask him yourself. I've got work to do."

"We want to ask you questions about Alicia Kraynak." Ukiah pushed the conversation back to Alicia. "We've been told that she came to talk to you last week."

"Yeah, she was here," Elaine shouted over the din. "Look, let me get these orders in, and I'll be back out to talk to you."

Elaine vanished into the kitchen, already calling out food orders.

Max leaned in close to Sam to ask, "Who is Ricky Barkley? Do you see him?"

Sam scanned the room. "If he's here, he's in one of the other rooms. He's a jerk. He went to school with my ex. Then again, almost everyone has some connection to Peter. He works the night shift at the flour mill and lives up on South Nye, just down from the Red Lion. I served him papers once on a bad debt. I haven't seen him in months."

"Any idea how he would know Ukiah?"

Sam shook her head. Elaine came sailing out of the

kitchen, holding aloft a tray of food in her left hand, and three plates stacked up her right arm. She delivered the food to a table on the other side of the bar from the booth, taking in new requests as she placed dishes in front of seated people. She came to drop drink orders at the bar, then turned back to them.

"Okay, the girl was here last Saturday night. She'd been out to the Tamástslikt and saw the photo of Magic Boy. I told my mother that was a bad idea and that Pap-pap shouldn't have loaned it out."

"And Alicia told you about Ukiah."

"Yeah, but I didn't believe her," Elaine said. "Magic Boy's been missing for like eighty years, and most of us didn't believe those family legends. Jared is one of the biggest unbelievers, so if stud muffin here"—she patted Ukiah on the arm—"has him convinced, that's good enough for me. I told Alicia, though, that there was no way he could be Magic Boy."

"What did *she* tell you?" Ukiah asked.

"She had a few beers, waiting for me to have time to talk, and she got a little sloshed. She told me how cute you are and how she had a huge crush on you and how some old Chinese-Hawaiian-White-Russian bitch snatched you out of the cradle when she had the decency to leave you there."

Max burst out laughing.

"Indigo isn't old," Ukiah protested. "She's twenty-six."

"Yeah, that's the name. Indigo. It didn't sound Chinese to me." Elaine gathered up drinks, preparing to move off. "And I didn't want to touch the White Russian bit with a ten-foot pole. Talk about old grudges."

"Did she talk to anyone else?" Ukiah asked.

"I don't know," Elaine said. "One of the other girls had called in sick and I barely had time to sneeze. Lot of the same people are here tonight. Maybe someone else noticed her talking to someone."

"Is it always this crowded?" Max asked.

Sam was shaking her head, even as Elaine said, "No, things are building up for the roundup."

With that Elaine hurried off again.

Max caught the look on Ukiah's face and laughed again. "Kid, you're fated to be thought of as much younger than you really are."

"Well, it's starting to really suck," Ukiah said. "What did she mean about White Russian?"

"Milk, vodka, and Kahlua," Sam said with a grin.

Max threw Sam an amused warning look that said "cute, but don't confuse the boy." "White Russians are a political party, like Republicans. Kraynak's grandfather went afoul of them in Czechoslovakia during the Russian civil war. I'm not sure if I followed the whole mess, but it's the reason the Kraynaks are in Pennsylvania instead of the old country."

"Chinese, Hawaiian, Russian? That's one mutt puppy you date," Sam said. "She's probably pretty, though. It's like God is trying to tell us something when the most beautiful people in the world are racially mixed."

"Like yourself," Max quipped, and then seemed to regret it. "Let's split up. If we descend in a herd, we'll spook people."

So they scattered, hoping to find anyone that saw Alicia the week before. More people were drifting in through the front door, making the place even more crowded as the private investigators drifted apart. Ukiah had worked his way into another room, flashing Alicia's photograph and getting no answers.

"Did you see this woman last week?" he asked a tall, dark-haired man with a scar running up from his eye like an exclamation point.

"Hey!" The man grabbed Ukiah by the front of his shirt, and shoved Ukiah sideways into a knot of men and women; who parted and regrouped to surround Ukiah and his captor. "This is the guy, Peter!"

Peter Talbot perched on a bar stool, flanked close by the watching locals, like a king and his court. "What the hell are you talking about, Ricky?"

"Sam's Harley was parked outside of the Red Lion all night, and then she came out with *this* guy." Ricky was heavily muscled and putting it to use to hold Ukiah still.

"Sam and him were all lovey-dovey and kissy-face in the parking lot."

A howl went up from Talbot's court, a dangerous sound, promising trouble. It attracted the attention of more men and women, who formed a second rank of onlookers.

"Sam finally got nailed," Ricky laughed. "Looks like you're going to be eating sloppy seconds, Talbot."

"Asshole!" Peter Talbot breathed a fog of whiskey in Ukiah's direction. "I told you to leave my wife alone."

"She's not your wife," Ukiah started to protest.

Ricky gave Ukiah a shake. "Shut up, adulterer!"

"I'm amazed that you can put that many syllables together, Ricky." Sam made her way to Ukiah's side, earning a laugh from some of the crowd.

"Shut up, slut!" Ricky pushed her back into the crowd. "You act so prissy, but you spread for the first pretty-boy Indian that came sniffing after you."

Sam hauled back and punched him.

Ricky went down and was pulled to his feet by his jeering friends. "You're lucky, slut, that I don't hit women."

"Well, then, this fight should be easy for me." Sam punched him again.

A second laugh went up from the onlookers, and one man called, "Get him, Sam!" but a woman plunged through the crowd, shouting, "You bitch!" to launch herself at Sam. Ukiah ducked a grab from Peter and a punch from Ricky but caught a jab to his left eye from one of Peter's court. There were simply too many hands to dodge them all.

There was a deep, menacing growl from behind him, and the smell of wolf hit him. The men facing Ukiah caught sight of what was coming and suddenly scrambled backward.

Ukiah turned.

Rennie Shaw towered over most of the men around Ukiah by a head. Black-haired, dressed in leather pants and a long, leather duster, he blended into the shadows except for the doglike gleam of his eyes. He stalked forward, men parting as if shoved back by an invisible shield. Ukiah knew

there was no power there except fear. The leader of the Dog
Warriors exuded menace that had even Ukiah backing up.

"Rennie!"

In a grab faster than any man could move, Rennie caught
Ukiah by the throat, thumbs crushing down on his windpipe,
and lifted him up off the ground.

"Wait!" Ukiah tried to say, but it came out as "Urk!"

"Did you sleep with his woman, cub?"

"I'm not *his* woman, and it's no one's business but mine
who I slept with," Sam stated, putting a gun to Rennie's
head, her voice tight but level. "Put him down," she ordered
calmly. "You're crushing his windpipe. You might kill him
even if that's not your intent."

Peter Talbot grinned from behind Sam. "You spend a lot
of time protecting your new boyfriend, Sammie Anne."

"Shut up, Peter," Sam said without taking her eyes from
Rennie. "Don't mess with me when I'm pissed. You know
what happens."

"Well?" Rennie asked, mind to mind. *"Did you have in-
tercourse?"*

*"No. We did sleep in a big bed together, but I was
wounded. Nothing happened."*

Rennie put Ukiah down. "Fine. Keep it that way."

Sam tucked away her gun, cautiously, swearing softly.

"Hey, you're not going to let him go?" Ricky reached for
Ukiah.

Rennie caught Ricky under the arm and flung him backward over the bar. Peter yelled and started for Rennie. Rennie reached under his leather duster and pulled out a
sawed-off shotgun with the flair of a magician producing a
rabbit. He leveled it at the local men, thumbing back the
hammers. The men jerked to a halt.

"Someone in this town shot my boy." Rennie growled
softly. "I'm here to make sure no one messes with him
again."

"I think it's time to leave," Max sang softly into Ukiah's
ear, pulling him backward. He had Sam by the elbow.

"What about Ukiah's father?" Sam sounded like she was

asking for form's sake, not like she actually wanted anything to do with Rennie.

"Let the maniac get himself out of this," Max said. "The more distance we put between us and him, the better."

They had left Sam's Harley by the courthouse park, with the statue of Sheriff Til Taylor watching over it. Max parked behind the motorcycle and they got out. Under the spread of the trees, the park was now a pool of dark stillness. Sam disturbed the night's calm by pacing the sidewalk, shaking excess energy out of her hands.

"What the hell was all that macho crap about?" she demanded, her voice tight with anger. "Why did he grab Ukiah like that? Why does he care if the kid slept with me or not? Why is everyone suddenly going apeshit about my sex life?"

Ukiah looked to Max, helpless to explain Rennie's attack in any reasonable terms. Rennie's reactions were wrapped tight around Ontongard biology, alien invasion tactics, and Ukiah's status as the only breeder ever created on Earth.

Once the Ontongard left their home world, they discovered that hosts on subsequent planets usually died, instead of becoming Gets. The Ontongard off-balanced this problem with newly stolen knowledge of genetic manipulation, turning weapons aimed at them to their advantage. All following invasions started with creating half-breeds, children with a mix of alien and native genetics, breeders able to mate with the native life and create children with certain genetic weaknesses. The breeders themselves could resist the Ontongard infection—too like their fathers to succumb—but the next generation made perfect hosts.

Ukiah had been the only breeder created before his father, Prime, destroyed the scout ship that brought Hex and Prime to Earth. The Pack had thought Ukiah killed in the scout ship's destruction and were horrified to discover he wasn't. Their first response was to try and kill him. Luckily, Rennie noticed that despite Ukiah's nearly two hundred years of sexual maturity, he had no children.

The Dog Warriors had been willing to let a nonbreeding

breeder live. They even allowed Ukiah to continue his relationship with Indigo, with liberal use of birth control.

The Pack would not, however, allow him to take a second lover. They would kill Ukiah first.

How to explain any of that to Sam?

"We warned you." Max pulled out his cigar case, a sure sign that he was rattled. "Shaw is dangerous."

"I just pulled a gun in a bar!" Sam was fighting to keep calm. "I can lose my carry permit over this. I can get arrested for this. I want to know why."

Max focused his attention on lighting his cigar. "Shaw has issues; they're between him and Ukiah. If I'd known he was coming, I wouldn't have asked you to take care of Ukiah. You're better off not getting involved with Shaw."

"Hello! I just put a gun to the man's head!" Realization flashed over Sam's face, filling her eyes with fear. "Shit! I just pulled a gun on a homicidal lunatic."

"Rennie won't hold that against you." Ukiah offered what scant comfort he could. "He'll probably respect you for standing up to him and appreciate you coming to my rescue."

"Yeah, sure." Sam shook a finger in Max's direction. "This is the same man that Max just called dangerous?"

Max took a deep drag on the cigar, and then breathed twin columns of smoke out his nose. Another drag and he had chosen his words, and began to speak. "Rennie's part of a paramilitary group known as the Pack. They have objectives you're better off not knowing. All their crimes stem from those activities. They're not crazy. They're not random killers. I wouldn't have left the bar if I thought there was real chance of Rennie killing those idiots. He'll rough them up, scare them good, and leave."

"You're sure of that?"

Max shrugged. "Reasonably."

"Rennie won't kill an innocent bystander," Ukiah said with some truth. The full truth was if Rennie couldn't avoid the killing, he would take anyone down, just making it quick and clean as possible. There just wasn't any reason, though, that Rennie would need to kill anyone at the bar.

"He *is* dangerous," Max repeated. "But by protecting Ukiah, you've probably earned yourself a great deal of immunity. Just don't sleep with Ukiah, and things will be fine."

"You're making that last part up," Sam said.

"No, he's not," Ukiah said quietly. "Rennie might have killed me if we had sex."

"Why?"

"There are some things you're better off not knowing," Max said.

Sam gazed at Max who screened himself with smoke. "Okay," she said, after trying to search his features for some answer to her questions. "I should have known when you weren't there chewing on Shaw's head for hurting your partner, that I didn't need to get all excited. I chose to pull my gun. You keep your secrets—I'll keep mine—this relationship is for a short haul. But if you lie to me, Bennett, I'll teach you the meaning of regret."

Max took another drag on his cigar.

Sam narrowed her eyes. "This is where you're supposed to say, 'Yes, madam, I won't lie to you.'"

"Ask me no questions, and I'll tell you no lies," Max said quietly.

"That's a shitty answer."

"It's the only truthful one I can give you."

"Men!" Sam turned to Ukiah. "Well, Wolf Boy? Do you have any oblique and obtuse comments you want to add?"

Ukiah shook his head.

"I thought as much," Sam grumbled, then headed toward her Harley. "I'm tired. I'm going home and sleep by myself!"

Annoyance flashed across Max's face. He raised a hand in farewell to Sam as she pulled away, sweeping them with her motorcycle's headlight.

"Sorry, Max," Ukiah said when darkness cloaked them again.

Max snorted, flaring his cigar tip to red brilliance. "The old adage applies here, kid—you can't pick your relatives."

The prickle of Pack sense swept over him, indicating that

Rennie had moved into his range of awareness and was looking for him. *Cub?*

"Rennie is looking for me. I should talk to him. Maybe alone—he might be fairly hyped by the fight."

Max cursed softly, not answering Ukiah directly. He went instead to the Blazer, opened the back and got one of the tracers. "Put this on. I want to be able to find you—especially if you're going to be alone with him. Call me if you need help."

Rennie came out of the shadows, his duster flaring out as he walked. He carried a small pack, which might have held clothes or explosives—one could never be sure with Rennie. Ukiah knew that the Pack leader probably had already secreted guns, ammo, food, and gear close at hand.

"You've been a tricky one to find today." Rennie dropped the pack and opened his arms, the sudden violence at the bar ignored since it couldn't be forgotten without bloodshed.

And despite everything, Ukiah found himself pleased to see the leader of the Dog Warriors. He hugged Rennie tightly and was pounded on the back with rough affection. Under cigarette smoke, spilled liquor, and coat leather, Ukiah could smell Rennie's wolf-tainted scent. The gruff welcome ended with a light bite on his ear, a slight reminder of his place as child among the Pack.

"You didn't have to come!" Ukiah said.

"Yes, I did. You are too alone here."

"I have Max."

"Cub, think. If you land in a hospital mortally wounded, as soon as you die, they will cut you open to see what killed you. Remember what happened to Janet Haze. They gutted her and took out all her organs and weighed them individually."

Ukiah shuddered, his individual organs reacting to such a fate. "Max will keep me—"

"Cub," Rennie caught Ukiah and shook him hard. "He's just a mortal man. One blow to the head, knocking him out, and he'll no longer be there for you."

Ukiah hunched his shoulders up against the idea of Max being hurt. "Why did you come alone, then?"

"I left the Dogs to watch over your little one," Rennie said. "The Demon Curs are the closest gang, but I trust Degas as far as I can spit him. I've given him plenty of reasons to hate me."

One of Rennie's memories darted through Ukiah's thoughts, and he caught hold of it.

. . . Cold rain pounded on Rennie's shoulders as he gazed down at Degas's body, blood pouring out into the mud. The watching Dogs and Curs growled at each other. He'd better check that, or they'd be at each other's throats in a moment . . .

"You killed him," Ukiah said as surprise jolted through him. The memory was from the 1930s, the last time Rennie and Degas fought against the Ontongard together.

This past June, Rennie had called a gathering of the five Pack clans for a desperate battle against Hex. For over a century, the Pack believed that Prime had destroyed the Ontongard mother ship. The truth was that the damaged ship had landed on Mars with the entire crew locked in cryogenic sleep by Prime. Hex had a remote key that would have allowed him to wake the crew—if the ship's protective shields were lowered. The Ontongard had manipulated the development of human technology for decades to bring about the Mars Rover, and then adapted it for their needs.

Only four of the clans fought Hex, and they nearly lost. The modified Rover lowered the mother ship's shields, and Hex used his remote key. Ukiah had replaced Hex's program, however, with one that self-destructed the ship— snatching victory out of the jaws of defeat.

The Demon Curs were the only clan missing during that battle. Considering Rennie's and Degas's history, Ukiah wondered now if the Curs' absence had been by chance or design.

"Chance," Rennie answered him. "Too much was riding on that. If Hex managed to wake the sleeping crew, Earth would have never withstood the following invasion. Much as Degas hates me, I know he would have set it aside to stop Hex."

Ukiah looked at Rennie skeptically.

"Remember, cub," Rennie turned to stare at him with eyes cold as gunmetal, "under it all Degas and I are nearly the same creature."

"If you're one and the same, why did you kill Degas?"

"To teach him a lesson. Your father's blood gave us the ability to be individuals if we're given the room. What we grow into depends much on the human that we were. Degas was a cutthroat pirate, devious and ruthless, with willpower made of steel. As a Get, he's extremely effective at fighting Ontongard—which is why I didn't destroy him completely."

"It just seems a little extreme to kill him. Did it help any?"

"Made me feel better." Rennie gave a wolfish grin. "And it did drive a point through Degas's thick head—stop trying to make massive numbers of Gets."

"So it worked?"

"Not completely." Rennie sobered. "There is necessary killing, and then there is wanton slaughter. Sometimes it's a fine line between the two. Those of us who were trained military men or law officers can walk the line—we do what needs to be done and no more. Degas often walks the wrong side."

Rennie jerked his chin in the direction of the Watering Hole. "Degas probably would have laid waste to that bar tonight and killed your gutsy woman friend on suspicion alone. You're lucky I'm the one that found you in June, not him."

Ukiah had Rennie's memories from the day that the Pack hunted Ukiah down and closed for the kill. He knew how much he owed to Rennie's compassion. "Degas would have killed me."

"Degas would have killed everyone that ever met you."

Ukiah staggered back, stunned. "Why?"

"Have you never questioned why the wolf dogs attacked Hex's Get disguised as you? How they knew it wasn't you and that Hex's Get meant harm to your family?"

"No," Ukiah whispered, suddenly afraid to hear the reason.

"Your blood has gotten into those dogs and changed them, cub. They nipped and bit and drew your blood, didn't they?"

"They're my Gets?"

"No." Rennie shifted uneasily. "I'm not sure what they are. Your blood should have made them Gets; at least it would have, if you were a normal breeder. Your father might be the reason."

"You think because Prime was a mutation, that I—I—I'm what?"

"You *are* a breeder. But your father's mutation has put a few spins on things. Certainly there's no memory in all of Ontongard history of blood crawling back out of a host before Hex tried to make Max into your Get."

Ukiah shuddered with the perfect memory of finding the syringe that had contained his own blood—and its needle tainted with Max's. He'd never known grief so great as that moment, when he was sure that his true Max was gone, replaced by an alien mockery.

Max's salvation was that very love that Ukiah had for him. All of Ukiah, every single half-alien cell of him, refused to harm Max. Instead of propagating through Max's body, Ukiah's injected blood gathered into a long, thin worm and crawled back out of Max.

"Thank God it did!" Ukiah said. "Maybe I can't make a Get! Maybe my blood will always—"

Rennie gripped his shoulder hard, to the point bones threatened to crack. "Don't even think it, because then you'll start believing it. The fact you heal up even from the dead and form blood mice says that you *can* create a Get."

"Okay, okay."

Rennie released the pressure and rubbed away the hurt. "The dogs can die, and they don't form mice."

"What did you do to my moms' dogs?"

"We only killed one."

"One! Mom Jo is going to freak!"

"If their blood were as dangerous as mine, wouldn't you want your family to know?"

"Yes! But did you have to kill one?"

Rennie shrugged. "It was important to be thorough."

"Oh, shit! I'm going to have to call her and tell her. Which one did you kill?"

Rennie gave him the dog's name, thankfully not one of Mom Jo's favorites of those that survived the June slaughter. This was still going to crush her; she thought of the half-breed dogs as unfortunate children, and had rescued them from shelters across the country. Ukiah imagined her pain and scrubbed the tears out of his eyes before Rennie saw them. Rennie, of course, noticed.

"That's why we let you live." Rennie rumpled his hair. "Because you have compassion. Yours is a human heart, and it's filled with a great deal of goodness."

"So, what did my alien blood do to the dogs?" He couldn't keep the bitterness out of his voice.

"It seems to have mutated them to something similar to what your children will be like—if you ever have any."

Ukiah winced. He had Kittanning, but his son was identical to him in every way except memories. He had witnessed his sister growing inside his Mom Lara and the joyful mysteries that surrounded her. What sex would the child be? What color hair? Even after she was born, the questions continued. How tall would Cally grow to be? Would she be good at school? What would she want to be when she grew up?

If he married Indigo, the only way she would ever experience the same wondrous unknown of a child would be by allowing another man to father it.

Rennie tipped up Ukiah's chin to meet his eyes. *Maybe one day you can father a natural child. Hex is dead. If we ever eliminate the Ontongard completely . . . children aren't a complete impossibility.*

For a few moments, he was pleased, and then realization slipped in. "So, like my kids, wouldn't the wolf dogs be perfect hosts for Gets?"

Rennie sighed and turned away. "Yes, they are."

"You made it a Get?" He caught Rennie's arm and pulled him back to face him. "That's what you did, didn't you? You made it a Get! But you said you killed it. As a perfect host, it should have easily survived the infection."

Touching, skin to skin, he felt Rennie's revulsion and caught a flash of memory: of having the dog before them, animal in intelligence, wolf in nature, Pack in every other regard.

"We couldn't bear letting it live." Rennie's voice was husky with emotion. "It was like holding a mirror constantly in front of you so you can see the monster that you are."

CHAPTER THIRTEEN

Pendleton, Oregon
Sunday, August 29, 2004

Max glowered as Rennie made himself comfortable on the hotel room's floor. In the morning, Max and Ukiah planned to drive out to Jubilee Lake. Sam had volunteered to play native guide, and Max gladly accepted. Rennie said nothing of the trip, but he joined them at breakfast at Shari's, making the normally cheerful waitresses nervous with his dangerous looks.

"This case has nothing to with the Pack." Max added milk to his coffee until it was tan. "If you come along, you'll probably scare the locals."

"I came out here to keep an eye on the cub. I can't do that from thirty miles away."

"I don't suppose I'll get any answers if I asked why he calls Ukiah 'cub'?" Sam asked the table and received closed looks from all the men. "Okay. That's what I thought. Why doesn't Ukiah take tall, dark, and scary to the Big Sink while Max and I question people at the lake?"

Max glowered some more at Rennie, obviously not happy. Finally, he sighed, "Fine! We'll take both cars."

But just as they were about to split up, Max pulled Ukiah aside and checked that he had the tracer on.

Whereas traveling south from Pendleton to the town of Ukiah had been a slow climb up into steep hills, going east up into the Blue Mountains was a stunning transition. At Weston, both cars turned off the almost-flat Route 11 and started to climb the first mountain on 204. Within five miles, they rounded a corner for a view that stretched for twenty miles out over the plateau. In another five miles, there was a scenic viewpoint, looking west into the heart of the mountains as if the plateau never existed. Pines leapt up, a hundred feet tall, crowding close to the road, and the wind-swept treeless plain was forgotten. Another ten miles, and they turned off onto a road of packed dirt, and civilization fell behind.

"This is the Oregon I remember," Ukiah said.

"This part doesn't look much different than when I first saw it," Rennie said as he gazed out the passenger windows.

Ukiah sensed that Rennie was scanning the mountains for something as they drove along the forest road. "What are you looking for?"

"What I always look for in Oregon." Rennie continued to gaze out the window. "The scout ship. There's a hole in our memory, of how it came down and where exactly it landed."

A hole would indicate that Prime had been injured and never recovered the memories. "Do you think it crashed?"

"Prime would have tried to destroy it before it reached Earth. It would make sense that he did something that made the landing rough. They certainly didn't land on the plains."

"You sure?"

Rennie barked a laugh. "No. We're not sure of anything. It's all mixed up and full of holes. Who knows what happened!"

Max had taught Ukiah problem-solving. Always make sure, he said, you knew what was supposed to happen before you try to determine where things went wrong.

"Well, we know how it should have gone," Ukiah said. "Hexadecimal—all six of Hex—was to explore the landing site of the mother ship. Check it for geographical anomalies. Secure it against native life, yada, yada, yada." To steal one of Max's phrases—the memories he shared with Rennie had a complete command list for the mission. "Prime managed to add himself to the crew." At that time, the Ontongard did not guard from attacks from within. They were, in essence, one sprawling creature. That part of itself would attack the whole had been unimaginable for the Ontongard. "We can recall the scout ship's approach, and then something must have gone wrong, because after that, Prime only remembers one Hex."

Rennie grunted an affirmation. "And Prime diverted that one Hex by sending him after the native life to start up a breeding program."

Ukiah found himself blushing slightly. "Which is where I come in."

Rennie scratched at his nose, thinking aloud. "Hex needed to get the Mars Rover within seven hundred feet of the mother ship in order to lower the shields. With human technology, the only way Hex could have positioned the Rover with that accuracy was via a transmission from the mother ship itself—sometime before the shields went up—giving its location."

"Knowing that the mother ship was intact on Mars," Ukiah followed the line of logic, "Hex probably would have taken the scout ship to Mars if it was capable of lifting off."

"But instead, he started a breeding program."

"So the damage was great enough that he committed himself for the duration," Ukiah said.

"Which leaves the question, where is the scout ship?" Rennie waved at the soaring mountains. "We've never found trace of it. They were aiming for the plateau prairie between the Cascade Mountains and the Blue Mountains. We think they missed, but they might have hit hard, somewhere close to a river, which later eroded the crash site. Or they went down in mountains. Our first outdoor memory from Prime is in the mountains, but he's already airborne and running at that point—and which mountains?"

"Coyote doesn't know?"

Rennie laughed. "Doesn't know, doesn't care. Despite the centuries he's been in human form, he's more wolf than man. What matters to him is *now*. He can't even tell us when Prime made him a Get. He spent countless days drifting as a Pack-blooded wolf, and then, once he started to change into a man, he lived years with the natives, mostly the Nez Percé. They're the ones that named him Coyote. He remembers Lewis and Clark, who came through Oregon in 1805, which gives us at least one date."

"Who?"

Rennie gave him a hard look. "Think on it a moment, cub."

So he did, and in Rennie's memories found a boyhood fascination with two explorers, the first white men to find passage to the West Coast.

"So, I was born before 1805." Ukiah glanced at Rennie. Rennie's boyhood had been in 1840s, shortly before the Civil War. When Coyote had found Rennie dying on a battlefield, Rennie had been in his early twenties. Rennie had "aged" less than a decade since then, but he was clearly a man, whereas Ukiah was arguably still a boy.

"Aye, cub, you're older than I am."

My life is so weird, Ukiah thought.

Rennie laughed.

Max and Sam in the first car turned off for Jubilee Lake. With Rennie navigating, Ukiah and Rennie continued until they found Forest Road 63, another narrow dirt track winding through the forest. Ukiah measured three miles via the trip meter and pulled off into a rough parking space.

It was the first time Ukiah worked with someone who could sense everything that he could. Rennie found where the women had parked Kraynak's Volkswagen and like two bloodhounds, they followed the grad student's trail. Where the girls separated, Rennie took Rose's track, while Ukiah kept to Alicia's trail.

Judging by the way the women had meandered over the valley, their directions had been not been very clear.

"What exactly were they looking for?"

"A hole in the ground, I think," Ukiah said.

"Are we talking groundhog-sized? Or something bigger?"

Ukiah stopped on an outscropping of rock. "Something bigger." He motioned down at the sunken earth before him. "Like that, I'm guessing."

Rennie bounded easily up the rocks to his side and whistled in his surprise.

Ukiah crouched down, picked up a pebble and tossed it out into the massive rocky depression. He knew it was only because they talked about the scout ship that this seemed to be a likely crash site. Both the Ontongard and the Pack had scoured Oregon, Washington, and Idaho—surely they would have investigated such an obvious spot.

"First time I've seen this," Rennie murmured, apparently reading Ukiah's thoughts. "I was on horseback last time I was in these mountains—this spot hasn't been this easily reached before."

Considering the rough dirt road and hike, Ukiah wouldn't consider it accessible. Surely, though, the ship's landing site couldn't be so well-known that two college students from Pennsylvania could so easily find it. And yet—

"Do you really think it's the ship?" Ukiah picked up fist-sized rock and sent it after the pebble.

"Perhaps."

"How can we find out if it is the ship?"

"I'd rather leave it lost and buried," Rennie said, "rather than dig it up and try to keep it safe from the Ontongard *and* the humans."

Ukiah looked up at him in surprise. "So why look for the ship, then?"

"To make sure that the Ontongard don't have it."

Ukiah chilled at the thought of the Ontongard having access to the scout ship, its weapons and technology. "Do you think that's why the Ontongard keep coming back to Pendleton? They know where the scout ship is?"

"Actually, I don't think they do. Hex would have focused all his energy into its repair instead of fiddling with the Mars Rover."

Ukiah frowned at the weak logic. "Using the Rover means humans do all the work of getting to Mars. To repair the scout ship to the point of being able to take off would mean exposing it to lots of curious noses, and not just the Pack's."

Rennie considered for a long time in silence, staring down at the massive depression that might be hiding the alien ship. Ukiah could sense Rennie's mind sorting through centuries of action and reaction, plots and sabotage, starting with Prime leaving the mother ship. Prime's nature of laying plan within plan was in fact an Ontongard habit, stemming from the fact they could think on multiple subjects at once. Luckily,

Prime's rebellion had instilled in Hex a self-paranoia; the creature mistrusted all its Earth-born Gets and limited his strategies to those conceived by the one wholly alien unit. Still, with hundreds of Gets to carry out his schemes, the sheer number of interwoven plots were staggering.

The Pack simply destroyed anything that smacked of Hex, without trying to step through the alien logic. Rennie now tried to see the greater design.

After a long time of thinking, Rennie said quietly, "Hex wanted *you*. If he had the scout ship, he could repair the ovipositor and make breeders based on his genetics. If he could hope to make a single breeder, he wouldn't need you. I've dealt with his Gets long enough to know that Hex would rather cut off his arm and burn it than to allow something of Prime's to live. Tainted as you are by your father's blood, he would have wanted you only if he had no other choice."

After searching the area thoroughly, Ukiah and Rennie rejoined Max and Sam, who were also calling it a day. All of the current campers claimed that they arrived after Alicia's visit to the Big Sink. There was simply no indication that the graduate students had ever been to the lake.

On the way back to Pendleton, they stopped at the Tollgate Mini Market and Café. The women that owned the store hadn't seen the girls, which, considering Alicia had filled the van on the morning of their trip, wasn't surprising.

Sam used the restroom as the men eyed plaster-cast footprints of Bigfoot hanging on the walls. The older of the two women was telling Max about the Bigfoot sightings when Ukiah's phone rang.

"Oregon." Ukiah moved off into the darkened café for a little privacy.

"This is Jared Kicking Deer. You wanted to see my grandfather?"

"Yes."

"If you come out to the farm, you can meet him."

*   *   *

Jesse Kicking Deer was the oldest man that Ukiah had ever seen. His skin folded again and again like a prune's. He sat on the edge of the folding lawn chair, seeming too excited to relax into the green-and-white webbing. Cassidy had claimed that her grandfather was nearly a hundred; Ukiah had expected someone fragile with age. Jesse Kicking Deer radiated health, from thick white hair, sound teeth, and long hard fingernails.

"Is this him?" Jesse asked.

"Yes, Grandpa." Jared leaned in the doorway of the back porch. He had greeted Ukiah and Max at the front door, shown them through the house to the back porch where Jesse and Uncle Quince waited, and yet paused at the door, as if not wanting to commit fully to their presence. "He thinks he's Magic Boy. We think he might be too."

Jesse considered Ukiah with fierce dark eyes. "His face is very familiar." His wrinkled hands came up and moved through smooth hand signs. "The eyes. The nose. It's been so long. I did not think I would forget a face so loved."

"Father," Uncle Quince murmured in Nez Percé. "Kee-ji-nah is dead."

Kee-ji-nah was Cayuse, not Nez Percé. Magic Boy. The liquid syllables struck something deep inside Ukiah that resonated. *Kee-ji-nah. That's my name!*

"I saw him," Jesse replied to his son in Nez Percé while Ukiah sat dumbstruck. "After your brother was born. I hunted elk in the mountains, and I saw him. His hair was matted. His eyes were wild as the wolves. It was Kee-ji-nah. He did not know me. He ran away, frightened."

"Father, I've seen the *photographs*." The last word, in English, jarred against the native words Quince used. "He is dead."

"Then what happened to his body?" Jesse asked. "Why did it vanish?"

"It vanished?" Ukiah asked, feeling cold. "Were they sure he was dead?"

They looked at him, startled.

"How was he killed?" he pressed.

They continued to look at him in surprise. Ukiah wondered

why, then realized that he asked his questions in Nez Percé. There was anger gathering in Uncle Quince's face, as if Ukiah had intentionally eavesdropped when they thought they spoke in private. Trying to outrun that storm, Ukiah turned to the old man.

"Please," he begged in Nez Percé. "I've lost all my memories but those of running with the wolves. I want to know about my mother."

The old man shook his head, and said in English. "You talk too fast. The young ones, they speak the tongue of the white man. They fumble with our own language. I have not heard our tongue spoken like running water for so many years.

"When I was born, Magic Boy lived with my parents, and he cared for me. He changed my diapers. He put me down for naps. He rocked me to sleep. He kissed the little wounds. He played baby games with me. I loved him as much as I loved my father and mother, my grandparents. He seemed old and wise and wonderful.

"Then I grew older, into a boy, and he became my guide. He took me to the best wading holes. He showed me how to fish. He taught me how to track. He knew the stories and jokes old as the Blue Mountains that I, as a child, had never heard.

"When I got older, I started to wonder. Why didn't Magic Boy go to school? Why didn't we celebrate his birthday? Why did my father and grandfather call him Uncle, when he was so young? Who had been his parents? At first, my parents said that they would tell me when I was older. Then, when I was fourteen, and starting to pass my old clothes down to Uncle to wear, they started to tell me.

"Magic Boy had been born before the white man came to Oregon. He grew until he was twelve, and then, never grew older, never grew up. His mother had been my great-great-great-great-great-great-grandmother. It was family tradition, that the oldest son, when he had a home of his own and children needing care, would adopt Magic Boy, and the cycle would start again. My grandfather had been raised with Magic Boy's help, and my father, as were my brothers and I.

"Eventually, Uncle became like my little brother, to be

loved but barely tolerated as I entered the world of being an adult. I had my friends and dated girls. I was the oldest. When I married, and after my children were born, I would have taken Magic Boy to live with me, to help raise my sons and daughters as he had helped raise me."

Ukiah shifted uneasily. His mothers had explained once why they had gone through much fuss and bother to have his little sister, Cally. It was not enough, as a lesbian couple, to help raise their nieces and nephews, to always be a second-rank voice of authority, and second place in the children's heart. "Magic Boy had no children of his own?"

Jesse looked surprised at the question. "He could not. When he was young, before they knew he would not grow up, they sent him out for the manhood rituals. He was to fast until he saw his totem animal. Again and again, he would go out, but he never saw his spirit animal. He never became a man. He could not marry." Jesse gave a slight shrug. "Perhaps it was because the spirits knew he would not grow up."

But he had. It might be a painful way to grow older, with beatings and death, but at least he could move on. He had a son. He might marry soon. He might father more children. He was no longer locked into an endless childhood. "So, how did you lose him?"

Jesse took a deep breath and slid back into the chair with a sigh. "We did not take Uncle often to Pendleton. We did not want the white man to know of him. That day, the roundup was at Pendleton. That day, we took Uncle to Pendleton. That day, we dressed him in his finest clothes and took a picture. Until all my aunts and uncles, brothers and sisters died, we still argued among ourselves. 'Ah, you were supposed to watch. No, no, you were supposed to watch him.' He had been the thread that binds, and when he unraveled, so did the family."

"What happened?"

"Who knows? One minute he was there, waiting for the parade into the ring, the next he was gone. There was a white man with a camera, he heard the screams and found Magic Boy's body. He took pictures. People came and saw and left the body alone and when they came back, it was gone, all gone except his bloody clothes. We knew it was him from the clothes."

"The ones he was wearing in the photo?"

"Yes. We looked and looked and found no trace. The white man law said, 'There is no body, there is no crime,' and would not investigate.

"Seventy years, and it still makes me cry. Perhaps because his body vanished. Perhaps because his killing had been so brutal. Perhaps because he would not be dead of old age now. He would have raised my sons, my grandsons, my great-grandsons, and on. He would teach them to track, how to ride, how to beat the drums and sing, how to be truly Cayuse, as the Cayuse were before the white man came. He was a family legacy of love, generations of care, a hundred years or more of tradition, and he was gone."

"He is dead," Uncle Quince said, looking not at Ukiah but at Jared. "There were others that looked like a Cayuse."

"None have looked like Magic Boy," Jared said quietly. "I've seen enough to believe. He is Magic Boy."

"I *was* Magic Boy," Ukiah said quietly. "Whatever happened that day killed that part of me. I'm a different person now. I want to know where I came from, but I can't go back. I don't remember the way."

Pendleton Public Library, Pendleton, Oregon
Monday, August 30, 2004

By Alicia's planner and Rose's account, the grad students had visited Pendleton only four times. They spent three nights at the TraveLodge, showering, washing clothes, buying food, and relaxing separately, before returning to the primitive comfort of the tent. The fourth trip had been only to stop for gas and directions to find Jubilee Lake.

Between the three private investigators, they had already covered all the known locations at which Alicia *had* visited. At breakfast, Ukiah, Max, Sam, and Rennie guessed locations where Alicia *might* have stopped. (Rennie, with his years of hunting out Ontongard, proved to have well-honed detective skills.) They split the resulting list in three, with Rennie shadowing Ukiah, arranging to meet at the library in four hours.

Although they didn't discuss it, they were quickly coming to a dead end.

The library opened at eleven a.m. When they gathered there, none of them had found anything new of interest.

Max politely requested that Rennie make himself scarce. Rennie had changed over to blue jeans and a T-shirt, but he still managed to radiate menace. Perhaps it was the number of mysterious bulges where he kept weapons hidden. Rennie grinned and promised to keep out of sight.

The library itself was nearly one wide-open room. The business area was divided off with walls of glass. The circulation desk was to the immediate left of front door, a long L-shaped desk. A woman in her late teens or early twenties, with a long blond braid lying on her shoulder, checked in a stack of books.

Sam ambled to the counter, saying, "The microfilm sign-in card is here."

The woman at the desk looked up, saw it was Sam, nodded and continued working. Sam returned the nod, leaned over to pull open a card file drawer, and pulled out a card. Sam glanced over the card, then held it out to Max and Ukiah. "Look here."

Alicia's name occupied the last filled-in line, dated August 21. Apparently she had come straight from the Tamástslikt and the discovery of the photograph. Sam signed under Alicia's name.

The woman at the desk finished up her work and slid across the workspace to beam at Sam. "Hi, Sam."

"Hi, Millie." Sam tapped the card, showing that she signed it.

Millie leaned across the counter and whispered. "Is that him?"

"Him who?" Sam tucked the card back into the card file.

Millie leaned closer to Sam. "The guy Ricky saw you with outside of Red Lion? I heard he's a cousin of Jared Kicking Deer's."

"Don't believe everything you hear." Sam ducked her

head, a flush of red crawling up her neck to spread across her face.

Millie looked at Sam's face and giggled. "He's cute, but isn't he a little young for you?"

Sam tugged on Millie's braid. "What? You think he's more your age?"

Millie glanced at Ukiah, saw that he was listening, and dropped her eyes quickly. "You need a microfilm lens?"

"Yup."

Millie leaned down and fished out a square box. Inside the box, the lens almost looked like gears out of a toddler's construction set.

Sam led the way to the small microfilm room hidden behind the reference bookcases. Between the newspaper-stacked bookcases, the two microfilm machines, and several pale green filing cabinets, there was barely room for the four chairs in front of the readers. Ukiah stopped at the door, letting the other two work in the cramped quarters.

"The big one is the *East Oregonian,* the local paper." Sam indicated the larger of the filing cabinets. "The smaller cabinets are papers from Pilot Rock and other neighboring towns."

The dates of the newspapers were clearly labeled on the drawer fronts. Max found the correct time range and opened the drawer. He tapped over the square boxes with handwritten labels. "1931. 1932. February, 1933. November, 1933 through—it's not here." He indicated an open slot between February and November. "It should be here."

Sam looked up from inserting the lens into the first machine. "You're kidding."

Max shook his head, slowly rechecking the boxes. "No. It's gone."

"Maybe Alicia misfiled it." She joined in the hunt. "Maybe it got replaced under 1943."

Ukiah scanned the room from the door, but everything seemed neatly in place. He turned around and glanced over the reference bookcase behind him. The words "Native America" caught his eye. *Native America in the Twentieth Century—an Encyclopedia, Mary B. Davis, R 970.004 N213.*

America, not American. What was the difference? Beside the encyclopedia was a book labeled *World War II—America At War, 1941-1945, Norman Polmar, R 940.5302 P776*. He stared at the library code on the spine. It was the same pattern as the cryptic numbers in Alicia's daily planner. He went off in search for the matching books.

OR 364.1523 B26 was a slim book, crudely bound, with only the number visible. He took it down and discovered the title. *The Death of Magic* by Hannah Barnhart. Alicia's presence salted the cover. She had handled it for a long period. He opened to the title page. *The Death of Magic: Injustice of the Kicking Deer Murder.* In the center were photographs. At first he couldn't grasp what he was looking at, they seemed surreally disjointed photos of body parts clothed in blood-soaked rags. It wasn't until he hit the beheaded torso that he realized they were pictures of a dismembered child.

"What's this?" Max asked as Ukiah handed it wordlessly to him.

"My death as Magic Boy."

Max glanced at the title page, found the photographs, and gave a slight noise of disgust. He shut the book. "God."

Ukiah wished he hadn't looked at the photos. They remained now in his memory, crisp and stark. At least they were black-and-white. "It's no wonder that most Kicking Deers don't expect Magic Boy to return."

"You okay?" Max gripped his shoulder.

"Yeah." He'd be better if he could forget. How had he completely forgotten his murder and everything—all one hundred years or more—before it? The most he'd forgotten since then was a few hours—recent memories bled away and not regained later. Memories older than a day were already genetically encoded. Unbidden, the photos surfaced, along with an answer, and he caught his breath. "Oh, Max, I know why I've forgotten everything. I'm not Magic Boy. I'm like Kittanning. I'm just a piece of Magic Boy."

"What?"

Ukiah glanced around to make sure no was listening. "When Kittanning was first formed out of my blood, he had all my memories, and Rennie's—back to the first of the Ontongard. All those 'old' memories are genetically coded but stored in a different area than Kittanning's own memories. Also they don't seem to be as . . . sturdy. Rennie describes the area like a temporary buffer space in a computer; old information is dumped in favor for new. Every time Kittanning undergoes a change, that area is overwritten, and he forgets."

"When Hex forced him to change from a mouse to a human, he lost a lot, but not everything—like you did," Max said.

"If he had stayed an adult mouse, he would have kept everything," Ukiah explained. "As an infant human, though, as he grows, he's losing memories. Every day. Every minute. In the past two months he's forgotten everything I know of you, my moms, and Pittsburgh. Rennie's memories are denser, but they're fragmenting too. I don't know if Kitt will retain anything by the time he's mature."

Max pinched the bridge of his nose. "Kid, please don't take this the wrong way, but your people don't make sense, evolutionwise. Why have genetic memory passed on to your children, only to have them outgrow it?"

"Ontongard don't have children," Ukiah said. "They reproduce by infecting other creatures. A handful of cells are injected into a host to profligate throughout the body."

"Well, this whole old-memory/new-memory thing—"

"—isn't normal in Ontongard. Rennie theorizes that it's part of what allows the Pack be individuals. We can tell where we as an individual end and someone else starts."

"Prime passed this mutation on to both you and the Pack?"

"Luckily."

"So, if you're not Magic Boy, where is he?"

Ukiah recalled the photos of the scattered limbs. He swallowed hard. "He might not exist anymore. There may be just parts of him, like me, left."

Max stared at him for several minutes. "Ukiah, this is fairly empty country. Someone's bound to notice four or five identical Wolf Boys running around. *You* would have noticed them. You've never said anything about remembering someone like you. Was there?"

Ukiah consulted his earliest memories. "No, there wasn't."

Max tapped the book's spine into his palm. "I would assume that any Native Americans picked up as a John Doe would have been taken to the reservation. No one has remarked on the similarities between you and someone else in the tribe. Maybe the rest stayed animals. There could be dozens of mice and such flitting around someplace."

With just one mouse, Ukiah could recapture his childhood. "I wonder where the murder site was."

Max lifted the book. "It's probably in here. I'm going to copy this."

Ukiah pondered if he wanted to look for the murder site and chance finding lost bits of Magic Boy. While Rennie's memories remained clearly delineated from his own, the memories he recovered from Joe Gary's cabin—lost for three years—merged seamlessly. What if he couldn't tell where Magic Boy ended and he began? Which one of him would emerge dominant? The private investigator who lived among the whites, or the Native American who had good cause to hate them?

Perhaps it would be best to stay ignorant.

Ukiah joined Sam in checking through the microfilm boxes.

She glanced up as he entered the room. "Where did Max go?"

"I found a book he wanted to copy."

Sam chewed on her lower lip before saying, "I'm sorry about this whole 'we're dating' mess."

"You didn't do anything."

She relaxed slightly. "That's sweet of you to say so."

After they checked all the boxes, including opening them and verifying the beginning dates, they checked with Millie. She came and quickly checked over the boxes herself.

"They *were* here!" Millie threw up her hands. "That girl was in looking at them."

"Alicia Kraynak?" Sam asked.

"Yes, her. She was in here, bawling her eyes out. I came over to make sure she was okay, and that's what she had up. September, 1933."

"When was this?" Ukiah asked.

"The Saturday before last. The twenty-first?" Millie went off to call some of the other staff to see if they knew the whereabouts of the missing film.

"So they were here, and now they're gone," Sam said.

"Alicia's kidnappers must have taken them," Ukiah said.

"Or Alicia herself."

"Alicia isn't that type of person," Ukiah said. "She forgot to pay for a pack of gum once, and we had to drive back ten miles to the store to pay the fifty cents."

"Forgot to pay?"

"She forgot she had them in her hand. She was—is really absentminded." And suddenly it was so awful that a few days short of vanishing, she had sat and cried for him. The nearly indestructible one.

They had a dispirited lunch at Taco Bell down the street from the library. True to his word, Rennie kept out of sight, but Ukiah still sensed him, roving on the edge of his awareness. It was a comforting feeling after viewing Magic Boy's murder.

Sam and Max talked over the logistics of comparing the arson suspects with the list of people Alicia had come in contact with. During their investigation, Sam had noted everyone the team had interviewed into a slim tablet with a brief description of their interaction with Alicia. Back at her offices, however, were the case files for the house fires. Those included employment records of the dead, insurance and arson reports, any arrest records of survivors, background checks of beneficiaries and area newcomers, and in some cases, even family trees. The result was measured in the square feet of paper. Sam's office, she said, would hold only two people with very little space to spread out paperwork. Neither Max nor Sam wanted to work in a public place such as the library or the hotel room. Reluctantly, Sam suggested that they retreat to her house to filter through the lists.

Arranging to meet at the park behind the library, Sam went off to gather her files from her office.

Max and Ukiah hit a supermarket for supplies, filled the Blazer's gas tank, and drifted back to the park. Ukiah sprawled on the shaded grass, trying not to think of the grisly photos, while Max made a series of phone calls, trying to keep their business back in Pittsburgh from unraveling.

Both of their part-time investigators, Chino and Janey, were good at stakeouts and trailing suspects without being noticed, which made them good for surveillance. They could hold their own in a brawl, which made them wonderful company while looking for skips or serving papers.

Investigative legwork, much like Max, Sam, and Ukiah had been doing daily in Pendleton, however, eluded the two. It seemed as if they couldn't conceive the next step to take once they reached the end of each task. Max needed to chop each case up into segments, talking them through each procedure.

"I know it's not because I'm a bad teacher," Max growled as he hung up. "I taught you fine. You understand how to follow leads and ask the right questions. They just don't get it."

"Why can't I find Alicia, then?"

"Working a case and solving it are two different things, the second sometimes having little to do with skill and much to do with luck."

They fell silent, and the wind moved through the trees, throwing dappled shadows on them.

"Alicia was doing a great job of finding my family," Ukiah noted. "She couldn't have known how close she was when she found that photo at the Tamástslikt, or even the book. The obituary would have listed Jesse Kicking Deer, and if she talked to him about me—" He fell silent, realizing where that thread would lead.

"It keeps going back to the Kicking Deers," Max murmured.

"No," Ukiah snapped. "They had nothing to do with Alicia's kidnapping."

Max spread his hands wide. "A hundred thousand dollars is a lot of money for most people. Maybe we should look into who gets the money if Jesse doesn't hand it out as a reward."

Ukiah leaped to his feet, unable to deal with his anger at Max. It was a foreign emotion, and he flailed about, trying to find a way to get rid of it. "It couldn't have been one of them.

Jared was with us when I was shot, and when the kidnappers went to Bear Wallow Creek to get Alicia's stuff. And it wasn't Zoey, or Cassidy, or Jesse, either!"

"I'm just saying that every time we turn around, there's something to do with the Kicking Deers."

"It's just because Alicia was trying to find my family." Ukiah flung out reasons. "And I'm trying to find them, and Jared's the sheriff. The man in the woods was blond and blue-eyed."

"Elaine Kicking Deer is blond and blue-eyed. Maybe the kidnapper is a distant cousin who has very little Indian blood."

Ukiah searched through his memory, finding the places where he made skin-to-skin contact with the various Kicking Deers. Zoey kissing Ukiah's cheek. Jared rubbing his thumb along Ukiah's newly healed radius bone. Cassidy brushing Ukiah's hair from his eyes. The siblings were too close to give a broad Kicking Deer "pattern."

He called up his visit to the hardware store, with the various Kicking Deer men. Had he touched any of them?

A stray memory leaped out from the flow.

Sam sighed at the news and tossed one of the candies to Ukiah. "One of the deputies, Matt Brody, lost his kid in June. He's one of my drowning victims."

"Oh."

"He and his wife took it hard . . ."

Ukiah stilled, as it triggered another memory, from later that night, as Max was cutting off his cast.

". . . One of Kicking Deer's deputies, he's one of those big dumb-blond ox types, has a theory that a hunter shot you, despite the fact it's out of season for just about everything."

"What is it?" Max asked, recognizing that Ukiah had thought of something.

"Jared's deputy." Ukiah whispered.

"Which one?"

"The big blond with the hunting-accident theory, the police scanner, the wife, and the drowned boy."

"Wife?"

"The female kidnapper."

"Oh, shit." Max's eyes scanned back through the days. "You haven't met him to do a DNA match on the kidnapper's hair."

"What's he like?"

"He's way beyond poker-faced. Wooden." Max took out a cheroot, moved downwind, and lit it. "He set off my creep alarms, but then they told me about his son, and I put it down to grief. I thought I knew something of what Brody was going through."

Max's wife had vanished without a trace. Months later, Max learned that she had gone out antique hunting and spun her Porsche off the road and into a lake. No one had seen the accident, and she had been so far from her normal area that no one thought to look for her in the lake.

"After something like that," Max said quietly, "you walk around with all your feelings shut down, because it hurts too much to feel."

"Except Brody's out kidnapping Alicia and shooting me."

Fury gathered in Max's face, and his eyes went cold. "Damn the bastard. He'll pay for this."

"I'm just guessing at this, Max. Until I compare his DNA with the hair I found, we can't know for sure."

"And then it will be your word against his. We'll need something more concrete than a stray hair before we can point fingers."

If Brody were Alicia's kidnapper, he had stayed one step ahead of them, carefully removing evidence. What had he done with Alicia? Today would mark a full week since her kidnapping. Ukiah tried to believe she was still alive, but all the deaths that Sam was investigating loomed up, condemning any hope Ukiah had for Alicia.

He peered at Max through his dark bangs. "You think Brody might have killed his own son?"

Max recognized Ukiah's fears for Alicia. He reached out to the boy and gripped his shoulder. "I'm sorry, Ukiah, but yes. There's been something about the man that raised my hackles from the start, so to speak."

Ukiah flopped back onto the grass to watch sunlight diamond through the shifting leaves. Obviously, Brody had the locals fooled. Max and he would have to play within the rules and find something that would nail Brody without obtaining it illegally. Ukiah cast his thoughts back over the last week, and found the hole in their investigation.

"We never found the sniper site of my shooting. Brody wouldn't have had a lot of time to set up, and he might have left in a hurry, to establish an alibi in another location. He might have left evidence."

"Good boy!" Max clapped him on the shoulder. "See. I'm a great teacher!"

"Change of plans," Max announced when Sam returned. "We're going south, one car, so we can talk."

Sam frowned at Max as she reluctantly got out of her car. "South?" She glanced to Ukiah, and read something on his face that Max managed to hide. "You've got a new lead."

"Possibly," Max said. "Bring your files."

Ukiah reached out to Rennie, who drifted on the edge of his senses. *"Rennie? We're going down to where I was shot."*

Rennie's faint reply grew stronger as the Pack leader moved to intercept them. *"I hear you. I'll tag along behind and make sure you're not followed."*

Sam shifted her case files across to the Blazer and they headed out of Pendleton for the national park. "What's up?"

Ukiah leaned over the front seat between Max and Sam. "Tell us everything you know about Deputy Brody."

"Matt Brody?" She glanced to Max and saw that they were serious. "Brody is a good cop. Yeah, he's gotten weird since his son died, but Harry's the second kid the Brodys have lost, and they can't have any more."

"The second one?" Ukiah asked.

"The whole family was in a car accident four years ago; a drunk driver hit them. Matt Brody lost one of his kidneys. Vivian Brody took massive trauma to her intestinal tract; they thought she was going to die. Their little girl—the car seat failed, and she went through the windshield."

"How did his son die?" Max asked coldly.

"He was the first drowning victim this year. June thirtieth. Vivian Brody reported him missing out of the yard, and he was found dead two miles away in the McKay Reservoir the next day. Coroner ruled accidental drowning sometime during the day he disappeared."

"No sign of being held under?"

Pain flashed across Sam's face for the dead child. "No. He was just five. The Brodys say he couldn't swim."

"So it wouldn't take much," Max said. "Just carry him out deeper than he could stand, and let go."

Sam glared at Max and took out her tablet to flip through it. "We don't have Brody on Alicia's list."

"If you do a search on the name 'Kicking Deer,' Jared is the only one that comes up," Max said. "The listing has him as sheriff of Umatilla County, no home information. Alicia could have gone looking for him at the sheriff's department and ran into Brody there."

"Is Brody on the other lists?" Ukiah asked.

Sam nodded reluctantly. "But I don't put any weight to it. All the fire and emergency people show up on the lists as being at the scene."

"What's his wife like?" Max asked.

"Vivian? She's just a little thing," Sam said. "A munchkin Martha Stewart."

"Five foot tall, a hundred pounds, and size five shoe?"

Sam said nothing, only stared out the window at the shimmer of sun on water. Ukiah suddenly realized that the lake they were passing was the reservoir itself. They traveled on in silence, each with their grim thoughts.

Sam broke her silence with, "Brody shoots at the same gun range that I use. He's got an M40." It was the gun that the Marines used as sniper rifles. "And he's good with it."

Umatilla National Park, Oregon
Monday, August 30, 2004

Your mind had been going round and round, cub. Rennie stood down wind on the cliff heights: The Pack leader had put his duster back on for the road trip, and the stiff breeze flared it out behind him. *What is it?*

It had only taken a short part of the trip from Pendleton to locate the sniper's location in Ukiah's memory. At first he couldn't pick up the muzzle flash. But then he paid careful attention to the direction of the rifle crack. By backing through his memory of being shot, he was able to pick out the small flare among the green. All that was needed was to stand on the cliff and line up the flash. Chances were that they would find only footprints and tire marks. Ukiah hoped they weren't killing three or four hours for so little, but it was all they had left to go on.

The remainder of trip, he tried to match Brody to the other crimes. Opportunity? In a squad car, Brody had eight hours of freedom. No one would find it odd that a policeman had a weapon in his car. His presence at a crime scene would go unnoticed.

Motive? What reason could Brody have for killing so many people, possibly even his own son? The possible grounds were so impenetrable, Ukiah found himself sliding off to another troubling question.

Did Alicia's investigation into Magic Boy's death in 1933 have anything to do with her disappearance?

"I was killed in 1933," he told Rennie. *"The day you came to Pendleton and found Degas covered in blood."*

Rennie cocked an eyebrow at him. *"You think Degas killed you?"*

Ukiah hadn't considered that. *"No. I think he might have killed the Ontongard that murdered me—and kept it from discovering exactly what it had just slain."*

"Their sloppiness is our gain." Rennie gave a wolfish grin. *"Hex and his Gets can't tell you from a normal Pack dog without checking closely."*

"You and Hellena couldn't tell at first either."

Rennie cuffed him. *"Why worry about it now, cub?"*

"If Alicia had found old evidence of the Ontongard, who better to take it and her than one of Hex's Gets?"

Rennie stilled, staring at him.

"There are thirty people dead in this county in the last two months," Ukiah continued. *"Whole families wiped out by fire. Individual family members drowned. This feels so wrong, Rennie."*

Rennie turned to look off to the north where Pendleton lay beyond the horizon, nostrils flaring as if to catch the scent. *"Hex? Here?"*

"There's no reason for Brody to do these things."

Rennie growled softly. *"Sometimes men don't need reasons."*

"You don't think it's the Ontongard?"

"You've been here a week. I've been here for two days. So far neither of us has caught the scent of them."

"I've actually spent much of that week holding down a bed in various locations."

Rennie grinned, then sobered. *"The sad truth is that sometimes, cub, men make perfect monsters without the influence of the Ontongard."*

"So what do we do?"

"What we always do—keep your eyes and nose sharp and be ready to fight."

Following the memory of the muzzle flash, Ukiah loped through the forest, Rennie by his side. Straight as a bullet, nearly half a mile from the cliff, they found where the sniper pulled off the road.

The shooter had pulled hastily under trees to hide any windshield glare. He had trotted a short distance to where he was screened by a fallen pine but had a clear view of the cliff. By the depth of the faint footprints, he had only waited minutes before Ukiah came into view. The sniper fired twice, the spent casings still glittering in the grass.

With Ukiah assumed dead, the shooter ran back to his vehicle and sped off.

"Do we call Jared or the FBI?" Ukiah asked Max, leaving the evidence for the police to find.

Max sighed. "You trust Jared, don't you." At Ukiah's nod, Max glanced to Sam. "You too?"

"He's as good as cops come."

"We call them both, and make sure neither of them use the police radio."

CHAPTER FOURTEEN

Pendleton, Oregon
Tuesday, August 31, 2004

The Brody home was a carefully kept brick ranch on Tutuilla Creek Road, perhaps a mile and a half from the interstate. Max and Ukiah followed behind a long convoy of
cars—FBI, State Police, Umatilla County Sheriff's Department, and Pendleton Police Department—as it ran along the
shallow Tutuilla Creek. Parking under a rare shade tree,
the private investigators watched as law officers broke
down the Brodys' front door and swarmed into the house.

For several minutes, the world sat in utter silence and stillness.

"It's clear," came a report over their hastily purchased police scanner, "There's no one here. We've got some blue
jeans here, though, with Celtic knots painted up the side.
Women's size fourteen, long. The girl was here."

Yesterday, their luck had held, and the FBI lifted a perfect
thumbprint from the spent casings and matched it to Brody's
prints on his permit to carry a concealed weapon. Still it had
taken nearly twenty-four hours to work through the legal
channels and arrange the search warrants for a number of locations where the Brodys might be holding Alicia, starting
with their house.

With the possibility of Ontongard in the area, Rennie had
kept close to Ukiah as the number of law officers allowed. It
was a fine line Rennie had to dance, since now was not the

time to be distracted by FBI agents trying to arrest him. At the moment, he was making himself scarce to the point of being beyond Ukiah's senses. Hopefully, with nearly twenty policemen nearby, Rennie's protection wouldn't be needed.

An hour after the FBI first entered the house, Ukiah's wireless phone rang.

"Oregon," he answered without looking at the display.

"It's me," Indigo murmured into his ear. Just her voice uncoiled some of the tension inside of him. "I've got that information you asked for last night. Of the Ontongard killed in Pittsburgh, two were identifiable as from the West Coast. One was a Portland native, reported missing three years ago. Another one was Pendleton native, a Jason Barnhart, reported missing in May."

"Barnhart?" Ukiah flashed to the author of the *Death of Magic,* Hannah Barnhart. "Who filed the report?"

"James Barnhart, his father."

A Jason and James. Ukiah couldn't help but think of the Kicking Deers and their inclination for naming boys with 'J' names: Jay, Jesse, Jared. Were these Barnharts part of his family?

"Okay. Thanks."

"How is it going?"

"The Brodys were the ones that took Alicia, but it looks like they've slipped through the net."

"I'm sorry. I hope this isn't more bad news."

"It might be."

"Be careful," Indigo said, and added, "I love you," and reluctantly said, "I've got to go."

"What if this turns out to be Ontongard?" Ukiah put away his phone. "It would have been better if we never came to Oregon."

"You can't fight the 'what if's.' " Max said. "You do what you think is right at that moment. Questioning it later only drives you crazy."

So they waited as the FBI scoured the house, collecting evidence for any eventual court case, knowing it might all be moot.

* * *

A little after five o'clock, the first of the neighbors started to return home to find the Brodys under siege. The local police took turns answering their questions. One could watch the horror spread across their faces as the realizations hit them. Their nice neighbors kidnapped a woman and possibly killed her. The people next door most likely killed their son. The killers still on the loose knew them intimately. More than one family packed up and left for safer parts until the Brodys could be captured.

Finally the men started to pack up, trying to move quickly in their race to find Alicia. Max got out and Ukiah followed.

"Think they'll let me in?" Ukiah asked.

"We'll check with Jared. Gear up."

Ukiah hated the idea of gearing up so closely to the numerous FBI agents and policemen who didn't know him, who had no reason to believe or trust him, who could drag him off and lock him up until he answered uncomfortable questions.

In the TV shows, it was always the police or the FBI that killed the aliens when they were friendly.

He left his pistol in the gun safe. The FBI didn't like armed civilians confusing matters. He could pick his pistol up later. He shrugged into his body armor and quickly disguised it with his windbreaker.

Fortunately, the strike force started to pull out as he threaded a tracer into his clothing and hooked on his radio headset. The last Pendleton police car pulled away, leaving Jared's county squad car as the lone marked vehicle. Ukiah locked up the Blazer and crossed the street, skirting the Brodys' front yard roped off with yellow police tape. Until someone gave him the go ahead, he had to respect the thin boundary. He stopped in the driveway, waiting.

The last FBI agent eyed Ukiah warily as he packed away his assault gear. Ukiah tried to look as harmless as he could, nervous under the casual inspection. The agent took in Ukiah's windbreaker, apparently recognized him from reports, and nodded slowly. Slamming his car trunk, the agent walked around to the driver's door and got in. Relief flooded through Ukiah.

As the FBI agent pulled away, though, the wind changed, bringing Ukiah the scent of evil from the house.

A growl started in Ukiah's chest. *"Rennie? Rennie?"*

Rennie had gone too far out, trying to avoid the FBI. Ukiah could no longer sense him. Max came out the back door with Jared, who looked shell-shocked.

"They found things from the Burkes, and the other hikers, and the Coles," Jared said. "Vivian has a brother over in Pilot Rock, and Matt has a sister up in Walla Walla. They've got a search warrant for both." Jared shook his head, looking young, bewildered, and disgusted. "This is like biting into rare-cooked steak a friend served you and finding maggots."

"Can Ukiah look around?" Max asked, apparently not noticing the smell. How could anyone not smell *them*?

Jared waved at the house in disgust. "Magic Boy might be the only one that can find her alive. Go on in, I'll cover for you."

Max waved Ukiah to the back door. "It looks bad, kid. Dr. Jekyll and Mr. Hyde meet Martha Stewart! You can almost tell when things went bad by the level of grime—like whoever lived here moved away and someone else took over."

"I can smell them from here. It's one of their dens."

Max cursed softly as Ukiah stepped through the back door into what had been a pristine white kitchen. The uppermost cabinets still gleamed from the sunlight coming through the windows. On the table, the counters, and the floors, were torn-open bulk packages of cereal and dog food. A yellow plastic tray held a well-gnawed chicken, with bits of bloody meat clinging to the still-connected bones, as if someone had ripped the package open and eaten the chicken raw while standing at the counter.

"Chicken eaten raw, dog food, but no dog," Max made a sound of disgust. "If you can't get sick from the filth, why bother cleaning up?"

Ukiah glanced outside at the neatly cut yard. "They do enough to blend in."

"Well, yeah, you certainly couldn't ID Brody on sight."

There was a splatter of blood beside the chicken bones. Ukiah brushed fingers over the dead blood cells. Matt

Brody's genetic pattern existed as a thin top layer, and underneath was another—alien—code. The blood was from several days earlier. "Brody must have been one of the people in the truck that hit me. He was wounded when he ate this chicken. Either Sam or Kraynak must have shot him."

"Why couldn't you tell that Brody was Ontongard from his hair?"

Ukiah considered the hair he had found, snagged in the tree branches. It reported only human DNA; a big, blond man. "The hair had been snapped off. The part I found was only old, dead cells. He must have been converted recently, the hair closer to the root would have told me he was Ontongard days ago."

Max cursed again. "Sam said the kid drowned June thirtieth. We killed Hex and his Pittsburgh Gets the third week of June. We reduced the Ontongard population in Pittsburgh, so Hex's Gets here kick into overdrive to replace them. They infect whole families, using fire and drowning to cover the fact that a huge number of people are dying from viral infection."

"And they pick up drifters, hikers, anyone that won't be missed."

Max swore. "Oh, damn. Alicia."

"They would have infected her the first day they had her." Ukiah had been braced for them to find Alicia dead for so long, he thought he'd feel nothing now. With his words, though, it was if someone wrapped a hand about his heart and yanked it out of his chest, leaving his ribs wrapped around a hollow ache. Every breath brought pain to that empty spot. "It's been a week. She's gone. Either the injection killed her, or she's one of them now."

"Let's find Rennie, tell him what's going on and get the hell out of here. There could be hundreds of them here by now. Anyone could be one."

"We should warn people."

Max caught Ukiah's shoulder and spun him around to face him. "And what do we tell them? Aliens from space are inhabiting the bodies of townspeople and now the Pack is going to kill them all?"

"I've got to tell them something." Ukiah pulled away. "Warn them. Both Sam and my family should know."

Max glanced sharply at him at Sam's name, and remorse filled his face. "Okay, we'll tap Jared on the way out, take him someplace quiet, and—I'll figure out something to say to him. Then we'll warn Sam."

"Thanks, Max."

They went out into the summer dusk. Jared's lone squad car sat at the far corner, facing them. The sheriff stood talking with a tall, thin, sloppily dressed young man. Apparently another neighbor was learning the truth about the Brodys' crimes. Ukiah trotted toward them to arrange a private meeting with Jared.

Communication had made the Ontongard effective as a species. Inside one body, the individual cells communicated to keep the whole body functioning. *Swap function. Repair this first and leave that damage until later. Change into this creature so that we can survive outside the host.* As the Ontongard spread across host bodies, they retained the link in a telepathiclike ability.

The Pack and Ukiah kept those telepathic abilities. They could speak mind to mind at a limited range. They could share memories mentally. If they focused, they felt each other at a distance, a prickly awareness across the skin.

And they could feel the enemy.

Jared and the stranger turned. Jared said, "This is Dennis Quinn, he lives next to the Brodys," and the enemy was there, looking at Ukiah.

Ukiah felt Ontongard awareness wash over him, recognize him as non-Ontongard. The hair on the back of his neck went on end and he slammed to a stop. *Oh, shit!* His body realized its danger, and reacted instantly with fear, as if terror was poured from a bucket over him, drenching him suddenly and completely! *Ontongard! Kill it! Run! It will kill without hesitation!* What was one cell to a full body? Or one body to a creature spread across many beings? So unlike a man, who would only fight while his own survival seemed likely, the Ontongard instantly fought to the death.

Ukiah started backpedaling, growling. Jared frowned at

Ukiah's reaction. With inhuman speed, Dennis Quinn reached out, caught hold of Jared's service pistol, shoved it slightly forward and pulled it out of the holster. Ukiah caught the Ontongard's thoughts. *Kill the witness.* The gun swept up to point at Jared's chest.

"No!" Ukiah leapt toward him with a howl of fury. "Don't hurt him!"

Ukiah felt Quinn's recognition of the oncoming danger. He welcomed the pain as Quinn spun away from Jared to fire at him. The bullet caught Ukiah in the bulletproof vest with a force that smashed him to the ground backward. A second bullet whined across the cement by his cheek as he rolled over and started to scramble to his feet. A third hit him in high in his back, still on the vest but barely, just inches from taking out his spine. It slapped him flat onto the street, knocking his human mind unconscious.

As the awareness that thought of itself as "Ukiah" blacked out, the collective whole—the independent yet interconnected cellular creatures that made up his body—took over. Not guided by human thought and operating solely on instinct, the colony scrambled to its feet.

Jared grappled with Quinn, trying to disarm him. While the county sheriff outweighed the Ontongard Get by fifty pounds, the alien shrugged Jared off. Max dove behind the rental car, shouting to Ukiah.

The colony intelligence ignored Max and dashed across the yard of the nearest house. As he ducked through a breezeway that connected the house to its unattached garage, a bullet splintered the trim of the garage's clapboard siding.

Jared staggered to his car and shouted into his radio. "Officer needs backup, shots fired. Armed suspect is firing at unarmed civilian. Suspect is Dennis Quinn, male, Caucasian, six-five, a hundred sixty-five pounds, brown and brown, wearing dark jacket and blue Levi's. He's chasing . . ."

Then Ukiah was out of earshot, half-tumbling down a steep hill to the interstate with Quinn in close pursuit. He came to running, the interstate somewhere behind him and the Ontongard on his heels.

Any normal man he could have outrun. His alien biology

gave him an endurance no human could hope to match. Quinn had his every advantage, in addition to a thorough knowledge of the area and an unknown number of allies. Ukiah sent mental shouts to Rennie as he ran, hoping that the Dog Warrior was near.

Quinn chased him through the stillness of the summer dusk, running footsteps matching his, yet seeming fractions closer every moment. It was all, he suddenly realized, a matter of stride. Quinn was tall, longer-legged than him. He couldn't win.

He veered off sharply to the right, onto a street he all but passed, hoping Quinn would overshoot it. He sensed that Quinn, still fifteen feet behind him, made the turn easily and even gained distance in the move. He turned left and then right blindly, unsure where the streets led, no clear plan in mind. The last lone Ontongard that attacked Ukiah did it in a police station, chewing through a dozen police officers to get to him. Indigo saved Ukiah with a bullet to the Ontongard's head—the only person willing to shoot the man to save Ukiah. In Pendleton, he was the outsider. The police probably would shoot him, and then it would be to the coroner's office and an autopsy—or worse, into the hands of the Ontongard.

Where could he go? Where would he be safe? Silence was coming from his headset, as if it was only so much plastic. Jared's siren sang far off, nearing only to grow distant again, as if Jared searched down random streets for them.

"Rennie!" he screamed.

"You stupid little puppy." A stranger's thoughts were in his mind. *"Your packmates aren't here. I'm going to cut you down to bits and burn you."*

Then the distance between them was a matter of two feet, and Quinn reached out and shoved him hard on the shoulder. Off balance, he went tumbling. As he came up, he stared into the muzzle of the pistol.

A woman screamed in rage. Quinn was smashed sideways even as he pulled the trigger. The muzzle flare nearly blinded Ukiah, but the bullet whined harmlessly past his ear. Quinn was turning, blood streaming from his forehead, to face his new attacker. It was Cassidy, swinging a baseball bat hard for second strike.

"Leave him alone!" Cassidy struck solidly on Quinn's upraised arm, which broke with a crack. "I'm not going to let it happen again!"

The pain and shock as the arm broke would have stopped a human. From just above the wrist, Quinn's right hand dangled at a strange angle. Quinn dropped his pistol into his left hand as Cassidy stepped toward Ukiah, thinking she had stopped Quinn.

"Watch out!" Ukiah knocked her aside, leaping for Quinn even as Quinn fired. Cassidy fell as Ukiah tackled Quinn to the ground, clamping both hands on Quinn's unbroken wrist, trying to keep the gun aimed away from Cassidy.

They were outside the hardware store, Ukiah realized as he grappled desperately with Quinn. In the deepening dusk, Main Street was weirdly deserted; all the stores were closed and dark. Where was everyone? Cassidy lay on the sidewalk, the smell of blood blooming from her. Had the bullet hit her? Was she dead? Was she bleeding to death? Someone, anyone, had to help her! But no one was coming.

Ukiah could feel Quinn's arm reorganizing, healing the bone break at a speed that amazed Ukiah—far faster than any of the Pack would heal. In a few minutes Quinn would have full use of the arm.

They rolled up against the street curb, on the steel grating of a storm drain. An inch beyond the gun was the open slot of the drain.

A memory surfaced. Hex's will pressing against Ukiah's mind, making him nearly spill out secrets he'd sell his soul to keep. Ukiah clenched hard at the hand holding the gun and thought desperately, *"Release!"*

And the hand obeyed him. The gun teetered on the edge of the storm drain, and then dropped into the wet darkness below.

"Ha!" Ukiah cried and then yelled in shocked surprise as Quinn spun under him and kicked him through the hardware store's window. Ukiah crashed through the plate glass, a stand of cheap Pendleton Roundup pennants, and landed hard beneath the stuffed moose head, which gazed at him sorrowfully.

Quinn came through the window and landed lightly among the shattered glass.

Ukiah scrambled backward, up the narrow aisle of the hardware store. He needed a weapon. Unfortunately, there were many at hand. Even as Ukiah snatched up a curve-bladed sickle, Quinn picked up a six-foot-long steel bar, flattened at one end into a narrow, sharp-edged wedge. Ukiah's moms used such a bar for clearing rocks and roots from postholes and ditches. The nearly twenty pounds of forged carbon steel smashed the blade through packed earth, gnarled wood, and stones with ease.

For a moment Ukiah hoped that Quinn wouldn't be able to handle the posthole digger with his broken arm. The Get, however, lifted the bar easily, holding it like a quarterstaff. Quinn's arm had already healed, a fact that filled Ukiah with despair. How could he win against this creature?

"You can't," Quinn hissed. "You fight the very essence of yourself. That's Prime's madness in you, denying the truth that we're many yet one, and one yet many."

"When we're done, you will be none." Ukiah slashed with the sickle, aiming under the bar for Quinn's groin.

Quinn dipped the posthole digger to catch the sickle. Ukiah slid the curving blade up the length of steel, hoping to cut Quinn's left-hand fingers. Quinn realized the danger, and twisted, yanking the top of the bar back, disengaging the sickle, while swinging the bottom at Ukiah's side.

Ukiah dodged the blow, turned his wrist to backhand at Quinn's face. Quinn jerked back, and the tip of the sickle cut a shallow furrow along the Get's cheekbone. Quinn struck Ukiah hard in the head, making him reel, and then in the chest with a blow that threatened to crack ribs.

Ukiah stumbled backward, and Quinn pursued. The bar gave Quinn twice the reach as the sickle. Ukiah grabbed things at random off the shelves with his free hand—hammers, pliers, and screwdrivers—and flung them at Quinn's head. Quinn dodged them with frightening ease, thrusting at Ukiah with blows Ukiah could barely duck.

Ukiah came to the end of the aisle and ducked around. As Quinn rounded the corner too, Ukiah leapt at Quinn, pinning the bar uselessly between them. They went tumbling backward, snarling, out the back door to store's loading dock.

The buildings neighboring the store hemmed in the area to make a large, nearly enclosed courtyard. A huge woodchipper sat in one corner, a mound of woodchips stacked beyond its exit chute. Cassidy's pickup sat parked beside it, the tailgate down, ready to be loaded with woodchips.

Quinn came to his feet first, swinging the steel bar like a long baseball bat. Ukiah ducked the swing, and swung the sickle, laying open a foot-long cut across Quinn's chest. Quinn swapped his grip on the bar cocked up over his shoulder. His left hand reached high on the bar, and with the full weight of his body, he rammed the pointed tip high into Ukiah's chest.

The steel cleaved under Ukiah's collarbone, clipped the top of his lung, and punched its way out his back. He felt the bar bite deep into the wood of the wall behind him, pinning him.

Leaning his weight against the bar, Quinn kicked the woodchipper on. It roared to life, its blade ringing.

"I don't know which Pack dog made you, puppy," Quinn said. "But I'm going to unmake you."

A growl wouldn't come. Ukiah couldn't breathe—his right lung was collapsing. The feeling was so like when Hex had shot him multiple times in the chest that he flashed to the memory of Hex picking up the mice forming in his spilled blood.

"You're going to help me take this world," Hex had taunted, "one way or another." *Oh God, the Ontongard will have hundreds of mice to work with!*

Quinn's eyes widened. "Who are you?"

"No one!" Ukiah whispered, desperately trying to hide the truth. *I'm just a pack dog. Just another one of Prime's rabid Gets.*

Quinn pressed fingertips to the blood welling from the puncture wound, and his eyes grew wider still. "The breeder! Prime's missing breeder!"

Ukiah gripped the bar, swung both legs up and kicked Quinn hard in the chest. The Ontongard Get flew backward—and landed on the woodchipper's intake chute. His torn sleeve caught in the blades and jerked him in. The arm vanished first, in a wet chopping sound.

Quinn screamed and jerked hard, trying to rip himself free. Bone and muscle linked him still to the blades. He smashed the machine sideways in his desperate throes. The exit chute swung until it faced the hardware store's back wall. Blood, bone chips, and hunks of meat splattered like an evil rain, stark red on the white. The woodchipper pulled Quinn's shoulder then head in, chewing him down. His screaming stopped, replaced by a dull, low, crunching of the heavier bones. Bits of cloth and leather joined the rest as the machine pulled the rest of the slumped body through. Finally the blades spun clean, ringing.

Formless, though, the Get still lived. Ukiah could sense all of Quinn's surviving cells communicating, desperately trying to take shape into something that could live through the massive damage. Ukiah's own blood was forming into mice. Remembering the speed at which Quinn healed, Ukiah was suddenly sure that he only had a few minutes before Quinn reformed—and he was still pinned, helpless to the wall.

He struggled weakly with the steel bar. *Rennie!*

Cub? It was a distant reply, he could barely hear.

Rennie! Help me, Rennie! I'm trapped. I'm hurt! One of Hex's Gets is here!

I'm coming, cub!

Jared and Max found him first, coming cautiously through the hardware store's back door. Jared stumbled to a halt to stare at the gore-splattered wall, slack-jawed. Max hurried to Ukiah.

"Get it out!" Ukiah whispered, tugging at the bar, sending shocks of pain through his chest that nearly knocked him unconscious. "Hurry!"

"Easy, son!" Max shouted over the woodchipper, catching Ukiah's hands and stilling them. He gingerly examined Ukiah, wincing at the damage he found. He turned, hit the kill switch on the woodchipper, and waited for the profound silence before trying to talk. "Easy. We don't want to hurt you worse by doing this roughshod."

Ukiah caught a newly formed mouse and pushed it at Max. "Quinn's reforming! He knows what I am!"

Max glanced at the bloody wall. The blood smear was gathering into larger clots, growing darker as the centers formed new organs. Hearts already trembled in the reforming masses, lungs sucked air through growing throats. "Oh, come on, what does it take to keep these guys down?"

"Fire. Acid." Ukiah struggled for breath. "Just get it out!"

"Acid?" Max gave a snort bitter laugh as he tried to pull the bar free of the wood. "Damn! He really nailed you. Jared! Help me get him free before—oh, shit."

The blood and gore had gathered into thirty or forty large clumps. Gravity pulled them down as they thickened, and as they tumbled earthward, black wings and feathers, dark eyes, and sharp beaks formed, and a flock of crows winged upward. They beat the air, a thunder of noise, and rose into a dark mob above. For several minutes they churned in the sky, an angry mass, gathering itself for an attack.

Ukiah whimpered, trying to free himself. Max shook himself out of his shock and pulled frantically at the bar. Suddenly, Rennie was there, a snarling, heavily armed presence. He emptied his handgun into the flock, so that it rained birds. The flock lifted, screaming their indignation while they fled.

"They left," Ukiah whispered, unbelieving. Ontongard usually fought to the death.

Rennie caught his thoughts, and shook his head. "It's difficult to override hard-wired instincts. It's in birds' DNA to be naturally cautious things. I could scare him off only because he hasn't tailored their responses yet. We better go, before he gets reinforcements."

CHAPTER FIFTEEN

Zimmerman Hardware, Pendleton, Oregon
Tuesday, August 31, 2004

Jared went off to check on Cassidy and returned with a new plastic drop cloth. He unfolded it as Max and Rennie freed Ukiah from the wall. "Cassidy is fine. I need to go. If Ukiah survived what happened to Magic Boy, he'll live through this—won't he?"

"Only if we keep him away from Quinn and the Brodys," Max grunted as they eased Ukiah onto the drop cloth. Rennie gripped the posthole digger close to the wound and pulled it slowly out. The Pack leader cleaned the blood from the bar onto the plastic, where it would have the best chance of surviving. As blood flowed from the wound, and shock set in, Ukiah found the situation more and more confusing. *Where had Quinn gone to so suddenly?*

Jared leaned down to grip Ukiah's shoulder hard. "Don't run off this time, and don't forget us."

Sam arrived as Rennie mummified Ukiah in the plastic. "I heard on the scanner that Dennis Quinn was shooting at Ukiah, then nothing. What the hell happened?"

"It's all over," Max said throwing the posthole digger, aside. "Ukiah's—fine, but Quinn got away."

Sam glanced at the steel bar, at the hole in the blood-stained wall, then stared at Ukiah, hand over her mouth. "Oh, shit, what did Quinn do to him?"

"He tried his best to kill the cub," Rennie said, picking Ukiah up like a child. "We need to go. Quinn will be back."

"The ambulance crew is out at Pilot Rock," Sam reported. "The FBI cornered Matt and Vivian Brody out there with his brother-in-law, Seth Bridges. There was a shoot-out."

"I wondered why we weren't crawling with police," Max said, leading the way into the hardware store.

Zoey was doctoring a swearing Cassidy as they entered, applying a butterfly bandage to a bleeding head wound while Cousin Lou looked on in concern. Jared's cruiser was pulling away from the front curb, lights going. The trio of remaining Kicking Deers looked up as Rennie carried Ukiah in through the back door.

"I'll follow you to the hospital," Sam said.

"No hospital," Rennie said.

"What?" Sam yelped.

"No hospital," Rennie repeated firmly. "We'll find someplace safe to hide and tomorrow the cub goes back to Pittsburgh."

Sam blocked the front door. "Are you nuts? He's got to go to the hospital. He's losing too much blood, he's in shock, and—and just listen to him breathe! It sounds like one of his lungs has collapsed. He *will* die if you don't get him to a hospital."

"Yes. That's a good possibly," Rennie said, jerking his head to indicate she was to move.

She stood her ground. "We're taking him to the hospital."

"*We* are not." Rennie shifted Ukiah and pulled out a pistol, which he leveled at Sam. "And you are slowing us down."

Ukiah tried to speak, but found he didn't have breath for it. *"Rennie! No! Please don't hurt her."*

Max caught hold of Sam and pulled her out of the way, putting himself between her and the Pack leader. "It's okay, Sam. You know I wouldn't let anything happen to Ukiah. Trust me. He'll be fine."

She gazed at Rennie, then at Ukiah in his arms, and finally at Max. There her face crumbled into anguish, and she buried her head against Max's shoulder. "You better be right because if he dies—if he dies—I'll come kick your ass so hard, you're going to have to stand the whole way back to Pittsburgh."

And she fled, as if running from her trust in Max, and her helplessness in the face of Rennie's determination. Ukiah tried to call after her, to let her know he'd be fine, but only a weak strangled noise came out. As he struggled to take another breath, she was gone.

"Shit," he hissed once he managed that second breath.

Max opened the Blazer's back and waited for Rennie to tuck Ukiah in. "Hang in there, son."

Ukiah struggled to take another breath, and forced out, "Something's in my lung."

"In? Something that will work itself out, or something that needs removed?" Max asked.

As if his body took it as a suggestion or perhaps a threat, Ukiah started to cough. Each cough was an explosion of pain, and he doubled over, trying to ease it. Something was forced up and out. He covered his mouth and coughed the wet, bloody mass into his hand. Immediately, he could breathe, and gasped in a huge sweet lungful of air. He slumped back in the seat, still cupping the mess, just enjoying the deep, unhindered breathing.

Max got some Kleenex and lifted Ukiah's cupped hand. "Here. Is this all—dead?"

Ukiah considered. "No. Something's alive in there."

Max carefully cleaned away dead tissue from living. The mass resolved down to a black cocoon, which shuddered open as the air hit it. An insect, looking like a cross between a wasp and a butterfly with too many legs crawled from the thin black silk.

Max gave him a look that clearly asked, What the hell?

"It's a v'vrex." Ukiah let Rennie coax the alien into inspecting a clean, empty Gatorade bottle. "It's from Prime's home."

"That's new." Max tucked the bloody tissue of dead-cells into the plastic wrapped around Ukiah.

Zoey darted to Ukiah's side and laced her fingers through his. "I know you're going to be okay. You're Magic Boy— even if you don't think you are. It's just that the scientist in me is at odds with the granddaughter of a medicine man. But that's nothing unusual. I think this time I better listen to the granddaughter."

"I'll be fine." Ukiah was glad that he could reassure at least one person. "You take care of Cassidy. She actually needs you more."

"Here, take this." Zoey slipped a small beaded bag on a thong of rawhide over his neck and kissed his cheek. "It wards off evil spirits."

"Evil spirits," Rennie said, as his big motorcycle rumbled to life, "are the least of our worries."

The Lyrids were falling the last time he really talked to Alicia. He had been doing a surveillance stakeout as the meteors streaked the April night sky in a rain of wishes. Since it was a matter of just sitting, and watching, it made sense that he and Max took turns.

Alicia came to him quietly, dressed all in tight black, shivering with cold and excitement.

"What are you doing here?" His breath smoked in the freezing night air. Alicia had not worked for them for nearly a year now, despite her frequent visits.

"I dropped by the office for a shoulder to cry on, or a ear to bitch into." She pressed a tall thermos into his hands. "Max said I could bring you something to eat."

He cracked open the thermos and found it filled with Max's beef stew, steaming hot. "What's wrong?"

"Oh, same old, same old." Alicia peered through his telescope at the storage yard he had under surveillance while he juggled cap, lid, and spoon to gulp down the first cupful. "I really should learn not to think with my hormones. Wild and crazy guys might be oh-so-hot, and great for messing around with, but they're not cut out for stable relationships."

He wasn't sure what to say to that. He was too new to civilization to understand the complex social dance everyone else breezed through. He wasn't even sure what "messing around with" entailed. "I'm sorry if you're hurt."

"I'm not hurt, just—pissed off—and mostly at myself."

She wrapped her arms about herself and rubbed at her arms. "Damn, is it cold!"

"Where's your coat?" He finished the stew and screwed the lid back on.

"It's screaming yellow. I didn't think I should wear it up here. I might give you away."

"Here." He started to unbutton his coat.

"I can't take your coat!" she protested.

He stood with his coat hanging open, unsure what to do, then said, "We could share it."

So she snuggled into his chest and he hugged her close. His coat barely covering her sides, he rubbed her back to warm her.

"You always smell so good," she murmured.

"It's the stew," Ukiah told her. "Max makes it with light cream and cashew paste, kind of like Indian korma."

She laughed into his chest. She smelled of arousal, but he had lots of practice around his mothers at ignoring the scent.

"How do you feel?" he asked, steering his mind and body away from her pheromones.

She looked into his eyes. "Safe."

He had expected "warmer" or "still cold" or something other answer. He puzzled over it. He supposed she felt that way because he wouldn't let anything hurt her.

"Look!"

Ukiah glanced up and saw another meteor streaking groundward. "Falling star, make a wish."

She laughed. "Don't tempt me."

"What would you wish for?"

She touched his face, tracing his smooth chin, and ran fingers over his mouth. "I wish you were older."

"Me? Why?"

She laughed, burrowing her face into his neck, and tightening her hold on him. "Oh, no reason. I'm just being selfish. There's time enough for you to join the cruel realities of the world. But when you do, I'll be waiting."

At the time, he didn't understand. Looking back, now he did. She was in love with him.

*   *   *

Ukiah woke in the stillness of late night, with the sense of Alicia all around him.

While mostly a blur to Ukiah, their retreat had actually been quick and orderly. Max paused at the garage where Kraynak's van was still under repair. Rennie broke in and confiscated Alicia's camping gear, and they headed out into the wilderness. The Umatilla National Forest covered 1.4 million acres land—even if the Ontongard knew it well, it would take them a while to search it all.

Ukiah now lay wrapped in Alicia's blankets, wreathed by her ghostly scent. What happened, he wondered with despair, to those that the Ontongard took over? Did their souls break free of the bodies no longer theirs to control—able to pass on to heaven? Or did they stay trapped—to be soiled by sins they had no power to prevent—doomed to hell if somehow the Ontongard died? Or were they somewhere halfway between? Pushed out of their bodies by the alien DNA and yet unable to pass on, did they cling like ghosts to the hair still caught in combs and the dead cells shed onto favorite clothing, the only DNA still solely their own?

Surely God wouldn't let such cruelty exist. There was, however, overwhelming evidence that the universe was full of such evil. Tortured by such thoughts, Ukiah slipped out of the tent and discovered the world beyond.

The campsite was high in the mountains, open to the stars. The campfire burned in a ring of stones, a low red eye in the darkness, scenting the air with wood smoke. Overhead the Milky Way crossed. The Big Dipper. The Little Dipper. Ursa Major. Ursa Minor. He gazed at the stars, homesick for Pittsburgh, Indigo, and his moms.

The campfire suddenly roared to life. It shot up as if feeding on gasoline, the flames shooting up as high as his chest. He backed away from it, looking for water or sand. A movement caught his eye, and he turned around.

A male grizzly bear towered over him.

It roared, a sound that filled his ears and senses. He saw the huge mouth open, the yellowed canines, the deep cavern of its throat, red rim of gums and the drool. The hot breath blasted over his upraised face. The carnivore smell of old meat. The spittle touched him with information on the huge beast before him, the ancient link with all bears and the twisting path down to this giant creature before him. The sound rippled over his skin, felt as well as heard.

It stood there, real in all his senses. But its eyes—its eyes were great pools of blackness filled with stars. And into his mind he felt the firm impression of something unreal, something huge and unknowable, something beyond anything he and any of his ancestral memories stretching back eons— had ever experienced. The bear, he somehow knew, wasn't truly there. And so, where he should feel fear jazzing over his nerves like electricity, he felt only serene awe.

Threading through his mind, quiet and elusive as the whisper of wind through pines, was a thought.

Protect your people. This is why you were born.

A rustle of fabric, and Max came out of the tent behind him. "Ukiah?"

Ukiah blinked. He stood with his back to the fire, gazing up at the stars. The bear was gone, vanished completely except for a ghost heat of its breath.

"Are you okay?"

"Yes." Ukiah glanced down at the ground. Dew covered the grass evenly with no mark of the bear's passing. The memory remained, perfect as always, filling him with peace. "I'm fine."

CHAPTER SIXTEEN

Pendleton, Oregon
Wednesday, September 1, 2004

If one thought about it, the Boy Scouts, with their "be prepared" motto, worked well with Max's paranoia. Every morning Ukiah and Max had stripped the hotel room of all their costly, high-tech equipment, loading it into the two cars in Max's belief that the cars were far more secure. They had left only suitcases, clothing, and toiletries behind.

Max decided that they would abandon everything at the hotel; while the police still searched for the Brodys and their known accomplices, unidentified Ontongard would be looking for Ukiah. If Ukiah and Max were lucky, they could slip out of Oregon unnoticed. If they were unlucky, the entire world might suffer.

After they woke at dawn, ate, and Ukiah absorbed back all his blood mice, Max made arrangements over the Internet, using his cover identity of John Schmid, buying five tickets instead of a telltale three in order to confuse anyone checking passenger lists at the Pendleton airport. Disconnecting his laptop from the Taurus's power, Max packed it away and scanned the campsite to make sure they were leaving nothing behind.

"I'm going to need at least a shirt," Ukiah said, fingering the holes in his shirt, crusted with dead blood cells, reluctant to put it back on.

"We'll see if Sam has something." Max handed his multi-pocketed vest to Ukiah.

Ukiah put on the vest and zipped it up against the morning chill. "We're going to see her?"

Max fished out the Blazer's keys and tossed them to Ukiah. "I'll get us down to the main road, and you can lead us to her place."

Ukiah caught the keyring. They had discussed Ukiah saying good-bye to his newfound family and decided it would be too dangerous. It had become common knowledge that Ukiah was somehow related to the Kicking Deers and the Ontongard could be watching them. "Isn't it risky to see her? Everyone knows we've been working together."

"You said that her place is fairly secure."

"She said."

Max allowed that difference with a lift of his shoulder. "I need to talk to her one last time. I'm trusting that she can shake anyone watching her."

Although his voice was low, he said it with an intensity that surprised Ukiah, as if his need equaled something much greater than simple talk. Ukiah considered the times he had seen Max and Sam together, and realized, between the moments of desperation, Max had been happier than he had been for a long time. It was possible, while Ukiah wasn't paying attention, Max had fallen in love.

If that were the case, then there was no way Max would leave Pendleton without Sam. Perhaps the five tickets weren't all a ruse.

"Are you going to ask her to come back to Pittsburgh with us?"

"I think I want to marry her."

"Really?"

Max laughed at his reaction and cuffed him. "Maybe. I don't know. Hell, I've known her for, what, a week? And I'm nearly ten years older than her. Indigo has nothing on me for cradle robbing."

Ukiah wasn't sure what to say. He and Max worked well as partners. During the last few days, there had been moments where he felt he was the one that was intruding, not Sam. Ukiah hadn't dwelled on it, because in the back of his mind he knew that he and Max would go home, and things would go back to normal.

But if Sam moved to Pittsburgh, then he and Max might never be the same again. "She would be a full partner?"

Max shook his head. "I'll offer her a job and moving expenses. I can't expect her to come to Pittsburgh without at least a job. No strings attached. No expectations. If she and I don't work out—well, we need another investigator anyhow." Max paused, and then looked anxiously to Ukiah. "That is, if you agree to it. You're full partner, you have an equal say in her working at the agency."

For years, he'd seen Max quietly grieve for his wife. Kraynak spoke honestly of a time, before Ukiah knew Max, when Max walked a suicidal edge. Ukiah couldn't say no, not to Max. "We need someone. There won't be any surprises with Sam."

"It might mean a lot of changes for you, kid."

"I plan on getting married to Indigo; I'm slated for changes already." Ukiah squinted as he considered additional ramifications. "Do you think Sam and Indigo will like each other?"

"Indigo and Sam?" Max shuddered. "God, one hopes that they can at least stand one another! Life could be hell if they can't."

"What are we are doing here?" Rennie's thoughts touched Ukiah's mind as they climbed the driveway to Sam's small, A-frame cabin. The Blazer's dashboard clock showed it was ten to five, and no lights were on.

Rennie trailed Max and Ukiah at a discreet distance on his motorcycle, watching to see if they were followed. When they turned off the main road, however, he closed in on them. Ukiah could sense Rennie's faint concern.

"This is Sam's place," he told Rennie, parking next to Sam's Jeep. Her Harley was tucked into a small half-filled woodshed. *"Max needs to talk to her."*

"All this madness, and still we have proclamations of love. Ah, humans are amazing."

Under the sarcasm, Ukiah felt Rennie's fondness for his birth race.

Max scowled at Rennie as he stopped his motorcycle beside the Taurus. "Could you give us a little privacy?" Rennie's eyes slid over to Ukiah and asked a silent question. "He's my partner. He's part of the deal."

Rennie grinned but swallowed down any snide remark that flitted through his mind, just out of Ukiah's reach. "Go pitch your woo. I'll check the main road."

He walked his bike backward until he could pull in a tight circle and head back down the steep driveway.

Max knocked on the door. "Sam?" He knocked again and glanced to Ukiah, who was on the other side of the doorway.

Ukiah listened carefully. "Someone's coming. Sounds like Sam."

It was an armed Sam that cracked the door and eyed Max warily. "Bennett?"

"I needed to talk to you before I went back to Pittsburgh."

"How did you find this place?"

Max tilted his head to indicate Ukiah, just outside her range of vision. "The Kodak kid led."

Sam flung the door completely open. "Ukiah! Oh, thank God!" She stepped out into the cold morning air and crushed him in a hard embrace, ignoring the fact she wore only a T-shirt, panties, and a nine millimeter in a shoulder holster. Her hands moved up and down Ukiah's back, as if measuring the whole of him, confirming he was all there and not a scarecrow dressed in his clothes. "I was sure you were dying. I kept kicking myself for leaving you with that lunatic."

"Thanks," Max said.

"I meant Shaw." Sam ran her hands over Ukiah's back again, slower this time, as if looking for something. Finally she pulled away from him, frowning, to zip open the vest.

"Sam," Max murmured. Ukiah couldn't tell if it was a protest, warning, or plea for understanding.

Sam ignored Max, silently examining the healed-over entrance wound, and then, pushing Ukiah through a half-turn, the exit wound. "Quinn put that steel bar through you."

"I heal quickly."

She framed Ukiah's face with her hands. "You were dying."

"No," Ukiah said, not sure what to admit to her. "It takes a lot more than that to kill me."

"Good." She scrubbed her hands through his hair, and then released him. Turning, she swatted Max on the shoulder. "You shit, why didn't you tell me?"

"I tried."

"Not in a way that I'd believe."

"What would have you believed?"

"How about the truth? Why are people I've known for years suddenly turning into serial killers? Why did all-life-is-sacred, tree-hugging, vegetarian Dennis Quinn chase Ukiah clear across town and nail him to a wall? Quinn never laid eyes on the kid before, and yet he stomps all over Jared and Cassidy, trying to kill Ukiah. Hate like that does not come out of nowhere. How does Mr. Most Wanted, Rennie Shaw, figure into this? Normally you don't need someone of his caliber for protection in Pendleton. And if the kid can get nailed that bad, and still be up and around the next day, why the hell are you giving up on Alicia Kraynak? Just level with me, Bennett."

"I-I don't even know where to start," Max said.

Sam crossed her arms over her chest. "Start by telling me what your partner is."

"My partner," Max said, quietly but firmly, his eyes like cold steel, "is a good, moral, decent person. He has exceptional abilities. He uses those abilities to help people. I can't count the number of times he's put his life on the line to save another person. Normally I wouldn't give a shit what people thought of his abilities. Now is not a good time, though, to be known as more than human."

"With everyone UFO-crazy since that thing with the Mars Rover?"

"Exactly. With the exception of serial murderers trying to kill him, Ukiah's never hurt anyone in his life. I'm not going let some nutcase, who has seen *Invasion of the Body Snatch-ers* one too many times, hurt him."

"Do you know what he is?"

"He's a good kid."

Sam laughed softly, a ghost of a chuckle. "*Your* kid, Ren-nie Shaw be damned?"

Max nodded slightly, and then clarified with, "My part-ner."

"And the rest of it? Come on, Bennett, you can't run out and leave me in the middle of this without a clue of what's going on."

"Come to Pittsburgh, then," Max said. "We still need someone to drive Kraynak's van to Pennsylvania. And there will be full-time position waiting for you, if you're inter-ested. Health insurance. Retirement plan. Two weeks vaca-tion. Paid sick days."

"You're offering me a job?"

"Yes."

"Is this an attempt to keep my mouth shut about the kid? Under your thumb, dependent on you for money?"

"No!" Max snapped. "Look, I just want you out of harm's way. Pendleton isn't safe any more. I don't want you hurt, and I certainly don't want what happened to Alicia to hap-pen to you."

"Sounds like you care what happens to me."

"I care a hell of a lot."

They stood staring at each other.

Max broke the silence first. "Say you'll drive the van to Pittsburgh. See what we have to offer. We'll pay for you to stay at a hotel, or you can crash at the office if you want, there's a bed there you can use."

"All business?"

"If that's the way you want it, yes."

Sam glanced behind her at the small, lonely cabin with the overstock flooring and mismatched furniture, then out into the thick pinewoods, with the double strand of electric-ity and telephone wires as the only mark of civilization. "Oh, hell. I pitched everything to come to Pendleton with my ex. I've tried hard not to hate this town because of him, but I haven't really succeeded."

"Come to Pittsburgh."

Sam looked at Max, then slanted a look at Ukiah where he'd stood silently this whole time. "What about you, kid? Do you have any say in this, or is it all his plan? Is he just saying anything to get into my pants?"

"It's his plan," Ukiah admitted. "But it sounds like a good one. We work well together. I don't think he wants your pants—they wouldn't fit."

Sam crowed in surprised laughter.

"She wants to know if I want to have sex with her, Ukiah, and please, don't answer her."

"Why shouldn't he?" Sam asked.

"His honesty cuts both ways. I haven't asked embarrassing questions about you, please don't ask embarrassing questions of me."

She sighed. "Okay, I'll drive the van to Pittsburgh. I'll check out the job, and if I like the offer—well, we'll deal with it then."

Sam found a T-shirt for Ukiah, then showered and dressed. The Volkswagen's keys were in Kraynak's personal effects at the hospital. By riding with them to Pendleton, Sam could get the keys and pick up the van without abandoning one of her own vehicles in town.

Rennie waited for them at the bottom of the driveway, tucked behind a large boulder that screened him from the main road. Max stopped beside Rennie to discuss plans for the addition of Sam to their group.

"Ah, tall, dark, and scary," Sam greeted Rennie. "I wondered where you were."

"They said I couldn't come up and kibitz."

"I see. You're out here, supposedly, to protect Ukiah. If I come to Pittsburgh, am I going to see you as much?"

"No, not likely." In Pittsburgh it was harder to spot the Pack as they kept watch over him.

"Good."

Rennie laughed, and said mentally to Ukiah. *"It will be interesting to see how this plays out."*

They stopped at the Chevron station just after six a.m. As the gas station attendant filled the cars, Max ducked into the convenience store to pick up traveling supplies.

Sam came to lean against Ukiah's door. "If Kraynak doesn't pay, are you guys going to be in a lurch?"

"A lurch?"

"Desperate for money."

"Max has been paying for this out of his pocket. If Kraynak pays him back, Max will make out. If not . . ." Ukiah shrugged. "Max feels like he owes Kraynak for sticking with him during the rough times after his wife died."

"I really hate to have to ask this, but you guys *can* afford to pay me to drive the car back, right? I'm not going to get to Pittsburgh and find everybody is dead broke after this."

"We can pay you, no problem." Ukiah wasn't sure how much money Max had. He had protested once over Max giving him half the company, which had assets totaling close to a million dollars. Max claimed that the company was nothing compared to Max's total worth.

"Good." She looked over Ukiah's shoulder. "God, your father is just like a dog, here one moment, gone the next, then back again."

Ukiah startled, thinking Sam meant Prime, and then remembered that they had introduced Rennie as his father. His so-called father pulled into the gas station, his mental hackles raised.

"What is it?" Ukiah asked.

"Crow." Rennie pulled out his pistol, aiming out over the river.

Ukiah spun and looked. The black bird sat several hundred feet away, watching with beady black eyes. *"One of Quinn's?"*

"Can't tell at this distance." Rennie pulled the trigger. The report shattered the early morning quiet.

Sam jumped in surprise. "Jesus Christ! What the hell?"

The crow exploded into a flurry of black feathers. It's

limp body, however, fell into the river. Both Ukiah and Rennie swore.

"Maybe it was just a bird," Ukiah thought.

"I'll go see if I can find one of the feathers." Rennie pulled out of the gas station and rode away.

"I don't know," Sam sighed, watching Rennie go. "I don't think Max can pay me enough to live in the same state as him."

Max had seen Rennie fire his pistol and then drive away. Ukiah wasn't sure what Max said to the clerk in the convenience store, or if this type of thing was common in Oregon, but whatever the reason, no police arrived to investigate the shooting. When Max came out, asking what Rennie had been shooting at, Ukiah tried to explain with facial expressions and gestures while Sam ranted about his lunatic father killing innocent birds.

When they pulled into the parking lot of St. Anthony's Hospital, Rennie drove up to join them.

"You *are* taking him with you, aren't you?" Sam asked.

"Sort of." Max ducked the truth. At the airport, they planned to split up, Rennie going to fetch the Demon Curs. Max glanced into the car beside the Taurus. "I thought I recognized it. Tell Shaw that the FBI is here."

Ukiah nodded and crossed to where Rennie was parking his motorcycle. "Did you find any feathers?"

"No," Rennie said, which was bad. Alien feathers would transform and crawl away before Rennie found them.

"The Crown Vic is a federal car. There's no telling where and how many FBI agents are inside."

Rennie frowned at the hospital. "Now is not the time I want to be messing with the FBI. When is your flight?"

Ukiah checked his watch. "In a little over an hour at seven-thirty. We're going have to hurry to make it."

Rennie sighed. "I would like to see you onto the flight, but you've got your partner, and his love, and I've checked out the local FBI agents. They're human." He started up the motorcycle, and it rumbled to life. *"I'm going to find Degas and the Curs to let them know that there's Ontongard in Pendleton. Make sure you get on that plane, even if it's without Kraynak."*

"I will," Ukiah promised. He reached out and gripped Rennie's shoulder. *"Be careful."*

Rennie leaned over and crushed him in a bear hug. *"Go home to your lady of steel and your little one. Keep safe. It's good to finally have children to return home to."*

"What do we tell Kraynak?" Ukiah asked Max as Sam paused at the café for coffee. Except for the occasional nurse, the hospital seemed empty, the slightest noise echoing up the hard tile hallways.

"Well, we'll have to tell him something close to truth, we owe him that," Max sighed. "Basically the same people that kidnapped the FBI agents in June also took Alicia. They injected her with the same virus that killed the agents."

Hex experimented with an immunity-suppression drug to increase the chances of host survival. The result had been a slower transformation rate that drove the newly made Get, Janet Haze, mad. She had lost the remote key to the mother ship, which Hex needed to release the crew who Prime had locked into cryogenic sleep. Ukiah found the key without realizing its importance. Sure that the key had been recovered by a law enforcement agency, Hex had first raided the Pittsburgh police's evidence room. When that turned up nothing, he kidnapped FBI agents and tried to make them Gets so they could retrieve the key from wherever it was being stored.

The agents died without transforming. As the homicide detective assigned to the murder cases, Kraynak would know what Alicia had faced.

Max shook his head. "He's not going to want to go home until he has her body."

"I can't believe this has happened."

"We've known Alicia was probably dead since you were shot."

"I know," Ukiah whispered as Sam came out of the coffee shop, still intent on stowing pocket change. "But this is worse than dead."

They had gone to Kraynak's room to find him gone. The nurse at the station told him that he had been signed out already and taken by wheelchair to the first floor. The private investigators hurried to the emergency-room exit first, as they had just come from the main entrance. When Kraynak wasn't there, Sam headed them toward a little-used side exit.

They were still two hallways away from the exit, when Zoey's voice, sharp and thin, echoed from around the far corner.

"His heparin lock needs to be taken out. I'm sorry I didn't notice earlier. Let me call the nurse."

"That won't be necessary." A woman's voice, familiar but flat, emotionless.

"Alicia?" Max caught Sam's arm, pausing her, as he looked at Ukiah.

It seemed inconceivable that Alicia's body could ever produce such a cold sound, but Ukiah sniffed and caught her scent. Hers, but not hers. Stripped of all the perfumes of soap and deodorant, thick with sweat and dirt, tangled with the Ontongard.

Ukiah froze, torn between running away and charging forward. "It's a Get."

"No, don't do that." Zoey sounded horrified.

He charged.

"Ukiah!" Max hissed, and then started after him, calling to Sam, "Call 911. Get the police out here!"

Ukiah reached the end of the hall and turned the corner. Down the empty, dim hallway, three people were silhouetted against the bank of glass doors to the sun-baked parking lot.

Kraynak sat in a wheelchair, dressed in street clothes, looking battered and gray. All the bruises that were faded and forgotten on Ukiah remained vivid on Kraynak's face and bare arms.

Zoey tugged at the wheelchair handles as a woman pulled the bloody IV tube from Kraynak's arm. Zoey looked up as

Ukiah rounded the corner, and relief spilled across her face. "Uncle!"

Kraynak, already smiling, only brightened at Ukiah's appearance. "Ukiah, look who popped up out of nowhere!"

The woman straightened and looked at Ukiah with dead eyes. How could Kraynak mistake this thing for Alicia? The creatures governing her face twisted it almost unrecognizable with sudden feral excitement. After the raid on the Brody house, all of Alicia's stylish clothes were accounted for. The oversized shirt and jeans that the woman wore had none of Alicia's flair. Beside Zoey—in her clean, starched, bright, tortoise-blue scrubs—the woman was rumpled, gray and dowdy. Even the way she held her stolen body was wrong, void of Alicia's liveliness.

"Alicia" Ukiah said. But it wasn't Alicia any longer. "Hex."

"I am Hex." She acknowledged the name with Alicia's voice and Hex's hard cold stare. "And I know you now, dog child. You stink like your father's Gets, but you're a breeder."

"We killed you in Pittsburgh," Ukiah said, edging closer, trying to get between Alicia and the other two.

"Was that what happened?" Alicia said. "I wondered at the sudden silence. No matter. You killed a piece of me, but I'm much larger than you can imagine, dog child."

Behind Ukiah, Max halted short of the corner, his gun coming out in a whisper of metal on leather.

Kraynak looked between Ukiah and Alicia/Hex, frowning at their stilted conversation. "What's going on?"

Ukiah nearly cried out a protest against Kraynak drawing attention back to Zoey and himself. Ukiah reached for his niece. "Zoey, come here."

Alicia caught hold of Zoey. "No, no, no. I wondered why people in this area made such good Gets. Your mother was changed in some way after she carried you in her womb—mingling her blood with yours—wasn't she? She went on to have many children after you, didn't she? That's why this little one called you Uncle."

"Let the girl go." Ukiah could smell a gun on Alicia, the

sharpened steel of a knife, and even the tang of C4. He and Alicia could survive almost anything, but Zoey and Kraynak could not.

Alicia twisted Zoey in her hold, pulling the girl's head back until Zoey's neck corded with strain. "You want her safe? Then we all go outside, quietly. You come with me, and I'll let them go free."

Ukiah caught the edge of a mental summons as Alicia called to Ontongard outside. He fought the urge to flee, pinned in place only by the pleading look in Zoey's eyes.

"Alicia!" Kraynak cried out, shocked.

Max stepped around the corner, gun leveled at Alicia. "No one is going anywhere."

"Drop your weapon or I'll break her neck," Alicia stated. "Trust me, I'm faster. Drop it."

"Like hell I will," Max growled. "I've seen how you keep your promises. I'd rather see the girl dead than your Get."

"Don't hurt her!" Ukiah cried, trying to hold at bay the inevitable. "Max, get back, she's got backup coming."

"So do we," Max said.

But Alicia's was already arriving in the form of a green work van pulling up to the bank of glass doors. The driver was a tiny woman that could only be Vivian Brody. The van's side door slid open, revealing five men with shotguns aimed through the glass at Max. The beefy blond man in a rumpled, stained, gray uniform was clearly Matt Brody. One of the others was Dennis Quinn, looking weirdly stretched and thin, as if he hadn't absorbed back enough body mass to recreate the familiar form.

"Max, get down!" Ukiah shouted as he felt the Ontongard's communal intent.

A hundred things happened at once.

The Gets in the van fired, flame and pellets blossoming from the ends of the shotguns.

Max shouted at Kraynak, the most vulnerable in the hallway, his pistol kicking in his hand as he returned fire.

Kraynak flung himself out of the wheelchair, diving for the cover of an alcove holding a water fountain.

Sam reached out and jerked Max back around the corner

just as the shotguns filled the corridor with metal, glass, and noise.

Zoey struggled in Alicia's hold, trying to break free.

Ukiah dove to the floor at Alicia's feet, hoping to wrestle Zoey from her in this moment of mass confusion.

Alicia pulled a pistol in that moment, as the sheets of glass sprayed out on either side of her and Zoey, carried by the shotgun blasts, glittering in the morning sun like thrown diamonds. She pointed the pistol down at Ukiah's head, and pulled the trigger.

Ukiah had one moment of awareness, all filled with sound and pain and muzzle flash. Then he was dead.

CHAPTER SEVENTEEN

The Mountains
Day of Shooting

The Wolf Boy came alive.

He was aware of a pain in his head from a small, neat hole in his temple, and a large, messy piece of his skull missing, and a tunnel through the gray mass between the two. Part of him wanted to sleep, reserving energy to heal. The rest recognized danger close at hand. He had to get up. He had to flee.

Normally his body shunted memories to his bloodstream, where they were encoded into his genes. While he had been dead, and his blood idle, his short-term memories had been purged as cells frantically dealt with mortal shock. So it seemed like black lightning had struck him. One moment he had been in the hallway of broken glass. Then, complete darkness flashed across his senses.

He woke sprawled halfway on a bare foam-rubber pad, the size of a toddler's bed, which lay on a old linoleum floor. A crack in the wall by his face let in air—mountain-thin, chilled, and scented with pine. A two-liter pop bottle sat by his shoulder, label peeled off, filled with sugar water. He sniffed it cautiously, and finding it innocent of poison, drank greedily. The carbohydrate intake barely touched the raging hunger in his stomach, brought on by the need to mend a badly damaged body. The sugar water would keep him alive, but he wouldn't heal.

A handcuff trapped his left hand; stainless steel looped

tight around his wrist, the other loop around a steel pole. He examined the pole and found that a hole had been hacked through the wood floor, a solo tube set down into the ground beneath the building, and the whole concreted into place. He searched for a loose nail or pin to pick the lock and failed. He gnawed desperately at the steel, at his wrist, and then finally broke the bones of his hand to collapse it down small enough to slip through the loop. He swallowed whimpers of pain—*they* were close, so very close.

The girl child of his mother's line whom he had come to love lay close. *They* crawled through her, changing her into one of them. *They* had started in her arm, and the flesh writhed as it converted. The change went up her neck, and flashed across her face. *They* were in her brain now, and she cried out as *they* established *their* dominance. He heard what she said, but couldn't understand the words any more. The head wound robbed him of that ability. He did know, however, that there was no saving her now, and he wanted to howl in misery.

The big male that he associated with friendship and safety was chained to another pole, sleeping. At the Wolf Boy's muffled sobs, the man startled awake and stared in amazement at the boy. He made a motion for the boy to come to him. The Wolf Boy could smell *them* inside of the man, under the veil of stale cigarette smoke and sour fear. He scuttled away from the man, growling. The door, though, was locked and solid. The only other exit was over the man's head, a dirty window showing a twilight sky, so he cautiously approached the man. The man spoke softly, not shouting for *them*.

Once closer, the Wolf Boy could see that the man had fought and delayed the injection. The man's immune system waged a feverish war with the alien invader, but it wasn't a battle he could win. The boy felt deep guilt now—if he had trusted the big man with the truth about *them,* the man could have fought free long before being hopelessly ensnared. As it was, the man had been happy to see *her* and had gone willingly and unknowing to his own destruction. The boy flung himself into the effort of freeing the man.

The big man caught the boy's chin, eyed the wound on his temple, and then turned the boy's head to see the damage in the back. The man's voice became a low growl of anger while the Wolf Boy examined the man's restraining band of steel. The metal cuff pressed deep into the flesh, nearly cutting off blood to the hand. Even breaking the bones of the hand wouldn't free the man. While the other cuff rode up and down the pole freely, giving the man some range, the pole itself was solid in the floor and ceiling.

The man caught and stilled the boy, silenced his whimpers with a hard look. He spoke for several minutes, words that the boy couldn't understand but would always remember. The man stood, opened the window over his head and motioned for the boy to climb out, into the gloaming.

There was no way to save them, but it felt wrong to leave them behind.

The Mountains
Day After Shooting

The Wolf Boy was so cold and so very hungry. He kept moving. He drank water when he crossed streams. He ate meadow mushrooms, lichen hanging from pine branches, late-seasoned blue elderberries, and huckleberries found as he ran. He could keep moving on what he found to eat, but not enough to either stay warm or heal.

During the night he used the pattern of the now-nameless stars to head west. He was being followed. He could feel it. The sense of *they* splintered even as he left the cabin, and some followed. By *their* very nature, he could not tell how many followed, or in what form. By the same means he knew *they* pursed him, *they* tagged after him, blindly following the tenuous link of shared genetics. But *they* did not have the Pack's wolf instincts, nor his Wolf Boy experience and intelligence. *They* could not hunt what *they* could not see, and so the night cloaked the Wolf Boy, protecting him.

Then dawn came, and the hunt started in earnest. He heard the crows calling as they moved through the forest,

growing closer. He was drinking from a stream when the
first one found him.

The black bird landed in a soft flutter of wings. They
eyed each other: the Wolf Boy in terror, the bird in eager
greed. The bird's eyes were all black—irisless—just like *His*
had been when *He* tried to kill the Wolf Boy days and days
ago, back home.

The similarity in his enemies' eyes triggered the boy to
action. He snatched up a water-smoothed rock and flung it
hard. He didn't expect to hit, and perhaps for that reason
alone he did. The crow hesitated, expecting a miss, and the
stone struck full on. Breastbone crushed and internal organs
ruptured, it fell out of the tree.

Blind hunger made the Wolf Boy leap the distance sepa-
rating them and snatch up the body. Hot fresh meat! He had
it nearly to his mouth, when he remembered the man who
nailed him to the wall. He flung the bird away from him in
revulsion. He couldn't eat it—it wasn't really a bird. Regardless of what it was now, at one time, it was human.

The bird shuddered, cells trying to work around the damage. Growling, the Wolf Boy picked up the body again, and
tore off the wings and legs from the bird, flinging them into
the stream. *There! Be frogs! Be fish! Be minnows! Leave him
alone!*

A small brook trout he hadn't noticed came out of a shadowed overhang, heading for the bits of alien bird. The Wolf
Boy's eyes went huge and he pounced, snagging up fish
with skill learned in seventy years of running wild.

They were getting close, so he ran, biting through the silvery scales of the fish to the delicious flesh below.

They had him cornered.

He had been running down the hill, and suddenly there
was a cliff. He caught hold of a tree to stop in time and
hugged it tight, panting. Trees grew right up to the edge,
screening the drop, digging roots into stone to lean branches
out over dizzying space, disguising the actual lip. As best as
he could judge, the cliff continued north and south for wrin-

kled miles. At the foot of a cliff, a river ran through a course of massive rocks, shallow and clear.

Behind him, toward the rising sun, he could feel *them* strung out, growing close. Before him the sheer drop; it would take great physical strength that he didn't have to get safely down. If a fall killed him, he'd be captured for sure. Nor could he afford to injure himself further; he could barely keep up the current pace.

He paused, panting, trying to think like the man he knew himself to be. As he did, his hand operated without thought, turning over stones and fallen branches. Five pillbugs scattered under the third stone. He prodded them with a fingertip, making them curl into tight balls. He popped them into his mouth. They crunched as he chewed.

He felt *them,* but he didn't know how many or what forms *they* were in. If only crows pursued him, he could kill them easily enough. It brought to mind the earlier crow, and the Wolf Boy grinned in savage delight.

It wasn't a crow. *It* was the big, blond lawman. Bullet holes peppered the heavily soiled deputy uniform, indicating that *it* had abandoned all pretenses of being human. *It* carried a shotgun, and the sight of the gun set the boy's chest spasming in perfect recall of being murdered by such a weapon.

The boy scrambled backward and away. *It* charged after him like an enraged bear as he ran parallel to the cliff, racing along the ridge. He sensed *them,* moving through the woods, making no efforts to cut him off. Why? *They* had him in an almost perfect trap.

It dawned on him that *they* didn't know the lay of the land. A plan came to him, based on an event that happened long ago, between him and a grizzly. He shunted the memory away, frightened that *it* would read his mind.

He veered east, racing down the hill, gathering speed, not thinking of what lay ahead. *It* turned and followed, *its* bulk and longer legs lending *it* speed, narrowing the gap between the boy and *it.*

And suddenly there was the cliff and the great empty space. He ran straight up to the edge and leapt . . .

. . . and caught a tree branch. He swung out farther into the void, and then up into the tree itself.

As he hoped, like the grizzly of long ago, *it* had been too intent on him. *It* realized too late that *it* was going to fall. Part of *it* reached for the tree trunk, and part of *it* leapt for the tree branch, and other parts tried to stop—but all of *it* failed and went sailing out into the air. *Its* howl of anger and fear ended abruptly with a wet, heavy thud on the rocks below.

Which only went to prove that there were some advantages to being a single individual.

The Wolf Boy swung back out of the tree and raced off.

The Mountains
Second Day After Shooting

He heard Max's whistle the next morning, after running all night without sensing *them*. The whistle went through him, piercing as an arrow. He jerked to a halt—torn between wanting to flee in mistrust of all living things, and wanting to go to the one he trusted completely.

In the end, he crept out of the woods and down to the forest road where a car sat. Max waited there, watching him come. Finally, his courage abandoned him; he crouched down, fifty feet from the car, and whimpered. Too scared to go forward, too afraid to run.

After a moment, Max made a show of stripping off his weapons and jacket. He pulled a package out of a bag, and opened it. The smell of roasted chicken spilled out of the package.

Then slowly, Max walked to him, chicken held out in peace offering. The Wolf Boy stalked cautiously closer, meeting him halfway, sniffing. The familiar, trusted scent, nothing alien added to it. The chicken cooked and cooled, the aluminum peeled back to show a brown, crispy skin.

The Wolf Boy crept nearer and put out a hand. Max crouched unmoving as the Wolf Boy's fingers pressed lightly to the back of Max's hand. Finding him wholly Max, the boy snatched up the chicken, burying teeth into the tender cooked meat. His eyes closed in the pure bliss of taste. He growled softly as he tore off the meat, gnawed down to the bone and sucked on the joints. The chicken, which seemed so wondrously large, quickly became a pile of clean bones. He licked grease from the aluminum foil, whimpering in distress that his belly still seemed empty.

Max spoke quietly, and then finger-talked. "Come."

The Wolf Boy sucked the grease from his fingers, and used them to speak. "Food?"

"Food." Max reached out for the Wolf Boy's shoulder then dropped his hand as the boy shied away. "Follow."

The rental car sat on the side of the dirt road, the driver's door hanging open, the tracking system quietly showing his position.

A second chicken, a fistful of candy bars, a jumbo jar of peanut butter, a loaf of bread, a gallon of whole chocolate milk, and a pack of beef jerky later, the boy allowed himself to be coaxed into the backseat of the car to be covered up with a wool blanket. It was frightening, but Max was here. He slept to the rumble of tires on dirt road, car engine, and the comforting sound of Max's breathing.

The Blue Mountains, Eastern Oregon
Friday, September 3, 2004

He was trapped. Try as he might, he couldn't get out! Trapped!

Ukiah jerked awake into darkness.

He was curled into a tight ball, the way he used to sleep, trying to copy the wolves' nose-to-flank slumber. He opened his eyes, a low growl rumbling in his chest, until he made out the steep roofline of Sam's loft bedroom in her little A-framed cabin. A dim light downstairs threw a pale halo on the ceiling beyond the loft's railing; one of the mismatched lamps by the angle.

A soft noise by his head drew his attention. A small old-fashioned steel cage on the nightstand held one of his black mice. The mouse struggled to lift the cage door, desperate to get to Ukiah.

Ukiah reached out and slid up the cage door. The mouse scurried up his arm to hide in his hair. It held an image of Rennie, astride his bike, driving off to fetch Degas and the Demon Curs. The thought of Degas triggered the low growl again.

Rennie wanted Ukiah gone before he returned with Degas. How long had passed since the shooting? Ukiah sat up in the king-sized bed, trying to count the lost days.

It was night—which night? Alicia had shot him on Wednesday, early in the morning. He had spent most of the day dead, awaking in the mountains at dusk. Or had he been dead more than a day? He didn't think so. With three captives to contain, the Ontongard would have infected Kraynak and Zoey immediately, quickly changing them from troublesome prisoners to allied Gets. Kraynak had just been injected, while Zoey was only in the first stage of infection. Thus only a short time had passed from Alicia shooting him and his waking into the cabin. The thoughts opened a floodgate on his memories.

Zoey lay beside him, denying the alien memories that were crowding into her mind, pushing her out. "No, that isn't me. I'm not that person. I don't really remember that! That didn't happen to me! Why is it so much easier to remember not being me?"

"Ukiah! Oh, God, kid, I thought you were dead! What the hell is going on? Ukiah? Ukiah?" Kraynak caught his chin and eyed Ukiah's temple wound. "Oh, shit, kid. Can you even understand what I'm saying? What the hell did these people do to Alicia? They've twisted her to hell and back. She didn't even flinch when she did this to you!"

Ukiah struggled to free Kraynak, not knowing what the man said.

"No, no, no." Kraynak caught hold of him, silenced him with a hard look. "You might have more lives than a cat, but you've used up at least three this trip. I dragged you into

this. I can't let you get killed. You're leaving now, without me. You go find help, and bring it back, if you can."

And he had gone, leaving them behind, without even looking back.

Footsteps thudded up the loft stairs. He rolled off the big bed and onto the mismatched wood floor. The intruder paused on the top step, and Max's familiar voice said, "Ukiah?"

Ukiah peered over the edge of the bed at Max.

His partner cautiously stepped forward and crouched so they were level. "It's okay, son. It's just me. You're safe."

Ukiah couldn't stop himself. He scurried over the bed with puppy whines of fear and self-loathing. He'd left Max's best friend behind, handcuffed and dying.

"It's okay. It's okay," Max crooned, tentatively taking hold of him, as if expecting him to fight or flee.

"I-I left Kraynak!" Ukiah whimpered. "He told me to go and I just left him there. I ran away and left him."

Max didn't seem to understand. He tightened his hold on Ukiah. "Oh, thank God."

"I left Kraynak and Zoey!"

"Hey, hey, hey! You did the best you could, and that was to stay out of the Ontongard's hands. Did you leave any mice behind?"

Ukiah considered his body at waking and what he just recovered. "No. Nothing's missing."

"Good." Then as if he really didn't want to ask, nor wanted to hear the answer, Max said, "How were Kraynak and Zoey when you left them?"

"Alive. Sick. They were both infected."

Max took a deep breath and sighed it out. "I figured that's how it would work out. Ukiah, you did the right thing. There was nothing you could have done for them." He rumpled Ukiah's hair. "Get dressed, kid. We've got an airplane to catch, although by now, they're probably wondering why I keep buying tickets and not using them."

"We're leaving?"

Max had laid out a set of Ukiah's clothes for him the night before. Ukiah struggled through changing out of his shorts and into them. He felt new to his skin, as if the brief run through the mountains as the Wolf Boy had stripped away the eight years of civilization.

"The sooner we get out of Oregon, the better." Max started to pace, jerking short when he nearly smacked his head against the sharply slanted ceiling. "The kidnapping of you, Kraynak, and Zoey was in the paper. It was too public to keep quiet. I'm not sure how we're going to explain getting you back while they're still missing, but I'd rather do it from Pittsburgh than Pendleton."

Ukiah considered those last few moments, the shadowed hallway, the sun-baked asphalt parking lot, and the blinding muzzle flare inches from his face. In those last seconds, he found Sam's voice, shouting out a protest. "Sam?"

"I didn't know if I was going to be able to get you back." Max said quietly. "I haven't told her anything. I gave her a thousand in spending money and sent her to Pittsburgh in Kraynak's van." A smug grin flashed across his face. "She's in for a surprise."

"This trip has been hard on my credibility as a normal human." Ukiah rubbed the new flesh on his temple. The bone underneath ached slightly. "I'm surprised she left. I thought she would have been the type to tough it out."

"Well, I led her to think that I was getting on a flight out yesterday, but only because she would be showing up in Pittsburgh on Sunday."

Ukiah puzzled through this a moment. Sam left only because she thought by doing so she was protecting Max. Max had pretended to leave only to protect Sam. Somehow this seemed twisted. "She left this morning?"

Max nodded. "She was hoping to make Salt Lake City today."

"She's going to be pissed when she gets to Pittsburgh."

"Only if she beats us there."

"I think she's going to be pissed regardless."

"I'd rather deal with her pissed than dead. What worries me most is that I haven't seen Rennie since we hit the hospital."

"He was going to get Degas and the Demon Curs."

"Degas? That's a new one," Max said after a moment of thought.

"The Curs didn't make the fight in June. Rennie is afraid that Degas will kill me."

"Rennie is afraid? Shit! Oh, this just gets better and better." Max paused, cocking his head. "Is that a car?"

Ukiah listened to the rumble of the approaching motor. "It's Kraynak's van."

"Damn that woman! I told her to go to Pittsburgh!" Max turned and trotted down out of the loft. Headlights slashed brilliance through the downstairs, and then snapped off, making the darkness more solid. The kitchen door banged open, letting in the soft chorus of night insects, as the van door slammed closed.

"What are you doing here?" Max shouted, outside, in the night. "I gave you money to drive to Pittsburgh."

"What am I doing here?" Sam shouted back, even though, by the sounds, they were only feet apart. "You send me off on a wild-goose chase, you break into my house, and you lie to me! You said you were flying to Pittsburgh! I stopped in Idaho and called Portland—do you *know* how many quarters that takes?—and you never got on the friggin' plane!"

"I'm getting on it! Tonight! I just wanted you out of firing range."

"Yeah, sure! I am not June-fucking-Cleaver here. I am a licensed private investigator and a damn good one. How dare you send me off while you play Rambo out for revenge?"

"I am not Rambo, you are not June Cleaver. You can drive me to the airport and watch me get on the damn airplane, if you don't believe me, but I want you out of here before all the shit hits the fan."

Sam gave a sudden laugh, as if caught off guard by Max's comment. "If the shit isn't already on the fan, I'd hate to see your idea of trouble!"

Max laughed too, then sobered. "I'm sorry, Sam. I shouldn't have lied to you. But I couldn't bear to lose you too."

Ukiah stepped out of the house in time to see Sam reach out and pull Max to her. They locked into a hard, desperate kiss. The rawness of it checked Ukiah, feeling like he was seeing something incredibly intimate. He was about to retreat when Sam caught sight of him, and she jerked away from Max with a gasp.

Max whipped around, reaching for his gun, and then relaxed, seeing it was Ukiah that startled her.

"I had a tracer on him," Max said as Sam covered her mouth and made a small guttural noise that could have been a sob. "Because of all the weirdness going on and with Rennie under foot. It just seemed a good idea to keep track of him. That's why I stayed behind, to find him."

Sam brushed past Max and went wordlessly to Ukiah. She reached for his head, and he shied back from the touch, his lip curling up into a silent snarl.

"Easy," Max said from behind Sam. "He's been through a lot. Go slow."

Sam carefully stretched out only one hand, and this time Ukiah suffered the touch. Her fingers explored the new flesh on his temple. "I saw her shoot him. I've seen it every time I've closed my eyes for last two days. She shot him. I saw it."

Ukiah felt the need to say something, but was at a loss for what. Finally he settled for a simple, "She did. I got better."

"I didn't know if I was going to be able to find him," Max said quietly. "Or what condition he'd be in, if I did."

"You're not human, are you?" Sam whispered.

"My mother was a Kicking Deer." Ukiah said.

Anger flashed across Sam's face. "So you're saying this is all Indian mystic bullshit?"

"No." He nearly whined his distress.

"Sam," Max said. "What I said before still holds true. He's a good kid. He didn't ask to be this way."

Sam saw that Ukiah was upset and smoothed away her anger. "It's all right, kid. I've just had a lot thrown at me the last few days." She considered him. "Rennie Shaw, he's like you, isn't he? It's why he doesn't seem to give a fuck if you've got a gun to his head."

Ukiah nodded. "More or less."

"And the Kicking Deers? They're legendary for being strong as bears and healthy as horses."

"They're only a little bit like me, not much at all." Ukiah looked to Max.

Max explained the viral transformation: Once exposed to the virus the person became virtually indestructible. "There are two types. Rennie has been exposed to the Pack virus, which makes him only vaguely anti-social. The Ontongard virus creates complete homicidal lunatics. Quinn, the Brodys, and Alicia have been exposed to it—and now Kraynak and Zoey."

Sam glanced at Ukiah. "But the kid is special. That's why you were hustling him out of the state once you realized what was happening."

Max explained Ukiah's unique position and the danger his capture created. "Because Ukiah's mom carried Ukiah first, then went on to give birth to the Kicking Deer ancestors, the whole clan has been affected. They make perfect hosts for the virus."

Sam gasped. "Oh, my God—Jared!"

"What about Jared?" Ukiah asked.

Sam spoke to Max, watching Ukiah as if afraid he would break under the news. "When I discovered you hadn't gotten on the plane, I called the sheriff's office, figuring Jared would know where you were. They told me that he's vanished. He called in for backup and when it arrived, all they found was the empty squad car."

"No!" It was the only human word Ukiah could force out.

Max gripped Ukiah by the shoulder. "Easy. Easy." Then softly, he asked Sam, "When was this?"

Sam seemed torn between wanting to offer Ukiah comfort and afraid he'd bite any outstretched hand. "Like four hours ago."

Max had tightened his hold on Ukiah. "It's too long. He's already gone."

"No," Ukiah growled through clenched teeth. He couldn't keep running away, leaving behind those he loved.

If he hadn't gone after Indigo and Max when the Ontongard held them, they would be dead now. He had to go.

Max gave him a shake. "You are not going after him, Ukiah. You had the Pack behind you in Pittsburgh."

"No." Ukiah ducked his head.

"Kid, if you go, you're going to have to face down Alicia. Do you think you can kill her and Kraynak in the hopes of saving Jared?"

The concept staggered Ukiah. He had barely been able to deal death to the Ontongard in Pittsburgh, wearing strangers' faces, to save Indigo. He had cringed every time he pulled the trigger, reminding himself that they were no longer humans.

He wouldn't be able to point a gun at Alicia and fire. Even knowing every cell of her had been replaced by a monster, that she would heal back even from dismemberment, that she would destroy everyone he loved without hesitation—he wouldn't be able to kill her.

He sagged against Max's shoulder. "Max, what do we do?"

"There's nothing we can do." Max hugged him briefly, patting him on the back. "Let's go home."

Max released him. As Ukiah stepped away from Max, something came out of the dark woods, a solid form moving silent and quick. Ukiah only caught the flicker of movement out the corner of his eye before it hit him, a hard collision of bodies.

CHAPTER EIGHTEEN

Blue Mountains, Eastern Oregon
Friday, September 3, 2004

Ukiah was slammed to the ground, his attacker on top of him. He felt leather, dodged a thin edge of steel, smelled wolf and man mixed together, sensed the pricking awareness of Pack. *Degas,* he thought, twisting and snarling, trying to escape the other. He had been taken too much by surprise. Faster than either of the two humans could react, he was pinned to the ground, a great weight on his chest, fingers like iron rods gripping his chin, a rumble of growl that felt like a motorcycle engine against his skin, a familiar awareness in his mind. It was Rennie, though, not Degas.

"Oh, Jesus Christ, Ukiah!" Max shouted in surprise and alarm.

Head thrust back by the hand that gripped his chin, exposing his throat, Ukiah could only see dark trees that loomed over them, a slice of moon, a scattering of stars and planets.

Submit! Rennie Shaw growled the single word directly into Ukiah's mind. Ukiah snarled back, too angry and frightened from the sudden attack to be relieved, the wildness flaring up in him.

Ukiah heard Max draw his pistol. Light flooded down from an overhead spotlight, bathing the entire yard in sudden sharp-edged brilliance.

"Shaw!" Max breathed in, and gave a growl of his own. "Get off my boy! I know shooting you will only piss you off for a while, but I'm not in the mood for this bullshit!"

"I'm not going to hurt your boy," Rennie growled. "I'm just making sure it's only him."

" 'Please' and 'may I' still work," Max said.

"Please, may I cut you?" Rennie said.

Ukiah snarled and fell back to a low, unending growl as he thrashed under Rennie.

"I'll take that as a 'yes,' since I'm not willing to take a 'no' on this," Rennie said. *"Degas and the Curs are close behind me. I'd rather be done with this before they arrive."*

I'm putting Max and Sam in danger by fighting, Ukiah realized and forced himself to go limp. He couldn't stop the growling.

"Go ahead and growl all you want." Rennie scored a thin cut across Ukiah's cheek and then licked up the welling blood. *"You don't have to like this part any better than what the Ontongard did to you."*

The mind-to-mind touch was too open and honest. He could sense Rennie's fears of what the Ontongard could have done to Ukiah while they held him, and the Pack's reaction to any additions to his genetics, and started to tremble. *"I was so scared."*

Rennie gazed down at Ukiah with eyes so dark blue they were nearly his father's utter black. There was a momentary stab of pain as Rennie entered his memories and relived those moments before and after dying. Rennie backed up and held the focus on those brief seconds of bright pain at the hospital, the awareness of blood, bone, and brain matter painting the glass behind him.

"Did you get this back?"

"Yes. Max had it."

"Good."

Ukiah sensed that Rennie approved of the man as well as the act.

"I would rather not have to kill him. Remember, the more you fight, the more your partner will try to defend you. For his sake, take whatever Degas dishes out to you." Even as Rennie gave his silent warning, he pulled Ukiah to his feet, but kept a loose hold on him.

Max holstered his pistol, frowning. "What the hell are you doing here instead of chasing the Ontongard?"

"We found their den two hours ago, but they'd moved already. The cub's trail escaping was two days old. There's an unbreakable bond between you and him, Bennett; he would head for you, and you would search until you found him."

"So you just looked for me."

"The hotels are full and public."

"I hate being obvious."

Rennie chuckled softly. "Hex's Gets missed their chance to warp the cub. We'll have to be sure they don't get another chance."

"We were just leaving."

Rennie cocked his head, listening. "Too late."

Ukiah listened with all his senses, and felt the Pack around him, familiar strangers moving through the shadows.

Rennie jerked his chin toward the cabin door. "Take her, Bennett, and get inside. You two can't get into the middle of this."

Max clenched his jaw in anger, but he pulled a protesting Sam into the cabin.

After Ukiah's recent brush with the Ontongard, the arriving Demon Curs struck him with their feral grace. Quinn and Alicia had the same strength and agility, but they lacked style. The Ontongard moved with robotic precision, wearing clothes like ill-fitting sacks over their stolen bodies. The Demon Curs moved with the elegance of dancers.

Embracing the biker-gang image, many wore jackets with a stylized crimson dog on the back, smoke curling from the dog's nostrils. For no other reason than it pleased the Curs, they tended toward black leather, tight denim with flashes of Chinese silks, and bits of silver jewelry. Savage and beautiful, they flowed out of the darkness, surrounding Rennie and Ukiah.

Rennie's early memories of Degas had him red-haired, sparsely bearded, with a sharply pointed chin. A century of alien blood had turned the red hair to Pack black, blunted the chin, and made the beard just a Pack memory. He and Rennie could be mistaken for brothers now.

Degas stared down at Ukiah, nostrils flaring to catch Ukiah's scent. "So this is the boy?" He stalked around Ukiah, stiff-legged, a slight snarl to his lips.

Ukiah turned in Rennie's loose hold to keep facing Degas. Rennie's distrust of the man stirred in him, a secondhand fear. "Degas." He nodded like a slight bow. Beyond Degas, he saw Degas's alpha female, Blade, and his lieutenant, Collin. He greeted them by name and nod. Rennie's hand rested on Ukiah's chest, over his thudding heart.

"The rest of the Pack has tested him, Degas," Rennie said quietly. "They voted. He's one of us."

Blending back into the shadows, Degas became two gleaming eyes, a growling voice, and a wolf-tainted scent. "Hex had hold of him since then."

"I've checked him," Rennie said. "Hex hasn't meddled with him. He's the same cub we found in Pittsburgh two months ago."

"Cub!" Degas spat. "It degrades us to embrace the wolf in us, Shaw. Even Coyote has lived nearly two centuries as a man compared to his handful of years as a wolf."

"All right," Rennie murmured. "Hex hasn't tampered with our beloved son."

Degas snarled. "He's not my son! I didn't screw his mother!"

"We are Prime!" Rennie snapped back. "Much as we beat our chests and claim that we're our own persons, we are Prime. We are Prime's genetic pattern, his memories, and his will. The boy is Prime's son, which makes him our son."

"He's a damn breeder," Degas said.

"He's Pack—with all that being Pack entails," Rennie said. "He has his own heart that knows right from wrong. In nearly two hundred years, Degas, he's not spawned a single child on a woman."

Degas considered Rennie's words for a minute, then said quietly, "On a woman. You're twisting words to serve your cause. We have to count the infant in Pennsylvania. Where there's one, there may be more."

Rennie's eyes narrowed in annoyance. "Hex blooded our boy and made that baby."

"And the boy should have taken it back!" Degas said. "You let sentimentality rule you, Shaw, and now we have two breeders to worry about instead of one. Face it, Shaw, every mouse the boy leaks out could become a full-blown breeder."

"And if every one of them is identical to him in compassion and fortitude, there is no risk."

Degas glared at Ukiah, safe in Rennie's protection. Finally, Degas growled softly, "Hex's Gets are here. A full-grown breeder shouldn't be. That's what is important."

"Degas is right," Rennie said. "Take your partner, cub, and get back home."

"Run home, puppy," Degas said with a smirk. "Let's make the Get and go back to hunting."

Rennie tightened his hold on Ukiah, growling now at Degas.

Get? Ukiah ignored his fear and the overwhelming Pack presence, breathing deep, nose flared to gather in the night air. A familiar scent, mixed with the faint metallic tang of human blood, tainted the night. *Jared!*

"You have him?" Ukiah gasped.

"He got in the way," Degas drawled. "Police have a way of doing that. Good thing they make good Gets."

Rennie read Ukiah's intention and caught him as he lunged at Degas, snarling. The Pack leader had a foot in height and nearly a hundred pounds in weight over Ukiah. Rennie held him firm when no normal man could.

"We don't have many rules," Rennie whispered into Ukiah's ear, holding him tight as iron bars. "One of them is *once a Pack dog has been tested and voted to live, you shall not kill the Pack dog except in a fair fight.*"

Ukiah choked on a bitter laugh. "Fair fight? How could I fight Degas and have it be fair?"

"If Degas attacked you, alpha male against a half-grown cub, it wouldn't be fair. But if you attack him, Degas can defend himself with all force. If he tricks you into throwing the first blow, he can kill you."

"And if I kill him in a fight?" Ukiah asked.

"Then your will holds sway." Rennie shook him. "You're

too weak, cub. That hand of yours is barely holding together, and a good hit will put you down."

"I can't let him have Jared!"

"Jared's guaranteed to survive the transformation, and he'll be Pack. Is that such a bad thing?"

"Do you think I don't know how much you miss being human?"

"Some, like Degas, don't mind."

"And that is why he rails so against the wolf taint?"

"Cub, I tried to keep these cards from being played, but they're on the table now. There's nothing to do now but accept that the game is lost and weep."

Ukiah could find not words to express the pain of giving up on Jared after losing Alicia, Kraynak, and Zoey. Robbed of language, he whimpered his distress.

"Oh, pup, I know this is bitter," Rennie said. "but you must swallow it."

"But—"

"Hush!" Rennie leaned close and whispered. "Do not give Degas an opening. You are not the only one at risk here. If he kills you, he'll hunt down your little one, claiming the right to kill *all* of you. For Kittanning's sake, silence."

Ukiah froze in fear. Kittanning who could fit in his cupped hands, unable to even to roll over. Indigo who would fight to the death to protect her son. Max who loved Kittanning. A cascade of people that would throw themselves between him and sure death. Hellena. Bear. Perhaps even Rennie.

"Yes, perhaps even me." Rennie rumpled his hair. "I caution you from putting me to any practical test, though. Depending on the conditions, I might not jump the way you hope I would."

Ukiah trembled with fury that he couldn't expel. "Fine. But if Jared has to be Pack, then I want him to be your Get, not Degas's. I want Jared under your control, not his."

Ukiah felt Rennie mentally flinch at his words. Rennie hated making Gets, stripping another person of their humanity and making them a pale shadow of himself. That very distaste was why Ukiah wanted Rennie to do it. Rennie would allow Jared to stay Jared as much as possible.

Rennie's eyes narrowed as something occurred to him, but he hid the thought away. He nodded slowly, as if it was a sane, everyday request. "I can only do this if you don't fight."

"No fighting," Ukiah promised.

Rennie released Ukiah then. Between Degas and Rennie was a silent clash of wills, and then, with a growl, Degas stalked away.

Wordlessly, Rennie skinned out of his duster, and then his long-sleeved shirt, revealing a body that normally would need hours of weight lifting to maintain. No scars blemished the skin, despite a hundred and forty years of warfare. A military tattoo bought on the eve of the Civil War had long vanished, a dim, human memory. At least Jared would receive perfect health in trade for his humanity.

Collin brought Jared out of the darkness. The sheriff sagged in Collin's hold, blood trickling from a temple wound, his eyes tracking sluggishly. In the absence of visible weapons and threatening behavior toward him, Jared seemed at a loss to understand what was going on. He recognized Ukiah, and deemed him safety, staggering into the pool of light to lean against him.

"Uncle, who are these people?"

"These are my father's people." Ukiah hugged him, silently saying good-bye. Over Jared's shoulder, Ukiah watched Rennie take out a small leather case, the size of an eyeglasses case. Rennie cracked the case, and the hypodermic needles inside glittered like diamonds in the harsh light. "They can be very ruthless people. I'm sorry. I can't protect you."

"Your father?" Jared slurred the words, glancing at Rennie. "This is your father?"

"I'm what's left of his father," Rennie murmured gently, tying a tourniquet to his arm. "His father was killed a long time ago by the one we fight. And if we didn't fight, then everything we love would be lost. Poets lingering over coffee, spinning words just for their beauty. The young women in their summer dresses, throwing you heated glances. Cats twining about your legs. Children's laughter. Even the simplest wildflower."

Rennie stabbed the needle into his vein and filled the hypodermic with his ruby blood. "It's a hard thing, to kill and lie and steal when all you want to do is live a peaceful life. You go on, only by knowing that ruthless as you are, the enemy is completely soulless."

"If his father is dead," Jared said, frowning, "how can you be what's left?"

"By a simple injection." Rennie caught Jared's arm, stabbed the bright gem into soft flesh and thumbed down the plunger. Jared jerked in Ukiah's hold. "Like that one."

Jared staggered back, holding his arm, staring at the bleeding pinprick. "What did you do?"

"Something that needed to be done." Rennie returned the hypodermic to its case. "You'll understand completely soon enough, and you'll know how sorry I am."

Degas drifted into the light. "The trail is growing cold."

"We're done here," Rennie said. *"This place is fairly safe, but leave as soon as possible, and avoid Pendleton. Drive to Idaho and catch a plane there."*

No other words or action. The Pack melted into the night, dark forms moving quick and silent. Seconds later Jared and Ukiah stood alone in circle of light.

"What did they do to me?" Jared asked.

"They're making you one of them. You'll get extremely sick, and when—when you get better, you won't be just yourself any more."

Jared stared at him, his jaw working. Finally he asked. "What's happened to my baby sister?"

Ukiah shook his head. "She—she's gone."

"What do you mean by gone?" Jared asked quietly.

"Those that took her, did the same thing to her as the Pack has done to you, only it's worse. You received a mutation of the original. You'll keep some semblance of yourself, your hopes and desires. Everything Zoey was will be stamped out."

"Matt Brody and his wife and Quinn?"

"Gone." Ukiah glanced to the cabin as the door creaked open; Max and Sam came out cautiously. They must have watched everything through the windows, for Max looked as upset as Ukiah felt.

Jared blinked at Ukiah, stunned, looking younger than Ukiah remembered him ever seeming. Lost and scared. "There has to be something we can do to get Zoey back!"

Ukiah swallowed down the growls but couldn't stop pacing, his hackles raised. "No, there isn't! It will spread through her like a cancer, only like a cancer of the blood, and the flesh, and the bone. You can't cut it out. It goes through her, making her into itself, and then she *isn't* anymore!"

"If it's like cancer," Sam said quietly, "quickly growing cells, can't we treat it with chemotherapy?"

"I don't know how that works," Ukiah said. They had talked about chemotherapy for his Mom Lara, for her brain tumor. It proved to be unnecessary, and the doctor spoke of her recovery as miraculous. Ukiah suddenly wondered if his blood had anything to do with her healing.

Sam explained. "You give a patient a toxic drug that affects the fastest-growing cells, like the cancer or hair. It gives normal, healthy tissue a chance to grow after the bad cells have been killed."

"I don't know if it would work," Ukiah said. "Many poisons don't work on the Pack. Our cells are able to recognize and adapt to the danger poisons pose. All that would happen, I think, is that the human cells will die."

"After two hundred years, I figure that the Pack has tried everything at least once, twice if it worked," Max said. "What happens when a Pack infects an Ontongard? Not that I'm crazy about the idea, but at least Kraynak and Zoey would be alive and somewhat individuals."

"The Pack tried once. It didn't work out," Ukiah said.

"Why not?" Sam pressed.

Ukiah had sudden sympathy with Rennie, being at a loss to explain the complexities of Pack and Ontongard to him. No wonder Rennie just gave Ukiah his memories. "Normally the Pack passes memories off to one another in the form of mice."

"Like what Rennie did with you?" Max asked.

"Yeah." Ukiah winced, remembering the hostile mouse that Rennie gave to him in a coffee can. It hadn't been pleased with being handed off to a breeder.

Max guessed at an outcome. "So, if you injected an Ontongard with Pack genetics, all that would happen is that the Ontongard would gain the Pack memories?"

"No. Not really," Ukiah said. "Rennie's memories made me sick because they and my cells were hostile to one another. Somehow the two reached a compromise. While I was dead, and the Pack was looking for the remote key, Rennie and Hellena couldn't absorb my memories—they refused to be taken in. There usually has to be mutual agreement before memories can be added."

"Couldn't Hex force a memory to cooperate?" Max asked, "Like he forced Kittanning to change from a mouse into a human infant?"

"He *what?*" Sam asked.

"It's a long story," Max temporized. "I'll explain later."

Ukiah considered the question. His gut reaction was that neither Hex nor his Gets would take a Pack mouse in, even if they could force it to merge. He fumbled for words to shape that instinctual feeling. "Hex probably would think it as too dangerous to consider. Prime wiped out the entire invasion force except for Hex. Prime registered on the Ontongard's senses as one of them. He managed to hide his individuality. Before we killed him, Hex was still bewildered by Prime and the Pack."

Sam was trying to keep up with the conversation. "The Ontongard can recognize Pack now."

"Recognize it, yes. Understand it, no. It's the Pack's experience that Hex's Gets will attack without hesitation, and fight to the death, regardless of the situation. Similarly, the Pack will attack and kill a Get—only they're willing to run away from a fight that they absolutely can't win. It's one of the reasons Pack have kept ahead of the Ontongard."

"What do you mean?" Max repeated Ukiah's phrase back to him. "The Pack tried it and it didn't work out? They tried to infect an Ontongard? What happened?"

"I was getting back to that," Ukiah said. "You sure you want to know?"

"Yes," Sam said. Max and Jared nodded.

Ukiah covered his eyes with his hands. "The Pack figured one mouse is a lost cause; the Ontongard cells would attack until it was gone." So many of Rennie's memories were cursed blessings. Ukiah discovered ignorance was dangerous, but so much of Rennie's past was horrific. "Hex had taken over a little boy, only like six years old, and the Dog Warriors didn't want to destroy the child without trying to save it. They killed the child in order to weaken the Ontongard."

Ukiah shuddered. The killing had to be brutal to be effective. Rennie loathed every second of it. "Then they injected a massive amount of Pack genetic material into the healing body. Several of the Dog Warriors donated blood."

"The child died," Max guessed.

"What survived wasn't a child, but a collection of animals, some Ontongard, some Pack. The boy's body just broke apart and fled in all directions. All the animals that were Pack returned to the blood donors, slightly diminished but unchanged. They hunted down the surviving Ontongard animals and killed them."

Sam held up her hand, trying to halt the flow of information. "Prime was your father, and Hex was the leader of the Ontongard. But they are both dead, so Rennie is now your father and Alicia is now Hex."

Ukiah and Max gazed at her, and then traded puzzled looks, helpless to explain better. "In very simple terms," Ukiah admitted finally. "That's more or less it."

"But you're special. How special?" Sam asked. "Can you change Ontongard into something else?"

"No!" Ukiah cried.

Max looked at him bleakly. "You told me that your blood has been transforming people and your moms' dogs without killing them or wiping out them out as individuals. You could counterinfect Kraynak and Zoey."

"Make them my Get?" Ukiah jerked away from Max, shocked that his partner would even suggest it.

"While I'm glad I'm just me," Max said, "if I had to be your Get or Hex's, I'd pick being yours. I know you don't like the idea, but if it's the only way to save them, maybe we should try it."

"No, no, no!" Ukiah backed away, waving off any possibility. "If I *can* make Gets—Max—exact cell copies! They would probably be breeders!"

"Maybe," Max said. "The wolf dogs aren't. Your mother wasn't. Your blood changed them, but not into Gets or breeders."

"But these are Ontongard Gets, Max!" Ukiah cried. "Think of someone like Hex, but set on spawning as many children as possible. They're brutal rapists of the worse kind: they use any force they need to take a female of the host race, no matter the age or willingness."

"As your Get," Max pressed, "they would mentally be like you, have your morals."

"I'm a genetic mishmash from an alien mutant!" Ukiah warned. "My blood has done things unheard of by the Pack. My Gets could totally retain their own minds—but in this case, the hosts are already mentally Ontongard."

"Or your blood could restore their human mind," Max said.

"Max, much as I love them, I can't risk it." Ukiah shook his head. "Besides, the Pack would never let them, or me, live."

"They're letting the wolf dogs live," Max pointed out.

"That's different," Ukiah protested. "That was an accident and they're not really Gets. Besides, I think only the Dog Warriors know. The Pack tolerates Kittanning because they know I didn't have a choice in his creation, and they're reasonably sure he'll grow up to be a good person. If I made a Get, they would probably decide I wasn't the person they thought I was—and kill me, Kittanning, and the Get."

Sam seemed ready to scream from the hopelessness of the situation. "I can't believe that your people came on a spaceship with all that advanced technology, and there's no way to reverse this."

"Why would they ever want to?" Ukiah asked. "Why would they want to unmake themselves?"

Max sighed. "Ukiah, there's no technology that could reverse the effects? No drug? No antibacterial, chemotherapy, retrovirus—anything?"

Ukiah opened his mouth to say no and then considered

harder. The ovipositor started as a weapon of war against the Ontongard. A race known as the Summ had welcomed the lesser-advanced Ontongard, confident that if a war became a matter of starship against starship, they would win. Only after a quarter of their race was dead or converted did they realize their danger. By then, telling friend from foe was impossible, and a racial cleansing would have needed to start at the heart of the Summ civilization. Recognizing that the war was truly being fought at the molecular level, the Summ worked feverishly to develop tools of genetic manipulations, only to have their lead scientists fall to the Ontongard and corrupt the technology to their use. "Well, part of the ovipositor did complex genetic manipulation. It would create a viable offspring between Ontongard and the native life, a child that could breed with the native stock and produce offspring that the Ontongard could easily infect."

"So we can use this ovipositor to do genetic manipulation—like to design something that will get Zoey back," Jared said.

Ukiah shrugged. "The ovipositor was on the ship, and Prime destroyed the ship."

"Was this where your mother was taken?" Jared asked. "Up in the mountains? Buried in the ground?"

Ukiah stared at Jared in surprise for a minute before answering. "Yes."

"It wasn't destroyed," Jared said. "It was damaged. You went back once."

"I did?" Two hundred years after puberty, and his voice could still crack. "You know this?"

"My great-grandfather Jay told me about it," Jared said. "The two of you had gone up in the mountains when he was young. Your mother had told you about finding her way home, when you were very young. She gave very vivid landmarks. While she was alive, she wouldn't let you go there, and she lived for a very long, long time. But after she died, you and he looked for it."

"And I found it?"

"Yes, you found it."

CHAPTER NINETEEN

Ukiah saw the excitement on Sam's and Jared's faces and winced.

Max, though, knew the truth. "Ukiah used to know where the ship was. He doesn't remember anymore."

Ukiah said, "I lost the knowing when Magic Boy was murdered. I don't have any memories of living with your family."

It hurt to see the excitement die out of Jared's face. Clearly, he felt betrayed and yet struggled to hide it. Worse, Jared had gone pale and trembling as Pack virus surged through him. Ukiah could feel the tendrils of it fighting Jared's defenses, finding ancient weaknesses created by the Kicking Deers' exposure to Ukiah's blood while Ukiah was in his mother's womb.

Ukiah scrambled to find some hope to offer Jared. The photographs had shown that Magic Boy had been chopped into many pieces. Hands severed from arms. Arms cut off at the shoulders. A nightmarish child's puzzle of body parts.

Some of Magic Boy definitely went on to form Ukiah. For his memory loss to be so drastic, he would have to start out as just a fraction of that whole. A leg, the headless torso, or perhaps just the arms changed, sometime, somehow, into Ukiah.

Which meant there had to be other parts, in some form or other. If he found one, he could conceivably recall the location of the scout ship—but would he still be Ukiah afterward?

"Maybe if I can find some memories," Ukiah offered weakly. Sam looked at him with confused, faint repulsion. "Exactly how do you *find* memories?"

Ukiah glanced to Max, who sighed and nodded agreement that the time had come to be completely upfront. "I'm not so much a person as a colony of cellular beings. If you cut off my hand, then my hand would reorganize itself into something that could survive. It would become a rat or a bird or a fish—and my body would grow a new hand to replace it."

Sam shuddered. "Oh, I hope you're talking theory and not practical experience."

"Theory," Max said.

"Actually," Ukiah reluctantly admitted, "maybe practical experience."

"Magic Boy," Jared hissed, his eyes unfocused as he made all the connections. "When Magic Boy was dismembered, all the severed pieces became animals and ran off. That's why his body vanished."

"Yes," Ukiah said.

Max understood the implications. "But there might be other parts of Magic Boy roaming around with his memories still genetically coded."

Jared blinked back into focus, surprised. "You don't think all the parts reassembled in Ukiah?"

"And why do you need them?" Sam struggled to understand. "Don't you remember? And if you've forgotten, wouldn't have they?"

"It's possible I'm only a fraction of Magic Boy," Ukiah fumbled for words. "I could be just his torso or one of his legs. There's no telling what I went through from the time he died to a time I clearly remember. I could have existed as two rabbits and a squirrel for a decade until they merged into something large enough to make a human child."

Sam's hand slid up to cover her mouth, and from behind its protective screen, she whispered, "Oh, that's soooo weird."

"When I became human, at that point, there's a change as

to how my memory is stored. Bird, squirrel, or fish—the piece of flesh was big enough to form an adult creature. When my cells decided to become human, they could probably have only formed a child—most likely there weren't enough of them to make an adult. And genetically, as a breeder, I have to grow to sexual maturity."

"And like Kittanning," Max applied what he knew to Ukiah, "your 'old' memories were lost as you grew up."

Ukiah nodded. "For Kittanning's sake, I'm glad how my father's mutation works out for us, but I wish I could have kept my memories of my mother and my family."

"What kind of animals do we need to look for?" Jared asked, already turning to the task at hand.

Ukiah spread his hands helplessly and guessed. "Mice. Snakes. Gophers. Dogs. Cats."

Sam stared at Ukiah, shaking her head. "I'm looking at you, and I just see a sweet kid. I can't believe what you're saying."

"He is a good kid," Max said. "Everyone has quirks. His are just weirder than most."

Jared ignored everything but saving Zoey. "Are you sure these lost parts will remember?"

"No," Ukiah admitted. "They've certainly lost some of Magic Boy's memories. How much depends on what's happened to that set of cells since the murder. The fewer changes and trauma, the more that piece will remember."

"These alien cats and dogs," Sam said slowly, obviously still struggling with the whole concept, "are they going to look just like other regular animals?"

Ukiah spread his hand helplessly. "They might be black. Certainly, they would be long-lived and nearly indestructible."

"Little Slow Magic, " Jared said.

"What?" Ukiah said.

"He's a family pet." Jared wiped sweat from his face with a trembling hand. "We've got pictures of him with my father as a baby. He's always seemed indestructible; he's lived through everything we've ever done to him, including accidentally running him over with a truck."

"What the hell is he?" Max asked.

"A turtle."

Jared vomited in the yard of the Kicking Deer farm. He had held out, growing sicker by the minute, until they arrived. The moment the Blazer stopped, he fought the door handle, tumbled out of the SUV, and threw up in the grass. After the first few wet upheavals emptied his stomach, he continued to dry heave, as if his body was trying to force out the alien invaders by any method possible.

Jared's mother and Cassidy were the only ones at the farm. They swung from being relieved at seeing Jared in one piece to alarm, as he lay sweating and weak on the lawn. Ukiah carried him into the house to a bedroom Jared abandoned along with boyhood. Fever heat poured from Jared, like he was transforming into a being made of flame instead of flesh. Already from his mind, Ukiah caught flashes of delirious thoughts, of rupturing to reveal a creature of the sun trapped beneath the sweat-slick skin.

"I'm sorry." Ukiah tucked him into the twin bed, dusty from disuse. "I'm a coward. I shouldn't have let them to do this to you."

"Could you have really stopped them?"

"I don't know. Trying would have been better than this."

"Cub, how would your dying save Zoey?"

"It wouldn't have." But at least he wouldn't have to listen to Rennie's words come from Jared's mouth.

Max waited for him in the dim, comfortable living room. "Jared's mother has gone for his grandfather; he's a medicine man of some sort. I've tried to explain something to Cassidy; I'm not sure how coherent it sounded, but she didn't ask a lot of questions. She and Sam are looking for the turtle now. Apparently they just let him wander around loose."

Ukiah closed his eyes and *felt*. As he suspected, Little Slow Magic felt much like Kittanning, a distant echo of himself. There was a difference, a deeper resonance to the answering note. "He's out back."

Max gave him a worried look. "Rennie's memory made you sicker than hell. You sure you're going to be okay?"

Ukiah wished he were better at lying; he was too scared to convincingly say, "I'll be fine.'" Max knew him too well. Since leaving Sam's cabin, implications of absorbing Little Slow Magic slowly filtered in from Rennie's memories. "I don't know, Max. The Pack, they try not to share too many memories back and forth; apparently it makes it hard to keep track of who you really are."

"You never said anything about Rennie's memories confusing you."

"There's enough difference between us that I can tell where I stop and he begins. I *was* Magic Boy; when I take in Little Slow Magic, I might go back to being him."

"Shit." Max rubbed at the stubble on his face. "I don't think you should do this, kid. You're risking your whole identity on the hopes to find a hidden space ship intact enough to pull out a piece of technology that *might* help you save three people who will kill you on sight, if we could find them before the Pack reduces them to ash."

For a moment he felt relief, forgiven by Max for refusing the danger. Then the memories crowded in. All the times they didn't warn Kraynak. Zoey's quick affectionate acceptance of him. Alicia in his arms, feeling safe.

Protect your people, that is what you were born to do.

Was this what the bear meant? The possibility helped calm the raging fear inside him. "I have to, Max."

"Are you going to recognize what you need? Do you know how to make it work? How to modify it?"

"Yes, and soon Jared will too."

Little Slow Magic was a large black turtle, and excited to see him. The turtle extended his leathery neck and bobbed his head in the closest thing to being rambunctious as he could get.

Because Sam and Cassidy had already been looking for the turtle, there were four pairs of expectant eyes watching Ukiah lift Little Slow Magic up, feeling that familiar shiver of joy welcome him. He never felt the need to hide taking back a memory before; suddenly the act seemed too intimate to do before two virtual strangers.

"I think I'd like to do this in private."

Tucking Little Slow Magic in the crook of his arm, he wandered off onto the prairie. When the house and barn were toy-sized in the distance, he sat down on the low grass. The turtle in his cupped hands, Ukiah waited with fear skittering around in his stomach like cold-footed mice.

And waited.

And waited.

It wasn't going to work. Unlike his other memories, there was no impatient want to merge. Ukiah sensed that Little Slow Magic was mildly lonely—part of a large, loving family and yet isolated by his very form. True, Little Slow Magic was happy to see him, but as a long-lost brother. The turtle had too long been an individual to consider himself only part of a whole.

Ukiah stared at the turtle in his hands, stumped. Rennie's mouse hadn't wanted to merge with him; the small crushable bundle of fur submitted only after he nearly killed it. Tearing the turtle into pieces would require a great deal of violence.

The happy burble from Little Slow Magic ended abruptly. Head, tail, and all four legs jerked suddenly into the shell, which snapped tightly shut.

Ukiah eyed the closed shell. Considering that Little Slow Magic was most likely supernaturally strong for a turtle—dealing with him just got even more difficult.

"I need you. Please. Help me."

It was like throwing stones into a well, straining to hear if there was water at the dark, distant bottom.

"I don't want to hurt you. Zoey is in danger. I need you to help her."

Ukiah focused on the girl, the bright smile, the dark eyes, the chin that cocked up in defiance. He remembered her then in the Ontongard shack, struggling to defy the viral alien within her.

"I need to save her."

From the dark well of Little Slow Magic's mind, images of Zoey echoed back to him, only these from floor level.

Zoey's bare toes absently rubbing along his chin. Green, succulent lettuce while Zoey droned on about the injustice of being a woman. Toenails, ten for Zoey and twelve for Little Slow Magic, painted to match.

"We," came the impression, not words, *"will save her."*

What was Little Slow Magic pressed against Ukiah's palms, and then seeped into him, cautiously joining with him. He felt the genetic links move through him, rushing with his blood, like someone opened his veins and poured lava in. He gasped in surprise and took in a deep breath . . .

. . . panting air clearer and crisper than any he remembered breathing. He was young, a baby of two or three, but pleased that he'd gotten so far from his mother's watchful eye. He stood on the ridge that would someday house the Red Lion Hotel and the I-84 overpass. On the far ridge, unfarmed prairie stretched out as far as the eye could see, golden grass waving in the wind. Huts of tule-reed mats clustered in the river valley, racks of drying salmon promised a winter of plenty . . .

A jump, memory lost.

. . . The wind outside was howling against the tule mats, making them rattle. His family lounged around a fire on furs. Four boys tumbled together like puppies. He was the oldest, but still very young. Eight? Nine? The other three boys were seven, five, and three years old. A woman sat with an infant at her breast. A man sat watching them with contentment in his eyes.

"Tell us about the crow people, Mother," one of the other boys cried.

"Yes, Kicking Deer," said the man. *"Tell us about the crow people."*

The woman breastfeeding the infant looked up, and he saw it was his mother. She was older than when Prime took her, a woman of her midtwenties, not of her midteens.

"Aiieee," she said, rearranging her clothing. *"Don't you ever tire of that story?"*

The boys cried out for the story, and she hushed them all. "The crow people came the summer before Magic Boy was

born. All winter the crows had night roosted in the river bot-
toms, closer to the village than anyone could remember, so
many more than ever before. It was like all the crows had invited their kin to come roost with them. Their klaahs drowned
out the sound of the river and the wind.

"Always, that spring and summer, when you looked, you
would see a crow. They watched us with their all-black eyes.
You could not leave out food or string or shells. They would
swoop in on black wings and grab it up. But if you picked up
a bow to shoot them, before you could nock the arrow, the
crow, he would fly away.

"One day, there was the sound of thunder in the clear sky,
and it went on and on. Mother called, 'Look, look,' and I look
up and see a thunderbird. It came from the setting sun, and it
carried a stolen firebrand in its beak, and the flames danced
all around the thunderbird, but did not consume it. Everyone
fell to the ground, afraid. The thunderbird swooped down
and landed in the mountains. The ground shook, and the firebrand put up a great plume of smoke. All the crows flew up,
shouting klaah klaah, as if they knew and were happy.

"We gathered around, asking, 'What does this mean?
Why did the thunderbird come without clouds? Why did it
steal part of the sun?' And we did not notice until later that
the crows had all gone away.

"The next day, the man of the crow people came. He was
naked, tall, with spindly legs. His hair was stiff and black as
a crow wing. And his eyes were all black, without any white,
just like a crow.

"At first we did not fear him. He was only one and we
were many. We had our bows and arrows, and he was naked.
We met him with friendly words, and offers of gifts. He did
not speak, only pointed, and the person at whom he pointed,
they would drop dead as stones. He pointed, and my mother
dropped. He pointed at my older sister Magpie Song, and she
dropped. My brother Willow Branch shot the man with an
arrow. The man pointed at Willow Branch and he dropped
like a stone. The man pulled the arrow from him and did not
even bleed. We saw we could not kill this man of the crow

people, and we ran away, scattering in all directions. I ran down to the river, and hid in the berry bushes.

"I heard a noise, and I think it was the man of the crow people. But it was Coyote. He crouched in the bushes with me, and he said, 'Little female, take this stone and swallow it. When the man of the crow people points at you, you will not die.'

"So I swallowed the stone, and it sank down to settle like a lump in my stomach. I went then to help my family. The man of the crow people was picking up the dead and putting them in a stone boat that sat on land. He saw me, and he pointed at me, and I started to turn to stone. I fell down and got all stiff, but the stone in my stomach protected me. He put me in the boat with the others, and the boat rose up into the air and flew into the mountains.

"Deep in the ground was the thunderbird. It had dug down into the roots of the mountain to escape the sun, but the sun had killed it anyway. The man of the crow people took us into the body of the thunderbird, where another man of the crow people waited.

"The crow people tied me down so I could not move or see. They poked at the stone in my stomach, and they talked in their harsh crow tongue. A long time passed and suddenly a voice whispered 'Little female, run! Run now, run away.' I was no longer tied, and there was sunlight seeping in from above. The mountains were shaking and dirt shifts in with the light. I climbed up and up and came out high in the mountains. I saw two boats of the crow people moving away. The crow people were shooting arrows with brilliant, long, red feathering at each other. They went toward the rising sun, so I went the other way hoping to find the village. I traveled for a short time when there was a great noise behind me, and the earth shook, and a fire roared up.

"I ran until I could run no more, and I slept, and ran more. Many days I traveled until I found my way back to the village. Those who were not killed had hunted down the crows and killed all that they could find.

"But I find that Coyote tricked me. The stone in my belly grew and grew, and after nine moons, Magic Boy was born."

A jump, memories lost.

*. . . must be the "white man" that they had been hearing
about. The traveling party had a score of men, and a woman
that looked like a Shoshone, a baby strapped to her back. By
count of limbs, eyes, nose, and mouth, the white man seemed
like any other man. He pressed through the crowd of vil-
lagers, fingers outstretched, curious to see if the men would
"feel" the same as other men, or would they would be totally
different, like a frog felt totally different than a fish although
both lived in the water. A woman's hand clasped tight on his.
Traced through her genes were many that matched his own.
"Uncle," she murmured, "don't draw attention from the
strangers. It is said that they go downriver next." Downriver
was where the various neighboring tribes sold slaves. He
gave her a disgusted look, partially because he wanted to explore, but mostly he could not imagine anyone wanting a
stunted freak like him, the boy that didn't grow up . . .*

No record of the woman's name, or her true relationship
to Magic Boy remained. Had her father been one of the little
boys that wrestled like wolf cubs with him? Or was she more
distantly related, a granddaughter, or great-granddaughter of
his brothers? There was no time to wonder, for even as one
memory snapped off, another blasted full bloom into his
mind.

*. . . They lay on the riverbank, dipping fingers into the
water, watching the minnows dart away. Far off, a train
whistle went unnoticed, yet recorded into his memory. The
boy beside him grunted, rolled onto his back, and watched
clouds drift overhead. "What do you think of Hannah?"*

*Magic Boy winced inside—it was the beginning of the
end. They always grew up to leave him behind, going on to
things he could never hope to have . . .*

A jump, memories lost.

*For once the memory caught him in a moment of reflec-
tion. He sat in high in the mountains, letting the teenager beside him catch his breath.*

At least one benefit of living for a long time, *he thought,*
is seeing the pattern of life, and taking advantage of it.

He thought then, of his mother's children, grandchildren,

great-grandchildren, great-great-grandchildren, and even her great-great-great-grandchildren. They numbered in the hundreds, being without fail healthy, wise, fertile, and long-lived. A strong law-abiding streak ran through them, and they became stuffy at an early age. Luckily, each generation had its troublemaker, and thinking of each in turn, from his baby brother to the most recent, Jay, he decided that he loved them most of all.

Take this adventure to find gold in the mountain streams. Jay's uncles and cousins would all argue that it wasn't worth the risk; a charge of claim jumping could land them both in jail, if they weren't hung out of hand. Jay only pointed out that Magic Boy could sense gold in the water just by touch, and thus they could find it quickly. Anyone watching would think they were boys on a lark, finding nothing. It was riskier than breeding horses, where a hundred years of experience allowed Magic Boy to coax superior colts out of only ordinary-seeming parents. In one day, though, they could find more gold than several colts would bring the family.

At my age, *Magic Boy thought guiltily,* I shouldn't have allowed my own boredom to let him talk me into this.

By then Jay turned and flashed him a grin that lifted away all sour thoughts. "Do you know, Uncle, I've been thinking."

Magic Boy laughed, knowing full well how this would end.

"What?" Jay asked, caught by surprise.

"Promise me, Jay, when it is your son that's dragged me off to some misadventure, you will not say 'Uncle, you're supposed to keep him out of trouble!' Ones like you cannot be kept out of trouble. In fact, I think it might be a mistake even to try. It would be like keeping fish out of water."

Jay laughed, showing the sound white teeth that marked him as a child of Kicking Deer. "I promise. Now, look over there." Jay pointed out the depression that later would be known as Big Sink. "Does that not sound like the rocks that your mother talked about when she climbed out of the thunderbird's body, fleeing the crow people? Let's see if we can find the way down to the thunderbird."

And off Jay went. Magic Boy followed, ambivalent about

the whole adventure. It sounded dangerous. On the other hand, Magic Boy could feel the strangeness in him. He was partly his mother, and in her many children he could find whispers of himself. He could find no match, though, for the other parts of him. Not coyote. Not crow. Not of anything that crawled in the dirt, swam in the water, ran the earth, or flew in the sky.

In the thunderbird's body, deep in the earth, perhaps there would be a clue of what he was.

It took all of Magic Boy's abilities to locate the narrow, chimneylike cave. Leaning down in, he found ancient traces of his mother's passage . . .

The memory ended. Only from what Jared told him did he have any hint that he and Jay actually ventured down the hole. Other memories were unfolding, competing for attention. Ukiah tried to hold onto the memory a little longer, treasuring the affection he felt for Jay.

Jared was Jay's great-grandson, he realized with dismay. Tiny flickers of memory gave him Jared's bloodline of Jay, Jesse, and then Jared's father, Jacob.

Then the next memory shared avalanched into his mind. This one thankfully degraded from the razor-sharp details of his normal memory—for Ukiah could only watch in dismay as Magic Boy pursued the lone Ontongard through the streets of Pendleton. His earlier version thought only of finally finding someone that felt just like himself, and forgot all the dangers of his conception. Lost was that moment when the Ontongard turned to attack, or how they ended up in the underground passages of Pendleton. The memories stuttered like a badly edited horror film as Magic Boy fled through the endless, twisting dark in an attempt to escape. The creature that only looked human chased him. Cornered him in the butcher shop. Reared over him. Ax. Ax. Ax. Ax . . .

Ukiah jerked away in horror from the memory and fell into another, saner one.

. . . he was stuck on the blasted doorstep again. The wood was deeply scored from the countless times he been there before, unable to climb up the height of his shell without repeated attempts. He felt vibrations of someone coming. He

blinked nearsightedly behind him, sniffing. Jared. He waited patiently, and sure enough a hand slipped under his shell and lifted him up to sit him on the kitchen floor.

"There you go, slowpoke," Jared rumbled far overhead, and then leaned down to tap gently on his nose . . .

Ukiah blinked at the memory.

Jared! And there—from the rhythmic creaking of bed-springs, to the break of Claire's water, to an infant's cry, to a toddler's curious fingers, to a boy's confidences, to a man's protective stance—unfolded Jared's life. This was a Jared he had only seen glimpses of, a man physically strong yet gentle, determined to do what was right and good, with a capacity to love deep and strong.

Oh, God, Jared! Ukiah threw his head back and howled the sudden and complete knowing of the nephew he had betrayed and lost.

Ukiah heard Max's hurried footsteps approaching, but couldn't take his hands from his eyes. His tears felt like fire burning under his eyelids.

Max touched him lightly on the shoulder. "You okay?"

Ukiah nodded.

"You know," Max said softly, "if the machine works on Ontongard, it will work on Pack too."

Ukiah looked up at Max, blinking, through the shimmering pain of unspent tears. "You mean change Jared back?"

"Yes." Max glanced about. "So it worked? You took in the turtle?"

Ukiah stood up, scrubbing at his eyes. "Yeah. I remember where the ship is."

Big Sink, Blue Mountains, Eastern Oregon
Saturday, September 4, 2004

Magic Boy and Jay must have moved rocks to block the hole, afterward, because a stack of stones blocked the entrance. Max, Sam, and Ukiah shifted the stack aside to reveal the opening.

Max measured the gas content of the fissure.

"You always bring all this to find lost hikers?" Sam asked, eyeing duffel bags of equipment.

"Hikers stick their noses into some of the most unlikely holes." Max clicked the detector to the natural-gas setting. "The dangerous thing about holes in the ground is that there's no good reason for oxygen to be present if another, heavier, gas has filled the hole up."

"And even the kid can't survive without oxygen?" Sam asked.

"I'd rather not test that theory." Max folded away the gauge. He took out his lighter, snapped it on and held it in the sheltered opening of the fissure. The flame flickered and danced. "The air is good down as far as I can drop the probe. There seems to be a strong updraft, so there must be another opening and this one is acting like a chimney."

"Great!" Ukiah cinched tight his climbing harness. "It's a going to be a tight enough fit without oxygen tanks—which we don't have."

"Oh, you don't?" Sam seemed amused by the lack.

"Not with us," Max explained. "You can't transport them on planes, and I didn't pick up a spare tank once we got here. I figured we would be working with the search-and-rescue team, which would have its own supplies."

"It can't be too bad of a climb if my mother got out, provided there wasn't a major landslide or fall afterward," Ukiah said. "Being that Jay and I got down into it and back suggests not."

Max looked at him hard. "You and Jay?"

Ukiah blinked. The memory was there, without having him dig for it—as if it was his own memory. "Jay and Magic Boy."

Max let it go, probably because there was nothing to be done for it now. Instead he flipped on the radio base. "Headset."

Ukiah slipped on his headset. "Testing. Testing."

"You're green across the board. Go ahead."

With Max anchoring off to control the climbing ropes tied to Ukiah's waist, Ukiah crawled into the hole and slowly rappelled down the steep rock chimney.

                              *   *   *

Only three people had made the climb prior to him: his mother, Jay, and Magic Boy. He found bits and traces of them, faint ghosts of their passing. Ukiah treasured those of his mother. For a woman seemingly chosen at complete random, his splintered memories of her revealed a person of great intelligence, compassion and wisdom. Unique as he was, he had been overshadowed by her in their family until her death.

"Mother, I'm like no other." He hid his face in her lap, her hands gentle on his hair.

"Ah, Magic Boy, let me tell you a story. Two coyotes met on a ridge looking down into a village. The first coyote grinned his sly grin and said, 'I am Coyote.' 'Well,' said the second coyote, 'so am I.' 'No, no, I'm the Coyote.' 'How can this be? We're both coyotes. I could be Coyote just as well as you.' 'Here,' said the first coyote, 'I'll prove it to you.'

Down the first coyote trotted into the village, and the people working there looked up and cried. 'Ah, it's Coyote!' And he trotted back to his brother and said, 'See. Did you hear what they called me?' 'That proves nothing,' said the second coyote. 'Here, watch.' And he trotted down into the village, and the people looked up, and said 'Ah, there's another!'

Magic Boy giggled.

"It is better, my little one, to be yourself, and not just another."

Outside the memory, Ukiah felt a powerful love for her. More than before, he could not leave Zoey and Jared to their hard fates. His mother wouldn't have approved.

They say God works in mysterious ways.

The alien scout ship made a controlled but hard emergency landing in the Blue Mountains, tucked up against a granite cliff. Either one of Prime's sabotage efforts—prior to or after the landing—or the landing itself had sliced open the hull exactly opposite of the crack in the granite. Superheated by the reentry, the hull had fused rock to glass where it touched, heat venting up through the chimney, keeping the vent open while reinforcing it with its forge-hot heat.

A bubble of space remained between rock and hull. Ukiah dropped down to the ceramic-covered hull and peered through the slash in the metal below. The hole continued down through a twisted mass of wires and circuitry boards.

"Well I'll be damned," Ukiah muttered over the headset.

"What is it, kid?" Max's voice whispered in his ear, barely reaching through the rock between them.

"This opens right into the ovipositor, nearly over the table Hex and Prime had my mother strapped to."

"So she got loose and climbed right out, just like she said."

"The room was intact when Prime last remembered it." Ukiah eyed the twisted equipment. "Prime must have done a lot of damage that I don't remember."

Max swore softly. "Are we going to be able to salvage anything useful?"

"Have faith," Ukiah murmured, easing himself through the ragged metal. Ukiah snaked through the tangled wires and swung down onto the dirt-coated floor of the scout ship. "Okay. I'm in."

He glanced at the table where his mother had been held captive. The restraining straps operated on magnetic locks. When the power failed in the room, they opened, freeing his mother. Since the ovipositor had its own independent, backup power system, only extensive damage like his father wreaked on the equipment itself would have caused it to fail.

He had thought during the trip from the Kicking Deers' to the Big Sink on what equipment they would need in order for this to work. He went first to the resequencer. The durable instrument front had been unscrewed and set aside. Stuffed into the heart of the circuitry was an unexploded detonator, looking as innocent as a can of soda.

"What is it, kid?" Max asked when Ukiah yelped in surprise.

"It's a bomb."

"Shit, get out of there, then."

"Wait. I think I can just disarm it." Ukiah peered cautiously at the detonator. Prime had apparently set the delay counter and tripped the arming switch. The power cell, though, was long dead, leaving no clue to why the detonator failed. Without an electronic pulse to trigger the explosion, the detonator should be inert.

Wincing, Ukiah picked it up. Nothing happened. Holding it at arm's length, he squinted and thumbed the arming switch to off. It clicked down. Gingerly he carried it to the waste disposal unit, unsealed the steel door and carefully placed the detonator inside. He sealed the disposal's door.

"Okay. I've gotten rid of it. I'm going to check to see if there's any others."

Ukiah had memories from Prime of shutting down the scout ship's damage-control systems. Judging from the damage he saw, Hex must have gotten them back on line as the string of detonators tried to rip the ship apart from the inside. Inertia fields had contained the explosions as they were detected, localizing the damage to spheres roughly twice the size of the soda-can shaped detonators.

Prime, with his layered backup plans, had placed all the detonators inside the equipment. So while the damage was minimal, the bombs still utterly gutted the equipment.

"Ukiah?"

"Most of the systems are toast," Ukiah reported. "One bomb failed to explode, and it was in the piece we need."

"Oh, thank God."

Ukiah knew that Max was just saying it out of habit. Still, he pressed his hands together like his moms taught him and said, "Thank you, Almighty God, for this blessing we have received. Amen."

"Ukiah!" Max half-laughed, half-scolded far above. And then explained to Sam, "He's praying down there. No, I'm not an atheist. Kid, are you going to be able to get it up by yourself?"

Ukiah considered the resequencer. "I could use help."

In some ways, Ukiah desperately wanted to know what had happened between Hex and Prime hundreds of years ago.

After leaving the mother ship, Prime had been wounded many times, reducing his last memories down to random snippets. Time and time again, the Pack had discovered the dangers hidden by Prime's lost memories. They had not known that the mother ship crashed on Mars. They had not realized that Hex could free the crew trapped in cryogenic sleep. They had not guessed that Kicking Deer lived to give birth to the feared breeder.

What else did they not know?

As Ukiah searched the ruined scout ship, looking for tools and equipment, he found evidence of Prime's systematic sabotage. Many of the doors had been fused shut and then cut open. The armory, when Ukiah cranked the door open using the backup manual system, was stripped completely. He found a stack of damaged weapon power cells by the trash compactor. The compactor was filled with crushed stunners. Laser burns riddled the bridge control panels. The lift to the bridge had been blown with a disrupter cannon jury-rigged into the ship's power system, apparently set to go off when the lift signaled that it reached a certain level. A landslide filled the open sled-docking bay with dirt, boulders, and tree roots.

Prime left a trail of emptied and smashed weapons. When Prime could no longer use a weapon, he made sure Hex couldn't either—usually by using it to beat a ship's control to pieces. All major ship systems were damaged in one manner or another.

Unless Prime was a horrible shot compared to Hex, then Hex probably had been as wounded as Prime. Ukiah reconsidered his last memory of Prime, fleeing the scout ship with Hex in close pursuit. Prime had been so hurt that he couldn't remember what he had done to the ship, or even which direction it lay.

Had Hex also lost the memory of where the ship lay in this manner? Or had some later accident robbed him of the knowledge? Without the store of weapons, Hex would have found the world full of hostile elements and hosts that would usually die instead of converting into allied Gets.

Good work, Dad.

In the end, though, when Ukiah found Hex's five other bodies cooked in their cryo-chambers—dry-roasted mummies—he was glad he didn't have all Prime's memories.

Ukiah gathered what tools he could find that his father hadn't destroyed and returned to the ovipositor room.

Max stood watching Sam pick her way through the wires when Ukiah returned.

"You could make a fortune selling haunted-house tickets to this place," Max said in greeting. "I think it's the creepiest place I've ever seen."

Sam dropped down beside Max and her eyes went wide.

Max shined his light onto bright, hanging pieces of the analyzing station. "Do I want to know what that is for?"

"It's for vivisection." Ukiah shuddered. His mother's tales were innocent of that horror. Had she been spared the knowledge of what Hex had done to her family members he had taken, or had she merely edited it from her story? "The machine would sample secretions and such from still-living— bodies."

"Well, that would win my vote for first thing to blow up too," Sam remarked on the fist-sized hole in the analyzing station's control panel. "Hopefully, we didn't need it."

"No. It's used to identify the reproductive systems on native life-forms and what is needed to be done to produce a half-breed child." Ukiah lead them to the resequencer. "This is what we need."

"And this machine does that?"

"If the Ontongard just injected one of their cells into an egg, it would consume it, not fertilize it. If that egg was placed into the human mother, the mother would be a Get, and there would be no child."

Ukiah pulled out the impregnation tip out of one of the wrecked stations. "They would use this extractor to take out a genetic sample. It would be put into stasis until needed. At that point, the sample cells are unable to act to save themselves."

Sam shook her head. "What irony. They operate on the good of the many over the good of the few or the one. Usually that's considered a positive trait for people."

"It's what makes the Ontongard nearly unstoppable," Max said.

*   *   *

Ukiah showed Max how to undo the connecting bolts and set him to work dismantling the damaged stations in order to free the one they needed. Max swore under his breath as he worked. Finally Max eyed the thin, oddly curled dismantler. "I saw Hex. He was human enough to pass. How in God's name did a race that humanoid create something like this? I don't have fat fingers, but I can barely get my finger into the hole to hit the trigger, and I can only grip it with these two middle fingers. Don't they have any clue to ergonomics?"

Ukiah looked up from stripping out a computer. "Oh, that. The Gah'h created those. They had tentacles for hands."

"Why didn't the Ontongard adapt the tools?" Sam asked.

"The Ontongard think of themselves in scales too small to see with your eyes," Ukiah answered. "And the next host race might have tentacles again. Why bother?"

In the end the resequencer was too large to take up in one piece. Ukiah roamed the ship but found no other exit. The numerous cracks that led to fresh air all narrowed to openings too small for him to climb out, let alone be useful. Finally, they simply dismantled the resequencer down to three small pieces, wrapped them in bubble wrap that Max had brought down, and hauled them back up the granite chimney. Power connectors and portable hydrofusion power plants followed. On Max's suggestion that their loved ones might prove "prickly" at the idea of being saved, Ukiah found two undamaged stasis field generators, and salvaged parts from three sabotaged ones.

"Is that everything?" Max asked when Ukiah climbed up out of the hole on the last trip, having made a clean sweep for anything they missed.

"Everything except the Ontongard." Ukiah moved the rocks back into place.

Sam came to help. "So how are we going to find Alicia, Kraynak, and Zoey? The FBI and the police are turning the state upside down trying to find the Brodys and Quinn."

"The Ontongard like to keep to places known to the people they've taken over. They don't like moving out into the unknown. They stand out more that way. If they keep to the habits of the host, then they can blend in."

Max swore softly. "Hell, we don't even know who is all Ontongard. There could be dozens of them."

"If we can figure out who they successfully infected," Ukiah said, "then we would be ahead of the game."

"Well," Sam said slowly. "The fire victims and the drowning victims are most likely the people that failed, so the families of the drowning victims—Brody, Walsh, Landin—could all be Ontongard."

"Walsh and Landin." Max cocked his head, thinking. "I saw those names listed together someplace."

"Carl Landin and Sonnie Walsh both drowned at the end of July." Sam considered. "But I don't remember giving you their names before. Between the hit and run, multiple shootings, and alien pod people, I haven't had time."

"They're distant cousins." Max said slowly, frowning.

Sam shook her head. "No, not that I know of."

Max snapped his fingers and leaned into the Blazer to root through their bags. "I know where I saw it. Here." He pulled out the photocopy of *The Death of Magic*. Max flipped a few pages and then gave a hard laugh. "Alicia had put her foot into it. They're all Kicking Deer cousins. The Ontongard are going down the family tree."

For whatever reason, the author had included a family tree, stemming down from Kicking Deer. Curiously, Magic Boy had been skipped in the first generation. Jay had been straight father-to-son line down from his eldest half brother. By Jesse's day the tree had a massive root structure, and very few of them were named Kicking Deer.

A sudden wealth of blood kin.

Sam frowned. "But Brody isn't here, nor Bridges, which is Vivian's maiden name."

Max took a sudden deep breath, as realization hit him. "The car accident. They probably had a blood transfusion."

"Yes." Sam said. "Matt and Vivian probably did, but Harry wasn't in the accident."

"Poor kid. He lost either way." Max sighed.

Sam took the bound photocopies. "Since Max and I aren't

going to be much help setting this machine up, why don't he and I cross reference this with my case files and see what we can turn up?"

Closing his eyes, Ukiah took out his favorite memory of Indigo, that first moment he became aware of their mutual attraction.

Her face transformed for a moment with surprise and something that could have been joy. She was suddenly beautiful, all hard lines softening to the point that looking at her took his breath away. She put out a hand to him and he took it. "Ukiah!" she breathed his name, gripping his hand warmly. "I'm so glad that you are alive!"

He could recall the soft strength of her hand in his, as if he held it now. Other treasured moments flowed after it, all filled with the steel sereneness that was Indigo. In the raw ache of losing so many he loved, he found solace just in his memories of her.

He had to call her, and warn her, and maybe, say good-bye forever. She answered with a smile in her voice.

"I just took Kittanning back to your moms'. They're all suntanned and happy. I'm glad you spared them all the horror stories. Where are you? Portland? Houston?"

"We're not coming back." It hurt to say it. "We think we might be able to get Kraynak, Alicia, and Zoey back."

There was a long silence from her end, and then, "Really?"

"Yes, we found the scout—"

"Ukiah!" Indigo drowned him out. "This line isn't secure. I just need to know: Do you want me there?"

"I want you here, but I need you there. If I don't call you back by dawn, Degas will be coming for Kittanning. Take care of him, will you? And don't try it alone. Get Hellena to help you."

Another long silence from her. "I'll burn him to ash if he hurts you."

He smiled at her cold steel promise. "I know. I love you. I'll try hard to come back to you."

CHAPTER TWENTY

Simms Quarry, Pendleton, Oregon
Monday, September 6, 2004

In the end, they found the Ontongard too late. The Pack had already found the den sometime before dusk and wiped them out. Ukiah, Max, Sam, and Jared arrived just as full night settled over the quarry. The Demon Curs moved through, cleaning up in a jovial, frantic pace. A bonfire had been built up, the flames throwing wild, shifting shadows over the rugged bareness of the gravel pit. Laughing and joking, the Curs doused the Ontongard dead with gasoline and flung them onto the roaring fire.

Here and there, the dead were reawakening and trying to flee in bodies too damaged to move. The Curs would leap upon the struggling body and club it back to death, and add it quickly to the bonfire. A shout went up when one body simply shattered into mice, which fled quickly in all directions, abandoning the form. The Curs chased the tiny bodies through the dark, snatching them up, crushing the life from them, and flinging the limp bodies in a high long arc into the bonfire.

Sick with fear that he was already too late, Ukiah raced to find Alicia, Kraynak, and Zoey.

He found Zoey, shot through the heart. Her mice cowered in her matted hair. The soft tissue was repairing the damage at amazing speed.

"I've found Zoey," he radioed to Max. "She's dead. She probably won't cause you any problems."

"I've got the position," Max radioed back.

Jared's four-door pickup swung cautiously up the drive. The Demon Curs nearest to the truck cut it off, recognized Jared as Pack, and waved him through. Jared pulled the pickup beside Ukiah, and Sam rolled the first steel barrel off the back. It landed with a deep musical thump.

Max got out, pulling on steel-mesh-lined gloves. "Let's make this quick, people."

Sam caught the gloves Max threw her. "Are you sure we shouldn't put air holes into this?"

"Can't." Ukiah pried off the drum's lid. "The Ontongard don't have the same sense of self as the Pack do. They'll splinter down to gnats if they have to in order to escape."

"But won't they suffocate?" Sam asked.

"Ukiah," Max asked. "How long can you hold your breath?"

"Depends." Ukiah caught Max's look. "A real long time."

"See?" Max said with the tone of a problem settled.

Sam helped Max snatch up Zoey's mice, dropping them into tall canning jars, while Ukiah and Jared quickly searched her for weapons.

Jared growled softly the whole time. He lifted Zoey up, small and limp in his arms. Ukiah could feel him fighting the urge to break the small body, destroy the dormant being. "There's so much of him that I can barely sense her—and I hate her for it."

"Not her." Ukiah took Zoey's body from him and slid it carefully into the steel drum. "Him." Ukiah slapped the steel lid back on the drum and tightened down the locks. "That's one."

"Damn, missed a mouse!" Max hissed as a mouse scurried toward the protective bulk of the pickup.

Jared stomped down on the mouse, reducing it to a dead bundle of fur and broken bones.

Sam startled at the brutality with a slight "Jeez!" of dismay.

"It will be fine," Max said, dropping a metal top and lid

on the canning jar and giving it a spin to twist the lid tight. "Just grab it and can it. Go on, Ukiah, find the others."

Ukiah loped into the darkness, casting about for familiar scents while Jared and Max lifted the barrel onto the pickup truck. Ukiah located Kraynak, extremely battered and very much dead, just as Rennie found him.

"What are you doing here?" Rennie said.

"Looking for our dead." Ukiah tried to ignore him, wishing he was better at lying and that Rennie couldn't read his mind. "Max, I found Kraynak."

Rennie grabbed him and hauled him around to face him. "I told you to leave!"

"I can't! I can't just run away and leave them!"

Rennie snarled into his face as the pickup pulled up. "Damn you, why can't you, just this once, use your head instead of your heart?"

"If you wanted him to use his head"—Jared climbed out of the pickup—"you shouldn't have left me with him."

Rennie pushed Ukiah toward Jared. "I left *him* with *you*—so *you* could keep him safe. It was the only way I could be both places at once."

"There was the small matter of puking my guts out for a day and a half," Jared said. "By the time I was seeing things from your perspective, things were too far gone."

"Totally." Sam rolled a drum off the back of the truck. "So can we stick with the plan? We secure the ones we came for and then talk, okay?"

Max helped her right the drum, unlock and pry off the lid, and ready it for Kraynak's body. "She has a point."

Jared reached for Kraynak. Rennie looked at him hard with a fleeting desire for him to be still. Jared froze, hand outstretched. Anger flared in his eyes a moment, and then it too was gone, washed away by Rennie's will. In that moment, two Rennies turned to look at Ukiah with disapproval.

"Stop it!" Ukiah shoved Rennie. "Don't do that to him!"

Rennie considered striking Ukiah a crippling blow and sending him away, making Ukiah flinch, and then discarded the action as too dangerous with Degas so close by. Jared's own anger flickered back into his eyes as Rennie released him.

"You're starting to sound like a spoiled brat," Rennie snarled.

"You knew Jared was part of my family before the Curs took him. Even if I had left before Degas turned him, I would have found out sooner or later. You know me. You knew how I was going to react. Why did you let them take him?"

"You know the edge I walk with Degas. You know there was no 'letting' or 'allowing,' just surviving."

Ukiah looked away, feeling like a thunderstorm filled him; dark rage, guilt, and hurt howled over a landscape pelted with sorrow and lashed with brilliant lightning strikes of fear. He trembled with the furious chaos of emotions, all of it wanting to escape into mindless violence.

"Just go. There is danger for us all here." Rennie pushed then, trying to shove aside Ukiah's own will with his own.

Oddly, Ukiah knew that yesterday he would have gone. He had been weaker then, just a wild Wolf Boy with a thin veneer of civilization. Deepened by Magic Boy and Little Slow Magic, he looked levelly at Rennie and shook his head. "No."

Rennie frowned, puzzled at the sudden show of strength. "What have you done to yourself?"

"I've found part of myself I had lost."

Rennie glanced about the flame-licked dark, trying to find Degas. "Take those you already found and go, before Degas sees you."

"One more," Ukiah said. "Alicia."

"No."

"Come, come, Rennie," Degas's baritone came out of the darkness. "Let the brat dig his grave a little deeper."

They turned. The dog-gleam of Degas's eyes reflected the bonfire's light. He came out of the night, holding a struggling Alicia. She fought to break down, flee. Degas's will held her in check, something Ukiah would have thought was impossible.

A low growl woke in Ukiah's chest as fear and anger twined together there in a tight, hot knot.

Alicia radiated hate at all of them. "Growl, you idiotic dogs! Tear each other apart! I keep hoping you'll embrace your nature and kill each other!"

"Not while we have you to hunt," Rennie growled.

"If I'd known what a thorn you would become, I would have found the damn ship, dug it free with my bare hands, and laid waste to the entire continent! You rabid, moronic beasts!"

Degas grinned. "I love having Hex helpless and ranting."

"She's not Hex," Ukiah said. "She's an innocent girl that Hex's tainted."

"Have you taught him nothing, Rennie? Or is he just as stupid as he is dangerous?" Degas shoved Alicia in Ukiah's direction. "Smell her! Listen to her! Only her hair and fingernails are human anymore! She's Hex's Get!"

"She's my friend," Ukiah said. "She loved me, and I care for her. Give her to me."

"Never." Degas clamped hold of Alicia's throat, choking her.

Alicia thrashed in his hold. Mentally she raged on. *"You imbecilic beasts! You'll never win this war! I'll kill you all like I killed Prime."*

"Cub!" Rennie pulled at his shoulder.

Dimly, Ukiah was aware that Max, Sam, and Jared had canned Kraynak and moved on to someone else, apparently hoping to save more than their three. The Curs continued to add Gets to the fire, almost absently knocking small burning bodies back into the flames. The smell of pine and burning tar mixed with singed hair, burnt fur, smoldering feathers, fresh-spilled blood, and roasting meat. The heat blasted nearly unbearable where they stood, some sixty feet from the flames, and the fire roared an unending deep growl, punctuated with cracks and pops as loud as gunshots.

The way that had been so simplistic in planning had been swallowed in the night. Nothing of that straightforward, *find the Ontongard and return them to human,* remained to guide him. He floundered on, pleading now.

"Degas, please, give her to me, give me a chance to save her."

"Save her? How in hell do you plan to do that, little Wolf Boy?"

"I found the scout ship," Ukiah said.

Degas's shocked stillness spread through the Pack until only Max and Sam moved through the darkness. Even Ukiah found his breath frozen in his chest.

Rennie shook himself free of Degas. "How?"

Ukiah forced a hard swallow and managed to continue. "My mother remembered the way, and she told me when I was young. The Kicking Deers had one of my memories, from before I got lost."

"The ship!" Alicia's mind pressed suddenly against his. *"Where is it? Where?"*

Degas snapped Alicia's neck with a quick, brutal move that silenced her. "What a dangerous little thoughtless brat, you are!" he said to Ukiah.

Ukiah continued, "We salvaged the resequencer. It's one of the few things not gutted. We think we can save the humans recently infected by the Ontongard."

"Do you plan to let Hex cook up breeders when you're done with it?" Degas said.

"You know that it's not enough for them to make breeders with," Ukiah growled. "It's useful only in taking back what Hex has stolen."

"No! They've transitioned, you twit!"

"Cub," Rennie urged in a low voice. "Forget this idiocy and go home."

"We can get them back!" Ukiah cried.

"The risk isn't worth it!" Degas snapped. "We must eliminate all of Hex: dig up the roots, burn the leaves, salt the earth."

"Kill the innocent with the monster?" Ukiah asked.

"Yes," Degas said.

"I don't accept that," Ukiah said.

Degas flung Alicia's body aside and snatched at Ukiah, catching him by the collar as Ukiah tried to jerk back. "This is my territory," Degas snarled into his face. "I lead here. You are just a cub better off dead. Push me, and I will see that it's so. Collin!"

Ukiah saw in Degas's mind that he was about to order Alicia's body burned. "No!" Ukiah twisted in his grip, striking out in anger and fear. Rennie yelled, "Cub!" as if trying to bring a dog to heel. He felt Degas's sudden eagerness, and realized there would be only one end; one of them would kill the other.

Guided by instinct alone, Ukiah's first blow struck hard, breaking Degas's nose into a sudden fount of blood. His second swing, more crippling, Degas dodged with a hard laugh. He used Ukiah's own momentum and the hold on his collar to fling Ukiah to the ground and kicked him viciously in the head. The blow sent darkness and stars whirling in Ukiah's sight. He rolled away from Degas's steel-shod biker boots and scrambled to his feet, shaking his head to clear it.

Degas slid a long knife out of a kidney sheath. "Come on, puppy," Degas laughed, motioning Ukiah closer with his left hand. "Let's end this, fast and clean."

Ukiah backed away as Degas came at him, fast and sure. The blade kissed him again and again as he barely dodged the strikes, shredding his shirt and his skin with long, shallow furrows. The heat of the fire spread across his shoulders, intensifying as Degas pushed him backward toward it, until it felt like it would sear the clothes from his body.

Every swing Ukiah took, Degas felt coming and dodged easily.

Suddenly Degas gave him an opening, and he took it without thinking. Ukiah felt Degas's blade stab into his side, just under his ribs, slicing through coils of gut. Degas, though, had overreached to score the blow. Ukiah caught the other's hand, pinning the blade inside of himself, and struck hard at Degas's arm.

The thin bones snapped. Degas screamed, and jammed his left thumb into Ukiah's right eye.

The pain was indescribable.

Degas jerked free his hand, leaving his blade still buried in Ukiah's side as the Wolf Boy reeled in pain. He kicked Ukiah in the right knee, shattering it.

As Ukiah toppled, screaming in pain, Degas lunged forward, bowling him over and pinning him to the ground. As

the Wolf Boy struggled to free himself, Degas looked into
his one good eye and laughed at his helplessness.

"I'm going to kill you and add you to that fire," Degas
whispered. "Then all those damn Gets you died for."

The Wolf Boy snarled, lunging up the few inches between
them that he could move, and bit down hard on Degas's jugu-
lar vein. Degas shouted in pain and tried to jerk away, but
Ukiah clung to him, sinking his teeth deeper into the flesh as
blood gushed into his mouth, nose, and eyes. Growling
against the prickling metal-tasting flow, Ukiah shook his
head, tearing free the mouthful of meat. Degas thrashed now,
desperate to put pressure onto the gaping wound to stop the
blood loss. They rolled on the ground as blood mixed with
dirt into a mud base alive with Degas's cells, now individually fighting for survival. Ukiah spat away the meat before it
could change inside his mouth. The blood he inadvertently
swallowed churned in his stomach, seeking escape.

Finally Degas went limp. Ukiah rolled away and vomited
up the contents of his stomach. Blood continued to gush
from the wound, ribboning now into a long black snake.
Ukiah crawled away, afraid it was poisonous and would
exact revenge on him. Collin, he noticed, was being checked
by Rennie.

"You know our laws," Rennie growled. "A fight started
by two, ends with two."

"He's a damn breeder."

"He's part of the Pack, and he's under my protection. You
want to fight me?"

Collin eyed Rennie and then shook his head, backing out
of arm's reach. "He won fairly enough."

"What do you want done with Degas?" Rennie called to
Ukiah, reminding him that he won the right to destroy Degas
completely—add him onto the bonfire along with the Ontongard.

The thought sickened Ukiah. "Nothing! Let him heal
back. I just want Alicia and the others."

Collin relaxed slightly at the news. "Let him take the
damn Gets and go."

CHAPTER TWENTY-ONE

Kicking Deer Farm, Umatilla Indian Reservation
Tuesday, September 7, 2004

Ukiah blacked out totally and came to in a rocking pitch blackness. Only Max's presence beside him kept him from striking out in alarmed confusion.

"Easy," Max murmured from out of the total darkness. "Mind your leg."

Ukiah lifted his head, blinking. A bandage covered his gouged eye. His good eye had been covered when his head rested on Max's shoulder, blinding him completely. He could make out Jared driving now, Sam beside him. In the headlights, a hay barn was growing closer, a large, hunched shape in vast, flat emptiness.

Ukiah sat sidewise on the bench seat, his leg splinted at the knee and sticking straight out. A blood-soaked bandage covered the stab wound in his side, and all his various wounds still stung from liberal use of antiseptics. He could remember fighting Degas, but the aftermath was a confusion of pain, centering mostly on efforts to undo the damage Degas had done to him. Wavering in and out of consciousness, he trusted only Max completely, thus the current seating arrangements. "What happened?"

"You won," Max said. "We've got what we came for, and then some."

"You do remember what you were fighting about?" Jared asked without turning, a trace of a smile in his voice.

"These trips never make sense until a couple days afterward," Ukiah complained, turning his head to compensate for his missing eye. "That is if I'm lucky and get all my memories rounded back up."

"I've got them." Max indicated a bulging pocket that radiated faint anxiety.

The barn loomed huge in the twin highlights. Jared swung the truck in a slowing arc away from the barn, stopped, and then backed toward the great doors.

Out across the prairie, a string of headlights moved toward them.

"They followed us?" Ukiah squeaked as he sensed the Pack presence emanating from the oncoming vehicles, mostly motorcycles with a car or two mixed in.

Jared gave a slight laugh, turning off the truck's engine. "They're not going to put a breeder in a car with five Ontongard and let it drive away to play with parts of the ovipositor."

"One could hope," Max got out, taking away his warmth, saying, "Stay." He returned a moment later with a bottle of warm Gatorade, a pack of beef jerky, six Snicker bars, and Rennie.

"Five Ontongard?" Ukiah asked after he gulped down the Gatorade.

"Quinn and a boy," Max named the two additional Gets offhandedly, his focus on Rennie. "How soon before Degas heals up and comes after Ukiah again?"

"Ukiah won the right to see if this works." Rennie stripped off Ukiah's bloody bandage and applied a fresh one. "And if Degas wants to deal with the cub again, it will still have to be a fair fight. Neither one will be up to that for a while."

Max scowled. "Which is to say he'll come after him once he's sure he can win."

"Perhaps," Rennie admitted as he picked bugs out of the bandage for Ukiah to reabsorb. "But he'll be on my hunting ground then, and things will be different."

Jared had gotten lights on in the barn and pushed the great doors open with a low rumble, flooding the night with the green scent of fresh-baled hay. The haylofts were stacked high, but the main floor was clear, giving them a large private workspace.

"Here goes everything," Max muttered, and went to lift the steel drums off the back of the truck.

They had no chance to mark the steel drums, and so they opened them on a luck of the draw. Zoey occupied the first drum—fully recovered and snapping. They quickly extended the stasis field over her. While she was completely immobile, they took a hair sample, weeded out a sample of human DNA, and ran it through the resequencer.

Or closer to the truth, Jared did. Ukiah found, to his distress, that in the finer details of working with resequencer and advance microbiology, he had holes in his memories.

"You're not full-grown yet, cub," Jared said without taking his eyes off the monitor. "You can't get the snot beat of you time and time again, and not lose some of the memories that aren't yours."

So Jared created their weapon of salvation.

Millennia before, the Summ had realized that the Ontongard's memory, its greatest strength, was also its weakness. Their cells didn't keep a record of what they experienced individually. If they did, a left foot cut off from the body would only know what feet commonly know: dirt, grass, carpet, socks, and shoes. Nor could a cell possibly handle that amount of raw data added to its genetic code.

Instead the cells shunt memories to the bloodstream. The information from the entire body is gathered in the blood to be encoded, and a condensed gestalt returns to be added to each cell's genetic memory. Each cell kept only a record of the full stimulus effect on the full body.

During that exchange, the Ontongard were vulnerable to a Trojan horse that slipped in and took over.

By returning the resequencer to its original function, Ukiah and Jared were able to fabricate a similarly condensed virus disguised as a memory package. Once accepted into the cell, the virus seized control of the memory handler. At that point, the Ontongard cell turned on itself, working to restructure itself into the human DNA blueprint recorded within the virus. The result would not be fully human—the certain construction mechanisms would remain intact—but they would be hopefully harmless hybrids similar to what Ukiah's children might be.

The Ontongard, after all, were basically no smarter than pond scum. Their intelligence came from their host bodies, which didn't have the ability to control their individual cells. It had been the host's weakness, which the Ontongard first exploited and then circumvented by having the cell communicate on an individual level. Now the virus took advantage of the weakness, immediately muting the besieged cell so no defense could be raised against it.

They injected the virus into Zoey at major artery points, while Hex's helpless rage glittered in her eyes.

It was then they realized their first mistake.

"Wait, what do we do with her extra mice?" Sam asked. "We've got four of hers in the canning jars."

"Oh, shit." Max glanced back at the trucks where they left the jarred mice. "We shouldn't have kept them separate."

"It's too late now, at least for Zoey," Ukiah leaned wearily against a stack of hay bales, wishing he could crawl off to bed. "We've already treated her. Her mice might reinfect the cells that transitioned to human."

Sam ran her hand through her short blond hair. "So how do we make the mice go back to being part of the body?"

"We destroy the mice," Jared said quietly. "It will be mercy, not to remember being hunted down and killed so brutally."

Ukiah nodded slowly in agreement. The Ontongard mice would flee rather than merge with the trapped body. "He's right. The mice will have to go."

Max looked down at Zoey, held still on the table. "How long do we wait before we take the stasis field off her? We're going to need it to do Alicia and the others."

"It's working quickly." Ukiah could sense Zoey's growing panic as parts of her body became mute, seemingly dead to the rest of the body. "It will slow down as the number of Ontongard cells approaches zero. I'll need to monitor the transformation. We might need to inject her multiple times to keep the process going."

"You? You're barely standing on your own power," Max said. "You should eat something more and go to bed."

"I'll watch over Zoey," Jared said.

Ukiah glanced across the barn at where Rennie shifted the next barrel into place beside the second stasis field generator. *Could he trust Rennie's Get with Zoey?*

"Me, Jared, will do this," Jared said. "I remember my baby sister, and I'm not going to let her go."

So you want to see the new baby, eh, slow poke? Well, there. No nibbling on fingers, no matter how much they look like little worms. How do you suppose, slow poke, you can love someone on first sight? I picked her up, and I knew I'd die for her.

Jared caught the flash of memory and recognized the source. He peered into Ukiah's eyes as if expecting to see the ancient turtle looking back out. "Little Slow Magic?"

Ukiah felt inside him, small yet brilliant, Little Slow Magic's love for the boy he had watched grow into a good man. Jared's face creased with pain as the newly made Get felt the adoration.

"Oh, God," Jared said, tears suddenly shimmering in his eyes.

"What's wrong?" Ukiah asked him.

Jared surprised Ukiah with a rough hug. *"I never knew how much that old turtle loved me before—and he's given himself to save Zoey."*

Alicia was last. All the damage Degas inflicted had healed, and she lay in her stasis field like a sleeping princess. Ukiah gazed at her with new eyes, feeling like he had somehow missed seeing the real her until it was too late. In his memory, he could find a thousand misunderstood words, glances, touches, and kindnesses. She had loved him and tried to let him know—and he had been blind to it all.

And with his new knowledge, he could look back to the Fourth of July picnic with only horror. He had been killed mid-June, and when he came back from the dead, he had vanished into hiding; the picnic was his first public reappearance. Alicia came early to the picnic, hugged him tight with tears in her eyes, and asked to go up to the attic alone with him, saying she had something important to tell him. Something she should have told him long ago.

Indigo, however, had come out of the house with a screaming Kittanning. "He just woke up crying, honey. I can't get him settled."

Ukiah took his son, settled him, and met Alicia's puzzled gaze. "Oh, Alicia, this is my girlfriend, Indigo, and this little guy is my son, Kittanning."

If any of it had been done intentionally, it would have been unforgivable. Even in all innocence, it had been cruel. Open pain flashed across Alicia's face, and then was hidden away. The worst of it was there would be no way to repair the harm. He loved Alicia as a sister or a close friend, but nothing more than that. Hopefully, she would not think of him as her prince in shining armor—because he couldn't be that man for her.

They lost Quinn. The process swept through him, but what was left behind couldn't function as a whole. They could only theorize that his splintering down into crows had made some global change that the process couldn't fix. He lay inert, a collection of tissue refusing to function together.

Two of the Curs took the body to dispose of it.

Ukiah limped painfully to where Jared watched over the sleeping Zoey. "Now you."

"Me?"

"We can make you human again. You've been changed the shortest time, and you haven't been hurt, so there's almost no risk."

"Uncle, how can I know what these things are, and what they want, and what they're willing to do to succeed—and go back to not being able to see them when they're standing in front of me?"

"But—"

"How many people died while I thought Brody was still himself, that Quinn could be trusted?"

"You can't blame yourself. There was no way you could have known."

"Because I was human then," Jared said. "I became a cop to prevent murders like Magic Boy's. It was Ontongard that killed Magic Boy. This is what I need to be to stop them."

"Jared! You can't stay this way. You don't know what it really means."

Jared reached out and tapped Ukiah's nose—a greeting of old to Little Slow Magic. "Uncle, I'm enough Rennie to know what this decision means. I'm also Jared enough to make it freely."

Zoey was fully recovered, not remembering anything that happened shortly after the kidnapping. She said she remembered being injected, of growing sick, and the beginning of odd dreams. Except for a tendency to jump at loud noises, and a slight, temporary clinginess, she seemed much her old self on every level that Ukiah could perceive.

Kraynak would be slower to recover. The Ontongard had not healed all the damage done to his body prior to his return to human. He took the ordeal stoically, talking about a long vacation once he got home.

The boy, Glenn, and Alicia both needed repeated treatments to overcome the Ontongard's hold on them. Even Degas, though, had to admit nothing seemed to remain of the alien taint. Grudgingly, he promised to leave the former Gets in peace.

Ukiah called Indigo with all the good news and for the first time, heard her weep with joy.

Pendleton, Oregon
Friday, September 10, 2004

They stayed until Friday for the sake of the recovering Kraynaks, and the Kicking Deers, who wanted Magic Boy to attend the roundup with the rest of the clan. Max made flight arrangements once more, buying tickets for Ukiah, Kraynak, Alicia, and himself. Rennie would travel with them, but he made independent arrangements, leaving Max wondering aloud where the Pack got their cash.

Sam was still driving the van cross-country and willing to *consider* a job offer once she got there. The smiles she gave Max indicated it would be more than a mild consideration, but she also wouldn't commit more positively than that. Max wavered through quiet terror and giddiness about her visit. At least, he stated, she had seen them at their god-awful worst and anything that happened in Pittsburgh would be simple. For Max's sake, Ukiah hoped that he was right.

The Kicking Deers gathered together clothing for Ukiah: moccasins, fringed buckskin pants, beaded shirt, and eagle feathers. He was combing his hair when Alicia found him.

"Hi!" He smiled at her, although he felt weirdly awkward around her. It was like he had opened a friend's diary and read her private thoughts—but in the meantime, a quiet, sad-eyed stranger had come and taken her place. Would this new Alicia even like him?

"Does she know?" Alicia asked.

She who? Know what? He looked at Alicia in confusion and then realized what she must be asking. "Does Indigo know that I'm—I'm not human? Yes." He considered things he could say to make things better, but they were small offerings. "You are my first and best female friend. I love you dearly, but I never thought of you in that way."

Her mouth twisted in a wry smile, but her eyes stayed wistful. "You were an innocent; you didn't think of anyone that way. She seduced you. She corrupted you."

He supposed it would be easier on Alicia to let it go with that: She lost out because she was the nobler woman. But it wasn't the whole truth, and letting false assumptions ride had caused so much harm recently.

"No. It wasn't all her, Alicia. I didn't have the words to describe how I felt the first moment I met her—she *did* teach me the words and actions—but the feelings were mine. I wanted to be with her. I couldn't stop thinking of her."

"O, my little Wolf Boy, you grew up and fell in love when I wasn't looking."

"I'm sorry. I never meant to hurt you."

"You haven't," she whispered and reached out to braid one of the eagle feathers into his hair. "I hurt myself. Sometimes it's like looking back and watching someone else; someone who was very good at deceiving herself. You were so beautiful and safe, and I was tired of being walked over."

"I still care for you." Ukiah caught her hand and squeezed it.

She laughed. "It wouldn't have worked out. I thought you were sweet and tame because you were young and overprotected. I figured you would change once you got older and your moms gave you more freedom. I wanted you as a wild wolf man, not the safe Wolf Boy. I saw you at the picnic— you're going right from sheltered Boy Scout to happily married man."

Ukiah thought of Jay, the mischief-maker, who Magic Boy had loved more than those that walked the straight and narrow. Alicia would have loved him too. "I've lived too long to be the man you really want."

"I know that now," she whispered. "I need someone that enjoys screaming in the face of conformity, who bangs out their own beat and dances to it. I know it's just my way of defying death because my parents died so young—but I don't want to change. And I don't want to change you either."

Last time he was at the roundup, he had been Magic Boy, and the world had been a totally different place then. Horses were still needed for transportation and to have many was a sign of wealth. All the Native Americans would come to the roundup mounted, and the parade into the ring was an endless stream of the sturdy Cayuse-bred horses.

RVs now sat next to teepees, and in both, people readied for the parade. Ukiah stood in the tiny bathroom of Cousin Lou's RV and looked at his reflection, acquainting himself with his new face. It surprised him to see a warrior gazing back at him. It was more than the freshly applied war paint, or the heavier lines of a man's face finally emerging, won through hard battle. He had grown beyond the Wolf Boy, and Magic Boy, and the cub, each with their little slice of humanity and alien. He was finally growing to be a man, something greater than all the parts that had gone before.

With a tap, Jared appeared at the door, and said in Nez Percé, *"Uncle, it's time. Coming?"*

Ukiah was pleased that Jared registered on his senses as Jared, and not Rennie, although there was no denying the Pack presence coming from him. He answered slowly, *"Rush. Rush. Rush."*

Jared grinned and tapped his nose. *"Try and not miss everything, slowpoke."*

So he followed Jared out, his feet already finding the ancient rhythm of the drums, to take his place with his family, his friends, and the Pack.